Summer Things

Joseph Connolly

W F HOWES LTD

This large print edition published in 2002 by
W F Howes Ltd
Units 6/7, Victoria Mills, Fowke Street
Rothley, Leicester LE7 7PJ

First published by HarperCollins *Publishers* 2001

A CIP catalogue record for this book
is available from the British Library

ISBN 1 84197 547 8

Typeset by Palimpsest Book Production Limited,
Polmont, Stirlingshire
Printed and bound in Great Britain
by Antony Rowe Ltd, Chippenham, Wilts.

To a fine brace of Michaels,
BOOTH and DILLON

PART 1

Before

CHAPTER 1

'Lick,' he said out loud and into thin air. 'Lick me.'

Norman Furnish was sitting at his desk in the largish and decidedly dated workroom that he shared with his sort of colleague, Katie: not really quite an office, as such – no, not really. The desk itself was very much in keeping – mahogany veneer, ex-Civil Service issue, could be; scarred and green old leather surface, blind tooling nearly eradicated now: In tray, Out tray, just the one phone.

'Lick me,' he said, staring dead ahead now at the calendar they received every bloody year from a struggling firm of quantity surveyors. Ann Hathaway's Cottage, this time: made quite a change from Monet's poppies.

A low and gurgling laughter from the girl beneath his desk and between his knees just then thrilled him immediately, but this was as nothing compared with the prickled and rippling sensation that soon overcame him, causing his eyebrows to jerk in their attempt to fly right away from his face.

'Urgh! Oh, *urgh*, good God!' came out of Norman

3

now, as a rhythmic drumming assumed its place in the way things were going – this from the energy in Katie's strappy and so-high-heeled shoes beating back against the modesty board on this good and commodious, fine old desk. Katie was really warming to her task – quite regularly cracking her head on the underside of the central drawer, she was, and Norman's eyes were raking the room, almost as if beseeching mercy or aid from some unseen deliverer, and as he took in spliced and glancing images of brown and beige filing cabinets, a diseased Swiss cheese plant and a thoroughly dented electric kettle, so did he feel more alive than even the last time and yet quite close to a heart-clutching death – and then the breathing did actually falter and damn near cease within him as the door to his workroom swung open, and now here was Norman aware only of a stopped-up cavity where once had throbbed internal organs and staring wild-eyed at the man who stood there before him in the passage of light – looking at Norman, just looking at Norman – as Norman caught hold of the desktop and kept on goggling back.

'You still here, Norman?' said the man. 'Thought you'd packed up hours ago.'

'Me?' queried Norman. 'Oh yes – still here. Still here, Mr Street. Howard. A few ends to tidy up, you know.'

Did he look normal, Norman? Was he betrayed by sweat on his face and lips, or was this just the lifeblood that had seeped down from his eyes?

Those eyes grew even larger now (Mr Street – Howard – had better be ready to reach up and out for a double catch, thought Norman fleetingly, for soon they were scheduled to pump out of his face like hard-blasted ping-pong balls from a children's fun-gun).

'Check out this property in the morning, would you, Norman?' said Mr Street – Howard – quite as if it didn't appear as if every vessel within Norman was now lithely poised to erupt spectacularly so as to spatter crimson into all four corners of the room. 'And get yourself *home*, for goodness sake, lad. All work and no play, hey? Anyway – holiday next week, yes? Have fun, if I don't see you again.'

Mr Street – Howard – dropped a buff folder on the surface of Norman's sinful desk, smiled briefly and strolled out of the room, softly closing the door behind him, leaving Norman to exhale in the manner of a small boy, red and victorious, light-headed and nearly hysterical at having broken his record at ducking under water. Because Katie, you see, hadn't stopped for a second – hadn't even paused: she was working on him now with a vigour that was singular even to her – and now as the big thrill flooded up, becoming full and gorgeously central before sending out tingling signals to parts that extended even beyond his finger ends, so did Norman heave before slumping as he lowed like some base creature and then slowly subsided into a thankful defeat, both without and within.

'God Christ,' he sighed, filled chock-full with all

5

sorts of relief. 'Jesus, Katie,' he implored now, as she clambered out and up to face him, 'what the hell did you think you were *playing* at? Christ – that's the closest yet. He'll *catch* us, you know. One day soon he'll bloody catch us for sure. I thought you said he'd *gone*.'

Katie was licking her lips. While any imagery concerning cats and cream may be seen to be going it a bit, lewdness aplenty was there all right – all over her face – dancing quite happily and well in tune with not just rude health but also the ruddy flush of unalloyed triumph.

'I thought he had,' she said simply. 'Anyway – I was very quiet. He can't have *heard* anything, or anything. Was it lovely? I loved it.'

'But what must I have *looked* like!' protested Norman in a wail in truth much closer to a whisper – didn't want Mr Street – Howard – barging back in again, did he?

'Oh – don't worry about it. He never notices *any-thing*. And anyway,' she tacked on, quite uncon-cerned, 'I don't know what you're getting so het up about – it's only *Daddy*.'

Norman rolled back in his chair and looked up into Katie's sweetly dark and glittering eyes and again became aware of danger. He might be just 'Daddy' to her, but to Norman he was the boss, the owner of the whole agency – and, more to the point, author of any putative reference that Norman would most surely one day be needing. Any minute now, if they cut this caper any bloody finer.

Mr Street – seemed a decent chap, really, and clearly pretty besotted with his seventeen-year-old and only daughter, Katie – had quite often insisted that Norman call him Howard, but, well – Norman didn't know, couldn't quite put a finger on it, but somehow, well . . . it just didn't seem *right*.

'Why are we using these glasses?' asked Howard of his wife, who didn't appear to have heard. She continued extracting with care a series of fairly bulbous golbets from crusty layers of candy-pink tissue. 'Elizabeth?' he pursued. 'Why these glasses, actually? It's only Brian and Dotty, isn't it?'

'It's not a question,' said Elizabeth now, setting down the last of the glasses on to the motley granite work surface, just west of the rather splendid triple sink in bright red enamel. Double sinks? Two a penny – but this, Elizabeth would ask you, was rather splendid – *non*? 'Not at all a question of just who's *coming*,' went on Elizabeth, a sort of smile coming into play – kindly imparting knowledge to a maybe lesser mind? Gently explaining the not-too-knotty ins and outs of the thing, really rather simple when you broke it all down. 'It's all about *effort*. Making everything as nice as possible. You want to be proud of your home, don't you, Howard? Proud of me?'

Howard poured whisky – tipped the neck of the bottle in Elizabeth's direction and accompanied the gesture with a questioning eyebrow, Elizabeth very briefly closing her eyes by way of reply.

'Course. Course I do,' said Howard, now taking a swig. '*Am* – course I am. Naturally.'

'And Melody's coming too.'

'Melody? Really? Didn't know.'

'I did tell you.'

'I'm sure – sure you did. One day I'll forget my own, er . . . oh God, you know – thing: head. Katie back?'

'I thought she'd be coming home with you.'

'Well I stayed on for a bit, as you know. Probably gone shopping. For her holiday.'

Elizabeth looked up sharply and glared at Howard – and he saw it, and he flinched, but God it wasn't *his* problem, surely, this Katie holiday thing? Surely this too was not to be placed fairly and squarely at his door?

'The least said about Katie and her so-called "holiday" the better,' said Elizabeth, tersely. 'But I suppose we'll be talking about nothing else all night.'

'It's that time of year,' allowed Howard, knowing well that was not at all what she meant. 'But you're looking forward to yours, though, aren't you? Ours?'

Elizabeth nodded. 'If I'm honest I can barely wait. I've never felt so much in *need* – you know? I really feel I need a break.'

Howard nodded. Break from *what*, is what he was thinking: what is it exactly that you *do*, Elizabeth? I've often wondered. He hauled out a chair now, and sat on that as he sipped a bit more whisky. Elizabeth, with her back to him quite a way away (the kitchen was big – people often remarked on it: more cupboards than you could shake a stick at) and squatting down on haunches that once had actually had the power to propel Howard into a narroweyed and lip-licking lust. Before things and the passing of time had changed all that.

'But isn't it funny?' said Elizabeth into the warm and freely-rolling shelves of the dishwasher. 'About Brian and Dotty?' She rose with her clutch of plates, hunkered down again for a further handful. 'I mean – of all places in the world!'

Howard nodded again – quite shortly, this time. It was not that he was wholly uninterested (*reasonably* uninterested, granted) – it was just that Elizabeth had said all this, done all this – they'd talked about all this before: most recently only last night, wasn't it? Maybe the evening before; anyway, not so damn long ago that he could face it all again.

'You'll never guess about Brian and Dotty,' is how Elizabeth had opened – and it was true, Howard never would: he had surely been married long enough to harbour few doubts on that score. So he said nothing – widened his eyes, maybe – and Elizabeth went on: 'They've only gone and booked their holiday in exactly the same place as we have!'

'Kidding,' Howard had said. 'Mind you, we did talk about it, didn't we? When we were round that weekend for that unspeakable casserole.

Remember? When Dotty burned the rice? We said – remember? – we were giving Portugal a rest, give England a chance – yes? That's where they got the idea. No originality, some people. When are they going?'

'But that's exactly the point!' enthused Elizabeth. 'They've booked for the very same week that *we* have!'

'Oh God no – *really*? Well who's going to keep an eye on the house, then? About the only really good thing about Brian and Dotty is that they live next door – keep an eye on things. Who's going to water the bloody garden? Christ – word gets out from that bent milkman of ours that *both* bloody houses are going to be empty, we might as well not bother coming back – they'll strip the place down to the foundations.'

That was weeks ago, all that. Elizabeth and Howard had more than once since discussed the likelihood of its having been a *true* coincidence – *can't* have been, averred Elizabeth: couldn't give a sod, thought Howard – but then when he had mulled it over for a bit he came to the conclusion that coincidence or not, the thought of this thing was now quite unbearable. The whole point of a holiday, surely, was the business of getting *away*, yes? Not to bring along the bloody neighbours. He had even tried to change his own booking, but this was a no-no, apparently, for all sorts of reasons that Howard could barely understand. And Elizabeth had set her heart on this English seaside holiday

– haven't done such a thing since I was *little*, she said (oh God, yuk). Anyway, she tacked on, it'll be nice to have Dotty to show off to: all my brand-new summer things. Dotty doesn't seem to have had anything new for simply *ages*: Brian's bad patch, I think. But *Christ*, Elizabeth, Howard had tried to reason – a whole week with Brian and Dotty! I mean OK, the odd evening, fair enough – but a whole bloody week! Morning till night!

Anyway. That's the way it was going to be, it surely did seem. And this very evening – now just a couple of days away from this famous jaunt to the coast – Brian and Dotty were coming over for one of Howard and Elizabeth's fab little dinner parties (they were renowned – just ask anyone local) and Elizabeth's friend Melody was coming too, apparently – quite good company, actually, young Melody (I do seem to recall) – and Katie, of course, if she ever bothered to show up. God – that girl. Messed up her GCSEs (no one else in her year managed it quite so comprehensively) – no plan at all as to what to do next, so Howard had given her some sort of typist's job in the agency: pro tem, he had said. Christ Dad, she had wailed (this was all the thanks you got), I don't want to be an *estate* agent! No, thought Howard, I don't suppose you do. I don't either, but there it bloody is. But Norman seems to keep her busy, anyway: memos and so forth. Good lad, Norman – going places, Howard shouldn't wonder (but where did an estate agent go?)

Thinking about it now, of course, Howard maybe understood Elizabeth having pulled up the drawbridge at the very mention of Katie's holiday, just a while back there (two large Scotches ago, if we're going in for counting). Katie, you see, had at first displayed reluctance for the very first time to join the family holiday. This soon became a point-blank refusal, at which point Elizabeth had said quite archly that in fact, Katie *dear*, there can be no *argument* here because you are only seventeen years old, not *quite* a grown-up yet, still a little girl, and anyway we can't possibly leave you alone in the house – *far* too dangerous – you'd probably set fire to the place and leave the windows wide open and Katie had said Fine, OK, fine then – I'll book up something with Ellie for the same week, OK, and when Elizabeth opened her mouth in protest Katie tacked on Actually Mum, Dad, I've already done it – it's fixed, OK? All booked and paid for.

And was it on the cards that the subject of summer holidays would raise its sandy and sun-kissed head during the course of the dinner party? You know, Howard rather thought it was. Oh well. At least the bloody thing was only a week – Christ, it had taken him hours, years, to make it just a week.

'A week!' had hooted Elizabeth. 'A week's no earthly good, Howard – even you must see that. You take nearly a week to *unwind*. It's hardly worth unpacking for just a week.'

For which Howard had not been entirely unprepared, so he took one of many deep breaths of late and launched into a fairly seamless catalogue of damn near watertight reasons why, in fact, contrary to Elizabeth's conviction, a week was the absolutely *ideal* length of time to go:

'For starters, you see, the drive down there's absolutely nothing so the holiday starts off straight away. *Plus*, as you know, we're booked into the very best five-star joint the place has to offer and so we can really do the thing in *style*.' And then he went for the clincher. 'And then, of course, there'll be time and money over for you to go shopping when we get back – get your winter wardrobe sorted out.'

Yes, that more or less had done it. But the real reason why Howard could not have contemplated more than a bloody week (didn't even know about Brian and Dotty at that stage of the game) was that Zoo-Zoo had looked so deeply unhappy when he had broken the news – when he said he would be leaving. And now – as Elizabeth silently checked on stuff in the Aga – Howard was smelling his fingers, and Zoo-Zoo still lingered there from just an hour ago. *Great,* he had thought, as he left the folder with Norman Furnish – if *he's* still here, he can lock up and all the rest of it, and I can just quickly go and see my little Zoo-Zoo, before traipsing back and facing this bloody farce of a dinner party.

And even now – as Elizabeth Street, perfectly made up and coiffed, was slipping those large and rather good pearl and gold studs through the holes in her lobes – so was Dotty Morgan still sitting on an unmade bed and staring into her wardrobe, the smoky mirrored doors slid open wide, the despair of the last, Christ, must be an hour, now accelerating into a not-too-far-from-tearful panic.

'I can't,' she whispered. And then louder she said: 'I can't – I just can't. I just can't face *any* of this. What can I – I can't wear *any* of this, I just can't. Brian – you go. You go on your own. I just can't wear that blue thing again – Elizabeth knows it by *heart*.'

'Don't be silly, love,' called Brian from the bathroom. 'What about the red jacket and skirt? You always look lovely in that.'

'That's the bloody *trouble* – I *always* . . . oh *Christ*, Brian – I've just got to have some new things or I'll *die*.'

No response to that.

'Did you hear what I *said*?'

If I go on saying nothing, thought Brian, she'll only become shrill.

'You know the position,' he said, quietly. No need now to yodel in a friendly chin-up-old-girl sort of a way, because a fairly wet-eyed Dotty was beside him in the bathroom.

'What you men never seem to *understand*, Brian – oh God *look* at you! Look at you! What on earth do you imagine you're *doing*?'

Brian was, in fact, holding high in his left hand a circular and chrome little mirror (normal on one side, lunatic on the other), his right hand poking

14

around with scissors at the back of his head while he tried to catch a glimpse of what on earth he imagined he was doing in the ajar and similarly mirrored door of the medicine cabinet.

'Just a bit of a trim,' he said.

'Oh God it's come to *this*,' moaned Dotty. 'You're even cutting your own *hair*. Why are you cutting your own –? And look what you've done! Look what you've done! There's a great chunk out of it there –!'

'Back's a bit tricky, if you want the truth.'

'But Christ, Brian – you're not a *hairdresser*, are you? God knows you can't even cut a piece of *wood* straight, never mind *hair*. I nearly broke my wrist trying to wrench open that latest stupid cupboard of yours.'

Brian squinted and swooped down with his shears on a little tuft of hair that he thought he almost certainly might have located jutting out above one of his ears (hard to say which, what with the mirrors, and all), but now his hand had moved (the circular mirror got a bit weighty after a while) and Dotty was partly obscuring the cabinet and blast and hell he'd lost sight of it now, damn near stabbed himself.

'Look,' he said, his eyes practically revolving within their sockets, so desperate was he now to see just what sort of tomfoolery his parting was up to, because although he'd done that side already, he was buggered if it didn't seem longer than the chunk he hadn't even got around to hacking. 'I *told*

15

you, Dotty love – economy is the name of the game from here on in.'

'But I'm no *good* at economy – *hate* economy: don't know how it *works*,' wailed Dotty. 'Oh *please*, Brian – can't we stop all this? I've got to get some clothes, got to – I mean, never mind *tonight*, tonight is bad enough – but what about the holiday? I can't wear the same old stuff – not if Elizabeth of all people is going to be there. Oh God – just the thought of it makes me want to *scream*.'

Well there was just no point in even *talking* to Brian, was there? So Dotty flounced out of the bedroom and flung herself on to the bed, piled high and slithering with possible-at-the-time but now discarded as hopeless outfits.

Brian continued to snip a little here, snip a little there (more to this lark than meets the eye) and tried not to hear Dotty's slow and gut-felt moaning. Poor Dotty – poor old thing. Wasn't *her* fault, was it? Wasn't her fault that everything they were used to had now disappeared. She had never thought – neither of them had – that they'd ever have to sell the house. The thought had never crossed their minds. God – the amount of work and money he'd poured into it. Had to take Colin out of school – that maybe had hurt the most. He'd been doing well, that boy – Christ, he'd only *been* there a year, not much more; he'd put so much effort into his Common Entrance and now look; hoiked out and stuck in the local comprehensive. Not happy there, you could tell: moped a lot, these days, and Colin

16

had never been a moper. And Dotty had no idea that worse was to come – oh yes, worse than this – and Brian for one had neither the heart nor the courage to tell her. At first he'd even said No to the holiday – was horrified when Dotty had said she wanted, had to have, just had to, a proper old-fashioned seaside holiday just like Howard and Elizabeth. Why didn't she understand (Christ knows he'd been over it often enough) that holidays were completely out for, oh Jesus, just about *ever*?

He gave in in the end – had to, she'd already told Colin, hadn't she? And Brian couldn't, could he (how could he? Could *you*?), take away from him anything else. So maybe, OK, maybe somehow we'll manage the holiday (just a week, mind – a week is tops) and then we've really really really got to knuckle down. I'll make it up to you, Dotty, I'm sorry, Colin, about the way things have . . . the way things . . . but I'll make it up to you, honestly: I'll make it all better, I swear it. I do love you both, for what it's worth.

'I really wasn't going to *get* the bag,' Elizabeth assured Howard, eyebrows arched, the better to demonstrate her lovable hopelessness – mouth now flattening down into the tacit acquiescence of a mutely accepting clown. 'But in the end I just *had* to have it because the colour was absolutely perfect. Am I *very* awful? But oh God it was so beautiful – you'll love it when you see it, Howard,

17

with the whole, you know – everything together. You'll just *adore* it.'

'I'm sure,' said Howard. What was she talking about now? Bag, was it, did she say? Something else?

'They'll be here any second, I should think,' went on Elizabeth. 'They're always exactly ten minutes late – it's so very sweet.'

She swished away from him and into the hall.

'Katie!' called Elizabeth, 'Are you coming down?! Does this dress look all right from the back, Howard? It feels a bit . . . Howard? Did you hear what I said?'

'Sorry, darling – miles away,' said Howard, thinking Wish I was, wish I was – and deeply into Zoo-Zoo.

'It's just it feels a wee bit tight on the hip . . .'

'Looks marvellous,' approved Howard, now more or less picking up the gist of the thing. 'Fabulous.'

'Sure? You're so sweet,' Elizabeth smiled – possibly at the sweetness of Howard, or maybe on account of her own adorable folly. 'Anyway I *hope* it looks all right because it cost an absolute – Katie! Don't ignore me, please! Come down!'

'Coming!' came back Katie's muffled response from a couple of floors away. Christ, she thought – I've only just got in. I'll go down in a minute – I've just got to finish sticking this stuff into – Christ, you know: not actually sure if it's all going to *fit*. It's bloody difficult packing for a city in summer because OK, it's going to be hot, sure – Chicago

18

is bloody hot at this time of year as *tout le monde* knows – but there were all the *evenings* and things and nearly all the outfits needed different shoes and it was these that took up most of the space – just look at them all. Maybe if she dumped the orange ones? Should she do that? Dump the orange ones? She could only wear them once – they only went with one thing – but oh God, I don't know, they are rather gorgeous and I've been *dying* to wear them . . . oh stuff it, I'll take them, what the hell: always bring another bag, if it comes to it. And passport. Mustn't forget my passport. You know, I'm pretty sure it's still in that travel wallet thing I got for when me and Mummy and Daddy had for some totally and utterly warped and deranged reason gone to EuroDisney in the spring which had been absolutely *gruesome*. Especially when Daddy had put on those stupid ears: *sooo* embarrassing. And God – I wish Mummy would stop screaming up the stairs! I'm coming – I'm *coming*. Christ – it's only Brian and Dotty: what's she making so much shit about? Right – OK, leave that now. Do the belts and scarves and things later. Probably *will* need another bag, by the look of it, yeah – haven't done all the make-up junk yet. Oh Christ – I didn't get that bloody lipgloss! Oh fuck – could've easily got that when I got all the rest of the stuff but I just didn't think of it. Oh well – pick some up at Heathrow: yeah, that'll be OK. Right, then – now let's face this bloody little dinner party. Why do Mummy and Daddy *do* all this? It's always so bloody *boring*. God, you know – it must be really awful to be old.

'I tell you – I'm not exaggerating – I can barely *walk!*' trilled Dotty, as she lurched into Elizabeth's drawing room with a hobble so cripplingly pronounced as to render her the victim of a recent and cruelly misjudged hip replacement, the possessor of a tin leg, maybe – or at least the noble bearer of the woeful aftermath of a semi-paralytic stroke.

'What on earth did you *do*?' cooed Elizabeth. 'Here – sit here – can you? There – is that comfy? How on earth did you *do* it, Dotty?'

Dotty bent both knees and slumped backwards into the frothy and down-filled cushions of one of the room's intensely floral and damn big sofas.

'Oh – it was one of Brian's cursed *manholes*, wasn't it?' huffed Dotty.

'*Man*holes?' screeched Elizabeth. 'You fell down a –?'

'No no,' put in Brian. 'Not the *hole* – the cover. She stubbed her toe on one of the *covers*, that's all.'

'Stubbed my –?!' piped up Dotty, disbelieving at Brian's airy dismissal, stung by so blatant a lack of care. 'I nearly *killed* myself, what are you talking about?'

'Drink, Brian?' said Howard, thinking Oh Christ this bloody woman – always whining on about *something*. Shame she didn't break her bloody neck.

'Thanks, Howard. Scotch, if you have it. She's not really hurt,' he tacked on softly – because this was for Howard alone (didn't want to start a bloody war, did he?)

Howard nodded briefly, moved over to the drinks trolley, and now with his back to the company – everyone seemed to be here bar Melody – he shook his head rather more languorously. Christ, what a woman: Dotty by name, dotty by thing, what was it? Nature.

'A drink will make you *feel* better, Dotty – *poor Dotty*,' soothed Elizabeth, her voice dripping with the Bisto-bolstered gravy of solicitude – quite the level of consolation that one would maybe dole out upon hearing that while he was away, some fellow's cat had – you won't believe it – stuck a claw into a mains wall socket and his thirteen-strong family had formed a conga chain and at the count of three all tugged heartily in a brave but misguided attempt to free the frazzling feline whereupon all were duly and fizzily electrocuted just seconds before the house blew up, taking with it a goodly proportion of the neighbours – not to say the better part of the corner shop, in whose rafters fancy pigeons were famous for roosting: something on those lines.

'What other man – I *ask* you,' beseeched Dotty, 'what sort of a man is it that collects *manholes*?'

'The covers,' said Brian, quietly. 'It's the covers I collect.'

'Well of course the *covers*,' snapped back Dotty. 'Of course you don't – I know you don't collect the

21

bloody *holes*, don't I, you stupid man? Have some *sense*, Brian.'

'Here, Dotty, here,' said Howard rather briskly, wrapping Dotty's fingers around her usual huge G & T. 'Drink. Drink it.'

Dotty did that, but now she was back up and off again:

'They're all over the house! You can't move for – oh hello, Katie – I didn't see you sitting over there. What do you think, Katie, what do you think of a man who collects huge great chunks of scrap iron?'

'Well,' said Katie slowly, 'you collect all those thimbles and things, don't you, Dotty? And plates, and spice jars, and those little china pigs.' And all the rest of the crap in your fucking awful house.

'It's not quite the same *thing*, though, is it, dear?' returned Dotty. 'Anyway – they keep arriving every month – I keep forgetting to stop them.'

'*Have* to stop them now,' blurted Brian, thinking Blast oh damn – she'll hate me now for coming out with that. 'Thought you *had*,' he added miserably, thinking will they fall for this, Howard and Elizabeth? Will they at least pretend to, just to save me? 'Thought you said you were tired of them. Dust-catchers, I thought you said.'

Dotty glared at Brian, and Howard (Well, he thought, I'd better say *something*) came up with:

'Why do you, actually, Brian, collect manholes? Covers. I've often wondered.'

Brian clutched the question to him. 'Some of

22

them have very interesting inscriptions . . . markings. You know, the *history* –'

'Oh *Jesus*!' wailed Dotty. 'Don't get him *talking* about them – sweet God, if he starts *talking* about them we'll be here all night. Oh Elizabeth, I forgot to tell you – Colin is coming over in about half an hour – I hope that's all right? He's got his guitar lesson so I left him a note.'

'Of *course* it's all right,' said Elizabeth, brightly. 'Haven't seen little Colin for yonks – have we, Howard?' You could, she thought, have told me *before*, though, couldn't you, Dotty? I mean, I *like* Colin – don't get me wrong – but I've set the table (and very beautifully, I might say) for *six*, and now I've got to bugger it up and lay another place. Thank Christ I made plenty of food.

'He's not so little any more,' simpered Dotty. 'Nearly fifteen, now. Seems no time at all since I had him in his pram. Oh dear – are we all *old*, Elizabeth? We're not, are we?'

Yes, thought Katie, you bloody are. Mm – I suppose Colin *must* be about that, now: never takes his eyes off my tits. Elizabeth for her part was thinking *You* might be old, Dotty – *you* might: God knows you're beginning to look it. What she said was:

'Let's all have another drink, shall we? Howard? Could you? Melody should be here soon – she said –'

Elizabeth broke off at the sound of the doorbell and everyone except Katie said 'Ah!' and actually appeared quite triumphant.

23

'Talk of the, er . . .' tried Howard. 'Talk of the – oh Christ, what is it? What is it, that thing?'

'Devil, Daddy,' said Katie, softly. Christ, Daddy – your mind.

'Devil, yes, right, that,' agreed Howard. 'Christ – my mind.'

It sounded as if Elizabeth and Melody were maybe conducting a screaming altercation in the hall – but no, this was just their habitual greeting: high-pitched whoops and cries, the hysterical and joyful shrieking of twins separated soon after birth and now newly reunited amid the full dazzle of a television studio. Christ, thought Howard, it was only last Tuesday the two of them had bought up half of Knightsbridge – Elizabeth, admittedly, the easy collarer of most of the spoils – the bringer home of the bulk of the booty. Thank God houses were selling again – during the recession Howard had had to not so much deepen his overdraft as mine it to its subterranean core, just to keep up with Elizabeth; and Katie, of course – Katie was no better, not a bit. God, between them – the *money* they went through! Howard didn't understand how it was possible. Still, it made them happy (I think) – and at least I get left alone. I wish, he suddenly thought – oh God, I wish I wish I wish that right now, this instant, the whole room, the whole house, was utterly empty and it was not Melody who was about to amble in, but Zoo-Zoo. Zoo-Zoo had never been to the house. It would be quite a kick, though, wouldn't it? Having Zoo-Zoo here? Where, exactly? How about there – right there on the golden Bokhara, now being rucked up by Dotty's stricken foot? Yes – yes indeed. That would do very nicely.

'Melody!' he called out now – for in she surely did amble (tuck away your dreams for the night, snuffle them out again soon). 'How very lovely you look. Come on in and have a drink.' And by way of welcome, Howard extended his arm as if hailing a taxi.

'I don't know *why* I do – *if* I do,' giggled Melody. 'I left in an awful rush – I thought it was an hour earlier than it was. I'm *always* doing that. Hi, everyone – hello, Dotty, Brian. Hi, Katie.'

As everyone mumbled their variations on a theme, Melody splayed the fingers of one hand across her chest (pretty fair chest, if Howard was any judge) and blew out her cheeks in mock exhaustion and maybe too in order to demonstrate to the assembly that she had, she had truly, run every single inch of the way so as to be here not too *very* late. She now fell as if felled into the squishy and damn big sofa right next to Dotty.

'Mind my foot,' said Dotty.

'Mm? Your foot? What's wrong with your –?'

'Oh Lord – let's not get into all that again, shall we?' Howard pleaded in practically a theatrically beseeching manner (back of his hand against his brow). 'Have a drink, Melody – usual? White, yes? Believe me, you do not want to relive the saga of Dotty's foot.'

25

'Don't be beastly, Howard,' admonished Elizabeth.

'If it was *his* foot . . .' muttered Dotty.

'Are you well, Melody?' asked Brian, rather quickly.

'I'm great, Brian. I'm good. You OK?'

'Just don't,' said Dotty,' get him talking about *manholes*.'

'I'm sorry?'

'Melody!' hailed Katie from . . . where was she – oh yeah: way over there. 'Never mind manholes – where are you off to for your holidays?'

Elizabeth stared pointedly at Katie, and Katie very nearly winked back. But oh look – Melody's brow is covered in ripples.

'Yes,' she said slowly. 'Bit of a sore point, actually.'

The doorbell sounded again.

'Ah,' said Dotty. 'That'll be Colin.'

'I'll go, shall I?' offered Katie.

'Oh *would* you, Katie?' implored Dotty, eyes dipping in supplication, quite as if Katie had just offered her one of her kidneys for a last-ditch (and minute) life-saving operation, thus enabling Dotty to continue to drink deep down into her God's clean air. 'I would myself, but my foot . . .'

Colin had not been expecting Katie to open the door. He had his bright, boyish and breezy grin fixed on for Elizabeth (he liked Elizabeth: she sometimes gave him money – don't tell your mother – and always smelled so nice. She loved his grin – she had told him so). But it stayed in place, the grin – if maybe rather frozenly. Oh God – he wasn't blushing again, was he? He was, he was – oh *Christ*, how did you ever learn not to? They gave him hell about that at school, the bastards, the rotten cowing bastards. At his new school, that is, the bloody horrible new school that, oh God, he hated hated hated: felt so scared each and every morning. Even the journey was awful.

'Hi, Colin,' said Katie, lightly. 'How was guitar?'

'Fine, thank you,' said Colin, stepping into the hall – the thought glancing across his brain, now: why, I wonder, did I just say 'thank you'? I never say Thank you, I always say Thanks.

'Good as Eric Clapton yet?' smiled Katie. 'Jimi Hendrix?'

Colin gave his joshing, throwaway smirk (Elizabeth loved that one too: she had told him so).

'Not quite.'

Look at him, thought Katie – he's looking dead straight at my tits: I don't think he even knows he's doing it. Shall I? Should I? Yeah, why not? Bit of a giggle.

Katie reached up on tiptoe to straighten a hat on the bent-wood stand, and somehow her left breast very slightly and swiftly brushed over and past Colin's blazing cheek. She followed him into the drawing room grinning broadly, her route well lit by the backs of Colin's mauve and luminous ears. Poor little sod – he's only, what, two-and-a-bit

27

years younger than me: maybe only just discovered the difference between boys and girls. Christ – I wasn't much older than him when I had my abortion. What was that bloke's name again? Dunno. Can't remember. Jonathan, was it? Or was it – no, not Damien, Damien was later, wasn't he? Or *was* it Damien? Dunno. Really can't remember. *Can* remember, course I can – can't ever bloody forget it. His name was Martin and he was such a shit – along with all the others – and I hate him, hate him for it and sometimes I . . . yeah, sometimes I even hate me, just a bit, but it's Martin I find myself *really* hating. Along with all the others.

And as Colin entered and beamed his greetings he was thinking oh Jesus Cowing Christ Almighty! She touched me with her tit and she didn't even notice and just the soft hard softness of it is dancing all over me and Jesus Jesus Jesus I can think about it all night and touch me for that fabulous tingling feeling and God I'd just *love* to do it to Katie – to really really *do* it, you know? Really *do* it to Katie. Yeah.

'Come on in and have a drink, Colin!' hailed Howard – and Elizabeth said: 'Colin – come and sit by me.'

Or to anyone, really. Yeah.

Brian had been pleased to leave the drawing room ('Come on everyone,' Elizabeth had rallied them, 'din-din time for boys and girls') because even since the last time he had been over – not that long ago, fortnight maybe – there were so bloody many new *things* – and Dotty, believe him, would have noted and begrudged every single one of them. There was that clock for a start – huge sort of brass affair, or maybe gold, who knew (Howard seemed to have endless resources; well – selling other people's property and helping himself to three per cent: nice for some). Oh God: that thought. That thought he had just had about Howard – now that wasn't very nice, was it? Hm? I mean, what harm had Howard ever done anyone? None, to Brian's knowledge – so why was he resenting his good fortune? He had a successful little business, right? Maybe not so little. And he reaped the rewards. Nothing wrong there that Brian could see – so what did it matter if he did buy new things (or Elizabeth, more likely, if it is accuracy we are seeking; Howard, left to himself, I doubt could care one way or the other)?

But this is the key to it, though, isn't it? Brian never used to think like this when he was flying high. On the hog. They say that, don't they? High on the hog. Christ knows what it means. But never mind all that, leave all that – where was I, actually? Oh yes: Howard, money – me, none. Yes. Actually, if I was just plain old flat stony broke it wouldn't be so bad. No. But it was the debt, wasn't it? The debt, the debt – huge as you like and mounting daily. At least if he could sell the house – free up the capital to stop them sinking. It wasn't as if no one had come to see it

29

– Howard had been very good like that (give the man his due): sent over droves of prospective, you know, buyers, purchasers – some, apparently, with cash in their hot little hands, ready to sign on the dotted line. Had it with other agents too, of course, but so far not a nibble. No one had even made an offer too ludicrous to contemplate. If there could be such a thing. In Brian's position, he doubted it. Did people maybe sense the failure that could now even have seeped into the very bricks and mortar? Maybe all they saw in the house was not soft furnishings but the most threadbare dreams – maybe they sensed not the warming fire, gas coals aglow, but just the unwelcome touch of the clammy mantle of desperation, laid across hunched-up shoulders by the damp and coolly insinuating fingers of defeat: could be.

Carpets. Carpets had been the undoing of Brian – and not just of Brian, no, but Dotty as well, yes – and Colin too. The lad deserves better – a better Dad, a *real* Dad – a *man*, for God's sake: but what can I do? All I can present to Colin is myself, and heaven alone knows what he sees there. I never thought of carpets, you know, as being anything less than a goldmine. Well look at it – when were you last in a house with no carpets? Everyone needed carpets, right? And God, for years I couldn't supply enough of the stuff. Bought larger premises, didn't I? Yes I bloody did – and did the extra expenses bother me unduly? Joking. I was making money hand

30

over fist – five blokes and a girl I had under me, couple of freelance fitters working round the clock. The mark-up was fantastic, so I could afford to plaster the windows with screamers: Free Fitting! Free Underlay! Free Delivery! Yeah – free bloody everything, except the carpet which will cost you a fortune.

So the recession comes along, but I don't believe in it. The middle classes will always want their carpets, you mark my words. And because retail outlets were soon going for a song, I bought a couple, didn't I? Yes I bloody did – and did this bullish expansion cause me any headaches? Joking. Even when sales began to fall away, I didn't see it. The word 'blip' was everywhere: I used it a lot. Started reducing the prices; didn't work. My suppliers started calling in the debts, the bank was looking worried – so what did I have to lose? Blips pass, right? It's in their nature. I stood as personal guarantor, didn't I? Yes I bloody did – and did they take me at my word? Not joking. They all closed in, and I closed down. Wood – that played a part. Even the people who could still afford carpets, they all wanted wooden floors, now. Crazy, really: I've been covering up wooden floors all my life. So I've got to sell the house. And then I'll be clear. Except we won't have anywhere to live. And I don't have a job. Apart from that . . . I'll be clear. Oh Jesus. You know, sometimes I think if it wasn't for the DIY and my manhole covers, I'd go mad.

'Brian!' called – was it Elizabeth? Yeah, Elizabeth.

31

'*Answer*, can't you?' urged Dotty. 'Always in a dream.'

'Sorry,' said Brian. 'Didn't hear.'

'I said,' said Elizabeth, 'if you can sit here next to Melody – and Dotty, you go next to Howard – no, other end, yes there. Katie, can you see to who wants what. Colin, my sweet – you come and sit over here and tell me everything you've been up to.'

'So, Dotty,' said Howard, flapping open his napkin and surveying the general lie of the land. Elizabeth has done us proud again on the table front – lots of little spherical twinkling lights (must be battery, I think – I think they must be, because there's no wire I can see) setting off all the silver, and the most wonderful – well, I would say flower arrangement, but just you take one look at it: there's peaches in there, if I'm not very much mistaken, and berries and twigs – flowers too, of course: ranunculas, anemones, those other things, can never remember the name of those other things, not gerberas, is it? Could well be – needn't be at all, of course – Christ: my mind. And there's a golden fir-cone right on top; where does she get her ideas from? The big glass goblets too – they do look nice, it has to be said, but goodness knows how Elizabeth can be bothered to go to all this sort of trouble – God knows, it's only Brian and Dotty, after all. Ah yes – Dotty:

'So, Dotty,' resumed Howard. 'Looking forward

to the bucket and spade and What The Butler Saw and bright pink rock and all the rest of it? Got your swimming cozzie ready?'

'I don't think it's going to be quite *that* sort of a holiday, Howard – I've heard that this resort is really rather select. I don't know – I've not been.'

'No – *we* haven't. It was Elizabeth who picked it out – recommended by someone or other, I gather. How come you did, actually, choose the very same place, Dotty? It really is a bit of a coincidence, isn't it? I mean – I don't *mind*, of course . . .'

'It was Brian who picked it,' said Dotty.

'Picked what?' Brian asked from across the way. 'What did I pick?'

'The holiday,' said Dotty. 'We're talking about the holiday.'

'Oh yes,' agreed Brian. 'Well – I say I picked it, I didn't really – I was just looking for the sort of holiday Dotty said she wanted, and this place seemed to offer what looked like the best deal, that's all.'

Not quite how it had gone, actually: that wasn't quite the way. Dotty had been to huge trouble to find out from Elizabeth the exact location and duration of her holiday, and determined to make hers identical. That way, Elizabeth couldn't, could she, afterwards infer that *her* holiday had been a *better* holiday – no she couldn't because they were going to be the *same*: same place, same week (and so the same weather), and therefore Dotty would be safe: an area of potential future hurt averted.

'Gosh, Elizabeth,' said Melody, 'this fish-cake is absolutely *divine*.' And she put a good deal of energy into the lip-licking side of things while Elizabeth acknowledged by way of a throwaway smirk of modesty, well laced with pride, the low chorus of appreciative grunts that had now risen up from hither and yon.

'There's seven different sorts of fish in it, actually,' she said. 'Including sole.'

'And the sauce!' went on Melody, rather gratifyingly. 'To die for, yes? It's just *too* dreamy.'

'More or less a basic hollandaise,' said Elizabeth. 'Fennel, of course. Are you enjoying it, Colin? Oh you are – you've practically cleaned your plate.'

'It's yum, actually,' approved Colin, chucking over to Elizabeth the sideways, chummy grin that actually could quite often be relied upon for an impulsive hair-ruffle, so he was none too surprised when she did it.

'Healthy appetite,' said Elizabeth. 'Growing lad. You're a growing lad, aren't you, Colin? Healthy appetite. It's good to see young people eating properly. Nothing worse – there's nothing worse, is there, than seeing them poke about at a lettuce leaf – or if they're faddy. Nothing worse than faddy – oh, I don't like *this*, and I can't eat *that*. But Colin's not like that, are you, Colin? Not like our Katie.'

'I *eat*,' piped up Katie, in her aggrieved tone that protested of wrongful arrest. 'I *eat* – who says I don't eat? I just turned against meat, that's all – I mean, I am *allowed*, aren't I? It is a free country.'

'You always used to enjoy your meat,' countered Elizabeth. 'Steak and lamb used to be your favourites.'

'I still eat chicken,' pouted Katie. 'Anyway, I don't actually see what business it is of anyone *what* I eat. I eat what I like, OK?'

'Yes, all right, Katie,' said Howard, in his let's-all-just-pipe-down-now-shall-we voice. 'Pass round the wine, will you? Dotty – have some more wine.'

'That's one of the best things about coming here,' smiled Dotty. 'Don't have to worry about getting home.'

A general sort of nearly-laughter rumbled briefly: it was just that she *always* said that – every time she came over.

'So anyway, Melody,' started up Katie. 'Oh sorry – do you want more wine? Oh – you've got. Yeah. Anyway – your holiday – what was it you were saying earlier?'

Melody was chewing fairly energetically on a chunk of French bread that she had just dunked into the last of her sauce (to die for, yes?) and made Katie aware of this fact by pointing a finger at her mouth, widening her eyes, and mock-chomping fit to bust; she put absolutely everything into the business of the eventual, gulping finale.

'Yeah well,' she said. 'Big problem, actually, because it looks like no holiday at all, this year. It's a bit of a bugger – oop, sorry – bit of a nuisance, because I took the time off work and

35

everything, but – well, if I'm honest, I just can't *afford* a holiday. I'm just so broke!'

Katie looked at Melody. Can't *afford*? What on earth could this mean? Melody maybe saw that a little elaboration was called for, so she opened her mouth to resume, but not before Brian put in:

'Expensive things, holidays. Very.' And he didn't actually care if Dotty was training lasers on him – didn't actually mind, in point of fact, because it was true what he said, right, so why not say it?

'You see it's *Dawn*, really,' went on Melody. 'Elizabeth – can I help with anything?'

'I can manage,' said Elizabeth, now standing and garnering plates. 'Katie – can you pass? Yes that – no, that. Yes.'

'I keep forgetting about little Dawn,' said Dotty. 'You never bring her, do you?'

If *I* had a little baby, thought Dotty, I would: I'd bring her everywhere. Carry her in my arms. Just like I did with Colin – and just like I did with my little angel Maria. Right up until the second she died, and then I went on carrying her still, rocking her gently to and fro, and stooping down to kiss those sweet, soft lips for the very last time – cool now, and emitting no gurgle to enchant me.

'Well you *can't*, can you?' expanded Melody. 'I mean, if I'd brought her tonight, I'd be upstairs *seeing* to her all the time – or else she'd be bawling her head off down here. I mean she's the loveliest thing in the world and I love her dearly, but she costs me an absolute *fortune* in nannies. Sometimes in a week I give the nannies more money than I get paid at the shop.'

'Oh but Melody!' deplored Elizabeth – back now from her brief foray next door, and wheeling a trolley piled high with what looked and smelled like damn good things. 'You *must* have a holiday. *Everyone* needs a holiday – God, I know I do.'

'Yes, well,' was Melody's comeback to that. All very well, Elizabeth – you've got Howard. Dawn's father didn't hang around for two bloody minutes, did he? And maybe you didn't hear me – I'm broke. Flat broke. If you or Katie have any conception what that means. The only reason I found the cash for a babysitter tonight is your amazing dinner: Christ, whenever I come here, I don't have to eat again for days. You don't know what it's like – no, Elizabeth, believe me: you just don't.

'Well I just think that's *awful*,' declaimed Elizabeth, placing on the table covered and glossy tureens, a swan-like gravy boat, a gondola of creamy and speckled sauce. 'I bet Colin is looking forward to his holiday, aren't you, Colin?'

'I am, actually,' said Colin. Just being out of that horrible horrible school is a holiday for me, but yeah – a week somewhere else will be nice. Shame it has to be with Mum and Dad, though. But apparently Howard and Elizabeth will be there too, so maybe he could latch on to them. Elizabeth, anyway.

'Now you'll all just have to be patient while

37

Howard *carves*,' announced Elizabeth. 'Here, Katie – madame's special order of chicken breast, because fillet of beef isn't good enough for her.'

'I didn't *say* –'

'Oh leave her,' put in Howard. 'If she doesn't want beef, she doesn't want beef. Here, Elizabeth – pass the plate down to Melody, will you?'

'But do all *start* when you get your plate, won't you?' continued Elizabeth. 'Howard is a very *good* carver, but he's just the teensiest bit slow – aren't you, darling?'

'Would *you* like to do it, Elizabeth?' Well *would* she? She wouldn't, would she? So why didn't she just shut up and let him get on with it?

'No need to get *sulky*, darling,' smiled Elizabeth, sweetly – opening wide her eyes and drawing down the corners of her mouth the better to tacitly convey to any of the company inclined to glance across – Ooh, don't look now but Big Mister Man is getting into one of his *moods*.

'Now there's some pretty decent claret for all those that wants,' said Howard (it's better to ignore her when she gets like this), 'or there's plenty more of the Chablis if you feel like sticking. You happy with your Coke, Colin? Does he want a drop of wine, Brian?'

'No,' answered Dotty. 'He doesn't.'

'I'm fine,' said Colin. I can speak for myself, you know. I don't actually *like* wine, if anyone's interested, so in fact I would have turned it down on grounds of taste, and not because I was shying away from some forbidden thing. Nor would I have rushed into accepting it because it was illicit – that would be, frankly, pathetic. I have tasted whisky, however, and I quite like that. With Coke, it can really be rather palatable. I wonder if Katie is aware that I have been looking at her? Probably not. Certainly she hasn't looked at me back. It's not that I mean to be rude – it's just that I can't keep my eyes off her tits. I wonder what they feel like. What do tits feel like, I wonder? Not for the first time. Elizabeth, I shouldn't wonder, also has pretty good tits, but she doesn't wear such tight clothes, so it's hard to tell. Of course, she's quite old. I wonder if old tits are different.

'You haven't had an English holiday before, have you, Colin?' asked Elizabeth. 'Or at least not since you were very little. You always went for France, didn't you, Dotty?'

'We got to know France quite well,' said Brian. 'Brittany, of course.'

'Is that where you went last year?' asked Elizabeth. 'I forget. Can I be awfully rude, Colin, and just stretch across you for the gravy?'

Colin didn't mind in the least because the action tightened the fabric of her dress and it was now as plain as day to Colin that the tit just east of his nose, anyway, was a very good tit indeed.

'Brest,' he said. 'Lovely.'

'It *is* nice,' agreed Brian. 'Anyway – couple of days and it's English seaside, here we come!'

39

'Yes,' said Elizabeth, 'but I still think it's fright-fully unfair about *Melody*. I mean, here we all are gadding off and Melody is left here –'

'—holding the baby,' grinned Melody. 'Oh Godsake – don't worry about *me* – I'll be fine. Catch up on some sleep.'

'Does anyone want more beef? Howard – cut more beef.'

'I'm stuffed,' said Brian.

'You eat too much,' said Dotty. Actually, he didn't – but look: why be sweet when the sour option's going begging?

'I wouldn't mind some, actually,' said Melody. 'It's absolutely *marvellous*, Elizabeth – so tender it just melts.'

'We're lucky we've got a good butcher locally,' said Elizabeth. 'Do you still use Turners, Dotty? They really are terribly good.'

'Oh God yes,' replied Dotty. 'I'd never go anywhere but *Turners*.' Haven't been to Turners for *months* – along with practically every other good shop in the world. God – the money I get from Brian now, it's amazing we're not all reduced to cat food. Give it time, and we will be.

'But Katie,' said Melody, 'what about *your* holiday? You're going off on your own this time, yes?'

'Well,' qualified Elizabeth, 'not quite on her *own*, no – some friend from school called Ellie, is it? Yes – along with meat she has chosen to give up her parents. We weren't *consulted*, needless to say – this is the way they are, nowadays. And don't

40

ask me what sort of girl *Ellie* might be, because we have yet to meet her. Katie never brings her home. Too ashamed of us, I expect.'

'Don't be daft, Mum,' laughed Katie. 'It's just that she lives quite far away, that's all. I told you. Hers was always the longest journey into school. But she's very *nice*, if that's what you're worried about. She's not common, or anything – and she doesn't do drugs or anything like that. She's very into architecture and modern design and all that sort of thing, and that's why she picked Chicago.'

'Chicago!' crooned Melody. 'Oh but Katie how *exciting* – I had no idea you were going to Chicago. It's fabulous, apparently.'

'Dangerous,' said Elizabeth.

'Not if you're careful,' soothed Howard. How can you do that, though? People don't get injured because they're careless – people get injured because they're *there*.

'When are you going?' asked Melody.

'Tomorrow,' grinned Katie. 'Can't wait.'

'Tomorrow!' hooted Elizabeth – eyes wide with genuine amazement: no play-acting in this one. 'Tomorrow! You're not going tomorrow, are you? It's the day after, surely? We're all going off the day after.'

'You might be,' said Katie. 'I'm going tomorrow. Ten o'clock flight – Heathrow to O'Hare. Can't wait.'

'Can't see it makes a lot of difference,' sniffed

Howard. 'Tomorrow or the next day – what's the difference?'

Elizabeth dropped her eyes. 'I suppose – I suppose that's right. I just didn't know, that's all.' It's true – of course it's true: what earthly difference could it possibly make? It's just that I *assumed* . . . I just didn't know that tomorrow she was going to America. I thought it was the next day, that's all. She's never *been* to America, and she's only young and oh God I hope she's safe. I don't *like* her going off – not coming with us – I don't, I don't: I don't like it at all. She's only a little girl, after all, and whatever she may think of me, I am her mother and I love her very much. I suppose I'd better start getting used to this – Katie, doing what she wants, when she pleases. Without me.

'Pudding,' she said.

First there were sorbets to cleanse the palate, and Brian – not hideously aware that he had a palate so filthy as to require such a thing – wolfed down his in a trice. Christ, he thought, I wonder if they eat like this every night? Must do – they're hardly likely to do anything special just to impress poor old Brian and Dotty, now, are they?

The subsequent tarte Tatin was truly wondrous (everyone said so) but here Elizabeth was fielding no bouquets:

'It's all down to the most *fabulous* pâtisserie in the High Street. They've got this wonderful old Frenchwoman there who does it all the old way, the real way. It's expensive – yes, I suppose it is –

but you can see how good it is. You still go there, don't you, Dotty?'

'Of course,' said Dotty. No. No I bloody don't.

'I've *just*,' trumpeted Elizabeth now, 'had *the* most brilliant idea!'

Oh God, thought Howard: never good news. Bound to cost a fortune, whatever it is. Blimey – do you know, I seem to have drunk that whole bottle of claret on my own. And made pretty fair inroads into that one, too. Do other people drink as much as I do? You never know, do you, what is normal and what is not. I mean, certainly no one round this table has come close – Melody, maybe – but then they were hardly typical, surely?

'Do tell,' urged Howard. Humour the woman.

'Right!' blazed on Elizabeth, her eyes on fire with at the very least evangelical zeal. What could she be about to impart? Maybe the absolutely wonderful old Frenchwoman in the pâtisserie had come up with the cure for all cancers in the oh-so-easy-to-take format of a light-as-air chocolate and almond croissant? Or could her bombshell maybe turn out to be less significant?

'Right – OK. At this hotel – this hotel you've booked, yes Howard? We've got a suite, right?'

'Right,' agreed Howard, slowly. What – she wants the entire floor?

'Well these suites in my experience are absolutely vast – far more space than you actually need. Now the sitting-room, right – they could easily move in another bed, couldn't they?'

43

Most of the table seemed pretty puzzled. What was Elizabeth up to? It seemed an odd moment to announce that she and Howard would no longer be sleeping together.

'Why, in fact –?' tried Howard.

'Because *then*,' went on Elizabeth triumphantly, '*then* – Melody could come along too! I just can't *bear* the fact that she can't go on holiday. It's just not *fair*.'

'Oh don't be so *silly*, Elizabeth!' hooted Melody. 'I can't do that! I don't want to crash in on your holiday! I'll be *fine*, I tell you – I'm used to not going away.'

Good, thought Howard. Why should I be paying for a suite and ending up with just a bedroom? With Elizabeth, trust me, you *needed* a suite: sometimes you just had to have somewhere to go.

'Nonsense,' was all Elizabeth had to say to that. This was her brainwave, OK – and it was going to happen, right? Believe her – it was going to *happen*. 'It's *perfect*, don't you see? It's all *paid* for – they won't charge any more for an extra bed, will they, Howard?'

'I shouldn't have thought so,' said Howard. Oh God. This is going to *happen*, isn't it? Yes – just take one look at Elizabeth: this is going to happen.

'But it's not *fair*,' protested Melody. 'It's *your* holiday – it's *your* suite. And anyway – it sounds a pretty ritzy place – what's the *food* going to cost?'

'Oh *God*, Melody,' swept on Elizabeth. 'What

44

can a little bit of food cost? We'll see to all that, of course we will – won't we, Howard?'

Oh *shit*. 'Of course,' he said. 'No problem at all.'

'Oh . . . I don't *know*, Elizabeth,' havered Melody. I do, though: free holiday – all that *food*. Yum.

'Well that's settled, then,' said Elizabeth, with a finality that Howard had heard before.

'But,' interjected Melody – oh bugger, I've only just thought of this – 'what about Dawn?'

'Ah,' said Elizabeth. Hadn't thought of that. 'Well she can come too! Can't she, Howard? It'll be lovely having little Dawn – and she needs a holiday as well.'

Oh *double* shit. 'I don't see a problem with that,' said Howard. Well what could he say? Hey? That the thought of being cooped up in a single bedroom with Elizabeth while a bloody little baby next door screamed its head off all through the bloody night made him want to fuck off to Chicago with Katie – or (bliss of blisses) just forget the whole thing and stay at home.

He'd never really been much of a one for all these summer things, if he was honest. I mean – take last year: Barbados. Paradise, right? Well yes I suppose so – but only up to a point. OK – there's the pale green sea, here's the white-gold sand. Am I in a hammock in the shade of a swaying palm? Certainly am – and in my hand is a huge and coloured Del Boy of a drink, bristling with paper and plastic silly things. Great. And one hour later?

45

You feel a prat. What – I'm going to be slung from a tree for a fortnight, am I, staring at the fucking sea and getting smashed on stuff I wouldn't so much as look at at home? You always end up doing stuff you don't want to on holiday. You get up in the morning – not because you had awoken eager and refreshed and keen to be up and at it, no. You get up either because you've been startlingly woken by a foreign woman with a Hoover letting herself into your room, apologizing, and backing out again, or else because you are traumatized by the fear of missing *breakfast* – which at home, of course, you don't even eat. And then you find yourself doing things like sitting on flyblown donkeys and stinking camels, or climbing three hundred and sixty bloody *steps* that lead absolutely fucking nowhere at all – or even (the worst) looking at *art*. You burn your arms, you overdose on calamari and your stools turn to slurry. And on the last day you haggle your way through markets in currency you don't understand with people you deeply distrust for garbage too dreadful to live with – and then solemnly agree over dinner that truly here is heaven and the thought of ever leaving is breaking your heart.

Howard was depressed, now, thinking about the misery of holidays. What if I –? Oh Lord, oh goody, oh boy – get a load of this! What a wheeze! But would Elizabeth wear it? She might, she might – it was all a question of approach.

'Shall we have our coffees next door?' said Elizabeth.

'Elizabeth,' cranked up Howard. 'I've had a rather *better* idea – about the holiday, I mean.'

'Katie,' said Elizabeth. 'Stop hogging the Bittermints. What about the holiday, Howard? It's all arranged.'

'Yes but look – if I'm perfectly *honest* here,' lied Howard through his teeth, 'I've been a bit worried about taking the time off work. Norman is off too next week, remember, and OK – Sam and Phyllis can more or less run the place with the temp I got in, but there are one or two pretty sensitive and, I have to say, Elizabeth, rather *lucrative* deals going through at the moment – isn't that right, Katie? – and I really wonder if I shouldn't be around.'

'But –?' interjected Elizabeth.

'No listen – hear me. Instead of Melody just bunking up in the sitting-room bit, she could take *my* place in a proper bed.'

'Oh God, Howard!' protested Melody. 'I couldn't *possibly* –'

'Listen, listen,' insisted Howard. 'It makes perfect sense – I can still drive you both down there, of course I will, and then I can see these, you know deals through – I'd really be easier in my mind, you know. Honestly, Melody, you'd be doing me a favour. And then, of course, I can keep an eye on next door. Not at all happy, you know, about both houses being empty like that.'

'Well,' said Brian, 'I'm all for *that* side of things. Wasn't too happy about it myself.'

Elizabeth was in two minds: what – go on holiday

without Katie *or* Howard? She'd never done that before. Which was appealing in its way because of course she wouldn't be alone because of Melody. And a week without Howard's moaning wasn't a too terrible thought.

'Look, Howard,' put in Melody, 'this is wonderfully *good* of you and everything, but I'd really feel too bad about it – I can't take your holiday!'

'Well look,' said Elizabeth, 'if that's what he *wants* . . .'

'I do, I do. As I say: perfect solution. End of subject.' Howard smiled as he rose and led the exodus from the dining room. 'This way everyone's happy.' Including, he thought, as he made his way to the Armagnac, my little Zoo-Zoo.

It was funny, Brian was thinking – back in the drawing room now, sipping his brandy, nice chair over by the window – it was funny, wasn't it, different people's attitudes as to what looked nice and what didn't. The things people chose to surround themselves with. Case in point – those two round-topped mirrors in the alcoves over there, one each side of the fireplace above those little tables. Brian supposed they were meant to look like sort of Georgian windows – glazing bars much in evidence, even a bit of a sill along the bottom – but he quite frankly wouldn't have given you twopence for them, while not doubting for a single moment that they had probably cost quite a good deal of money; most of the stuff in this room gave off the air of fairly stiffly lavish expense.

Now next door, Brian had very similar alcoves to these (they could be twins) but had he stuck up a couple of mirrors? Very much not. No, what Brian had done was got out his Workmate from the garage, banked up the Black & Decker power tools, took a little trip down the woodyard and then got back and got cracking. What you do, right, is form your basic casing out of blockboard (you need inch, inch-and-a-half if we're talking load-bearing) then score a sort of a plate groove in each shelf with a very special slotting attachment that he had been pleased to pick up at Homebase one January sale for a fraction of the recommended retail price – silly money, really. You drive bolt holes through the sides of the carcass, see, so that you can screw direct into the flanking walls and then the chimney breast. You can get these very thin strips of veneer to cover the fronts of the shelves (blockboard, Brian would own, is unsightly in profile) and within a remarkably short space of time – all of Saturday and a fair part of Sunday afternoon – you've got a pair of very smart display units, though Brian says it himself. He was the only one who *did* say it, mind, because when Dotty got back (she'd been off somewhere for the weekend – sister's, pretty sure – would never have tolerated the noise and dust) she took one look at his handiwork and said Christ Almighty, Brian, I do hope this is some sort of *joke*, is it, because if you think I'm going to live

49

with a couple of coffins made out of packing cases you've got another think – *Christ*, Brian, actually – what is it in fact that is *wrong* with you, hm? I mean, what are you – *blind*? Colin, Colin – come here, come in here. Will you just look at what your father's done *this* time! I mean *Christ*, Brian, what do you want to go making up *driftwood* for?! Look, he had mollified, listen: it may not look very much now, but you just wait till I put up the manhole covers! So you see what I mean: people have different ideas.

'I don't know, I'm not sure,' Dotty was saying to Elizabeth. 'I'll ask Brian. Brian – what *floor* is our suite, do you know? Will we be near Elizabeth?'

This hauled Brian back quite sharply. He had been expecting something on these lines for some days now – amazing it hadn't come before – but still he had composed no adequate response. Might as well just start talking, then, and see what came out.

'No. Yes. I meant to mention that. We're not actually *in* The Excelsior. Not as such.'

'Not?' queried Elizabeth. 'Oh but Dotty, I thought you said –'

'I did,' said Dotty softly, the fear of something, don't know what, passing into and out of her. 'Brian –?'

'You see the thing is,' said Brian, 'I thought we'd be a little bit different.'

Dotty looked at him. What *is* it – oh God would someone just tell her what *is* it about Brian? She had *told* him, *explained*, over and over, that the whole *point*, the whole point of this thing was that it must must must be the *same*. And no – no, Brian, no, since you ask, I *can't* actually put into words why this should be so, I just happen to feel it, and if you do this one thing for me – it's not much, is it, not much in the light of everything you have taken away – then somehow I shall, I know I shall, feel protected. She told him, she told him: it all had to be the *same*.

'Different,' breathed Dotty.

'The Palace,' said Howard, 'is equally good, I'm told.'

Dotty was still looking at Brian. 'Palace?' she enquired.

Brian shook his head. 'Surprise,' he said. 'I'm keeping it as a surprise.'

'Does anyone want more drinkies?' piped up Katie.

'God,' croaked Melody, 'I actually feel quite sloshed.'

And she did, actually. Don't normally drink like this because I can't normally afford it. And now look! I've just landed an all-expenses-paid hol for me and Dawn! Shame about Dawn. Could actually have a much bloody better time without *Dawn*, but there's no way I can stretch to a live-in nanny for a week. No way on God's earth.

'I think,' said Dotty, 'we must go. Where's Colin?'

'Oh don't go, Dotty,' urged Elizabeth. 'Stay.'

And already Dotty could hear it in Elizabeth's voice. They hadn't even gone, hadn't even *packed*, let alone come home and compared notes – and already Elizabeth just knew that *her* holiday was better. And here was just the beginning – here was only the hint of a graze, but if Dotty were to betray the true extent of her fear of goring, then Elizabeth, she just knew, would become insatiable and bleed her, bleed her.

'Where's Colin?' said Dotty again.

'I'll find him,' said Katie. 'Actually, folks, do you mind if I say all my goodbyes and happy hols sort of stuff *now*, cos I've still got quite a bit of packing to do.'

This was generally acceded to (have fun, send us a card) and then Elizabeth said:

'*And*, Dotty, I haven't told you how lovely you look this evening. I meant to say it the second you walked in, but all that business with your *foot* . . .'

'Ah,' said Dotty. Very good. Now everyone was reminded that Dotty had completely forgotten about her foot.

'That red outfit really does suit you, you know,' went on Elizabeth (had to be loving it, didn't she?) 'You're *so* lucky you can still get into it.'

Yes indeed. The blood-letting had begun.

Katie thumped once on the downstairs lavatory door and called out Colin, I think your Mum and Dad are about to go – but the door glided open and it was dark and vacant within. Where *is* the silly little sod, then? Oh well bugger all that – I've got packing to do. She wouldn't have gone into Howard and Elizabeth's bathroom, but the light was on and the door ajar. Colin was standing by the basin, his nose hovering over a large glass phial of scent, its globular stopper aloft in his hand.

'What on earth are you doing in here?' said Katie.

Colin put down the bottle. 'Katie. Hello. I'm sorry – I just used the lavatory. I do, usually. It's nicer up here.'

Katie shrugged. It made not one bit of difference to her what lavatory Colin chose to use.

'It's pretty nice, that one,' said Katie, picking up the scent. 'I sometimes borrow that. I think I'll stick some on now.' Katie idled the moistened stopper up and down her neck. 'Mm – gorgeous. Want to smell?'

She bent down to Colin, purposely pushing out any part of her that would jut: hee hee. Colin came forward and his nostrils were flickering just half an inch from Katie's throat when he felt the gentle insistence of her breasts against his shoulder and he just had to look down, then, didn't he? Just had to do it.

'You can touch,' whispered Katie. 'If you want to.'

Colin's eyes underwent a quick-spliced spasm of shock and then darted up to meet Katie's and enquire of them Am I mad? Did I hear you say . . . ?

Can I *really*? He reached out with a paper hand and felt it smoulder on contact with the silky feel of whatever it was that Katie was wearing – burst into flames as he quickly clutched. Suddenly his ears were assailed by Katie's screaming.

'What in Christ's name do you think you're *doing*?! Take your fucking hand *off* me you disgusting little shit!'

Alarm was all over Colin, now – alarm and mortification. Oh God Jesus! *Am* I mad? Am I? He turned and fled downstairs, his whole head crimson – ran right into his mother in the hall, hadn't looked back, hadn't seen on Katie's face the huge and fleshy grin of malicious pleasure that hung there still as she closed behind her the door to her room.

'Oh God my *foot*!' wailed Dotty. '*Colin* you clumsy little idiot – that was my *foot*!'

'Oh dear,' sympathized Elizabeth. 'Poor Dotty – your foot really is having a *beast* of a day, isn't it, poor love?'

'Oh dear,' confided Brian to Howard, quietly in the corner. 'Dotty's not best pleased about things – you can tell. She's bound to start up when we're home.'

Howard opened wide his eyes, and compressed his lips into what was meant to be a sympathetic gesture indicative of his powerlessness to offer the slightest help on that score. When Brian then asked Howard what on earth he was meant to *do* with the woman, it was Howard's turn to augment the eyes and lips thing with a shrug of shoulders that said in equal measures Don't ask me and Leave me out of it.

'She hasn't, has she –' whispered Brian, quite urgently, '*said* things about me, has she? I mean to you, or anything?'

'*Said* –?' checked Howard, puzzled to a degree – but in not much more than a couldn't-frankly-give-a-sod sort of a way. '*Said* things? No, no she hasn't said things – not to me, anyway. What sort of things?'

'Oh,' said Brian miserably, assimilating the distance between himself and Dotty. Seemed OK: she was still laying in to Colin. 'Just things. Last January, I happen to know, she went around saying that I had burned her Christmas presents. Her presents to me, I mean. She told everyone that she had given me two beautifully wrapped Christmas presents and that I had set fire to them – burned them.'

'And . . .' began Howard, thinking Christ Almighty it's difficult to say which of them is more beyond hope – Dotty with her plethora of common or garden neuroses, Brian with his fucking manhole covers. '. . . *Did* you, in fact, um – burn them?'

Brian turned his eyes full on to Howard, now, urging the man to be a part of this:

'Well of *course* I did. Yes, I did – of *course* I did! She gave me a scented candle, didn't she? And a packet of twenty cigarillos.'

Howard looked back as directly as possible, the

possibility of a smile tugging at him, difficult to subdue.

'But you don't smoke, do you, Brian?'

'I *don't*,' agreed Brian, with passion. And then, more reasonably, 'but you've got to show willing, haven't you? They made me very ill, those cigarillos. Only did it to *please* the woman.'

Howard nodded – tried not to focus on Brian's spectacularly awful haircut. Oh Lord oh Lord – I'm so so pleased that I'm not going to the seaside. Zoo-Zoo, Zoo-Zoo – keep your bed warm for me, he nearly sang out – just as the thought glanced across Brian's mind that he could just about get down not being a winner any longer, could just about bear to take that on board, if only he could just get back all that which he had lost. But here, of course, he was forced to acknowledge with a weary and aching helplessness, here we have the very essence of loss: all the stuff is gone.

Howard was back now from having driven Melody home – mixing his last Scotch of the day, bar top-ups, and insisting just the one more time to Elizabeth that he had in fact been in a perfectly fit condition to drive, thank you very much – that it would take considerably more than a couple of drinks to render Howard in any way incapable of sitting behind the wheel of a car, he would have her know.

'But it *wasn't* just a couple of drinks, was it, Howard? All that wine at dinner – God knows how much brandy afterwards. And what about the Scotches before? Christ, Howard – you could have killed the both of you.'

'Well I didn't. As you can see.'

'And what if you'd been stopped? Christ – your breath would've turned the crystals *tartan*. How on earth could you *exist* without a car, Howard? You couldn't, could you? You just *couldn't*. It's just not worth the risk.'

'Well I *wasn't* stopped, was I?'

But she was right, of course she was. It had been bloody stupid – but there had barely been any traffic, went right through. And anyway, taxis never wanted to go to the dark and more than faintly horrid bit of London Melody elected to inhabit. Howard for one didn't blame them. But it had been an interesting little trip, in its way. What with one thing and another.

'Thanks for doing this, Howard,' Melody had opened, once they were both in the Jaguar. 'Where's the other bit of this belt thing? Oh here – got it, it's OK. Gosh, I do actually feel quite woozy – it was *you*, Howard. You kept on filling my glass.'

Howard eased the car away from the drive.

'Why would I do such a thing?'

'I know why you *used* to,' came back Melody.

Howard smiled. 'I don't recall that we needed any of that. Sometimes we didn't even get the bottle open before . . .'

Melody sighed. 'I miss all that, Howard. I miss you.'

'That was then,' said Howard. And then, more slowly: 'It's different, now.'

'Doesn't have to be,' pouted Melody.

'Oh it does, Melody – believe me, it does.'

Nearly a mile of road thudded away beneath them before Melody came up with Why?

'Because,' said Howard. God will you look at that – bloody cyclist and no bloody rear light – Jesus I could've flattened him. Which wouldn't be good: I've had a hell of a lot to drink. 'You took up with someone else – remember? It was your choice – I didn't want you to leave.'

'Always the same ground – you always keep going over the same old ground.'

'You can't brush it aside, Melody. You *lived* with the man.'

'You were *married*. You weren't going to leave, were you? You weren't ever going to leave Elizabeth.'

'No I wasn't – as I made clear again and again. Anyway, she's meant to be your friend.'

'Yes but what was in it for me, hey? I mean, what – I'd just go on getting older and you come on over whenever you feel like it –'

'Oh *can* it, Melody . . .'

'– and meanwhile Elizabeth sits in the lap of luxury thinking oh what a great *husband* she's got.'

'I doubt she thinks that. Anyway, Melody – I know all this, you've said all this. You made a decision. You met a bloke and you lived with him and you had a baby and then he buggered off. End of chat. It's only since he's been gone that you say you miss me. Or when a bill comes in.'

'I *do* miss you – I *do*. If you go left at these lights it's probably quicker. I never really *cared* for him, you know – it was true when I told you that.'

'He didn't chain you down, did he?'

'Don't . . . be crude, Howard. Oh look – there's a place right outside.' And then – as if inspiration had newly dawned: 'Howard – drive into the bit around the side.'

Howard cut the engine and turned to face her. He released his seatbelt.

'Why?' he said.

Melody laid her fingers on his knee, and looked at Howard in a way he well remembered.

'Please,' she said.

'Melody . . .' he tried (Christ – the touch of those fingers – just so little a thing reaching all over him like it always had done). 'You're not *serious*? It's been years.'

'So?' said Melody, sliding her hand around his thigh. 'Come on, Howard. *Please.*'

'I'm half cut,' he said – but his hands had made contact, though he surely could not recall having willed them to do so.

'Howard,' said Melody, more darkly, 'move the car.'

Howard sighed in despair – he was not quite sure of what or whom – fired the engine and swung the midnight-blue Jaguar into similarly inky shadows alongside the house.

'I don't know about this, Melody,' said Howard, with lukewarm foreboding. But he was out of the car and opening the rear door, so he maybe had an inkling.

Even when Melody's flat had been quite available, she and Howard would quite often do this. It was, said Melody, the urgency that she loved; that, and the creaking of the leather.

'Put your hand there,' breathed Melody. She was astride and facing him, and Howard felt with almost fear the flood of warmth from that always plump and even tender place right up tight between her legs. 'I miss you,' she sighed, as she pulled his trousers asunder. 'Oh I've missed you, missed you . . . really missed you.'

Now he was up her and Melody stared at him as if amazed by a revelation. She came down hard on top of him – harder now with every stroke. Howard felt hot and scared and mightily courageous and he plunged his damp and prickled face into Melody's breasts, pulling at the centre of her bra with clenched and nippily eager teeth. Just as he felt the stream, the swell of rising pleasure beginning to play and tease, poised on inundation, so did Melody place both of her hands across his mouth and bear down on him as if to grind him out.

'Kill me!' she hissed. 'Oh kill me kill me kill me!'

The sudden and hideous shriek that pierced the silent air all around them had Howard jerking upwards in unalloyed terror and coming hard into a frightened and hotly pleasured Melody as the word Cat then rasped out of him: *Cat*, he said, it was only a cat – husking now with just dismissed humour and this full and aching crush of exhaustion. Melody laughed and hugged him, and then she kissed his lips.

'I've always loved you, Howard,' she said. 'And I always will, I know it. God – I wish it was *us* who were going to the seaside, sharing the suite – not me and Elizabeth. It's *you* I want, Howard – *you.*'

M'yes, quite possibly, thought Howard, as he tugged himself sort of together. But what you are unaware of, Melody – what neither you nor Elizabeth *knows* is that I have no longer a desire to be with either of you, ever. This was just old times' sake: even now, Melody, as I inhale your sweet-hot and deep inner milky juices, I am thinking only of my little Zoo-Zoo, and waiting for us to be together again.

Right, thought Katie, surveying her room with a critical eye. I think that's just about everything I can do for tonight. Tooth stuff and all the rest of it in the morning (must set the clock) – slippers, and so on. *Did* need another bag: inevitable. Could easily have filled up a fifth, but there was no way at all she could heave along five, even with help.

Elizabeth had just been up, asking Katie if everything was all right. I mean, she qualified, you've *got* everything, have you? Passport? Money? Got everything?

'Yep,' answered Katie, really quite breezily: now I'm all packed I just can't *wait*. 'Don't think I've forgotten anything.'

'I really *didn't* know you were going tomorrow, you know,' went on Elizabeth. 'For some reason I really had it fixed in my head that we were all of us setting off the day after. Oh God. I'm not at all sure I even want to go, now. Poor Howard. He may not get away at all this year, now.'

'It's true what he was saying about work, though,' said Katie. 'There is a hell of a lot going on at the moment. Lots of lovely money.'

'Yes but your father *needs* a holiday – everyone does. I do hope he'll be all right on his own.'

'He will be,' said Katie. Yes, she thought – he will be. She didn't know, couldn't quite put it into words, but she just felt sure that Daddy would be all right, very; and maybe not on his own at all.

'I really think you ought to phone this person – *Ellie*, is it?' said Elizabeth. 'I mean obviously she would have phoned you if anything was – you know, if something was wrong, some hitch. But I think you should make contact.'

Katie nodded. 'It's on my list – I'm just going to ring her now, and then I'm going to bed. Got to be up at seven – six-thirty, safe side.'

'Well I'll be around to see you off. Good night, Katie – and Katie,' added Elizabeth from the door, 'I know you think I *fuss* and everything, but you will won't you be *careful* out there, hm? Always get taxis. Don't wander round late at night. Promise?'

62

And don't, will you, do anything at all with *men*: I wonder if you do already?

Katie smiled: dear old Mum. 'I'll be *fine*,' she said.

When Elizabeth had gone, Katie picked up her mobile.

'Hi, it's me – OK?' she said into the mouthpiece, with the other hand flicking back a flap of duvet. 'All set? Ready for the big day? . . . God – yeah, OK. Me? Can't wait. And whatever you do don't be *late*!'

Norman Furnish smiled as he replaced the receiver. 'I won't,' he had said. No – won't be late: now it's come I'm really looking forward to it. Apart, of course, from the money side of things. That and the white-hot freezing fear that Mr Street – Howard – would somehow get wind of this whole wild and scary caper. (Incidentally, Katie hadn't phoned this person – *Ellie*, is it – for the perfectly valid reason that Ellie didn't exist: one of Katie's better strokes, the creation of Ellie. Well look – how on earth else could she have played it?)

The awful truth is (Norman could never understand it himself) he had actually been asleep when Katie had called. Not really credible – million things to do, been putting it all off for, oh God, hours. And Jesus knows I'm pretty bloody nervous about this whole damn – wait just a minute, hang on, won't you: nervous? Did I say that? Did I say I was nervous? Well I'm not: I'm terrified.

63

Absolutely terrified about this trip (never been to America before – never been anywhere much – not really one of life's pioneers, am I? Let's face facts when they are staring us in the, yeah – face) but what I'm really maybe terrified about is – yes, must be – Katie. Not terrified *of* her, no (although sometimes – my God – *sometimes*, the risks she takes – the danger she puts me into . . . !), but terrified by all that I feel for her – awed, I am, yes I suppose I am: awed by the sheer hugeness of everything that I feel for her.

And just look around Norman's really rather dingy bed-sitting room (only the one bulb working now – just never seemed to get around to . . . not even sure I've got any spares; sixties, are they? Or hundreds?) Just look at the piles of stuff: clothes he's decided he's *definitely* taking (or at least I think I am, pretty sure I am – I am for now, anyway), clothes that are completely and totally out of the question, for one reason or another (too hot, too old, too plain yuk disgusting) except maybe that blue sort of shirt over there, just possibly, and I maybe can't wholly rule out the one underneath. And one of the locks on the suitcase seemed to be a total write-off, which is odd because as far as Norman could recollect it was working perfectly well not all that long ago, when he had hoiked it down from the top of the wardrobe in the last place, this really rather seedy old case – more like caved-in cardboard than anything, which actually I think is exactly what it is – in order to cram into it all his rather tired and ugly clothes and one or two other bits of stuff so that he could finally move out of the last place (truly dowdy – pleased to see the back of it) and into the new place, this place, not much better, hardly any better at all – in fact I don't think I'll actually be here much longer.

And yet in the midst of all this I fall asleep. Nerves. Yeah. I reckon it's down to nerves, you know. Blotting it out, sort of thing. But I *am* looking forward to the holiday, of course I am – never been alone, not truly alone, for whole long nights, with Katie. Once – few weeks ago – Norman had asked her back to his room. Up till then, it had all been just these very carnal – exciting beyond measure, let's be clear here – and actually fairly aggressive bouts and sessions in the office. Katie really seemed to go for it. And I think – you know what I think? I think that last evening – under the desk, remember? Hard to forget – I think, I'm pretty sure, actually, that Katie knew that her father, Mr Street – Howard – hadn't yet gone home. She *knew* he hadn't yet gone home and that's why, I'm sure, she went for it the way she did. Now you see here is one of the many huge differences between Katie and me: I *genuinely* believed that he'd gone (why? Because she told me. I see. And Katie never lies, is that it? Oh get *real*, Norman: I must grow up soon, I really must) because, yeah, if I had had even an idea as to the *possibility* that Mr Street – Howard – was still in the office then I wouldn't have come within a hundred yards of Katie – but Katie, Katie was different, very.

Anyway, as I say, I asked her back – couldn't have been more than a fortnight ago, if you put me on the spot – and Katie had said Where is it, actually, Norman, in London that you live? Norman had told her, and Katie had said Where in the fucking world is *that*? So Norman had filled her in on what boroughs and tubes were nearest but it was clear she was none the wiser. It took a lot of persuasion to get her here. Can't we go to a *hotel*, Norman? No – no we bloody can't. Every penny I own – oh God, don't get me on to this money thing. *Yes* I'll address it later – got to pay it all back, haven't I? – but I can't get into it all now because if I do, if I do – well, never mind packing, never mind holidays: I'll just crawl under the bed and stay there, all hunched up with my hands over my eyes, and praying to anything at all that hasn't deserted me that they won't come and get me, won't find me and haul me out and make me face things and deal with them because I *can't*.

She came, Katie. She took one look at his room and said I don't *think* so, Norman – and left. It was she who picked this holiday (of course it was): if you want me like that, then it has to be on my terms. Right, said Norman: fine, OK, right – whatever you want, Katie – whatever you want I'll try to do.

Because this is it: I love her. I truly truly love her. And actually I *don't* want her like that: that's not

66

the way I want her at all. Shall I tell you how *I* want it to go? Shall I? I want it to go like this: 'Well Mr Street – Howard,' I say (don't think I haven't been over this in my mind, because I'm here to tell you that I have). 'Well,' I'll say, 'I expect what I have to ask you will hardly come as a complete surprise.' Mr Street smiles quite kindly at this point, which he can do, actually – I've seen his smile, it's kindly, he really is a pretty good bloke. 'I should be honoured to take your daughter's hand in marriage, if she'll have me.' Katie hugs my arm at this point (did I say she's there, hanging on to my arm? Well she is) and then she kisses me once on the cheek. Mr Street – Howard – he grips my shoulder, grasps my hand, mumbles something about 'Delighted, dear boy,' and then suggests we go to his club that very evening – 'Discuss a few of the practical points over a single malt or so. You'll be wanting somewhere to live: I'd like to help with that. Son.' And I'll say Oh *thank* you – thanks ever so much, Mr Street. Howard. *Dad.*

And I don't actually see what's so weird about that. I mean, OK, Katie is appallingly young (seventeen! I nearly died when she told me she was just seventeen – you know what I mean?) but I'm not exactly an old codger, am I? Twenty-six next birthday – that's not old, is it? So *why*, Katie, *why*? Why can't we do it the pure way, the sweet way? Why does it all have to be such a *sin*?

And is what *I* am doing not a sin, then? Not with Katie, no (it can't be truly bad if you're in love, can it? Because love is good – everyone says so), but what I am doing with the *money*. Mr Street's money – God, it must be so much, now: I can't even bear to look at the figures. Oh Jesus – I'm screwing his daughter while I'm screwing him blind and he hasn't got a clue about any of it. And he *likes* me, I'm pretty sure; Christ, if he ever did find out, he'd kill me – fire me, sue me, break me, run me down – banish me from the company of Katie: amounts to the very same thing. And he's a good bloke, Mr Street – he's all right.

Christ in heaven, what is it I imagine I'm *doing*? And just how long do I think it can last?

PART 2

During

CHAPTER 2

John and Lulu Powers were lolling on loungers just alongside the sauna rooms in what were described in the brochure as extensive grounds. Or so it might seem for the duration of a glance – but just take a closer look at the two of them. Lulu – no problem: she was at ease, all right – apparently not a care in the world. She'd just had her massage, her hair was entwined in towelling and the ten glossy red and sunlit sparkling tips on feet as sweet as hands at the end of honey legs told you all you needed to know about Lulu's keen appreciation of the true lift and value of a halfway decent pedicure. But John was less comfortable, you could tell that immediately – you only had to look at the way he was lying: ready to toss aside his copy of *Hello!* and bound to his feet and in all possibility with a fair deal of force come right out with the truth that he for one had had just about enough of this.

It did in fact very much look like he was about to speak. Certainly one side of his mouth was twitching as with evident impatience he looked quickly across at Lulu; impossible to tell what she was thinking – even whether or not she was awake.

71

Rose and thickly wet-looking lips pointed up at the sun, oil-black wraparound sunglasses effectively screening any hint of expression. She had this ability for motionlessness that John really did use to admire – envy, even; drove him mental, now. How can any intelligent person be disposed to just lie there – just lie there, not talking, not reading – just lie there hour after hour after bloody fucking hour? Not natural, is it? Can't be. She did it on beaches, too. 'But this is the whole point,' she'd say, when he tackled her about it over dinner – which he had done, repeatedly, every night since they'd been at this Christ-how-can-they-even-begin-to-justify-these-prices so-called bloody health farm. Six nights – seven days of doing absolutely bugger all – and there was more than a week of it to come! What had possessed him to book a fortnight? The only way – there was only one way on earth you could for two whole weeks just lie around on a recliner, lie around in a sauna, lie around on a bloody massage table and then spend every fucking early night lying around on a bed and that's if you were already embalmed on arrival, with very little choice in the matter.

'It *can't* be the point,' John had retorted tetchily. 'How *can* it be the point? Christ – we can do all the hanging around we want in the *garden*. Don't have to spend a sodding fortune doing it here.'

'Oh dear. Johnny isn't a happy bunny, is he?'

John looked at Lulu and said quietly, 'Johnny is close to becoming a serial killer. And first on the list will be that, what is she called – are they *nurses*, these women all over the place? Or what are they? Anyway, that one – the one with the bun, you know the one. Every time I slope off to the smoking room she gives me that *look* – that bloody look she gives me. Christ it makes me want to smash her face in. When I crack, when I finally have had it, she'll be the first one to go, I promise you.'

'Oh God's *sake*, John – we're meant to be here to *relax*. Unwind. God when you're like this I could just scream! This is meant to be my holiday too, you know. I've worked bloody hard this year –'

'Oh and I *haven't*, I suppose,' shot back John, the blue touchpaper now truly red and lit. 'Christ you have no *conception* of the number of crappy bloody articles I've had to put out for that woman this year alone. Same old bloody stuff, year in year out – drives me *mental*, I'm telling you. But this is no sort of a holiday at all – I mean you have to *think* all the time. There's nothing to stop you *thinking* and I don't want to think. I've *done* with thinking. I want –'

'So why don't you ever write *better* articles, Johnny? And *what* is it that you want? Tell me.'

'I don't write better *articles*, Lulu, Christ damn you, because my bloody editor doesn't *want* better articles, does she? She wants articles that start off' – and here John assumed the voice he thought best approximated to that of an idiot – '"Most people would have been daunted by the ramshackle state of the old and forgotten vicarage over-grown with

73

bracken but to Gideon and – oh God I don't know – bleeding *Nancy* it was love at first sight and they weren't afraid of hard work and with the help of an architect friend and a doolally local builder . . ." – see! See! I know the bloody crap off by heart. Or would you like my 101-Ways-To-Brighten-Up-Your-Fucking-Little-Kitchen - For-Easter piece? And as to what I *want* – fun! I want some bloody fun! Christ – everyone around here is old or fat or both and I'm bored bored bored! Christ, Lulu – I'm going out of my mind with boredom! But aren't *you*? You must be – you *can't* want to stay here another week!'

Lulu sighed, and slid down her sunglasses as far as the bridge, the better to peer at Johnny. He wasn't going to leave it alone, was he? He would only get worse – and what sort of benefit would she even have a dream of reaping if he was sounding off like this all the time? Over lunch – yesterday, she thought it was – she had said without any hope at all:

'Look, John – I can *understand* if you feel like this. You've never been to a health farm before – OK, maybe that was my fault: I thought you'd enjoy it. So why don't you try to book yourself in somewhere else for a week, mm? Go and *have* your fun, if that's what you want.'

John had become predictably silent.

'You know I can't do that,' he said, eventually.

'Why, John? Why, actually?'

John breathed out and looked down. 'You know why,' he said.

74

And Lulu was sighing again now because yes, she did know why – it had dogged every day of the nearly two years they had been married. John would never leave her side because he was convinced (he had even said it once, one night – half drunk, he'd been, but still) that Lulu would one second later be surrounded by *men* and she'd smile at them and play with them and John couldn't *stand* it – *couldn't*, you hear? Just couldn't bear the thought of it: I love you too much to chance it, Lulu.

'That's not love, John,' Lulu had replied.

'It's my sort of love,' said John. 'It's the only sort of love I have to give you.'

When he comes, thought Katie – if he comes – then I shall simply kill him. Again her eyes swept in as much as they could take of the crushed and vilely urgent airport terminal and – oh wait: there, yes? Over there – that was, was it? Finally? No – no, it wasn't. Wasn't him. That was about the fourth time she had hissed in breath, the better to let fly at him right close up – but no, yet again, it was just some other wild-haired and hopeless man with cases.

Never before had Katie been in such a position. She couldn't even check in and head hotfoot for the lounge, because guess bleeding who had the tickets? It was always, wasn't it – it had been just the same at school: some things, she guessed, would never change – it was always the other people who

75

messed you up. No matter how well laid the plan (no matter what you put into it) if there was just one more human being built into the scheme (and hey – if you think about it, when in life could there not be?) then you could bloody depend on it that he'd be the bastard to fuck things up.

Everything had gone quite perfectly up till now – well, I say *now*: Katie had been both hot and standing there next to her trolley for what? Getting on for a bloody hour, that's what. *And* she'd made a point of hanging around for a bit in the loo so that she could be just eight minutes late for their meeting in order to make the most of guaranteed (mawkish, maybe) pre-holiday and joyous greeting. At first she had been no more than miffed; miffed had soon segued into irritated and then – following a very fleeting and fast trampled-on instant of anxiety – absolutely beside herself with the sort of Katie-like fury that didn't really bode all that well for Norman Furnish. Wherever it was that man might be.

That morning, Katie had actually woken (click! Just like that) exactly five minutes before her alarm clock had bleeped. This happened, sometimes: if something good was on the way. And so everything was done by the time Elizabeth had wandered in for whatever reason people do at such moments as these. (I know it will bore Katie terribly, Elizabeth thought, I know too that it will diminish me if again I go over all my warnings and reservations, but what else could mothers utter in the face of such daunting mornings? What else but what they felt deep down?)

'So you're absolutely sure, now, Katie. That you've got everything you need? And you will be sure to phone – hm? The minute you land, yes?'

Katie was watching the taxi driver load up her bags. Hope to God I get a trolley at the other end or else I'm completely buggered. There was always Norman, of course: yeah – Norman could lug it.

'Told you, Mum,' she said again. 'Got everything – money, toothbrush, passport – condoms.'

Oh *God* Katie could only enjoy the sight of her mother's chalky complexion (no face on yet) pale even further before colouring up with shock, her eyes now brighter.

'*Joke*, Mum. Joke – honest!' sang out Katie. She kissed her mother lightly and dashed into the taxi before she burst out laughing. Poor Mum! That'll keep her worrying all week! But Howard, *Howard* – she'll go – Do you *really* think she was joking? You know Katie, Dad will reply – probably thinking Who actually gives a toss? And anyway, Katie defended herself, as the taxi puttered away, I *was* joking: haven't got any – never do. Hate them.

Norman simply couldn't believe it. You're *kidding*, he kept on saying – but the man in the white short-sleeved shirt (fairly jaunty epaulettes) had been shaking his head for so damn long now that even Norman had to face up to the fact that here could be no vestige of a gag. As if they *would* gag, he sort of semi-thought, as he grabbed at his bags and started off at a canter. You ask people directions – is this the way he said? This can't be right, can it? I've got to cross a *road* – you ask people directions – oh yeah, oh God yeah, thank God, there's a sign, there's a sign – now does that mean straight on or up this way? It's not *clear*, is it? You ask people directions – Christ I'm having a heart attack, why do they always make these places so bloody *hot?* Oh look – that's it – there: Terminal One. Thank Christ. You ask people directions, they're not going to lark *about*, are they? Whenever you say 'you're kidding' of course you just know that they're *not* – you always know that because why in Christ's name would they? Oh God, Katie's going to be – Jesus my hands are so slippery I can barely hold the – is that her over there? God, she'll be wild. So if the man *says* Sorry chum, wrong terminal – then you're in the wrong bloody terminal, right? No good accusing him of having a *jape*. That *is* Katie, yes – I think I'd better put on speed. I think if I truly gallop up to her like a soon-to-be-glue carthorse and practically expire at her feet then maybe she won't be quite so up for putting me down.

'Katie!' he gasped, dropping his bags as ballast, and goggling open-mouthed at her like an apologetic seal. 'Katie! I'm *so* –'

'Where the fuck have you *been?*' hissed Katie. 'I've been standing here for bloody *hours* – the flight'll be called any bloody minute, you moron!'

'Katie!' is all Norman could wheeze. He felt now

as if his heart was tugging at sinews in a bid to be up the man's throat, splurging its way through wet and gabbling lips and then out and free and shot of him for ever.

'Oh come *on*,' husked Katie, more intensely irritated than she could say – and not least because of the sight of him: in Katie's eyes, Norman had all the allure of a char-broiled vagrant. 'Let's just check *in*, Godsake. Christ Almighty – look at your luggage!'

Norman looked down at the cardboard suitcase and the plastic bag. Yes, since you ask, he *did* possess another case, a smaller case – canvas sort of holdall affair – but he wasn't quite sure where it had landed up since his last trip to the launderette and also he had over*slept*, if he's honest, and – oh look, it's a long story but the upshot was that he had grabbed the Tesco bag as a last-minute thing and shoved stuff in because otherwise, if he didn't, he'd be *late*, right? And late he had been quite determined not to be.

'Oh God,' moaned Norman, as soon as he saw what she meant. It wasn't so much the plastic number – although you could depend on it that Katie would have more than something to say on that subject in not too very much time – no, what I think engaged her more was the benighted and bashed-in suitcase: that damn iffy lock had sprung (he'd hit it with a shoe this morning: seemed all right) and some fairly livid woollen things appeared to be as eager to be away from

Norman as had (several aching lungs ago) his very own beating heart – now having simmered down apace, grudgingly content with thumping sullenly.

'Oh God,' repeated Norman. 'Have you got any string?'

Katie just looked at him. 'Have I got any –?! *Norman* – let's check *in*. *Now*, Norman – now. Christ, if I *did* have any string I'd wrap it round your bloody *neck*. Where the hell do you think you're going now? Club check-in's *this* way, dimbo. Can't you read?'

'Ah,' said Norman (seeming now quite interested in his shoes – did actually mean to give them a bit of a clean). 'You see, you see – the thing is –'

There was no more than a beat before Katie said: '*Norman*.' The word glinted like anthracite before fading back into black.

'No,' said Norman – maybe unconsciously putting up his hands to his face – 'I can explain. The thing is, is – um. *Look*, Katie, have you seen the *price* of Club Class? I mean, Jesus, look, you're only sitting *down*, aren't you? I mean it's not as if it's any *quicker*, is it? And –'

'Norman,' said Katie, very slowly. Not easy to say a short name slowly, but Katie pulled it off with room to spare: lingered forever, to Norman's ears. 'We agreed. We did this. We talked about it. We marked the brochure. All you had to do was bloody *book* it. I am *not* –'

'Katie –'

'– *not, not, not* travelling Economy. Is that clear, Norman? I hope it is clear, Norman, because if not –' Katie broke off to snap at a small and pink-haired old lady who could barely believe it: 'What the hell are *you* staring at?!' – her valedictory Fuck Off sending the woman scurrying away in search of paramedics, while Katie resumed her assault on Norman: '– if *not*, Norman, then I walk straight out of this airport and you never see me again. And I mean *never*. Have you *got* it, Norman?'

And this speared him. A hurt that was almost hunger assailed him sharply, dulling only into a blunt and more generally aching void. Whether she meant it or not, Norman simply couldn't bear – never mind the thought of it, no – he couldn't even bear to hear the words.

'But what can I *do*?' he implored. 'I've got the *tickets*.' And he flapped them around. I want, he thought, to die.

'Oh God it's no good *crying* about it, Norman.' He wasn't crying, wasn't – but God, thought Katie, he didn't seem far off; men can be so *stupid*. 'Upgrade, Norman – you upgrade.'

'I do?' checked Norman. Upgrade? He had never before heard of such a thing in his life. 'How, um – how do I do that, Katie? I'll do whatever you want. Will it cost much? Only I don't have much, what with . . . everything.' This was a terrible discussion to be having in the middle of an airport – but then, where else would you?

Katie explained – they were well on their way to the bookings counter now, Norman pushing the trolley, dodging Americans and cocking an ear – that in *some* cases (if you've got the right job, the platinum plastic lozenge hanging from a bag that believe me, Norman, does not at all look like yours – even, sometimes, if you're just wearing the right clothes and attitude) then the upgrade comes free. I think all that frankly leaves you standing, Norman. In your case, the only way is to pay.

Yes, thought Norman, I have discovered this before. He approached the bookings desk ('Be *quick*, though, Norman, Chrissake – that was the first call!') and conducted what looked like to Katie from a distance fairly earnest discussions with the oddly coiffed and elaborately tranquil woman there – big on lipstick – and various bits of paper were being folded and pored over, and soon Norman was back again, face heavy with the mask of bereavement.

'No good, I'm afraid. I'm terribly sorry, Katie, but Club is booked solid on this flight and the next. Nothing anyone can do.'

Rushes were flickering behind Katie's eyes, but there seemed no point in splicing them into a feature, let alone putting it on general release. Without a word, she directed Norman and the trolley to the Economy check-in. They queued. Katie seethed. And Norman quivered with relief because at least he had got away with something:

there *had* been space in Club (maybe I can pitch for seats so far back that Katie won't notice – please God let this happen) but the extra cost would have wiped him out. And how would Katie have acted then? As it is it's tight.

Norman was fraught, it is fair to say – and nor was he the first person in his circumstance to have been struck by the glancing thought that God, you know, if I ever get through this, I'm really going to need a damn good holiday in order to recover from all the *stress*.

Brian was on his hands and knees in the hall – vestibule, Dotty now called it, since she had ordered from a catalogue a thermal-lined and fully washable heavy-duty velvet curtain which Brian had slung from a pole four or five feet from the front door, some way down the hall, hence creating what Dotty now chose to call her vestibule. *And* that curtain had been bought way after Brian's strict and serious dictum: no more household or personal expenses beyond the absolutely necessary, is that quite clear to you, Dotty? I tell you, Brian, she had replied – looking at him in that way she had, as if she had never laid eyes on him before (and maybe wishing that this were the case) – I tell you, Brian, and I tell you now: I just won't be able to *cope* with this. I can't *bear* to live like this – there *must* be more money, *must* be: what's wrong with you at all? Why can't you find more *money*? There's only one way there's ever going to be more money

83

in this house, Brian had reflected, and that's when you go back full-time to your job as a secretary, or whatever it was you did. Hadn't told her, of course: at this stage it hadn't been mentioned. Get the holiday done, get the holiday over, and hit the poor cow with it then. She won't like it. That is the strongest Brian can put it without succumbing to a fit of trembling. And even that presupposes she could even *get* a bloody job; last time she had one, Brian doubted there were even computers.

Economy, as Brian had said and said, was the name of the game from here on in. That very pole he had put up for the curtain is a good case in point. They've got some lovely ebony-looking poles in John Lewis, Dotty had said, with sort of nice ball things on the end: get one. But no: Brian did it his way, right? The clever way. What you do, right, is you get yourself down to the woodyard and you select a length of decent dowelling (we're talking broomstick – softwood is totally fine in this case because we're anyway looking at a central support, aren't we? This sort of span, you need it.) Next on the agenda is a pair of perfectly simple L-brackets – plug the wall, ram them home nicely – and now here's the really artistic bit: a dab of Evo-Stik secures to either end of the dowel your bog standard ping-pong ball – no, *not* joking, actually, Mr Clever-Clever – because if you think about it: it's not as if anyone's going to *touch* them, is it? Not at that height they're not. Then a lick of primer, nice coat of Humbrol glossy black and quite frankly you can *stuff* your John Lewis curtain pole: we're talking very fetching, here-and-now, and maybe a sixth of the outlay.

And here was Brian now applying the very same principle (the reason, if anyone wondered, why he was on his hands and knees in the hall – or, and we now know why, the vestibule). Let him just ask you this: have you seen the prices they charge for cat-flaps in this day and age? Well have you? And do not even risk a migraine by enquiring what your local firm of cowboys is going to want for putting it in. What you need, right, what you need to do is to do it Brian's way: let him talk you through it (telling you – once you get the hang: nothing to it – piece of cake).

OK: I'm not going to lie – for this job you definitely need a fretsaw attachment on your basic power tool. It *can* be done with a twist drill, hacksaw and a rat-tail boring rasp, I'm not denying, but for clean finish and next to no time spent, your power fretsaw is your man. First you mark it out – not so low as you're into a draught situation, nor so high that your moggy has to do a flying leap (and not so large, either, as to admit undesirables – dogs, foxes, burglars, etc.). Once you've got your hole (see to the edges with a bit of wet-and-dry) you're needing a piece of board just ever so slightly larger, and a short length of old carpet or upholstery webbing to act as a hinge. You *can* use brads for fixing, but for a job you can stand back and be proud of you're looking at

Araldite and dome-top japanned screw fixings with casing cups – inch is plenty, eights in gauge, maybe. Couple of bits of self-adhesive foam strip to keep everyone snug (and Dotty's curtain will play a part here, I'm not saying otherwise) and what you have, my son, is a very smart and functional cat-flap in no time flat. Cost? Zero. All made from odd bits lying about the place, wasn't it? You have to learn to see the potential of everything around you: that's the trick. *Plus*, of course, home improvements of this order are money in the bank – you just ask anyone; might even prove to be a Unique Selling Point to the sympathetic punter.

And where was Dotty while all this craftsmanship was taking place? In the bedroom – in despair. Could someone please explain to her why, if they were all meant to be leaving for a week at the seaside first thing in the morning (and it was well into the evening now), why in fact it should be, then, that Brian had at this moment elected to manufacture a cat-flap? Was Dotty expected to do absolutely everything, then? And Colin's stuff – she hadn't started on Colin's stuff, yet – but God, you'd think at his age he wouldn't be completely incapable: at least he could lay out what he wants to take. But no: here was Dotty surrounded by suitcases and all her summer things (oh those clothes, those same dusty, boring, horrible old clothes – maybe if she went back *Years*, Elizabeth wouldn't remember them?) while Colin slumped on his bed as the whole house throbbed like a headache to the boom-boom bass of whatever truly terrible CD he had most recently acquired. Brian? Making a cat-flap. Sometimes Dotty thought she could lose her mind. God Jesus: it's not even as if they had a fucking cat.

'But Howard, *Howard*,' worried Elizabeth, 'do you *really* think she was joking? Is this turquoise too similar to the green?'

Howard was settled into the small sofa in the bay of their bedroom, sipping a whisky and watching the extraordinary sight of Elizabeth packing, while hugging to him the thrill of being not one part of it.

'Of *course* she was,' he came back. 'You know Katie. She just does it to wind you up. It's very *naughty* of her, but that's Katie, isn't it? And you should know, Elizabeth, that if anything of that sort was going on between Katie and some boy, she'd be at very great pains to say *nothing*. Basic psychology.'

'Well I hope that's so,' returned Elizabeth, partly mollified. 'She *is* only seventeen – and I know you *read* things, but –'

'Elizabeth – relax. I'm telling you – I know my own daughter, and so should you. If anything of that nature was going on, I'd just *know* about it. You live with someone that long, it's instinct.'

Elizabeth smiled briefly, blew a kiss. 'You're sweet, Howard. What do you think – the turquoise: too much like the green?'

Howard smiled too. Thank God he'd got her off that tack. For one, it actually disturbed him to think that Katie could . . . could even *contemplate* . . . no it was silly, she couldn't: impossible. And he meant it when he said he'd just *know* – he would, he knew, the first time Katie ever did . . . then he'd feel it, he would, he'd feel it deep down – and it wasn't a feeling he yearned to embrace.

'The green is very lovely,' he said. 'But the turquoise, yes – that would bring out your eyes. Take them both – they're both quite delightful.'

'You're *so* sweet, Howard. I *wish* you were coming. Are you *sure* you're going to be all right here on your own?'

'I'll be working most of the time,' smiled Howard.

Elizabeth came across to him, which was odd in itself: once Elizabeth was packing, Elizabeth was packing. She bent down, the finger she drew down the side of Howard's face tucking under his chin and lifting it; she touched his lips with hers.

'Can't work *all* the time . . .' she whispered.

Howard for one was very pleased when the cordless squawked – made him convulse as if stun-gunned, true, but it certainly did cut through what could well have become the teensiest problem because *yes* he wanted to send off Elizabeth as happy as you like, but there was, it should be understood, a limit here. As to that instinct thing that Howard had referred to a while back in context of Katie – well Elizabeth, Howard had years ago been very relieved to observe, possessed absolutely none of it whatever, and some things, some states, you very much want to stay the same – no? Think I'll lay low for the rest of the evening.

'Oh it *is* you, Katie, thank *God*!' Elizabeth was shouting into the phone (America was a long way away, right?) at the same time pointing at the receiver and mouthing to Howard Kay-Tee. 'I'm so pleased it's you because – can you hear me? I say I'm so pleased it's you because it rang earlier, the phone rang earlier and I said to your father oh thank God, that'll be Katie, she's safe – I *know* I'm silly, I know – you *are* safe, aren't you, Katie? You are *there*? Good – I'm so pleased, darling. And was the flight . . . ? Really? Oh that's good. Oh that's sweet. And give Ellie *my* love too – how sweet of her. Shall I have a quick word with her? Money? Well can't you reverse the . . . Katie? Can't you reverse the . . . ? Katie? Katie?' Elizabeth looked over to Howard, and replaced the receiver. 'That was, as you gathered, Katie. She's there and she's safe, apparently. Ran out of coins. Isn't that Katie all over?'

Howard caught sight of the gelid tear in Elizabeth's eye gathering force and glazing just before it began to roll.

'Think I'll just refresh this drink,' he said briskly, making for the door. 'I'm sure Katie'll have a wonderful time – stop worrying, Elizabeth. *Your* holiday tomorrow, isn't it? Get packing! Chop chop!'

Elizabeth smiled in a conciliatory way. 'Sweet,

Howard. And you've told Melody what time we're picking her up, yes? Good.' She sighed. 'No I *know* it will be fun, I know it will – it's just that it's so odd without you and Katie, that's all. Strange. But I do *need* a break, I do.'

Break from *what*, is what Howard was thinking. What is it exactly that you *do*, Elizabeth? I've often wondered.

'I can't wait,' she concluded.

No, thought Howard: nor can I.

So Katie is in Chicago after what we gather was a no-problem flight, then – yes? Or is there just the slightest frisson detectable here? Maybe in just the set of her shoulders – Norman some inches away – as the cab noses slowly away from O'Hare and into the surrounding chicken-wired wastelands before swinging hard on to the highway and hitting it.

They're not talking. Odd, no, that they shouldn't be talking? I mean – neither of them ever been to America, and here they are just minutes away from one of the most fabulous cities of all – and yet: no chat. Katie isn't even criticizing him, listing his shortcomings. No, well – there's a reason for that: she's barely stopped laying in to him since last they were sighted back in London in the check-in queue – a bit nearer the action, yeah, but not by very much – let Katie leave you in no doubt on *that* score. They could have been there, oh God – another *year* if only their flight hadn't been so heart-clutchingly imminent and those women, Katie doesn't know what they're called – those women who do all the checking-in thing (checker-inners? Hardly likely) were now urging everyone on Flight 708 to Chicago O'Hare to the head of the queue. Katie and Norman were the only ones, it hardly needs saying (everyone else – anyone not travelling with *Norman* – had sailed through bloody ages ago), but still this didn't damp down a fairly good deal of disgruntled tutting from those ahead of them – and in particular a rather angular and red-faced woman with Swissair and El Al stickers all over her cases.

'This is not *fair*,' she said, really pretty audibly, as Norman bumpily slid and lifted one, two, three – oh my God she's got *four* cases, I can't believe it, on to the conveyor belt. '*Germans*.'

Katie rapidly answered all the questions by rote (No, not a known terrorist, Not a drug user, Not carrying a single bomb) while hustling across the tickets, her passport, Norman's passport (yes, the thought had crossed Katie's mind too, but Norman *had* in point of fact remembered to bring his passport – and yes, it was even in date. Just as well, because otherwise, well, it wouldn't really have mattered because the only place on the itinerary for Norman would have been Hell – and Katie, rest assured, would have seen to all the travel arrangements.) Then she wheeled round to the red-faced woman and said:

'Germans? What are you talking about *Germans*

– we're just late, that's all. We're not *German*.'

'Sorry,' put in Norman.

The woman narrowed her eyes. 'You *look* German.'

'Excuse me,' piped up the woman, the other woman – the woman who checks you in (the in-checker? I don't really think so) – and it was Norman she was talking to. 'Did you pack this bag yourself?'

'Yes,' admitted Norman, looking down on it in sorrow. 'But it seems to have sort of come half unpacked on its own since then. Do you have any string? By any chance?'

The last call for the flight noisily Tannoyed out nasally just then, and all sorts of folk were jumping about on Katie and Norman's behalf – taping up the derelict suitcase, applying swing tags, sending it away to be gobbled up by black and rubber-flapped gullets – all this concentrated attention doing nothing to appease the red-faced woman, now a good bit redder.

'You really do *look* German,' was her parting shot.

'Yeah?' hailed back Katie as they scuttled along to Departures, 'well you really do look hideous, you mad old bat! Heil Hitler!'

They got the flight, yes they did – just – but the *pain* of having to rush right past Allders duty-free shop because Katie simply *needed* to buy Paloma Picasso, didn't she? Yes she did – and she also needed Calvin Klein and Jean Paul Gaultier and they never had such a good selection on the plane

– and now they were on the plane, yes – here they were, and oh God the *looks* everyone gave them (people crossing the Atlantic in five-and-a-bit hours don't care to waste a minute, you know) and of *course* their seats had to be right at the very bloody back, didn't they? But naturally – next to the luggage, next to the bogs. The curtain was sort of half pulled to up at the Club Class end, so maybe Katie hadn't noticed large and well-spaced empty places? One can but pray.

And for Norman, soon, praying was very much the order of the day. Even Katie observed that all was maybe not well with Norman: as the plane began to taxi, so did he squirm in his seat. Katie stopped all that with a single reprimand, but she got a further inkling of unease when finally the four engines boomed on the runway – the moment when some of your stomach flutters elsewhere and then tatuens as the boost makes strips of green grass fast rewind before your eyes until a brief and surging lightness pinions back your shoulders into the angle of climb and outer London recedes into and then becomes a slanted route map. It was something to do with the way that Norman was clutching the seat so tenaciously as to threaten an eruption of finger bones through tight and shock-white skin, only barely pinkly dappled; the way too his eyes were screwed shut as if in the face of tear-gas – and look at how his teeth seemed to bite on a bit in a final and vein-busting attempt to restrain a racehorse.

'Oh Christ,' said Katie, flatly. 'You're scared. You've got this thing, haven't you? Fear of flying. This is all I bloody, bloody need.'

Norman's head flailed in denial this way and that – wasn't giving up on that racehorse, though.

Behind them (directly behind – Katie never knew people could actually sit this far back on a plane) someone was banging around behind a curtain. They had yet to level out and the orange seatbelt sign was still aglow (accompanied by the odd and inexplicable bleepy sort of gonging noise) and so this person had to be one of those – oh God, Katie didn't know what on earth *these* women were supposed to be called, either: used to be stewardesses, but not, now. (Why, actually, was such a job ever considered *glamorous*? I mean – you *serve* people, right?)

'What you need is a drink,' said Katie, arching back to flip aside the ash-grey curtain and half-yell through it: 'Hello? Anybody there? My friend would like a drink.'

A woman reluctantly approached and assumed the expression well known from hospital nurses of the old school when enquiring of a prickly-faced and incontinent old wreck of a man what on earth he thought he was doing out of bed.

'The trolley will be brought round in due course,' said the woman. 'We're still climbing.'

God, thought Katie, they never said that up in Club Class; she also thought Christ just look at

94

her: I wouldn't wear a hat like that if you paid me in cash.

'Yeah but look at him – he's not well: needs a drink.'

The woman gazed at Norman, and maybe twitched a bit. It could possibly have been his Dulux (eggshell) eau-de-nil and plasticky complexion – skin stretched tight across the cheekbones – that in the end convinced her. Lowering her voice into an unselfconscious and therefore mildly hilarious now-look-it's-more-than-my-job's-worth and conspiratorial undertone, she muttered to Norman:

'Gin? Whisky, brandy, vodka? Champagne?'

Norman swivelled his distended and glassy-eyed face towards her, and exhaling for the first time since take-off gasped out:

'Oh God – yes *please*.'

The woman glanced nervously at Katie, and not only was uneasy enquiry packed into that glance, but also a good dose of My God In Heaven I've got five-and-a-half-hours of this, and here are the two of them right by the galley.

'Bring a selection,' suggested Katie, quite kindly – practically winking and patting her hand.

John Powers was practically at his wits' end, and he didn't at all mind who knew it. Maybe what had finally tipped the balance was that when he woke up this morning at about five-thirty (usual, surely, when you go to bed at nine, having exhausted every conceivable byway of activity or conversation, save indulging in some other brainless and filthy sweat-inducing bout of state-of-the-art loafing around, followed by the twentieth nice cool shower of the fucking day in order to get clean again) the first thing he was aware of was a light rain glancing off the window-panes. Right, he thought: *right*. That's truly it. The only thing that had got him through so far was walking (and then walking back – how stupid can it get?) or else sitting under a parasol on that terrace that was handy for the smoking room. If he was to be confined to this hideous and ill-thought-out string of Victorian conversions and plate-glass extensions while simply yearning for mealtimes – when the poor bloody slimmers paying three hundred quid a day could gorge on rocket and envy the life out of the equally highly screwed epicureans on the other side of the chevron screen busy getting their laughing gear around sometimes a whole leg of chicken – then he would quite simply kill himself – or, conceivably, others. Starting with that one – you know the one, the one with the bun who gave him all those looks. Might kill her anyway, just for the hell of it: work up a filthy sweat hacking her fucking head off, followed by a nice cool shower in order to get clean again.

John glanced across the bed at Lulu – God, it was barely light, but there were the undulations of her, wondrous as ever. She had swapped her wraparound sunglasses for a black and lacy sleep mask – Christ, he could barely remember the last time he had looked at her eyes: whenever – if ever – they made love, she shut them tight (blanking out what, John wondered: blanking out what?) Look at the way that hip of hers roundly eased up the counterpane into so perfect a hillock. She's mine, he thought: that woman is mine. Was it too early to wake her? Oh Christ of *course* it was – look at it: five forty-five. It was too early to be *alive*, Jesus damn. I don't know, though: could do with the sweet tenderness of knowing her again. But there's no point, is there? There's no point. All she'd do is moan in that put-upon and when-will-my-suffering-end voice of hers and start explaining as if to a willing but dim school leaver that the whole *reason*, didn't he see, the whole *idea* is for us both to get *rest*. Well no he *didn't*, as he has expressed before: rest at home, couldn't they? Could *fuck* at home too, granted (though not nearly as much as they used to: it wasn't like then, when she was hot and all over him) – it's just that right now, right at this God-forlorn dawn and dusty hour the most tempting facilities in this plutocrat's stalag were all the warm and yielding (soft and downy) ins and outs of Lulu. It's about the only time since he'd got here that he really did feel like working up a filthy sweat, followed by a nice cool shower in order to get clean again.

John screwed up tight his eyes as if denying a vision of horror. Sleep sleep *sleep*, he commanded himself – pleaded, really. Or if not: rest rest *rest*, then – because this, apparently, is the whole *idea*.

Failing that – die die *die*, God damn you, and preferably before the rain comes down even more mournfully. Turning on to his side, he sighed loudly and from so deeply within him as to newly arouse self-sorrow, and possibly too to induce in Lulu a slow and languorous semi-awakening – arms maybe reaching up, if not towards him; didn't, predictably. John's eyes were now wide and staring at the just-ajar bathroom door, willing the shadows to become less ashen.

It was the heavy drone of the aeroplane's engines that had lulled Norman Furnish into a dropsical and boom-headed semi-slumber – that and about a quart of raw alcohol – but now there was talk overlaying the talk of his dreams, and one eye soon was focusing hard upon the drop-down plastic table before him, the other one coaxed into completing the set, but only in its own good time.

'I love you, Katie,' he slurred. Did I say that, he thought, or did I dream that too?

'Oh shut up, Norman,' said Katie. 'Look – wake up. Do you want any duty-frees?'

Norman stirred himself from his ow-Christ-my-back-is-killing-me curved-spine slump (hell of a head, felt a bit queasy) and tried if only for Katie's sake to become a little human. Her lap seemed piled high with cellophane-wrapped and shiny boxes, and beyond her was a trolley with not much more than a carton of Marlboro left on it. She had got her Calvin OK, but they'd run out of the other two (that's how it was, being at the back) so she'd bought four other perfumes she had vaguely heard of, and also a Mont Blanc ballpoint which she'd thought was pretty nice.

'It's no good looking at the card,' went on Katie. 'Christ you look awful – how do you feel? It's no good looking at the card, Norman, because nearly everything's gone.'

'That,' said Norman, pointing. 'I'll have that.'

'You're joking,' scoffed Katie. 'You are *joking*, Norman?'

Norman shook his head. 'I want that. How much is it?' he asked of the footsore woman, resignedly weary from having hauled and braked her deadweight wagon the length of the plane, dispensing to the surly and the spoiled various glamorous scents, narcotics and hooch – and now, God help us, this.

'Twelve pounds, if you're paying in sterling, sir,' she said, placing into Norman's cold and clammy hand the small and fluffy teddy bear with the goggles and the flying jacket – and isn't that little white scarf just *too* adorable?

'What in Christ's name,' demanded Katie, now the trolley and its dolly were behind the curtain, replenishing, 'did you want to go and buy *that* stupid thing for? Christ I worry about you, Norman. What am I in fact *doing* here with you, thirty-five thousand feet up? Are you going to be like this for the whole of the holiday?'

'You're here,' sighed Norman, 'because you love

me. God – is it *really* thirty-five thousand feet? Oh my God.'

'Ha! Big joke, Norman. I really wish you'd pack in this "love" crap. I've told you and I've told you – "love", whatever that is, simply doesn't enter.'

Oh! The cold pain when Katie did that! Thank God in heaven I am partly numbed. 'Don't. Please don't say that, Katie. I'd do anything for you, you know that. I thought,' he added on, placing the pilot teddy into her hands, 'you'd like it.'

'Yeah?' shot back Katie, dumping the thing back at him. 'Well I *don't*.'

'I need to go to the loo,' said Norman, darkly. 'I feel a bit . . .'

Actually, having sent out a posse of scouts to explore the many areas of deep-down bad feeling coursing in and around him, Norman now realized that he needed to go to the loo *and* he felt a bit . . . Yes: at least both of those.

Katie had on her cat-like face now – which was, Norman adjudged, not great timing.

'Norman . . . ?' she said (playfully? Toying with him, certainly). 'Norman, listen to me.' And now her fingers were tingling lightly at his crotch. Christ, he thought, thank God we're at the back: anyone could *see*.

'No listen,' he said, with some urgency, 'I mean I really *have* to go because not only do I have to *go*, go – but I also feel a bit . . . oh God, Katie – I've got to go *now*.'

'*You* listen,' insisted Katie – had his thigh in a

grip that was not so much affectionately sexy as approximating to a wringingly heartfelt Chinese burn. 'You go to the loo, right . . . ?'

'*Right*,' agreed Norman with passion, making to rise – and oh Jesus: she was touching him *there* again.

'. . . and then leave the door unlocked. I'll follow soon, OK?'

'But *Katie*,' moaned Norman (I mean Christ, you know how it is – any *other* time . . .)

'*And*, Norman,' she whispered, her eyes now dancing – even cavorting. 'Leave yourself open for me.'

Norman smiled weakly: really did feel a bit . . . but at least she'd let go of him now, so he eased himself up a bit – but before he was even close to standing, it was then, then that she did that thing: she did that thing that he would never ever in his life forget, could barely believe had happened. She quite deliberately upended her glass of Christ-I-don't-even-have-a-*conception*-of-what-she'd-been-drinking right into his lap and Jesus that would be bad enough at any time but when you're wearing pale khaki chinos and you've simply got to got to got to get up and go – and not just that but you feel a bit . . . and Christ I *can't* go now, not looking like this – look how I look! (the stain was spreading). But I've got to oh Christ got to go – oh God now I'm up and that man's face, American must be (Coca-Cola baseball cap – has to be, doesn't he?) That face

101

of his is right at the level of my bloody groin and no – *yes* he's registered, he's staring at me now with open-mouthed revulsion (and who can blame him?) and thank Jesus only that the loo is near and I'm at the door, in now – I'm in now (should I sit? Or hang my head down into the hole? I feel I could burst at either end) and Christ Almighty that Katie! The risks she sometimes takes – the danger she puts me into!

So from what we have learnt, it should have been Norman who was none too pleased with Katie for the duration of the cab ride into the city and not maybe the other way round – particularly in the light of what had happened next. Norman's bowels and bladder had been copiously evacuated, and now he was peering down into the steel-grey bowl (having flushed – there is a limit) whose soil pipe led out where, exactly? Probably directly connected to Norman's luggage, he shouldn't at all wonder – it was that sort of day. He didn't like this little cubicle, not a bit. It swayed and resounded, enclasped him coldly but wanted rid of him, he could tell. Norman felt I *suppose* a bit fresher now that most of his internal organs had been clatteringly dispatched to kingdom come, and so now he slid back the bolt – actually, at this moment, this horribly rude idea of Katie's didn't seem half so bad – and while he was waiting, dashed some water across his face, this having the effect of making his whole head feel grudgingly nudged to just several inches left of centre. He sat down and waited. Katie would tease him until it became unbearable – Norman knew this and (yes) loved it. He spread wide the flies of his I-don't-see-this-stain-coming-out-in-a-hurry trousers and rummaged around inside for a bit (give the girl a head start – why not?) Things were now assuming a life of their own, which is always nice (God, never been like this in a plane before – all right, yeah: never *flown* before, OK, but there's no sense in broadcasting it, is there?), and now, Christ, I'm really excited about all this. Come on, Katie, come on – I need to feel your hot soft lips around me. Why didn't she come? Was she coming? Why didn't she come?

Norman continued to idly play with himself for another, oh – could have been three or more minutes, was beginning to think oh Christ if she's not going to come, then, I might as well finish it off for myself – quite in the mood, if the truth be told. And then (oh great) the door opened gently (God I need you) and Norman looked up with a good deal of himself between his hands and screamed out once when his eyes connected with that man's face, American must be (Coca-Cola baseball cap – has to be, doesn't he?), and that man for his part stood as if pole-axed before spitting at Norman really quite throatily and stamping back out and leaving Norman to cope with piping tears gurgling down from the hot tap of humiliation and he stayed there, stayed there for as long as he could bear to, left with his head hung low when he could no longer stand the rush of enclosure.

'OK, Norman?' was all Katie had to say, as worm-like, he squirmed back into his seat.

'Why didn't you *come*?' he whispered urgently through the side of his mouth.

Katie shook her head, and beamed with gorgeous malice. 'Why didn't *you*?' she laughed. And she went on laughing, holding her nose – packing it in from time to time, looking sidelong at Norman, and then again letting it rip.

Norman just stared at the window and wondered. Apparently it had been vodka and cranberry that Katie had been drinking: would be. Can you see what he looks like? Can you? Christ Almighty on top of everything else he looks as if he has been cruelly surprised by a heavy and particularly vexing period: maybe explains the tension earlier.

But now as the suburbs of Chicago shouldered in on them, in their wide and bouncy cab – the billboards more shrill and insistent – it was Katie who was so pointedly Not Talking – because, Norman supposed (didn't know) – but maybe it was because he had wept his heart out during that bit of turbulence as they were coming in to land, and God – the screaming force of the landing itself had caused him to grind down his teeth to the point where he was practically gnashing at gums. Plus he had been completely flummoxed by the bewildering scale of O'Hare, with its glass-covered tunnels and monorails and walkways and travelators and God I can't begin to tell you – so it had been Katie doing all the This Way, Norman, and Down Here, Norman, and Come Bloody *On*, Norman, You Fucking Cretin type stuff. (Hard to believe she's only seventeen, isn't it? But it's true – that's all she is.)

But I suppose, yeah, if I'm honest – what really must have got her goat was that little misunderstanding at Immigration. There they were, all herded behind a yellow line – God, *acres* from the row of booths, each of them womanned by an unsmiling official. When it was nearly Norman's turn, he had apparently let one foot idle over the line and Christ! This huge black policeman – no uniformed airport employee, mind, not a security person – this was a real-life Chicago policeman, complete with badges, belts and fury – bellowed at him to Get Back Now, *Boy*! And the *gun*: the handle stuck out sideways, menacing and dangerously ugly, and Norman could barely believe it – and all this was truly terrible because he had anyway been ducking attention (holding fast his Tesco bag, hard against his plumstained genitals) and now wasn't everyone *looking* – and God, if that American man (you know the one – you can't have forgotten: Norman hadn't, that's for sure), if he sidled up for a quiet word with the policeman, then this officer could well take it into his head to save the time of whatever judiciary it was around here that dealt with filthy perverts and blow his head off right here and now (look: this is *Chicago* we're

105

talking about – think Cagney, think de Niro).

But the worst bit came when finally Norman had been granted leave to approach the booth, Katie had already been through – and there she was on the other side, tapping her foot and *waiting*. Norman handed over the immigration form that he had filled in on the plane, but was perturbed to say the least when the boot-faced old cow just flicked it back at him and yelled out: 'Fill It In!' Did *everybody* in America have to shout? It was, to Norman's way of thinking, very nervous-making. Well of course he *had* filled it in and he said so, but the only response was the woman becoming if possible even *more* vile and antagonistic and repeating more loudly and with added venom: 'Fill It *In*!' – and by now the black policeman's fingers were twitching close to the butt of his gun – and he wasn't coming *over*, was he? Norman could only babble at this unforgiving hag that he had, he *had* filled it in and by now he was so rattled that when she screamed out 'Sex!' Norman all but burst into tears and barked back Mind your own fucking business! This practically caused an uproar and if Katie hadn't come over and sorted things out, then Norman truly did believe that a gang of janitors, as we speak, would still be engaged in expunging from the airport's vast and granite floor the final cloying traces of Norman's blood and guts.

'You didn't fill in the box marked "sex",' explained Katie, petulantly, afterwards. 'I ticked "male" for you: was that right, Norman?'

And now as the cab rumbled on, Katie suddenly sat forward and shrieked, this causing Norman to jerk visibly: he was not at all sure that his mind and body could take too many more shocks like this.

'Oh *look*, Norman – oh God *look*! Isn't it *wonderful?*'

And Norman peered forward through the jail bars separating him and Katie from the driver, and there beyond the windscreen was (sure enough) Chicago. Suddenly, the whole soaring and glistening city had leapt up at them like the centre spread in the most fab and titanic pop-up book in the whole wide world.

'Chicago!' squawked out Katie, getting him in a clinch around the neck. 'Ready or not – here we come!'

Idly stroking his pilot teddy bear, Norman smiled, gingerly. Would have put more into it but why, since we're delving, was it *his* suitcase that had to go missing? Katie's quartet had made it safely, so why not his half-crippled effort? Maybe the sniffer dogs turned up their noses at it. Could be the baggage handlers refused to touch it. Whatever way, if all you had (bar the Tesco bag containing bugger all) was what you stood up in – this encompassing the pruney bloody chinos that said to the world Hey look *guys* – my balls have just exploded! – it wasn't that easy to be chirpy. Also, if he was honest, he felt a bit car-sick. Holidays, Norman surmised, were maybe something of an art form – yes?

CHAPTER 3

'I believe,' said the man to the sort of reception-ist girl at the vast and curvy counter in the foyer of The Excelsior, 'you have a booking for me. McInerney.'

'Bear with me, please, Mr McInerney,' responded the girl, damn near whispering for some reason or another, drawing down a fingernail the length of an invisible list (maybe awed by the sweep of the place, could she still be? Marble columns topped by gilt Corinthian capitals, much deep-fielded Oxo-brown panelling – you know exactly the sort of place we're dealing with here). 'Ah yes,' she announced brightly, as if she'd just won Pass The Parcel and was pleased with what she'd got. 'Miles McInerney. Double room, sea view, balcony – right?'

Miles McInerney nodded curtly, almost sighed – glanced up briefly at the crystal chandelier; look – he'd done all this a thousand times, OK?

'If you wouldn't mind just registering,' went on the girl (who had the weary and faintly distant air of having done it quite a lot herself). 'I'll just get someone for your bags. Seven nights – correct?'

'Correct,' confirmed Miles, adding a scrawled signature to the hastily filled-in boxes on the card. (I have *signed* things before, you know: takes up most of my day.)

In the lift on the way up to Miles's room, the porter – hands clasped at crotch level as if in prayer, or else in readiness to line up with his team-mates and jointly deflect a pounding penalty – broke the drumming whoosh of the ascent by observing in a voice that had well-meaning painted all over it:

'You've picked a lovely week, sir. Hottest day of the season, yesterday was.'

Miles regarded the man sideways – tugged on the half-mouth-jerk-smile: the one that discouraged cats from settling on his lap, deterred sticky-fingered children from coming any nearer – the one that repelled declaiming lunatics, and made the trussed-up doorway homeless know better than to ask him to spare any change.

Miles stood four-square at the centre of his room, splayed hands to the back of his hips (elbows jutting sharply) – could have been readying himself for an energetic bout of knee-bends, but no: here was Miles in critical survey mode. He strode over to a mirror and touched its top – could he be searching for bugs? No no – checking for dust: seemed OK.

'The minibar,' said the porter apologetically – seemingly yearning for approval, or maybe just to be let off a cuff round the ear, 'is just –'

'Yes,' interjected Miles. 'I think I'll find my way

109

around.' He dropped a pound coin into the man's pink and bashful hand.

'If there's anything you need or wish to know . . .' tailed off the porter: seemed a bit dim to say Just ring down to Reception because he would do, obviously, wouldn't he?

'Well obviously,' said Miles, very much putting the tin lid on that one.

Once he had shooed away the porter and locked the door behind him, Miles let out a great, deep and throaty sigh of utter satisfaction – as if he had just unexpectedly been mugged by an orgasm – which he hadn't, naturally enough, but by the end of the day, if all went well (and didn't it usually? Did indeed, did indeed), then who could say or tell? Who knew what might come up? That was the joy of it, that was the joy.

Miles carefully extracted a couple of suits from the navy nylon garment bag (maroon piping, and 'M.M.' embroidered loopily) and hung them in the wardrobe. One of them (Italian) was pearl grey and faintly iridescent – ideal with a French blue shirt and possibly that yellow woven silk tie he got in a Hugo Boss sale (hadn't worn it yet). The other (Italian also) was very nearly black – quite high buttoning, and a guaranteed puller: it spoke sophistication (or it did, at least – Miles would aver – when it's all six foot two of me that's bloody inside it!) plus it murmured money – which considering what it had bloody cost him (an arm and a leg doesn't come into it – we are talking quadriplegic

110

damage here, minimum: believe it, son) was pretty subtle of it, don't you think? Yeah: should be shouting it from the, wossname – rooftops, yeah. Course, he'd got all the summer-type gear as well: polo shirts, cotton trousers, deck shoes, towelling socks – all of that. But a suit of an evening in a place like this can work wonders, you know: has them eating out of your hand – most people, men anyway, they don't change, see, these days: come down to dinner in something stripy, hands deep down into the pockets of fairly foolish trousers. Miles comes in in the Italian number and whoosh! All the girls (and the women – the women, the older ones, they were actually easier), they all think that suddenly a holiday romance maybe isn't such a daft idea after all. And the moustache helped: why do you think he'd bloody grown it? Women might *say* they didn't go for facial hair – bang on about clean-shaven – but when it come to it (and in Miles's experience it did, quite often, come to it) then he wasn't hearing any complaints, was he? They were up for it, let him tell you: they were up for it, all right – don't you worry.

They could smell success, see – women. Smell it a mile off. And was Miles successful or was Miles successful? Joking – only top salesman overall for the third year running: *third*, mark you. The others – they were just little kids, compared to him: playing at it. For Miles, selling was like a war. He actually psyched himself up each morning into thinking that if he didn't win that day when he was

111

out there in the field, then – just like in war – he'd be killed. Sometimes, he came close to believing that if by the end of a given day he had failed to reach his own self-imposed targets then he would quite literally expire. Took it out of you, stress of that order – but Jesus did it get results. Which is why he had won yet another week in a luxury hotel, all expenses paid (He'd got a Harrods hamper at Christmas – didn't go a bundle on the duck breasts in jelly, it has to be said), while all the others – Peter Brady, Ken Carter, Dave Ridley, bloody losers the lot of them – they were all traipsing off again to some cut-price crappy little Spanish dump, or something, and trailing the wife and kids along with them. Miles had a wife (yeah – Sheil, she was called – fucking pain in the arse) and he had a couple of kids, and all (Damien, six – and little Mark, nearly about five, now: nice enough lads – but blimey, you didn't want to be around them for too long at a stretch – the bloody noise they made, it'd kill you). So winning this holiday, see, was the perfect way to get off out of it – holiday's only for *one*, love: *course* I'd love to take you, *course* I would – *and* the kids – but there's no way I can afford a hotel like The Excelsior for the four of us, not if you want that conservatory and the staircase doing. Is there? Hey? So look – you go off down to your mother's, right, and come autumn I'll take us all to EuroDisney – promise: how about that? Worked like a charm – sweet as a nut. Yeah: you fuck off down to your mother's and leave me alone to do what *I* wanna do. And what do I wanna do? Dunno – haven't met her, yet, have I? EuroDisney? Get out: come autumn, pressure of work'll hit that one on the head. You've got to plan ahead: see things coming. That's how Miles got to be where he is.

Right: I think a drink is called for. Always check out the bar: golden rule. Settle into a seat where you can see the foyer, for preference – keep an eye on the comings and goings. You learn a lot about women when they don't know you're looking; soon as they're aware – the second they catch your glance out of the corner of their eye, then you're watching someone else entirely – the woman they want to be seen as: from there on in, it's pure theatre. But you catch a woman rushing in from the rain (stopping and batting at the wetness of her hair) or losing her temper with whoever she's with – or (best of all) just sitting alone somewhere, waiting – catch her like that and you know what you're dealing with: makes the initial approach just that little bit easier.

Right. That salmony-coloured Ralph Lauren polo shirt, I think should do it – slap on a bit of pong, and I'm there. It's a good one: Chanel – Egoiste, it's called – bought for me by that Jenny from work, after I'd given her a major seeing-to up at her place when her Malcolm was off on a job in the Midlands. She said it was a joke: didn't get it, but it's a nice pong. Now I'll just put everything away into drawers, and I'm on. Shirts up here, socks and pants in this one – ties I've hung up –

113

and down the bottom I'll keep these rather tasty fur-lined leather handcuffs and the riding crop I picked up at that boot sale down Crawley way. Time they had a bit of an outing. Right: drink.

Miles used the stairs – take in a bit of the lie of the land – and cruised into the foyer with very practised ease (he rehearsed the amble in front of a mirror – once even thought of videotaping himself just taking a stroll, see if there was room for improvement, but the logistics just weren't worth the candle, if you want the God's honest truth). And well well well – what have we here over by Reception? Two women, with only one man: always a good sign – women hated being the odd one out, didn't they? More than anything, they hated that. The bloke's probably with the older one, I should think – don't much fancy the older one. Other one looks all right, though (good legs, nice little bum – can't see the tits yet cos she hasn't turned round); bar was over there on the left, wasn't it? Seem to recall. Oh but dear oh dear – look at this: she's got a bleeding baby. Oh fuck me – a bleeding baby, that's all I need. What a shame, what a waste – and Christ, tits are pretty good, actually, now they're in profile: just thrown away on a bleeding *baby*. Never mind, Miles lad: early days. I think a Campari and bitter lemon might just hit the spot – and not before time: bleeding baby's only doing what babies are largely famous for, isn't it? Bawling its fucking head off.

'Melody,' said Howard as kindly as he could,

114

trying to make no big deal of having to raise his voice. 'Can you just keep her quiet a bit? I can't hear what it is the girl's saying.'

'*Obviously* I can't, Howard,' countered Melody with petulance. What – he thinks I *enjoy* this? I have to *live* with it, Christ's sake. Jesus, we've only just arrived and already my little treasure is screaming. What's she screaming for? What's she got to scream about? It's a lovely hotel. God, I'm really going to enjoy this; at least I would, if it wasn't for *Dawn*.

The sort of receptionist girl who had checked in Miles McInerney was now round the other side of the counter, making goo-goo eyes at baby Dawn (mauve-faced by this time, the ranting now ripping out of her – elfin punchball at the back of her throat wetly engorged and on such full vibrato that you knew this baby surely meant it).

'Ooze a lickle crying ickle bubby, den?' enquired the girl rhetorically if bloody stupidly: evident, wasn't it? Dawn, plain as day.

'She does this,' said Melody.

'OK,' shouted Howard to the man who was now dealing with it all, 'well that seems to be everything, then. Elizabeth – they're just getting someone for the bags, and – are you all right, Elizabeth? What's wrong?'

Elizabeth had one finger to a temple, her eyes veiled and flickering. 'I'm not sure,' she confided to Howard as softly as was reasonable in the, well – she did actually find them rather trying circumstances, 'that Melody bringing Dawn was maybe such a good idea.'

Howard smiled. Could have told *you* that, darling, the second you thought of it. The good thing is, I – unlike you – will very soon be out of here and singing along to *Don Giovanni* on my peerless quadrophonic system in my fabbo Jaguar and almost certainly breaking speed limits in my extreme eagerness to be away from the shitty seaside and back in London with an empty house and nothing whatever on the agenda with the glorious exception of my little Zoo-Zoo. (The business deals? Couple of phone calls – they're done.)

The girl was talking to Dawn again:

'Izzoo a naughty, naughty ickle baby girly, den? Izzoo? But ooze a *lubbly* ickle babba, izzuntoo? Yes oo izz, yes oo *izz*.' All the while the girl had been mugging like a simpleton, and repeatedly jabbing a finger towards Dawn's midriff, this producing in her a new and awful state just this side of apoplexy. And then the floodlight of concern turned full up on Melody's face. 'Do you think maybe she ought to be changed?'

Melody nodded. 'But I didn't keep the receipt.'

The girl's eyes blinked. 'I'm sorry?'

'Nothing!' yelled back Melody (if there was one thing Dawn could not abide it was any form of competition in the volume stakes). 'Joke! Forget it!'

'Maybe,' suggested Elizabeth, 'a drink?' She surely looked as if she could have used one –

was even walking in the direction of the bar. 'Did anyone *hear* me? I said –'

'Yeah, I heard you!' bellowed back Melody, 'but we can't take *her* in there. Look – let's go up and I'll try to quieten her down.'

Elizabeth nodded, and came back over to Howard (grin as wide as his face, wrist energetically engaged in an epic session of car key jangling). 'Well we'll say our goodbyes now, then, darling.' Her cheek very nearly touched his. 'Now phone me when you're home, yes? Promise?'

Howard promised, and then Elizabeth said goodbye about four more entirely different ways until at last, finally, he was able to make the break.

'Have a good journey back!' Elizabeth called, as the tang of the sea reached in for him, mid-revolving door.

I will, I will, he thought, as he headed for the car. Can't be as bad as the journey coming, can it? Christ that bloody baby had screamed non-stop from start to finish – no wonder Elizabeth was just about shredded. And twice they had to stop because she'd been sick over just about everything, and then they stopped a third time for Howard to get out and be sick because the stench in there, I'm telling you, God – it really got to you no matter how hard you tried to blank it out. They squirted around quite a lot of Elizabeth's Arpège body spray, eventually – overdid it, actually, and *that* became fairly heave-inducing after a while. Didn't seem too bad now, though. I wonder if

117

this twinkling little resort can throw up a halfway decent bar? Couple of Scotches, and home. Yes!

Brian Morgan could well have done with a Scotch or two himself, as it happens, but precious little chance of that for some time yet: serious diplomatic bridge-building was called for right now, as even Brian couldn't fail to see, and with Dotty, of course, this was never the work of moments. In truth, she seemed so exercised about this particular – how did she phrase it? *Disaster* is the word she used – that it was pretty much touch and go as to whether he would emerge from this latest little fracas with all his limbs intact. Well, to be fair, there was no way she was ever going to be *pleased* about this, was there? No way at all.

And Howard thought *his* journey down was bad! He should have tried cramming himself into the rented Vauxhall Cavalier along with Dotty and Colin and a truly preposterous amount of stuff – I mean look, we were talking about a week at the seaside, not moving house, God help us: what *is* it with women? Even the car itself was a point of contention:

'But why can't we take our *own* car, Brian? I don't understand.'

'Told you, Dotty. In for its service. Apparently the clutch wants doing. I told you.'

'Yes but you must have said you're going away and you *need* the thing, didn't you? I mean why couldn't they put a move on?'

'That's what *I* said,' averred Brian, cutting himself a hefty chunk of Dotty's vexation. 'But look . . .' he tacked on – and yeah, let's just leave it hanging: you can't *reason* with these people, is the gist of what he was attempting to put across – and what could Dotty do but shrug? Their Volvo was out of action, and so it was down to the seaside in this none-too-new little Cavalier. Would she leave it now? No, not quite – one more bit:

'And the *colour*! Wasn't there anything less –?'

'This is what they had,' said Brian.

'It's like – it's the colour of a blood clot,' Dotty now decided. 'It'll be like sitting in a *scab*.'

'Look,' placated Brian (can't make a big deal out of the car – let her score any point she likes and enjoy her discontent over the car: nothing to what was surely coming soon). 'Look – it's only for the week, right? It'll be fine for a week – set of wheels, isn't it? A to B.'

Colin dropped a rucksack by the boot.

'That's the last of my stuff,' he said. 'But Mum's right, you know, Dad: it is horribly vulgar, this car.'

Thank you oh so much, son of mine: she was just getting off the car thing, and now you have to stick your twopence-worth into the mix.

'Clutch shouldn't even *need* doing,' grumbled Dotty. 'Car's less than a year old.'

I know, thought Brian: that's why I got quite a good price for it. Oh heaven defend me! Joys to come.

'Anyway,' said Dotty briskly. 'Let's be going if we're going, shall we? At least the weather's lovely. Now Brian – are you sure everything's *off*?'

Brian nodded. 'Checked everything, and double-checked – all present and correct. Tank drained, gas off, back door bolted – milk and papers cancelled, all done. And Howard said he'd look in every evening – he's got the spare set, so that's OK. So let's all stop *worrying*, shall we?' he implored (yeah – let's for God's sake stop moaning – let's just *get* there, shall we? That'll give you something to moan about.) 'And yes, before you ask, all the windows are locked and bolted too.' As is my cat-flap, not that I'll mention it. Two little chromium latches left over from when I converted the landing cupboard into my tool store (along with a proper place for my beer-making stuff) round about the time I relagged the copper. Always just chuck these little things into a big old Quality Street tin and it's amazing, you know, just how often they come in handy: there's all sorts in there.

'You go in the back, Colin,' said Dotty. 'I would but it's my foot.' She settled herself into the passenger seat (not at all *liking* it) and suddenly said out of the window to Brian: 'You know, since you did that, you look just like a *match*.'

Brian was fairly used to deciphering Dottyisms but was all at sea on this one.

'Like a *what*, Dotty?' he asked, opening the door at the driver's side, patting his pocket the way he always did whenever setting out for

120

anywhere, he knew not why. 'Since I did *what*, actually?'

'Since you gave yourself that stupid haircut – it's made your head look all sort of *round* – and because you're so skinny anyway you look just like a matchstick. It has, you know – I don't know if you used a pudding bowl, Brian, but it's changed the whole shape – it's given you a round head.'

Brian the Roundhead had the Cavalier at the point of engagement, and following a prolonged disagreement over the selection of gear, man and machine were now at one. Once he'd cleared that terrible ringway system beyond the flyover – but hadn't yet had to face the inevitable bottle-neck at the junction which had, in all Brian's driving experience, the shortest light in London (two – three cars at most got through: I ask you) – he thought he might go in for a bit of levity. Wagging his head and widening his eyes in order to indicate that whatever was about to emerge from his mouth was, in fact, intended to be, OK, if not *funny*, then surely in holiday spirit, at least, Brian suddenly piped up only vaguely in tune:

'Oh I *do* like to *be* beside the *sea*side . . . !'

To which there was no response whatever, bar Dotty gazing up at a series of grim and rain-stained blocks just beyond the overpass and muttering Just imagine *living* there . . . while Colin continued to tab at podgy buttons on whichever hand-held timewaster currently had him in its clutches. Bloop, said the machine: bleep blap blop *bloop*.

121

Brian sighed, and tacked on much more quietly, Tiddle-ee-om-pom-pom; he was thinking – you know, I wonder sometimes, I really do wonder just why it is I bother. It was *Dotty* who insisted on this holiday, wasn't it? Could make a bit of a bloody effort. But as the low-built factories and the high-rise offices gave way to steep and grassy banks deeply chamfered by wide and dead straight roads, so did Brian begin to feel fear. Signs to their ultimate destination were springing up now, and so it was only a matter of time before . . . oh look, Dotty was turning to him now: here it comes, so make room for it.

'Do you want a mint?' she asked.

Not this time, then. Not quite yet. Brian shook his head.

'Colin?' pursued Dotty. 'Mint?'

While Colin was thrusting his fist into the bag, Dotty turned to Brian and said:

'Brian – just explain to me, will you, one simple thing.'

Now, then.

'Mm?'

'Why, when I asked you – oh Colin, do you *have* to play that blasted thing all the time? It's so – can' you turn the sound off?'

'No fun without the sound,' sulked Colin.

'Well isn't there anything *else* you'd like to play with?'

Yes, thought Colin: Katie's tits, but they're not on offer, are they? Currently resident in Chicago along with their rightful and crazy bloody owner. 'I'll read,' he said.

'Anyway, Brian – what was I saying? Oh yes – one thing. I'd like you, if you can, to just explain to me *why*, when I told and told and told you that I wanted this holiday to be exactly the *same* –'

'I thought you just meant the *place*,' put in Brian. Crap, of course: Brian had understood precisely Dotty's intention, while not remotely understanding it: had even booked a suite at The Excelsior, directly beneath Elizabeth's – did it out of fear. But then he thought of the *money* . . . well, he cancelled. Just a couple of days ago, if you can believe it.

'But that wasn't *it*,' maintained Dotty, becoming shrill: shrill was here now, to help us all along our merry way. 'I mean I could understand if The Excelsior was fully booked – OK, it's that time of year . . . but we're not going to the Palace either – and you won't tell me where we *are* going, that's what worries me. Why is it such a secret, Brian? Oh God, knowing you you've probably booked us into some ghastly little b & b a mile from the front with some ghastly *landlady* telling us what to do all the time.'

'It's not a secret,' qualified Brian. 'It's a *surprise*. Look, Dotty, we're not going to a b & b – of course we're not. Promise. Nobody'll be telling us what to do. Promise.'

Dotty looked sidelong at Brian. 'Really? *Really* promise?'

Brian nodded. 'I'm *telling* you, aren't I?'

Well what could he do? What could he do but postpone the awful moment? Which was now here. Yes, the miles had fled, the resort was reached (Look Colin, look: look at the *sea* – see?) and then, much to Dotty's consternation, they were right through the place and out the other side – more fields, now, punctuated by frankly in Dotty's view rather shitty little houses all with strange and pointy stuck-on *porches*. Dotty drew in her breath, but then this scattered little estate passed away too, and then at the sight of a small blue sign strapped on to a tree (Dotty missed it – what was that?) Brian turned off to the right, and the road now was narrow – banks of gorse near brushing the flanks of the car, the roar of the main road faded and gone – and Dotty was just on the point of saying that she found this sudden jolt of *rural* really rather lovely, when the lane they were bumping along opened out on to a clearing and here, closing his eyes (all but arranging his neckwear so that the executioner could better find his mark), Brian cut dead the engine. All that was heard for some seconds was the trill of birds, high up and soaring higher. Then all that was heard was Dotty:

'Brian –!'

'Dotty, listen,' said Brian, hastily. 'It's not as bad as you think, honestly, Dotty – you mustn' have a closed mind. It'll be great! Look – get out of the car and –'

'Brian!'

'Oh God,' sighed Colin from the back. 'Oh God oh God – this is just the end.'

'Shuttup, Colin,' snapped Brian. God, though – you would, wouldn't you, you'd expect a *bit* of support from your own son, wouldn't you, from time to time – instead of all this wholesale *moaning*. 'Think of it as an *adventure*, can't you? God – I would've been thrilled with a holiday like this, when I was your age.'

'Brian,' said Dotty, in carefully measured tones, while Colin rolled up his eyes and stuck two fingers down his throat. 'Listen to me, Brian, because I am saying this only once. Turn the car round – turn around this horrible tinpot bloody *car*, Brian – and drive straight back into town and book us into a hotel. Any hotel. Failing that –'

'But *Dotty*,' Brian tried to reason, 'at least have a *look* at it. I mean – you might *like* it when you see it, you never know. It's *different*, isn't it? I mean – holidays are meant to be a *change*, yes? Colin – come on: help me with the bags. I'm telling you both, you'll love it when you're inside.'

It took a hell of a while, but eventually Dotty was persuaded to leave the car (which she hated) to confront this place (which she hated) and listen to the latest urgent out-pourings from Brian (for whom hate was, believe her, too small a word). She stared, not quite trusting the vision, at the small and rounded duck-egg blue caravan, whose axles rested upon four brick stacks set into concrete, its wheels having been summarily amputated. Next to it was another, very similar. As far as the eye could see, damn near identical pastel little caravans fanned out in all directions, separated by sometimes as much as four feet: thus were formed intersections and treeless avenues. Dotty stared. She took in the two cemented steps leading to the door that Brian – being his height – would crack his head on every single time (hope it splits his skull). She saw little cream and ruched crossover net curtains beyond the rain-spattered window. She stared. Now she was conscious of what appeared to be an outboard motor bolted on to the rear of the caravan, close to which emerged a broad white plastic pipe which led into a sort of butt: it didn't bear thinking about. Dotty just simply stared. It was the sight of the movement to the right of her that broke into her trance-like and horrified state.

'Brian,' she said slowly – the word sent out as a feeler, much like one would a hand in a coal-dark cellar. 'That woman – she is filling a bucket from an outside tap.'

'Only because – well, she must *want* to, Dotty: doesn't have to. They've all got *water* and things – course they have. Cookers, heating – everything. Why don't you go inside, hm? I think you'll love it, once you're inside. I think you'll both be pretty impressed.'

Colin yanked open the door and stuck his head inside – Brian jerking a thumb at him and raising his eyebrows at Dotty.

'See – you see. He'll love it, you'll see. You can't

judge a book by its *thing*, can you Dotty? Well Colin – what do you think?'

Colin was rattling around inside for a bit, before his deadened voice wafted back out:

'Oh my *God* . . .'

'Brian,' snapped Dotty, turning on him eyes as cold and dull as those you hate to see on a fish on a slab. 'This is a *disaster*. I could – just now – *kill* you. Do you know that?'

And before Brian could conjure up any other bloody stupid thing to say, Dotty howled as her bad foot connected in a kick that had been aimed God alone knows where but collided hard with his knee and had him exhaling swiftly and buckling (thought he could save himself – Jesus what a curious pain) and then caving in and falling heavily on one side (thought I could avoid it – wrong again) and the woman filling the bucket was entranced – maybe thinking Thank Christ: something round here I can actually *talk* about – and as the water coursed down the sides and made boggy the grass, so Dotty (could have needed to be somewhere secret, the better to do her weeping) stamped up the steps and banged shut the caravan door behind her – which, Brian observed from his vantage point of all over the ground, swung wide open again – but it was probably nothing: hinge wanted tightening, drop of oil, work of a moment. Lucky, really, I brought my tools.

At long last, Elizabeth was about to get her drink

– and talking of which, she had meant to make Howard promise her faithfully that he wouldn't, would he, stop off on the way, no matter how tempted. You can drink all you want at home, Howard, she would have said, but when you're driving it's different. Not that there would have been any point, she supposed: he only would have nodded and then done as he pleased. But in Elizabeth's humble opinion she actually jolly well *deserved* a drink – God, quite apart from the interminable journey, there had been very much the Dawn side of things. Look, don't misunderstand: I *love* babies, love them dearly – although I have to say Katie was such a handful I was in no hurry to *repeat* the whole exercise: put me off the entire business. That, and the pain. But little Dawn is something else! I mean, it truly did appear as if the child would never stop her screaming: never heard anything like it. I'm not at all sure who was the most pleased when one of the hotel's nannies eventually arrived – herself or Melody. But certainly the sudden silence was palpable. God knows what it's going to be like tonight, though. Anyway, Melody – let's go down to the bar, and then we can get out and see a bit of the place.

Fine by Melody. She *adored* the suite, just adored it. Never, if she's honest, seen anything like it, outside of a Fred Astaire film. And the view! To die for. Melody couldn't *wait* to get out and just smell that air. So this is the way Howard and Elizabeth did it, hey? All those times when Howard would say to her – Look, Melody: got to take her away for a few days, few weeks (once it was a whole bloody month: Thailand), but I'll be thinking of you all the time: miss you already. Got to do it, though, love: keep Elizabeth quiet. Balls: I bet he loved every single minute of it – and Christ, if they always stayed in places like this, why in hell wouldn't he? Meanwhile, Melody was expected to make do with a quick pasta and an even quicker fuck in the back of the car (a Mercedes, in those days: the Jag was very new).

Anyway, she was here, now – let's give Howard's bank balance a run for its money, shall we? Maybe I can even outspend Elizabeth – but God, just looking at those clothes, I doubt it. Melody's clothes were quite good: anything left over from nannies went on them, and she certainly looked after them. Jaeger was a favourite, and Escada for parties; used Next and M & S as well, of course, and generally managed to look pretty good, even if she did say it herself (shoes were her real weakness – but Harrods sale was very good for that). But just take one look at all of Elizabeth's lovely summer things: Joseph and Kenzo and Chanel – and so much Armani it made Melody want to cry! And most of it looked brand-new. Howard never looked after *me* like this.

Miles McInerney didn't appear to have clocked Elizabeth and Melody as they entered the bar (hey – the man's a pro, right?) but of course he took it all in. Had this knack of watching people without even looking: comes with years. Yeah, I was right – couldn't fancy the older one, but the other one really *was* all right – but oi! I'm not so wet behind the ears as to get caught up with some slapper with a bloody baby: they're all looking for husbands, that lot – but where was the kid's father, ay? Buggered off is where, which tells you all you want to know.

Ordering another Campari allowed Miles just the movement necessary to sneak another look at the woman down the other end who really *was* something: Christ, those endless and silky brown legs of hers, and wonderful slender and bony hands, nails all long and red and shiny: can you imagine what she could get up to with hands like that (and just you leave the legs to Miles, OK?) Trouble is, she's with a bloke, isn't she? Lucky bastard: touching her arm – looking at her in that way, what was that way – Christ, sometimes Miles just couldn't find the, oh Christ, things – words. Solicitous? Yeah – that'll do: caring. Wasn't going to let her out of his sight, was he? And yet they didn't seem to be newlyweds: those you could spot a mile off. Maybe the bloke was being like that because he had met types like Miles before: maybe he just smelled the presence of one of the breed. Yeah – that was probably it. Well so what? It's not a problem. Just takes a bit longer, that's all. Right: knock this back and bugger off down to the front – see what's cooking. I'll just do my famous amble past this woman, suss out any reaction.

The bloke was talking when Miles sauntered up to and away from them – and yeah, she did, the woman: just glanced almost up for practically no time at all, but you noticed these things, when you were looking. Christ – she was even better, close up.

'So you see,' John Powers was saying, as Miles wandered out of the bar, 'they've got absolutely everything here that they had at that Christawful health place – saunas, pools, hairdressers. Massage. But at least it's not a dead-and-alive hole in the middle of a field. Oh and by the way: there are only *masseuses* here, Lulu.'

That had been the last straw, actually. I mean yes – he had decided that he just had to get out of the place while he still had possession of his mind – no idea where to go, though – when Lulu had just let slip (cool as you like) that the person who had been giving her her daily massage was a nice young chap called *Paul*. A bloody feller! John could barely believe it – that every day for a week while he had been smoking and cursing and trying to remember where he had left off in his Frederick Forsyth, Lulu was being handled (naked! Jesus, it made him froth to even *think* about it) by a man! A bloody fucking man! *Right*, John had said, that's it. He'd gone straight to the local guidebook, picked out the best hotels in the two or three nearest seaside places, and got phoning. Drew a blank just everywhere, at first – packed bloody solid, they were. Then someone mentioned the Palace just down the road from here and the girl there rather thought they *did* actually have a room if he could only hold on just a sec. John held on (never mind 'sec' – more like five bloody minutes) and it turned out it was a poxy little single round the back. Have you tried The Excelsior, the girl suggested. No he hadn't – hadn't *heard* of The Excelsior, had he? She gave him the number, and not expecting much, he rang it. Actually sir, we have a very large and beautiful *suite* – sea view, everything: last-minute cancellation. Right, said John – I'll have it; no messing about – didn't even ask the price (OK, it'll be a fucking fortune, but so what? I get out of the bloody concentration camp, and the fucking masseur gets to maul someone else's fucking wife: if I see him before I leave I'll dot his bloody i's for him.)

'Oh *God*, John,' sighed Lulu, twiddling the stem of her champagne flute between what Miles had been quite correct in assessing as truly elegant fingers. 'Don't keep going *on*, hm? We're *here* now, OK? You got what you wanted now leave it. You've talked of nothing else but Paul since we got here – and in the car coming down.'

John's whole face flinched away from this blow.

'Don't call him *Paul*!' he hissed.

'Oh John you're being truly childish here now, you know. Why shouldn't I call him Paul? Paul is his *name*.'

John was pleading with her now – eyes heavy and tilted in supplication (can't explain what I

132

feel, how much it hurts me, can only beg her to stop). 'Please,' he said softly. 'Please just don't.'

Lulu's eyelids fell and she yieldingly smiled at John, quite as one would with a child who had newly proffered a skew-cut birthday card alive with glue and felt and glitter, that he had made with love when he got up at dawn, just for you, and you alone.

'Come on,' she said. 'Let's walk.'

John and Lulu put on their apologetic smirks as they coincided with these two women at the too-narrow-for-four bar door. Lulu had noticed them earlier – one of them had on the most divinely simple pinky-beige linen sun dress, must be from somewhere good: Nicole Farhi, maybe, Lulu surmised. The woman was saying to her friend:

'I do hope Katie calls this evening – she never gave me a number, you know. I hope she's OK.'

Lulu smiled as she and John made for the glass doors and the white bright sunshine beyond. It was funny, in places like hotels, overhearing little titbits of other, unknown lives. Who and where was Katie, she wondered. And is she OK?

Well actually yeah – she's doing good (they say that, here). Fagged out after a whole day of doing really dreck and touristy summer things – but God, Chicago was *so* thrilling. Katie had no idea just how amazingly tall the buildings actually were – pictures gave you no idea, it just didn't come across in films. She'd dragged

Norman to the top of the Sears Tower, which he hadn't enjoyed at all.

'Can't we just get me something to *wear* first?' he had asked, without much hope. Whenever Katie had that gleam – and not just in her eye, either: at times like this, Katie's whole *face* seemed to gleam – there was never really any of that – hope. It's just that, God – they'd got to the hotel so late last night, and Jesus he had felt so *ill*. Maybe it was, oh – I don't know – it was just *everything*: Norman had really had it. Didn't even want anything to do with Katie, which had frankly disgusted her (God in heaven, she was thinking, if Norman is no good for sex, then what the fuck is the point of him?) And he'd gone to sleep in his clothes and now here he was in a lift, shooting up it seemed like the firmament and he was still wearing the same old grotty old stinky old clothes – and God it was *hot* in this town, let him tell you that. The airline had apologized and assured him that ninety-eight per cent of lost luggage is eventually recovered – but that presupposed that the case stayed shut for the duration of its global misrouting: Norman might well get back the suitcase, but any contents seemed unlikely. And was he insured? Well ask yourself: was he?

Norman simply refused to believe the view from the top of the building. I mean, yes – he'd been up tall things before: the Eiffel Tower comes to mind (he had lost a rather natty dark blue beret that he had only just bought – Christ it was gale force up there – and later he had dumped the onions because it didn't seem funny any more, not without the hat). But up here the sheer – I mean: *look*, can't you? There is no way there can be a view like this unless from an aeroplane – and it was a bad move thinking that, very, because now he felt sick and traumatized again and he scattered, oh – scores of Japanese in his determination to gain the lift and be down and out of there in double quick time.

'We'll go to the Magnificent Mile,' announced Katie, once the two of them had reached terra firma – and even now, you know, there was a sort of tingling in Norman's toes: hardly dared let his feet reach all the way to the ground for fear it was illusory and would swallow him up (oh God – maybe I should have stayed at home).

'Where's that?' asked Norman. 'What is it?'

'It's not its real name,' said Katie. 'I read about it on the plane. It's actually called, I *think*, Michigan Avenue – I think that's what it said. Anyway, it's dreadfully famous and packed with fabulous shops, so we're bound to get everything you need from somewhere there. And there's a Gucci, which is great, because in London you can't get the loafers in all the colours. I want pink and orange, if they've got my size.'

'Doesn't have to be *fabulous*,' muttered Norman. Can't be, he was thinking; anyway – all I want is something *clean*. 'How do we get there?'

'All American cities are really easy because it's all avenues intersected by, um, things that *aren't* avenues – and anyway this one's huge so we can't miss it: it's near a bridge.'

Well they managed to miss it for well over an hour, and Norman was dripping like a carthorse and fed up to the back teeth with saying again and again to the fast-moving rear view of Katie *Look*: why don't we just buy a *map*, Godsake?

'Because we don't *need* one – oh stop *complaining*, Norman. You're always *complaining*: you drive me crazy.'

After a further forty minutes even Katie had had enough – Christ, bloody shops'll be *closed* at this rate – so she stopped a man on a corner and asked directions and he told her to go buy a map, lady (which wasn't very nice). Suddenly, Katie caught sight of Bloomingdale's, looming – and she'd heard of Bloomingdale's (Big Brown Bag – famous, yeah?) and so she piped up Oh look it's OK, Norman – Bloomie's is huge – got everything; oh Christ look – this *is* Michigan Avenue: *see* – I told you we'd find it, and you didn't believe me.

Katie became a transfixed person in such shops as this: Norman had seen her with her mother just as they both stepped into Harrods – it was like nothing so much as a matched pair of Dr Jekylls performing impromptu their famous party pieces.

Katie suggested they split up and meet back here – right here, Norman: look around you, memorize it, right on this spot – in what, say – hour, hour-and-a-half? Hour's probably enough: one hour, Norman, right here: got it? Norman replied as leadenly as he dared *Yes*, Katie – think I've just about assimilated that. Trouble was, if he underdid the irony (as now) she missed it completely; go the other way and she'd quite likely maim him, so what could you do?

He was pleased about the splitting-up arrangement, though – couldn't buy a thing with Katie looking on. God – once (that Harrods trip, actually – first and last) she had tried to get Norman to buy a tie that cost sixty-five pounds. Sixty-five pounds! Jesus Almighty – you go down to your local Mencap and for that you'll get a three-piece suit, a greatcoat, some barely-worn brogues and a bag to put them all in (actually the source of his, yes, um – suitcase). Ties? Christ – they practically threw in *ties*. *Sixty-five pounds*? Please don't make him laugh. Who on earth would even *contemplate* spending such a sum on a tie? And oh dear – suddenly Norman found himself in a vast department positively alive with just such people, plucking up armfuls of what Norman could now see were very expensive clothes. I don't suppose the Magnificent Mile runs to a thrift shop, does it? No, don't imagine so: and it wouldn't do to ask.

Right – a bit of quick thinking called for (have to be *very* quick if Norman was going to meet Katie in just an hour – a touch over fifty minutes, now). He bought a pair of socks – twenty-two dollars plus sales tax (Jesus! Maybe he could wear one today and one tomorrow and just get used to hopping.) Then he did the cheeky thing – almost certainly would never have had the nerve in London, but hey – he was a foreigner, wasn't he? Never have to confront them again. He asked for a bag – the biggest they'd got. And *yes* the salesgirl sneered (didn't even tell Norman that she just *lurved* his accent – to be fair, no one else ever had either) but he did obtain his objective: one Big Brown Bag, as advertised (a wino could practically set up home in it).

Norman raced out of the building and dashed down a series of side-roads – surely this city has a seedy area not too far away? Not *everyone* in Chicago can be a millionaire, can they? Eventually he found more or less what he had prayed for – a truly disgraceful-looking shop, seemingly hastily set up in the front half of someone else's bankrupt premises. There were piles of horrible striped sweatshirts, virtually transparent T-shirts (the very cheapest were printed I'VE BEEN TO HICAGO), thick and formless denims, acetate bombers with the word BULLS on the back (well why not? Better than COWS, anyway), iffy chinos and all manner of two-tone sneaker. Great! Plum and turquoise were much in evidence – those and fag-ash grey: Norman bought three of most things – hundred and fifty bucks the lot (thought of haggling a bit, but the bloke doing the money was built like a dump truck so best maybe let it go, I think). He crammed it all into the Bloomingdale's bag (Katie would never think that it was all atrociously naff and ugly – not if she believed it had come from

Bloomie's) and now he had just – what was the time now? Just coming up to quarter past, right: exactly nine minutes to get back to *there* – right there, Norman: right in that spot, got it?

And nine minutes would have been ample – would even have given him time to assume a what-kept-you and laid-back slouch against a mirrored pillar – yes, easily time enough if only he had set off at a sprint in the right direction. He was busy thinking Look – that street, that Mile place, Michigan Thing: vast, right? Can't miss it. I mean, Bloomingdale's alone was the size of a small town – and that other huge building he'd shot past – said Wrigley on the front – anywhere else it would tower over everything. It was the *scale* of the place that was half the trouble – that and the fact you had to run while looking straight upwards at the glassy and vertiginous gleaming shanks of buildings that could blind you – it was the only way to have a hope of spotting something you vaguely recognized, but the down side was that you kept slamming into people, some of whom appeared quite murderous (oh God – maybe I should've stayed at home).

He ended up staring out at what looked like the sea. How could this be possible? Five minutes ago he was in an avenue which made Oxford Street look like some back alley, and now all of a sudden he was by the seaside. How did people live here and not go mad? He asked a woman to please tell him where Bloomingdale's was but her reaction could not have been more astounding were he

139

brandishing an axe: she simply fled. He asked a man the same question and the man in return asked him one: Hey, man – do I look like a cop to you? To which Norman seriously contemplated responding (*Not*, since you ask) but he'd gone by then, at the fairly standard hundred miles an hour that people seemed to move in this place.

Eventually Norman found someone who did indeed look like a cop (oh Christ – the time, just look at the time!) in that he had jackboots and a gun and sin-black Ray-Bans – frightening as you like. If that wasn't enough he was perched up on a bloody great horse and so even bawling up at the man meant a further strain on Norman's aching neck. The policeman directed him this way and that by way of flourishing a glossy black club that had everything going for it save a six-inch nail through the end, but Norman had lost his drift way before the end and didn't like to ask for an encore for fear of the man shooting him dead, or at least doling out a damn good bludgeoning.

It was, anyway, too late: even if he knew where to go, he'd never make it now – and there was no question of Katie waiting for him: Katie would never wait. Norman stared down at the *lake*, according to Darth Vader the cop (only in America, Norman supposed, could lakes look like oceans), and wondered should he save Katie the trouble and just jump now and end it all? No – seemed a waste (now that he'd got his fab new clothes, and all). No – I'll just go back to the hotel and await her wrath:

face it like a man. Right. Oh Christ. Where's the bloody hotel? And Norman was close to weeping when the next thought assailed him: what was the bloody *name* of it? He knew it began with a B, but what – he was going to approach another policeman, was he, and politely ask directions to that hotel, you know the one – the one that starts with a B? I don't think so.

Norman ambled around for a bit, this way and that (can't actually think of any hotels in the *world* that begin with a B, now I put my mind to it – Borchester, Blaridges, Bitz: doesn't work, does it?), when quite suddenly he found himself in a broad and lofty tree-lined avenue, and several seconds later, slap outside Bloomingdale's. He went in with heavy heart and Big Brown Bag (more for old times' sake than anything) and there, predictably, was the very spot he had been due to meet Katie, bereft of any sign of her. Well what did Norman expect – he was forty-five, nearly fifty minutes overdue: what a joke. After all that airport fiasco. Katie would have given him ten seconds leeway and then she would have been off.

It was then that she strolled up behind him and ruffled his hair and said:

'Hi – I'm a bit late. Let's get back to the Sheraton now, Norman – I've got a rather exciting present for us both.'

Norman fell into step, and off they went. He was content to be lost in the slipstream of Gucci chatter and Prada prattle and very wisely put in little. He was more hot and wet when eventually they got back to the Sheraton than he could ever remember being – and no matter how vile his new wardrobe, at least it didn't stink – shower first, and then change: bliss.

Funny, though: could have sworn it began with a B. Maybe thinking of bleeding Bloomie's. Wonder what this rather exciting present could be? With Katie, you never could tell.

'Well I think it's a perfectly *charming* idea,' Elizabeth was saying. 'Perfectly charming.'

She was standing among maybe a dozen or so people in a room just off the main hotel foyer, fooling with a glass of champagne and addressing the not-quite manager of the place: submanager, undermanager, deputy manager – managerette. Whatever these people called themselves, these days.

'It's something we like to do,' said the person – he's actually got his name on a tag thing on his lapel but God, there is simply no way Elizabeth could read that from here. 'Often, you know, people come on holiday and they feel they can't approach people,' he went on. 'All very English. But we find that new guests quite like to come to these little parties of ours. Apparently some lifelong friendships have been formed in the past!'

Elizabeth smiled at his spurious delight in a way that needn't at all have been sweet. Yes well, she was thinking – let's not get *too* carried away, shall we? I mean a glass of champagne with a few new people was one thing – I think I'll just sidle off for another of those rather yummy canapés, actually, give me a chance to get away from this person (perfectly pleasant, but a bit of a bore): I've had one of the salmony ones so maybe I'll go for a prawny one this time. Yes, as I say – a drink with some people is one thing, but I don't quite see it as a *marriage* bureau: what can the man be thinking of? And where was Melody? Ah there she was – over by the buffet and talking to some man: would be. A bit man-mad, Melody: Elizabeth did not know quite why she thought this, but she did. And shouldn't Brian and Dotty be here by now? With Colin? I did *say* six o'clock.

They wouldn't be long: just parking the car. Touch and go whether they came at all, though, because Dotty was quite literally at her wits' end (wild-eyed and flushed – even a bit of dribbling): what on earth could she tell Elizabeth? Not the *truth*: couldn't tell her the *truth*. What? And be vanquished at a stroke – truly a Head of John the Baptist stunt that would be. No, she had to think of something brilliant. But for now, just phone her – give her a ring as she made you promise faithfully to do, the moment you got there (I just have to know you're *safe*).

Problem Number One with their delightful little home on wheels (except, yeah – no wheels) was that there wasn't a bloody telephone. So down to the local pub in the hateful little car (and God

143

you should have seen the *pub* – more like the recreation room in a reform school: banks of livid and belching games, fronted by callow simpletons) – just so she could make a phone call (they used to have a mobile, but Brian said the rental was way too high). Oh God what a wonderful holiday this is going to be! And yes of *course* Dotty contemplated going straight back home – but what on earth was she to say to Elizabeth *then*? And Colin, poor Colin – he needed a holiday, poor lamb. Although he did say quite openly to his father that in his opinion this caravan was the shittiest place he had ever set foot into in all his life on earth.

She had confronted Brian (confronted him? Ooh – came close to really *braining* him, insufferable little man) but he had actually got up on his high horse (can you *credit* it?) and made clear in no uncertain terms that This Is It: no more *money* – clear, Dotty? How many times and in how many ways? No more *money*. So there it was. Anyway, she'd phoned Elizabeth at The Excelsior (oh God – The *Excelsior*, just think of it) and Elizabeth had said Look, they're putting on some sort of a cocktaily effort for new arrivals this evening so come to that (do) and then we can go somewhere to eat; actually the restaurant here looks pretty good so we'll maybe try that. And *yes* Dotty accepted, of course she did – anything to get out of that poky little tin can that Brian seriously seemed to believe could comfortably house three people for a week. But then later – oh God, oh God: what to wear?

What to *say*? What to wear? What to *say*? Would have called it all off but the thought of entering that frightful little pub again was simply too much to even contemplate.

Anyhow – they're here, now. Colin, come over here – your hair's all up at the back; and honestly, Brian, what you think you're doing turning up to a cocktail party in that quite hideous tweed jacket I simply do not know. Dotty herself was got up in a perfectly all right navy blue cotton coat dress – short sleeves, wide and contrasting white reveres, all very nautical and really rather nice – and the bag and shoes were an almost match. Of course, le tout ensemble was terribly *old*, but summer things don't really change all that much, do they? Oh *please* don't say they do, because this one thought was all that Dotty had to cling to. If only Elizabeth didn't *say* anything about the outfit, then she'd be OK; but she would, of course – being Elizabeth, she'd be bound to.

At that moment, Elizabeth was more concerned with the canapé table: actually, I think that chickeny thing was rather nice too, but I really must be careful because they're all rather moreish and if I go on being piggy I shan't have room for dinner; could maybe just manage a starter and a pudding.

'Hello,' said a voice to the left of her. 'I'm John.'

Oh dear, someone's talking to me. It's all so odd talking to new people like this but I suppose one had better show willing.

'Elizabeth,' said Elizabeth. 'These canapés are really rather good. I recommend the prawny ones.'

John Powers nodded. 'They *are* good, actually. I'm not normally great on nibbles, but I must say . . . Are you down here for long?'

'For a week,' said Elizabeth, brightly – rather as if supplying the punchline to a joke. 'And you?'

'Same. Just arrived. Actually, this is a sort of second holiday for us because my wife – that's her over there, Lulu – she'd booked us into one of these health farm places – I don't know if you've ever . . . ?'

'I haven't, actually. I've thought of it, but I've never actually –'

'Well *don't*,' cut in John, drawing a finger across his throat. 'Hell-holes. We couldn't wait to get out. So really, coming here was a totally unplanned thing – but it seems very nice.'

Where are Brian and Dotty? Why isn't Melody talking to me? *I* don't care about this man and his stupid health farm, so why's he telling me about it?

John was just in the process of popping one of the commended prawny things into his mouth, when he froze – mid-pop – and just stared across at Lulu. Right – got to put a bloody stop to that! She was talking to that bloke – that bloke with the moustache who'd been in the bar a bit earlier on. And she'd *looked* at him, then – she may imagine I didn't notice, but I am here to tell her that she's *wrong*. I simply chose not to comment (all right,

146

yeah – store it up, feel it fester, let her have it later) – and now she was bloody *talking* to him, bold as you like.

'Will you excuse me?' he said to Elizabeth, already having left.

'Yes of course,' responded Elizabeth, to his swiftly retreating form. 'Ah Dotty! *There* you are – I was beginning to think you weren't coming. How divine you look – *what* a lovely dress, such an old friend. Colin, my darling – come and say hello. What's wrong with you, Brian? Why are you walking like that?'

'Oh leave him,' said Dotty, dismissively, thinking well that didn't take too long, did it? To rubbish this accursed bloody rag: maybe give it to the V & A.

'I assaulted Dotty's bad foot,' said Brian, drily, 'with my knee. A glass of champagne would actually be most welcome.'

Elizabeth got everyone drinks (Pineapple juice, Colin! I used to *love* pineapple juice when I was a girl), glanced across at Melody (talking to some *other* man, now) and then got down to business:

'So tell me, Dotty – your hotel. Is it near? Is it divine? Our suite is very lovely, I have to say.'

'I'm actually bowled over,' Dotty happily admitted – glaring with menace at Colin (he had been firmly and repeatedly briefed all the way here in the car, but young people had this awful habit, didn't they, of just coming out with things: sometimes even the truth). 'Brian has done this very sweet

147

thing and actually rented a country property – it's just on the fringes of the town. It's quite *ravishing*, actually, and so sweet of him to have kept it secret – such a lovely surprise.'

'Oh but Dotty how *wonderful*,' trilled Elizabeth. 'Oh how delightful – Colin, you must be so *pleased*.'

'Great,' said Colin, looking down at the floor – while Brian for his part concentrated on milking all the interest there was to be had from the ceiling. I think, he thought, I shall fill my face with food, to stop me from opening my mouth. If only Dotty wouldn't see this lack of money as some sort of chronic and disfiguring *disease*; I don't know, though – maybe it is: certainly the shape of things has changed, and I don't see it getting any better.

'Sorry,' murmured Brian, to whosever shoulder he had brushed against at the canapé table.

'Quite all right,' allowed Miles McInerney, who was thinking Yes, yes indeed, interesting, very interesting – that Lulu woman was a bit of quite all right – and Miles, believe him, knew a bit of quite all right when it came his way, make no mistake. She was cool, though – didn't see any green lights. If I'm honest, there wasn't even a flicker of amber – and the way she kept looking over at that bloke, Christ. And then he only comes over and more or less tells Miles to piss off out of it, doesn't he? I mean – Jesus. Behaving like I was bloody raping the woman on the floor! Which is a tasty thought. Mm.

Could be tricky, this one – could take time, and I haven't got too much. Maybe best forget it, ay? Save yourself some grief. Well depends – depends, doesn't it? Depends on who else turns up. If there's no one in the frame by morning I'll just have to go for it because I am not in the business of mucking about. If you get my drift. That other one's a bit gorgeous too – Melody, she said her name was – but oi! Do I *look* like I was born yesterday? No I *haven't* forgotten the bleeding baby, no I bloody haven't. Right – I'm out of this little vicarage tea party; bite to eat, check out the clubs.

'Bye,' he said lightly to Lulu, as he passed her.

After just a beat, John turned those eyes of his (oh God, those eyes – how many times had Lulu had to deal with those eyes?) full on to her face and said in that strangulated way he had at times like these (equal measures of disbelief, hurt and molten fury all oiled and glistening and grappling with one another):

'What did he say "*bye*" for? Hm? How does he get off saying "bye" to you, hm? What did you *say* to the man?'

Lulu half closed her eyes: could she really go another round of this?

'I imagine he said "bye", John,' she said, with I-can't-believe-I'm-hearing-this quasi despair, 'because he was *leaving*. People generally do, you know, say that when they are leaving.'

'But what did you –?!'

'I said *nothing*, John – I've told you. I said nothing. He was going on about being a salesman of some sort and he'd won a holiday as a *prize*, or something: I really wasn't listening very closely. He was actually extremely boring and very conceited, if you must know.'

John eyed this lifeline with half-hope – sniffed around the thing before reaching out to touch it with just one finger.

'Really? Was he? Was he really?'

Lulu smiled and leant over to John and kissed his cheek. 'Come on,' she said, 'I've had enough of it here. Let's see what the restaurant's like.'

John was all for that: thanks Lulu, thanks for jerking me out of it yet again – this awful thing that eats me up.

'Bye,' he said to Elizabeth, as they left. And then briskly to a genuinely amused Lulu, her eyebrows arched into irony: 'Just being *polite*.'

'Who was that?' asked Dotty.

'Hm?' queried Elizabeth. 'Oh him – oh God *I* don't know – banging on about a health farm, or something. Bore of the century – I thought you'd *never* arrive and I'd be stuck with him.'

'Nice wife,' said Brian. *We-ell*, he thought – why not? Why shouldn't I? Don't get many pleasures in life, do I? Not these days, I don't.

'Certainly dresses beautifully,' observed Elizabeth – well of *course* Dotty's scowling at you, Brian, you silly little man in your ghastly little jacket: do you wonder at it, coming out with something like that?

My Howard never would. 'New season Jil Sander, I think.'

Right, thought Dotty – we'll get off talk like that right this minute. 'Come on, everyone,' she rallied, 'let's go and have dinner.'

'Mm,' agreed Elizabeth. 'Hungry, Colin? What do you feel like getting your choppers around tonight?'

Well as I intimated earlier, mused Colin, Katie's tits – but as I quite appreciate that this is at the very least a logistical impossibility, I should be quite prepared to settle for yours, Elizabeth – which, certainly in what you are wearing tonight (those little lacy panels) appear very much more fetchingly buoyant than ever they have before.

Colin shrugged. 'I'm easy,' he said, tossing off the grin. 'So long as it's hot and tasty.'

Norman Furnish was lying full-length in the vast and peachy bath in the marble-clad bathroom just west of the bedroom in which the possibility of getting up a really good game of five-a-side rugby could by no means be dismissed. Yes: expensive, very – it was preying on Norman's mind (don't think it wasn't) during those cold and scary unguarded moments when he let it. But he had other things to think about just at that moment, thank you very much – chief among them being quite how he was expected to keep this little Sony camcorder both steady and focused upwards on the tits of young Colin's dreams, while at the same time Katie was coming down on him with the full force of her pinkly wet and sloshing pelvis (and yeah – let Norman leave no one in any doubt on the matter: when Katie straddled you, right, and then came *down*, well believe him: this sweet baby came down *hard*).

'Gnuh!' was more or less the noise that Norman gave out now, because Katie's last thrust had *really* connected, and the epicentre of his body now began to rule him as he struggled to keep the camcorder up and dry while taking in too Katie's sharply exhaled and increasingly breathless instructions (her eyes like a teddy bear's: hard and bright).

'My face!' she rasped. 'Focus on my face, my mouth – do it – as I come! Ugh! Now down, go downwards – get the shot of you – in me, up me!'

God that struck Norman as an impossibly thrill-whippy thing to say and I'll do that, yeah, I'll do that, he thought – but he was losing grip on this bloody machine (all of this was far from easy – not too straightforward, not any of this) and gah! Now there was a ripple deeper than anything else inside him and as his eyes beseeched Katie to be a big part of this dreamy thing, so Norman flipped the camcorder on to the bathmat and gave himself up to all fleshly pleasures and as Katie screamed out and fell forward, so was Norman propelled beneath the welling surface (drowning without, drowning within) and as he drank in both slick, wet, hard and conical nipples, along with half a gallon of bathwater – so did he think Oh Good Christ, when and if the hour came to entertain the spectre of oblivion, then surely it was into this here and now that he could be most blissfully ushered? He did not actually think that – of course not – but given both time and maybe a poet's turn of mind, who can say to what degree Norman Furnish might best express these few vital seconds of so soaked and fluid an orgasm?

'Christ,' he moaned – rallying, gasping, spitting, pushing upwards at the soft and half-beached weight of Katie, his recent open-armed welcome to the Angel of Death now decidedly frosty. 'There's more water on the floor than in the bath.'

'That's not,' said Katie, clambering out slappingly, 'a very sexy thing to say.'

Norman nodded, and swept back his lank and wringing hair. I know, he thought, I know: I have all those thoughts while impaled by the during – after is just after, as far as I'm concerned.

So how was, in fact, Norman finding this holiday of theirs? Cheap clothes and a vastly expensive hotel would appear to be the order of the day, so – what? Howard taking care of the business end of things, is he? Subbing his darling daughter's Stateside vac? But what of the mythical Ellie? He wouldn't happily have forked out for her as well, would he? No. The fact of the matter was that Howard was paying for none of it. Um – let Norman rephrase that, slightly: Mr Street – Howard – was (oh God) paying for *all* of it, yes –

it's just that he had no idea that this was the case. Well *Norman* couldn't, could he? Only his second two-bit job since leaving that hopeless 'university' (where he had read, oh cripes, Economics) and Katie, well – ever since he'd got involved with her (months, now – impossible to think of life without Katie: God, he loved that girl so much) – she had been putting *demands* on him, hadn't she? As may have been divined by this stage of the game, Katie had mighty big ideas.

At first it had been OK: she wanted to have dinner at the latest trendy places, so all right – dig into savings (what money is for, yes? That's what everyone says). But then it got to her expecting presents – not just for birthdays and things: Christ, Norman had yet to deal with one of Katie's birthdays – he'd have to knock off Fort bloody Knox for that one (maybe roll it into this little trip to America). No: every time they met, went out, she'd expect something – and we're not talking *token* presents, either, oh no, not with Katie. He'd left a single, red, long-stemmed rose on her desk at the office, one time. Know what she said? What happened, Norman – lose the other twenty-three in the street, did you? Well look – the man was so besotted with her that he took all this at face value, and soon he was buying her watches and clothes and scent and all sorts of expensive trinkets from shops with the right names; he'd never *heard* of most of them before, but he could list the lot off by heart, now – they knew him, in most of the places:

Norman, God help him, was a regular. And the meals! More dinners, matey, than you've had . . . yes, well: you get the idea.

The savings went. Took no time at all, really (well, they never were very huge), and then Norman had taken to selling the few vaguely valuable things he owned: an early Victorian bookcase his grandfather had left him, few books – the gold Omega he'd got for his twenty-first. (Hurt, that, actually – parting with that had hurt him, a bit, because his mother had given it to him, you see, and she never did have much, Norman's mother: it must have been a struggle for her to get it. It didn't raise a lot: enough for lunch and a taxi and a bottle of fizz for after. Sad, really.)

So then he did the next big thing. Mr Street – Howard – kept this petty cash box at the office, and so Norman had thought Look: if I just sneak out forty (make it fifty) just to get Katie this new Gaultier scent she's been on about, and then if I pretend I've got a cold or something and not take her out for a week and not eat in the meantime anything at all and not use things like electricity and the phone and things, then when my next month's salary comes in from Mr Street – Howard – I can pay back, er, Mr Street. Howard. Trouble is, I *can't* pretend I've got a cold or something, can I? Because then I can't come into work and that means I'll be paid money for *not* working by someone I stole from and need to pay back and all this arises out of the fact that I am broke as a

155

result of being so helplessly in love with this same person's daughter. Some days, I tell you, Norman's head was in quite a spin.

So anyway, he did that: lied about the cold, sat in the dark in his horrid little room for a week, crying out from the sheer pain of hunger (eating those beans with a cocktail stick, one by one, to make them last). But it didn't work, did it? At the end of it all, Katie insisted upon taking him somewhere absolutely divine to cheer him up and to celebrate his recovery from his nasty old cold (joke was, he was now sure he was really in for one – so God knew what was going to happen *next* week) and Norman had allowed himself to be dragged off to one of the most blindingly expensive restaurants in London, knowing full well that it would be he who would be dumped with the bill at the end because, look: it always was, wasn't it? Oh God! Katie would exclaim: I've left my thing at home again; *you* get this, Norman, can you? And I'll pay you back after. She never did, not once (Norman never even discovered what this 'thing' was that she kept on leaving at home: could have been a snow plough for all he knew), and of *course* he never mentioned it again after, did he? Well – you don't like to, do you? It just doesn't seem *right*. So what with that dinner and the taxi back to the office – yes, they used the office at night, too (Norman used to say Look, Katie, there's always my room, you know, but Katie said I would prefer an open sewer to your room, believe me, Norman), and then the inevitable *present* (a mini Hermès scarf, this time, which Katie wanted to tie around the handle of her handbag: aren't women funny?) and then Katie's taxi back to her place and Norman's taxi back to *his* place (the last bus was history) – well look: it should be perfectly plain as to just what Norman is *saying*, here. Not only could he not pay back the sixty (yeah – he had made it sixty, in the end) but his entire salary for the forthcoming month was, at a stroke, so much dust.

So Norman had taken to inventing journeys and non-existent clients and dipping into the cash box fairly frequently after that (someone's *bound* to notice, sooner or later) and in truth it was from there a short and fairly natural step to doing the really big, bad thing. Of course, Katie being Katie, she never bothered to wonder where all the money *did* come from (Christ, she must know what Mr Street – Howard – pays him). She just went on taking, and went on asking for more. Then Chicago came up.

'I don't know why I want Chicago and not New York,' she had said. 'I just do. It sounds wicked and glamorous. *Great* shopping. Look – I've got us all these brochures. This is the best one – and that's the hotel: I've marked it. Just think, Norman – all those nights somewhere fabulous together. No more office floor! Book it. I've written down the dates.'

Norman gazed at the brightly-coloured fait accompli before him, and then his eyes travelled

157

down to the *cost*. He simply could not believe she was serious – the way Katie wanted it done, Norman was looking at, what – eight months' salary? Except that he'd spent his salary for about the next forty years. On the other hand – he loved her, right? And just think, Norman – all those nights somewhere fabulous together. As we have seen, he drew the line at Club Class travel (do I dare? Have to, have to – it just won't run to it) but everything else was just what the doctor ordered.

And the money? For the holiday? Yes – the money. Norman even now can barely stand to think of it, so he'll be brief, if that's all right: he had been on site with a client, one morning, whose fantastically expensive house had been on their books for so damned long that Norman (whose baby it was) had more or less forgotten about it. The owner had requested a meeting – wanted to show Norman how he had improved the property since first it had gone on the market, he said.

'Double glazing. Doesn't come cheap. Also I've repainted the outside – well: front, anyway – and there are those tubs, see them? One each side the door.'

'OK,' said Norman. 'We'll get a new photograph. Might help.' Don't much care, he thought.

'Yes but really *push* it this time, will you, Mr Furnish? Hm? I tell you – I'll be honest with you: my ex bloody wife, her bloody solicitors, they're on at me night and day. I've got a bridging loan that'd bring tears to your eyes. I'm telling you,

Mr Furnish, I'm desperate. I'd just do *anything* to sell the bloody house. Every day I own it, it's killing me.'

And Norman found himself saying it before he'd realized that such a thought had even entered his mind.

'Look,' he opened – eyes narrow, now: show the man you mean it – 'I'll tell you what I'm prepared to do. But first it must be understood that there are conditions, and absolute silence is one of them.'

The man was hooked, you could tell. No stranger to what might be termed unorthodox business practices, Norman shouldn't wonder.

'Go on,' he said, the eyes egging on Norman to do just that.

'I'll reduce the agency commission to one-and-a-half per cent . . .'

The eyes were flickery, now: you'll do *what* . . . ?

'. . . and I promise you I'll send round as many people as humanly possible, right?'

The man nodded slowly, his eyes not leaving Norman for a moment – almost as if in fear that if he did so, then Norman might thaw away to an icy trickle, or maybe even levitate. And the eyes? The eyes were alive and poised, squinting up at the sun while keeping the wicket, and waiting for the catch.

'When we sell the house – and we will sell it, and soon I promise you – the commission is payable in cash directly to me. You then formally instruct the agency – and you've got it with others, haven't you?

159

Yes – well you tell all of them that you have sold the property privately. Right? And that is that.'

The man nodded, and a smile meandered over his face. 'Got you,' he said, fielding so graceful a shot with ease. 'Done.'

And that – Norman can hardly believe it even now – is exactly what happened. He had sent just everyone to view this house, whether it was suitable or not, and the minute he smelled the hover – a would-be buyer havering – he more or less demanded of the owner a substantial price cut. OK – it ate into Norman's share – but a bird in the hand, right?

Norman got the cash – booked a five-star holiday in Chicago, where in fact he is right now, capering amid the considerable fruits of his larceny – sprawling, if we are seeking pinpoint precision, with Katie on a bed that might be eight feet square, and engrossed in a gorgeously frank if jerky video recording (plus titanic soundtrack) comprising himself in a vast and peachy bath with Katie making waves as she rudely comes down on him hard. (Crime may not pay – as they say – but who could doubt its compensations?)

On the table to the left of the bed was Katie's powdery Amex card, lying among the leftover traces of two chopped-out lines of coke; a fifty-dollar bill curled up alongside, with the air of being truly out of it.

'No *way*,' Norman had said. 'Now listen to me, Katie – there is no way – hear me? – no *way* that I am going to take that stuff. And nor are you. Christ Almighty – where did you *get* it?'

'Oh come *on*, Norman,' sighed Katie, rolling into a tube the fifty bucks. 'I got it on Michigan Thing – you really *can* get anything there. I got it as a *present* – I thought you'd be pleased. You liked the *other* present, didn't you, Norman?' She grinned, with mischief. 'You liked the video thing, didn't you?'

Norman smiled involuntarily. 'Yeah,' he admitted. And then he rallied. 'But that has nothing to do with *this*. Now I'm telling you, Katie – look, OK, a bit of grass – a bit of grass, that's one thing – but this –!'

'Oh come *on*, Norman!' exploded Katie. 'You sound like an old *man*. We're meant to be on holiday, right? So bloody act like it.'

But Norman was going to be firm: she just couldn't get away with this, not this one – not now, and not ever.

'Katie –!'

'*Nor*-man,' said Katie, slow and deep. With one hand she was proffering the little green tube, while the other took up the full weight of his soft and heavy genitals – now beginning to lighten up and show a bit of interest.

'OK,' shrugged Norman, and he snorted up the whole line with ease.

His eyes blinked and then opened wide in such a way that Katie became totally committed to catching him up and in no time at all the two of them were transformed into multi-limbed creatures of bright steel and rubber, in bed and in heaven. When the mood shifted, Katie made for the remote, fast-forwarded to the frames where Norman's rod was glimpsed emerging from her tight and nearly hairless cunt during a tidal retreat and just prior to her once more coming down on him *hard* – and then she hit the freeze: it did look as if the two of them, now, were chronically cold, numb and stiff, yet barely shivering. Katie now put the comcorder into Norman's hands, and then slid down the length of him. She looked up full into his face.

'Film this,' she said, shortly. Dropping her eyelashes, the better to concentrate on the job in hand, she took a good deal and then all of him into her mouth. Norman surrendered to the enveloping heat and the advent of sensation – until suddenly he was aware that she had withdrawn (the disappointment was close to nearly dying).

'What are you doing?' he gasped. 'Why have you stopped?'

'It's OK, Norman – I'll do it more in a minute,' giggled Katie. 'I've just got to make a phone call.' She briefly kissed the very gleaming tip of him, and then was punching out numbers on the pale blue phone. 'I know it's hard on you,' she said.

It took no more than two beats of her heart for Elizabeth to become conscious of this new

162

and terrible, piercing invasion as the telephone shrilly pealed beside her – but it was the huge and defeated groan (an earthy blend of please-don't-let-this-be-happening and real disgust) from Melody just feet away that alerted Elizabeth to the full and awful horror of what had just been done, and she was out of bed and colliding amid shadows with Melody who had done that too – and hang the phone, who could it *be*, curse and damn them – never mind that: just get next door and try oh please God to save it. But no, it wasn't to be – Elizabeth was still yards away, Melody not much nearer, when the air was rent yet again by the pitiless rant of Dawn, now duetting with gusto with the unremitting phone, as it continued to scream out into the dark. Melody quietly beat her forehead against the jamb of the door, too utterly drained for words or even sobbing, while Elizabeth – feeling more wretched than ever in her life, sighed from deep within and cut into at least half the cacophony by resignedly lifting the receiver.

'Christ,' she heard Katie slur, 'you took long enough.'

'*Katie*,' exhaled Elizabeth, practically weeping. 'What are you phoning *now* for – oh God, there's nothing *wrong*, is there?'

'Nothing's wrong,' said Katie. 'I just thought I'd ring, that's all. You said to phone.'

Please, Elizabeth heard Melody imploring, oh

163

please please *please* stop screaming! I just simply can't stand it any more.

'But *Katie* – it's the middle of the night!'

And all those miles away, Katie looked up and away from Norman's fevered groin and into a sunlit window.

'Snot,' she said, vaguely amazed.

'Oh *God*, Katie – we'd only just got that accursed little baby off to sleep. We'd been *walking* her and *changing* her and *singing* to her . . . oh God, we'll never get her off again now.'

Sleep yelled Melody from way over there. *Sleep*, God damn you, or I'll bloody well *kill* you.

'OK,' huffed Katie. 'I'll hang up, then.'

'But it doesn't matter *now*, Katie,' explained Elizabeth – now having to sigh at the top of her voice, and casting a limp hand through lifeless hair. 'Why are you making those awful noises? Are you eating something?'

'Not really,' came back Katie. 'I'm just sucking something sweet. Quite yummy, actually,' she tacked on, as Norman launched into an abrupt but heartfelt farmyard impression.

'What was *that*?' asked a startled Elizabeth.

'It's Ellie. She's got a really stinking cold.' And now Katie was sounding like a steamship, so strenuous were her efforts to not give in to dirty laughter.

'Look, Katie – oh God, this noise, it's killing me. I just can't go through a week of this, I'll *die*. Look, Katie – we'll speak again, yes? Can you hear me? I say we'll speak again, hm? I've got to ring off now because my head is splitting.'

'OK, Mum,' agreed Katie. 'Oh – and, Mum?'

'What *is* it, Katie?'

And now the rich chortling just *had* to emerge. 'Sweet dreams, yeah?'

Elizabeth replaced the receiver and slumped back into the king-size bed, gathering pillows around her face and bunching her fists up tightly; Melody now was wailing at the enormity of this injustice, sounding utterly spent – and all the while this other-worldly and full-throated Dawn chorus went on ripping into them both, shredding too all that was left of the still just black night.

When finally the insistence of the telephone split into fragments the clung-to flickerbook of Howard Street's frankly madcap dreams, he felt sure it had been ringing for quite some time. It wasn't yet even light; not completely dark, but by no means had the deep and fuggy air been stirred by anything close to the brashness of morning.

'Elizabeth . . .' he murmured, thinking no, she can't, can she? Elizabeth can't pick up on the bloody thing because Elizabeth isn't here. He stretched out for the phone, beat it (it clattered) and more or less had the thing now and made a noise into it.

'Howard thank God!' is what made him flinch. 'I thought you were *dead.*'

'Elizabeth . . .' he murmured, thinking yes, she can, can't she? Elizabeth can phone me on this bloody thing because Elizabeth isn't here.

'Look, Howard, I *know* it's early – God *knows* I know it's early – but it seems as if the night started *years* ago and I just had to talk to someone because it's still too soon to go down to breakfast and I can't even *bear* the thought of even *looking* at my face in the mirror – I feel about a hundred years old –'

'What's that noise?' put in Howard – this having the absolutely immediate result of Elizabeth's voice cranking up a good few notches from strung-out and crazed to out-and-out hysterical:

'What's the –?! The *noise*, Howard – that *noise* that you can even hear from the next room is *Dawn*! It's been going on all night! All night! It's *Dawn*!'

Howard was now squinting at the clock. She's right, he thought: it bloody is.

'Oh God – it was *Katie*,' went on Elizabeth, the jagged edge now reduced to a help-me whimper. 'We'd just got her off! Just got her off! And then Katie rang.'

Got her off? Got her off what? Who, actually?

'Is Katie all right?' grunted Howard.

'Oh she's fine – fine. And why wouldn't she be? Oh God, Howard – look I'm *sorry* I've woken you up, darling – I just didn't know where to turn.'

166

Howard eased himself into maybe twenty per cent of the available stock of soothing sort of there-there noises (like Christmas decorations – saved from last time) while not, in truth, actually understanding the problem; and given time, it seemed to be working.

'Yes, Howard, yes,' she allowed herself, 'you're right – I know you're right. But I'm already dreading tonight! Oh God – and I really *need* this break: I really do.'

Break from what, actually, Elizabeth? What is it exactly that you do? I've often wondered.

When the sounds of Elizabeth ebbed away as far as they ever did, Howard promised her three times that he would take care, and carefully replaced the receiver. He sighed, and slumped back into the bed, hauling in the duvet around him.

'Elizabeth,' he said – quite without expression.

'I gathered,' said Zoo-Zoo, from somewhere within the mound beside him.

Howard smiled, and tugged back the covers. It was maybe first thing in the morning that he felt most weak at the sight of the fresh-limbed warmth and cool of Zoo-Zoo – the long, dead straight black hair around that angel's face forming a softly chaotic tousle of graffiti, scrawling across the white of pillows. He closed his eyes and some sweet radar guided him on down to dark pink and so-full lips, charged with body-heat.

'How wonderful that you are here,' whispered Howard – and Zoo-Zoo kissed his fingers. 'I worry,' he said then, 'about Katie, you know. In America, I mean. Only seventeen, after all.'

'Well,' sighed Zoo-Zoo from the languor of still-dreaminess (snaking a slender arm across Howard's chest and snuggling up to it). 'That's still a year older than me.'

Howard turned his head, his mouth elongating into tacit agreement. 'I know. But it's different,' he said, with gentle decision, reaching over to caress the shine of all that dark wild hair. 'It's completely different for you, Zoo-Zoo: you're a boy. And boys can look after themselves.'

CHAPTER 4

Dotty reached down from the little cupboard above the little sink in the little caravan ('we will have to,' she had drily observed the night before, 'just learn to wash one fork at a time') the packet of teabags that had formed part of the haul from a deeply depressing shopping trip to the out-of-town superstore that was the very sort of thing that Dotty had come on holiday to avoid. She shut the door of the little cupboard, whereupon it sprang back open and smacked her in her little face and that was all it took for Dotty to lean down over the little draining board and cover her eyes with a tremulous hand. The first time the door had done this, Dotty had assumed this pose as a give-me-strength-and-save-me-from-despair sort of gesture – and one that had been observed by all, for the simple reason that in this caravan no one could ever be much more than a yard or so away from you. But now, this bleeding door had bashed her so bloody often (and did she see it coming? No she did not) that she was decidedly on the brink of serious headache time, and hence the hand-over-eyes bit was now rather

169

more than histrionics. Even the furniture, she was thinking – even the fittings are attacking me.

'What it just needs,' Brian was saying, rubbing straight fingers up the thickness of the door, as if gently planing a silky surface, 'is a bit of adjustment to the catch. These magnetic jobs are never as heavy-duty reliable as the ball catches of the old days. Do you remember those, Dotty? Used them in that bathroom fitment.'

'Oh *yes*,' roared out Dotty with a big-chested enthusiasm so thoroughly clad in the tongue-and-groove of wooden irony as to be able to be worked on and shaped with a Stanley tool. 'Oh *God* yes, Brian – how could I ever forget the ball catches on the bathroom *fitment*? They form some of the fondest memories of my entire life on *earth*. Christ, Brian – for as long as I live –!'

'I'll just give it a tighten,' said Brian – could even have been a gesture of appeasement. 'Budge over a bit – can't quite get a purchase.'

'For as long as I *live*, Brian, I will never, ever, ever forgive you for this – do you hear me? And *yes*, since you bring up that bloody cursed little bathroom fitment – yes indeed, Brian, yes – I *do* remember, I remember it *very* well. You needed the strength of a *horse* to heave open that stupid little cupboard and when you *did* finally get the thing open everything fell out of it – broke that lovely atomizer of mine. And then the handle came off, didn't it? Just before the whole bloody thing fell off the *wall*.'

170

'Well,' allowed Brian, 'the room needed doing anyway. No my point is, Dotty – those catches never sprang open: catch my drift?'

'Brian –!'

'I think that should do it,' said Brian, eyeing his handiwork and speaking with the cautious confidence of a noted surgeon. 'I might just replace the washers on the taps, now I've got the bag out. They're not dripping *now*, but you never can tell, not with taps like this, you can't.'

Dotty just watched him set about it, as she had so many times before. Christ Almighty, by the end of the week Brian would have this bloody rusty heap in concours condition, Dotty would be led away simpering in a straitjacket and Colin would file an action against his parents on grounds of child abuse at least. And where *was* Colin, actually? Hadn't seen him since, oh – since about dawn, when Dotty had given up any remaining hope of ever dropping off again on the padded shelf stuck up against the ceiling in which Brian had assured her she would sleep like a queen. She had fried some bacon; wasn't, in truth, very hungry – not after that huge meal at The Excelsior the night before, that Elizabeth had insisted she pay for, and there was Brian raising no objection. Had maybe a bit too much wine – but then the muzziness she was feeling could equally be down to having slept for maybe twenty-five minutes or, since rising to greet the promise of a freshly-minted day, being repeatedly beaten about the head by a delinquent door.

171

So she'd fried the bacon and the whole place had filled up with smoke and Colin had set up a wail ('Oh *Jesus*, Mum!' And can you blame him? Well can you? Young boy on holiday?) and so Dotty had hurled open the caravan door but it was bitter out because even the sun had not yet seen fit to rise so she shut the door and they all settled down to weeping amid the acrid smoke until the door flew back open again and Brian said Hm, now that's a very funny thing because that hinge was perfectly fine after I looked at it yesterday: I'll just get my tools.

So where was Colin, actually? Standing outside a caravan. Not *the* caravan, no – not Home Sweet Home – but some other caravan, pretty much identical, bit bigger maybe: orange sort of striped what-do-they-call-them, blind thing, shade, sticking out of the front of it. And why was he there? Why was he *there*?! Don't ask *him*: he had just walked, right? Well look at the options – he couldn't drive, could he? Oh God, oh God – if only he could *drive*. Why did growing up take so long – and why were the people who'd got there always so terribly *childish*? Forever messing things up. Well they might, but he wouldn't – not Colin, no sirree: but if only it would just *happen*. Why did it take so *long*?

So what would you have done? Stayed in the rickety cash box with Brian and Dotty? Or walked? Colin will tell you exactly what you would have done: you would have *crawled*. Anything – just

172

anything – to get away, right? Trouble was, you walk on a caravan site and what you get is *caravans*, all filled with murmuring people (maybe they're all locked in). All they ever seem to do, these people, is queue up at a tap for water; amassing enough to drown themselves? Understandable. And talking of water – they were supposed to be at the seaside, right? So where was the bloody *sea*? Hadn't even seen the sea.

Colin walked and walked, up and down avenues of shiny metal homelets – it was as if the panicked and chain-clad Mayor of Toytown had rushed through the paperwork for a prefab suburb the colour of bonbons in the wake of the news that many more gollies, teddies and sundry bumpy dogs were heading south for work – and even this left out of the equation the influx of elves and the recent and phenomenal explosion in population among families of brightly striped skittles.

Eventually the caravans petered out into a patch of indeterminate grassland, maybe a disused mine-field, and then after a gravel nearly-path, a sheer and unprotected drop down to possibly a beach below – Colin didn't trust himself to get close enough to see. Great, he thought – now I'll bloody walk all the way back again. Oh hang on – over there: *can't* be, can it? Colin had given up all hope. It was, you know – a little knot of human beings, and youngish too, by the look of them from here. I'll make for over there, then, thought Colin.

As he approached, Colin could see now around

the edge of a hillocky thing just why all these people (well – I say all these people: four – five at most) were clustered about. A lovely old traditional ice-cream van – and now it pealed out its clangingly awful and quite irresistible come-along-you-kiddies jingle, and yeah: now Colin came to think of it, he wouldn't at all actually mind an ice-cream, or maybe a lolly or a drink. But mainly just to be with people.

Colin ambled down the slope – the sun in a quite blue sky was beginning to warm him, now – and then stepped up the amble into a touch of hurry-up because the queue had diminished to just two, and if he didn't get a move on there'd be nobody left and then the van would shove off and what was Colin supposed to do then, then?

He was fairly breathless when finally he fetched up at the thing – just one girl being served, now (can't see her face, but her hair's nice – thick and reddish), and I think yeah, a drink is what I want – or maybe one of those lollies, what are they, with fruity stuff on the outside and gooey stuff in the middle, or maybe – Oh Christ look! Oh God just look what's happened now!

'Oh *no*,' apologized the girl. 'Oh God I'm most awfully sorry!'

Yeah well – what could Colin say? She must have, what, spun round too quickly, didn't see him standing there, eager to get back to her parents or friends? Maybe she's just generally cackhanded, this girl, who's to say? Only just

174

met her. The upshot anyway was that Colin had a fair deal of whippy white ice-cream all down his shirt, and shards of flake were hanging there.

'I don't even have any tissues,' went on the girl, vaguely dabbing with two fingers at the mess.

'S'all right,' Colin assured her expansively (what – you think this is the first time I've been on a sand-dune and had a 99 dumped all over me? Happens all the time). Then he smeared a manly hand across his chest, rather in the way that Arnie might have shrugged off a gaping and near-mortal wound – and this proved to be quite the most stupid thing he could have thought of because his hand and wrist were thick with the stuff, the once localized slick of ice-cold sticky yuck now just all over the place, and maybe that is why the girl began to laugh.

'Oh look I'm most terribly – I don't *mean* to laugh, it's just that – oh *God*, what a mess. Look, my caravan's just over there . . . you could . . .'

'No no – I'm fine,' said Colin. Well – couldn't do much else now, really. 'Let me buy you another ice-cream.'

'Oh but –'

Colin thought she was probably about his age – fourteen, fifteen, something like that – and her face was pretty. Pretty? Yeah, pretty. Not too bad, anyway. Wasn't in a position, was he? Soon they were sitting side by side in a little hollow, each working away at their 99s, Colin as casually as poss wiping the back of his hand in the scrubby grass alongside.

'How long are you down here for, Carol?' asked Colin. Her name, it had transpired, was Carol.

'This is the last week,' said Carol. 'It was OK at first, but it's a bit boring, now.'

'I'll say it is,' agreed Colin with gusto. 'And I've only been here a day. What on earth do you *do* in a place like this?'

'Well we've been out sailing, most days. My Dad's got a boat. I'm down here with my brother and my Dad. He's divorced. Are your parents divorced?'

Colin shook his head. 'No. They're just mental.'

'I come down here in the evenings. Most evenings. Round eight or nine. It's very peaceful and you can hear the sea come in. Or going out. Anyway – you can hear it.'

Colin had been about to say something just then (of course he was) but as he opened his mouth, a raw and braying boy's voice (so like all those voices at school) was roaring out above him:

'Oh God *there* you are, Carol. Come on – Dad's waiting. Let's get a move on.' The boy looked down at Colin. 'Who's this?'

Colin wanted to meet the boy's eye – yearned to – but he knew he couldn't: he was big and at least a year older than Colin and already he could feel that he was being hated, just as he always seemed to be, these days.

'This is Colin,' said Carol, getting up and beating at the seat of her jeans. 'This is my brother,' she added on for Colin's benefit, rather as if announcing a death. 'Terry.'

Terry sneered at Colin as he and Carol turned to leave.

'Your boyfriend's a very messy eater,' he said. 'Teething, maybe.'

After a few paces, Carol fluttered back briefly and whispered quickly to Colin:

'I like you, Colin. You have lovely hands.'

Colin smirked his thanks. She hovered, and then as Terry set up his bawling, turned to go.

Yes, Colin was aware that he should have delivered some sort of compliment in return, but all he could think of – when she said I like you, Colin, you have lovely hands – is Thank you, Carol, I like you and you have lovely tits – but as is known, it is simply not done to talk about tits: such things are, thought Colin, more to be felt.

John Powers was unable to dissuade Lulu from having a swim, and had therefore been forced to have one too. It's not that he disliked swimming – oh no, quite the reverse: about the only exercise he ever got – no, it was just that, well, even in a fairly exclusive hotel such as this one, right, even at this time of day the pool was hardly likely to be *empty*, was it? Most unlikely that there should be no one else at all. And . . . look, OK – it was difficult for John to, you know, *verbalize* all this: wouldn't actually *be* like this if he had any choice in the matter, you know. OK, look – if you really have to have it, John just simply couldn't bear it if there was some *man* around when Lulu was swimming. Well, let's face it – he couldn't bear some man around when Lulu was *breathing* – but the way that Lulu cleaved through the length of the pool, I'm telling you: well, it always set *John* on fire, so what would it do to someone who had never glimpsed such a thing? And when she climbed the steps, water coursing away from her perfectly plain, perfectly simple, hideously expensive black Lycra one-piece costume, when those silver rivers of water ran away down her honey-coloured thighs as she blithely blotted her face with a hand towel, blinking, bunching back her gold and streaming hair – eyes lighting up, now, as she caught sight of John (watching, lurking): well, what man could fail to be stunned by such a sight? So John, you see, just had to be there: to guard against this sort of thing.

It was much better in the sauna, after. Well, better from the standpoint that at least in this vaporous poaching box there could only ever be the two of them – but in all other real senses, true hell. I mean, *God* – wasn't natural, was it? Wasn't natural to sit on a plank in the sort of temperature that you could safely entrust to render piping something tasty and quick from Marks & Spencer? John's eyes stung him – felt as if they were braising. Aren't your *eyes* burning, Lulu? Lulu – eyes closed – smiled serenely and gently shook her head. Oh God she was so lovely, so lovely – oh God

I could just die for this woman, I love her so much. Kill, if I had to.

Can't take much more of this, though – Christ, I feel like a candle: my head's on fire, and everything else is just trickling on down to the sconce at my feet (quite good, that, actually – might let the subs cut it out of some fuckawful piece). Leave, shall I? Get out, yeah? There's the latch on the door, temptingly near – air as fresh as dew just beyond (not to say a packet of fags) so make a break for it now, shall I? Can't. Why? Can't. Yes but why? Just *can't*, that's all. Really? That's all? Can't is an answer, is it? Oh all right, all right (Christ, you don't give up, do you?): I can't – *leave*, right – because sometimes, not now as it happens, but sometimes – Lulu lets fall the little towel snug around her breasts and tucked in neatly to her hips; sometimes this towel just falls away (is she aware? Is she? John could not tell you – could never be sure) and I do not have to remind anyone, do I, that these fetid and tropical garden sheds come ready fitted with a little window, right? Well – self-explanatory, then, isn't it? Steam notwithstanding – just *anyone* could happen by, couldn't they? So John, you see, just had to sweat it out: guard against this sort of thing.

He would have preferred to have had his shower back up in the suite, but Lulu didn't care for it, that way; so; not to appear too much of a sentry, John subjected the rare-to-medium soles of his feet to the slime of the slats and gave himself up to the

179

nimble scourge of wire-thin water as cold as he could honestly bear it.

And now here was Lulu in the hotel foyer – the glowing warmth of her face, the sparkle of her expression to John's eyes the most precious jewels of all, caught between the bright white froth of a terry turban and the deep shawl collar that she hugged around her.

'I just want to see if they've got a *map*, darling,' she said over her shoulder. 'I'll be up in just a minute.'

John hesitated – glanced to the left and right of him with a furtive instinct that brought even him to his senses: the place was teeming with people – couldn't vet all of them, could he?

'OK,' he agreed, briskly – as he strode on over to the lift thinking See, it *can* maybe be conquered, all this stuff: I'm walking, aren't I? Alone? And she'll be up in just a minute. There's nothing wrong or *odd* about this, John, so why can't you see it? Well I'll try, I'll try – I *will* try, actually, because I sometimes sense the faint odour, the powdery traces of inherent erosion in the things that I do, and sound foundations of course are vital, when all you ever really want to do is build; it is important that I guard against this sort of thing.

'You of all people,' insisted Miles, smilingly, to the receptionist as she slotted coloured postcards into the perspex counter spinner, '*you*, surely, should know all the hot spots in town?' He brought his

180

face close to her name tag as if to sniff it. 'Pauline,' he tacked on. 'Nice name – Pauline.'

Pauline smiled more or less in the manner they had all been told to (remember they're the punters, but don't get too pally).

'Atchy, I haven't been here that long. Don't really know the town well at all.'

'Well that's even *better*,' expanded Miles. 'We can discover it together. How about it? Pauline? A spot of dinner, maybe.'

The smile became a bit tighter as she more energetically than earlier went on cramming in too many postcards (and oh piddle, *look* – I've done them in all the wrong slots, now). On the other hand . . . if he was going to spend *money*: Christ, I can't hardly remember the last time I had a decent meal out.

'Yeah? Well I dunno. Might be nice. Thanks. Don't get much time off, though, Mr McInerney. And when I *do* get out, I never go far, or anything.'

'Miles,' said Miles, low and confidingly.

Pauline stared at him. 'No,' she protested. 'Mostly just round the corner to the pub.'

What, thought Miles, is the dozy little pillock talking about? Oh Christ, if something better doesn't show up soon . . .

'Excuse me,' cut in Lulu – who had been hovering and half hearing all this for *quite* long enough, thank you – 'but I wondered whether you might have a map – a town plan, yes?'

'Oh certainly,' agreed Pauline, chucking a maybe intended to be conspiratorial glance over to Miles – who had by now forgotten this tedious little receptionist's existence on earth: well well well – just take one look at what we do have here: if it isn't the lovely Lulu (all gift-wrapped and ready for bed, by the looks of her: very handy, I must say).

'Hello again,' he said, cocking a brow.

Lulu looked around: hadn't noticed which particular oaflike member of the male gender had been standing alongside, but now she dimply realized: it was the salesperson oaf, was it? The holiday-winning oaf? Well that's nice for him. She had her map, and she made for the lift – Miles just managing to edge in between the satin steel doors before they sighed and closed.

'Swim?' suggested Miles.

'I'm sorry?' commented Lulu, looking up from the map, a faint air of irritation about her.

'Had a nice swim, have you?'

Lulu glanced down at her attire. 'No,' she said. 'I've just been skiing.' What an insufferable person.

'Hah! Like it – *like* it! Joke! Like that in a woman.' The lift was whooshing on: not much time to lose. 'And,' Miles went on, 'what a *lovely* woman . . .' And she was – Christ, you only had to look at her.

Lulu snapped on her tried and tested Don't-even-think-about-it-and-now-drop-dead look – but just before the lift slowed and settled wheezily, maybe just a few seconds before the orange floor number pinged alight – Lulu was amazed by Miles reaching out a hand to her cheek, her jerked reaction away from him causing the turban to come loose and she dropped her map and while she reactively stooped down to retrieve it her gown fell open to the waist exposing a breast and just as the silver doors slid away so did her eyes meet with the wild and disbelieving face of John who just went on staring as Lulu hastily covered herself and stepping out and unravelling the turban with fever in her voice said John, John, *listen* to me, John – don't, John, *don't* – it's nothing at all as it may – look, John, come on, come on – let's go to our room, hm? John? And right up until Lulu yanked away her stunned and practically palsied husband, so did he continue to goggle into the lift until the doors eased shut again – but not before Miles had formed his index finger and thumb into an 'O' of certitude and then said 'Bye' – before his so-what face was hissingly squeezed right out of the picture.

It was as the door of their bedroom clicked shut behind them that John snapped out of it and now ripped into her: his eyes were molten and his fingers were bunched – he could have been ready to pounce, howl or disintegrate.

'John –!' Lulu tried again. She was angry – frightened too (she knew how John could be) but angered, yes, by so stupid a thing – so vile and rude a man had dared to – and now all this! It was

183

Lulu's fury John should understand: he should not be poised on venting his own.

'*What*,' he began heavily – closing his eyes and batting away Lulu's further attempt at intervention – 'just what in bloody Christ's name did you think you were *doing*? Hey?'

'Doing? *Doing*?! *I* wasn't doing anything, it was –'

'Just what sort of a fucking tart have I *got* here, then – hey?'

Lulu was lashed by this, and hot tears broke through all else as she stood before him.

John's eyes blazed as he came at her.

'A quickie, was it? Quick fuck in the lift with lover boy, was it? What – made the arrangement last night, did you? How did it go? Hey? What did you *say*, you –'

'*John*!' pleaded Lulu. I need help, she thought, I need help, and I need it soon.

'Shut up, tramp! How was it? "Just let me get my husband out of the way for a few minutes" – was that it? Was it? Map! "Oh looky-look, John – I've got to get a *map*." It wasn't a *map* you wanted, was it? Wasn't a fucking *map*.'

Now he was upon her and Lulu squealed as he dragged at her hair and hurled her hard just anywhere she'd go – and now she skittered across the room and fell over a rug and hit the side of her head on a stool and John was hard on top of her now and both wings of her robe were away from her and John had her cheekbones squeezed tight in this grasp which forced wide her mouth and eyes and now he reached up to a half-empty bottle of Moët, clanked it wetly out of the bucket and it sizzled as it spilled across Lulu's breasts and stomach and a gurgle of fear of pain and ugly sickness rattled away from her slackened mouth as the bottle was brought down between her legs and she saw him ready to force it into her.

'Is – this – how – it – was – for – you?' grunted out John, his hard grip on her face now sloppily glazed with saliva and tears. Then he turned abruptly away and hurtled the bottle against the far wall.

'You're just not worth it,' he rasped, near inaudibly.

Lulu brought in all her limbs so close to herself, her soft brown shoulders heaving at first convulsively, and then with a slower rhythm, made disjointed by shuddering. John glanced at those shoulders, and saw the faint golden hairs there, sparkling in the light as each involuntary spasm assailed his Lulu – Lulu oh Lulu! John's chest came close to crushing him as he raged in pain and wept until he was nearly choking. Lulu – oh God, Lulu – I love you more than life itself – I *love* you, Lulu my darling – I'd *die* for you my angel, you know I would do anything to keep you, my sweetest sweet. There is no end to the depth of my passion: how can you *do* this to me? Why can you not see just how much I love you?

'Does it *hurt*?' enquired Elizabeth, tentatively –

hesitant fingers wavering just in front of Dotty's face.

Dotty was practically crying – not only from the pain in her nose, but more maybe just at the sight of it. She had this very minute clipped shut her handbag mirror, quite unable to believe that what she had seen there could really be true.

They were all sitting or lying on towels – not just Dotty and Elizabeth, but Melody and Colin as well – in the crook of a sheltered cove just on the southern tip of town – fine and not too crowded expanse of sand – and yes it was golden, just as advertised. They had been half in and half out of the shade, when they arrived, but the sun was unremitting now, one of the by-products being the almost too extraordinary crimson of poor old Dotty's nose.

'But didn't you put anything *on* it?' urged Melody. 'I'm covered in stuff – aren't you, Elizabeth?'

Elizabeth nodded. Yes indeed – just after first Dotty and then Melody had dropped off to sleep, Elizabeth had asked Colin if he'd mind doing her the most enormous favour. Would you, Colin? Just for me? Could you bear to rub this cream all over my back and shoulders? I'll just undo the strap. And you should be wearing some too, you know – it's going to get really hot, later. Colin had eased the cream into every pore – and do you know, it was terrible of her, yes, Elizabeth supposed it was – but at one point she had wanted Colin to slip his hands around and forward and cup her breasts so

186

that they could feel both protected and charged. I *told* you it was terrible! I mean – look: this was Dotty's *Colin*, for heaven's sake. But there's nothing quite like the fingers of a young boy – that's what Elizabeth thought. The firmness, the deep and goading pressure of a man's hands – that was one thing, and not to be dismissed; the feather touch of a woman – this too could be quite delightful; but a boy was something else. After, Elizabeth had stroked the lotion over Colin's back, but he wouldn't turn over and let her do his chest – just wouldn't; maybe it was just the heat, but Elizabeth longed to be quite sure why – had yearned to discover.

'Well of *course*,' replied Elizabeth. 'I *always* do, nowadays – God, you read such awful things. Why didn't you put anything *on*, Dotty?'

'I did, I did,' protested Dotty. And she had, she had – given herself quite a basting: all but used a spatula.

'What factor is it?' pursued Melody.

Dotty threw her a puzzled look. '*Max* Factor, pretty sure.'

'What – the top one?'

'Well it wasn't *cheap*,' came back Dotty – thinking what on earth is Melody *talking* about? *I'm* the one who looks like a bloody circus clown and here she is banging on about *labels*. And I'd really been quite enjoying myself up till now. The weather was *so* beautiful – just as good as Italy, or somewhere – and so when over dinner Elizabeth

187

had suggested that next day they all go down to the beach together, Dotty had been all for the idea: ooh yes – *lovely* – what a perfect summer thing to do. Colin had shrugged his compliance, and Brian was simply not consulted. He had decided not to, the following morning (If I get roped into buying lunch for that lot I'll be done for), and so Dotty had had to spin Elizabeth and Melody some tall tale concerning Brian being more eager to explore the intricacies and range of the flora and fauna within the grounds of their estate (which by now Dotty had ratcheted up to something on the lines of Blenheim Palace) and try not to eye with apprehension an impassive and supremely indulgent Colin kicking up sand as she did so. Truth was, she had left Brian on his hands and knees beneath the tiny flap-up table in their poxy little caravan, attempting to discover why it persisted in flapping down again when anyone laid on it so much as a plateful of fucking digestives.

They had arrived quite early, to get a good place ('At least we don't have to worry about *Germans* here,' Elizabeth had quipped. 'I very much doubt if Germans have ever *heard* of the place'), and Colin had altogether enjoyed watching Elizabeth stretch out in her Liza Bruce bikini, not wholly loathing it either when Melody displayed her High Street knock-off of the very same number – her three most interesting bits now well signposted in highlighter lime. Melody already had a smouldering tan (Clarins, she had confided, loudly).

Dotty had gazed up at the white and quite blurred sun through tortoiseshell Wayfarers (a relic from better days – old-hat now, but at least a recognizable brand: *something*, isn't it?)

'You know,' she had said, 'that sun is so warm, I could just have a snooze, right now.'

'I'm completely knackered,' muttered Melody.

'Why?' asked Dotty. 'Did you not sleep?'

Melody made a face like a bloodhound and threw across first to Elizabeth and then – with a slow sweep of the neck (hunched up, so as to suggest that her head was as lead) over in Dotty's direction.

'*Don't*,' she said.

'We didn't,' glossed Elizabeth, with complicit irony, 'have the *best* of nights. It wasn't the poor little thing's fault, but Dawn was just a little bit –'

'She yelled the fucking place down,' mumbled Melody miserably. 'Sorry, Colin,' she added on. You do that, don't you, if there's someone young around: fuck knows why. 'All night long.'

'Oh – poor little *Dawn*,' lamented Dotty – with real feeling in her voice. 'Maybe it's just being in a strange place, could it be?'

Melody shook her head (Mm – this sun is really gorgeous: I'm just going to lie back and let it toast me). 'Nah,' she said. 'She's always like that. Bloody always.'

'Let *me* take her,' blurted Dotty, suddenly – and yes she was aware that Colin had gone so far as to drag his eyes away from Elizabeth's tits and was looking at her sharply. She did not know herself why she suggested such a thing – it had just come out of this wide and vivid blue. Maybe it was no more than the fleeting vision of a little baby girl: crying, crying – crying so piteously all through the night, just as in those dark and terrible final days my little angel Maria had done, and all of us in some awful way clinging onto each of her fearful shrieks as if to a life-raft in crashing rapids, each one of us knowing that when eventually the agony came to an end, then so too would little Maria.

'What do you mean?' asked Melody gingerly – though with hope that was rising like mercury in hell. Elizabeth was all ears too.

'Well,' expanded Dotty, breezily (what exactly *do* I mean? Let's just see what comes). 'What I mean is – *we* could take her. For a night. Let you get some sleep. I don't mind. I'd love it.'

Melody glanced at Elizabeth as if to say Yippee – think we've caught a big one here; don't jerk the line or we'll lose it – just have the landing net ready.

'It's an *idea*,' approved Elizabeth, warmly – with not much caution at all.

'Yeah,' enthused Melody.' And you could just stick her in the East Wing or the butler's pantry, if you couldn't stand it.'

Dotty smiled. I must not catch the eye of Colin – but I can already feel its burning – as would, soon, her nose. After, she had given herself up happily

190

to sleep – this towel, this sand: so much more comfortable than that bloody padded shelf stuck up at the ceiling. Melody too was soon dozing, and not much later Colin was actually getting to *touch* Elizabeth all up and down her soft and warming, flawless back, and holding back impulses with the help of a thousand harnessed horses – but oh! Just to be able to slip my hands around and forward and hold on hard to those knockout tits. Later still – oozing as she oiled him, face down and rigid – he had practically fucked the beach.

It was sunny and warm in London, too – rather *too* warm, thought Howard as he replaced the receiver on the main phone – the black one – on the broad old desk in his office. His eyes were narrowed and his lips were pursed – looking as if he was just bursting to say out loud: *Een*-teresting – vary *een*teresting. Which is more or less what he was feeling; but no – couldn't be true, could it? Not Norman Furnish. No – he was a good lad, Norman: Howard had always said so. Going places, Howard shouldn't wonder (but where did an estate agent go?) No, the gist of the call he had just received – well, the tail-end part, really: almost nothing more than a postscript – was that word had it that Norman was pocketing commissions. It was a rival agent who had rung (some offer on a property they were handling jointly) and he had just sort of slipped it in at close of play. Howard had chuckled, indulgently. And then he

191

had started to peruse the records – even glance at the petty cash book (a thing he never did). Hm. A couple of houses that Norman had been handling had apparently been privately sold. And Norman certainly seemed to have been taking a lot of trips, just lately – and long ones, too. I mean, good God – the agency only covered one fairly small if affluent area of London: some of these fares would get you to Inverness in a taxi. But Norman did get results, let's be fair – sold that Northwick Avenue semi just last week (Howard had thought they'd never get rid of that one: wrong side of the road) and God knows Howard didn't pay him very much. Shame he's on holiday, actually, or I'd confront him directly: can't stand mysteries – don't care for the shadows of things that might or might not be going on. Not, of course, that one ever really did know what it was that any given person was really up to: you only had to look at Howard and Zoo-Zoo.

Hadn't planned it, you know: never done anything like it before – well, odd fumble at school, but you expect that. No, the first time, if Howard is honest, that he supposes anything of the sort arose was when he and Elizabeth had been in Thailand, that time. Hell of a holiday, that was: whole month (Melody went nuts – on and on at him, she was: you never take *me* anywhere – all of that, on and on; just as well Melody finally did meet that other bloke, I think, all in all: she was becoming just a little bit of a *pain*). Anyway, yes – where was I?

Christ – my mind. Can never keep track of – oh yes, got it, I've got it: Thailand, yup. Yes, as I say – didn't actually *do* anything, or anything, but did sort of notice all these young boys around (lovely limbs – some of them wearing make-up which yes Howard *did* find quite arousing, in point of fact). So something of all this must presumably have always been there within him, lurking. Actually, I've just thought – what I *did* do in Bangkok was find a very lovely bar girl, while Elizabeth was off somewhere buying another shipload of stuff. By Christ, there wasn't much *that* little bag of tricks wasn't up for: like a contortionist, she was – lovely. Anyway, I, er – oh God: lost it again, done it again. My *mind, my mind – had* it just a second ago and now it's completely – oh no, I've got you, I've got you: yes – the boys in Thailand. Mm. No – completely went out of my mind (God – as things do!); didn't give it another thought. And then we got this new team of cleaners at the office. Filipino, they were – thought we'd give them a go. Christ – they couldn't have been worse than the last lot, moaning old biddies – usually late, often ill and always bloody useless. So they arrived – sometimes two women, sometimes three (think they're sisters – not sure) – and then one time one of them brings her boy along: finished school, can't get a job – usual thing. So I said well look, there's always a bit of filing to do, round here – generally getting all the bumf off the floor: couldn't offer much, but if the lad is at all interested . . .

193

Yes. And that's my Zoo-Zoo. I call him that because it suits him so well: his lips always look as if that is just what he is poised to say: Zoo-Zoo. I bought wigs for him to wear when he's with me – love long hair – and of course I give him money. But I think there is real affection there on his part – think so. He hates it when I go away, certainly. We don't actually do that much, physically – if you want to go into it. I don't: want to go into it, if you see what I mean – that's not at all it, for me. No – I just love to touch his slim and muscled limbs, and I love for him to hold me tight. In a strange way, he's all I really want, I suppose. Never really felt completely happy living with anyone, you know – I am actually pretty domesticated – don't find running a house a particularly daunting thought. Melody – this is funny – Melody once truly believed that I'd actually leave Elizabeth for her. What a laugh – if I ever left Elizabeth (which is impossible, now – maybe once, but not now: what would be the point?) – but if I ever did, then it wouldn't be to live with anyone else at all. No – I'm really quite happy on my own. And – at tender times – then maybe with my little Zoo-Zoo.

I don't feel any shame, though – no guilt: why should I? Although, er – obviously I don't actually want it, you know – to get *about*. Well – it would be the end, wouldn't it? Just the end. There is this awful stigma, you see. Zoo-Zoo looks so like a girl, you know – I wish you could meet him. Which is funny, isn't it, really? I mean, I could be wrong (open to correction) but I should have said that if a chap is attracted to another chap who actually *looks* like a chap (you know – tall, big muscles, beards and boots: all that sort of thing) well then, well then – well then you really might have a problem. But it's not like that – not with me and Zoo-Zoo.

Right – no more chat. Oh God, just look at the time – might just be OK if I step on it. Got to show a prospective buyer round a house (no rest for the wicked); Brian's house, actually: maybe this one will bite – God knows the bugger deserves a break. Quick whisky, maybe? Not really the time: have one later. Now – keys, keys – where are the keys? Ah – got them. No – wrong ones. Here they are, yes – right: roger and out. But Christ, you know: my *mind*.

When eventually (quite late) they all traipsed back to the hotel, it was really only Melody who was attracting the glances of admiration: she looked splendid – hair not at all frizzed or gritty from the beach – sleeker, if anything, than it had been that morning. The tan was rich and even ('I told you, I told you,' she laughed: 'all down to Clarins – nothing to do with *me*') and the sashay was well from the hip. Didn't do it for Colin, though, for the simple reason – you can see it coming, yes no? – that for all her evident lusciousness, Melody wasn't that great in the tit department, right? And if you're Colin, OK – then Tits R Us. Elizabeth looked fine – felt really good (braced? Is the word braced? It

195

sounded good) after all that sun and an awful lot of sleep. Dotty? Well, Dotty – with her radishy face and nose well anointed by random blobs of cold cream – Dotty looked like nothing so much as a last-minute substitute in some ancient and maybe Maori sacrificial rite. Colin was tugging at her arm, which caused her to howl – oh God, oh God: she felt cooked and flayed.

'What *is* it, Colin – oh God don't *touch* me, don't *touch* me.'

'*Look*, Mum – what did you think you were doing, saying all that to Melody? It's impossible enough trying to sleep in that bloody rust bucket without a screaming *baby*.'

A tooth of Dotty's was sucking on one of her lips. Of *course* that was true, of *course* it was. She hadn't given a thought to Colin when she'd offered to take in Dawn (can't *wait* to see her, hold her, have her); and as for Brian – he hadn't even entered.

'OK, Colin, OK,' she shushed. 'I'll think of something, OK?'

'Wish I could stay *here*,' moped Colin.

'Well maybe . . .' – and light sprang into Dotty's eyes now, rendering her not unlike a battery-powered Mrs Potato Head – 'maybe you can. We'll see. Elizabeth! Here – listen to this: isn't this just kids all over?'

'I'm going to the bar, Dotty,' returned Elizabeth. 'Come on, everyone – let's all go and have a drink. My God it's packed in here tonight. I can't see a table. Oh there – over there, I think we can all fit –

196

bit of a squeeze. Excuse me,' Elizabeth now said to the woman with downcast eyes at a table easily big enough for five (just get another chair from somewhere), 'would you mind awfully if we . . . ?'

'Oh no of course,' replied Lulu – God: voices. She had been absolutely years, centuries, eons away: what I mustn't do is cry again. 'Please . . . sit. Of course.'

Elizabeth remembered Lulu from the previous evening – well, she remembered the lovely could it be Nicole Farhi she had been wearing: rather nice trousers on this evening – and a beautifully cut military-style shirt in heavy silk, sort of tawny colour. Obviously knew her stuff, this woman – but wasn't she with that awful and tedious health farm bore? It was always odd, wasn't it? The men women got.

'Well I don't know about anyone else,' said Elizabeth, plumping herself down and directing people, 'but I really do feel like a glass of champagne – is that all right for everybody? We are on *holiday*, after all. Just get that chair from over there, can you, Melody?'

Various appreciative murmurs went up, though Dotty indicated Colin – but no, Elizabeth wasn't having any of that: oh no nonsense, she said – everyone can drink champagne, champagne's not *drinking*. The steward came and went, and Elizabeth called after him Oh and can we have some olives? Black? And maybe a few nuts, or something: great.

197

'Colin was just saying,' started up Dotty, chattily.

'How's your poor *nose*, Dotty?' enquired Elizabeth, solicitously.

'Mm? Oh it's fine, fine. Well – *not* fine, obviously, but it'll be fine, I'm fine – honestly. No listen – typical, this, isn't it? We've got this absolutely unbelievable country house to stay in, right?'

'Yeah,' put in Melody, flatly. 'You told us.'

'*Right*,' agreed Dotty, determined not to be deflected (she could be quite sardonic, that Melody, if you let her), 'well Colin is only saying oh *God*, I *wish* I could stay here with Elizabeth – it's the most beautiful hotel I've ever *seen*! Kids are just never happy with what they've got, are they?'

Colin looked away and blushed, as Elizabeth swooped in with her response. That's *not* what he had said at all, was it? No it wasn't; could kill Mum, sometimes. And Dad (nearly always).

'Oh but of course you *can*, Colin!' enthused Elizabeth. 'What a perfectly brilliant idea – because we've already got a proper bed set up in the sitting-room bit, haven't we, Melody? Oh yes – great fun: we're all swapping children for the night, what larks! Not,' she tacked on gravely, 'that I suppose for one minute you enjoy being referred to as a *child*, Colin: I think you are very manly. More grown up than most grown-ups are.'

Well that was worth Colin's impish, hundred-watt and fully fashioned grin, now, wasn't it? Yes

198

indeed – very good value: and Elizabeth appreciated it, you could always tell.

'Would you *like* that, Colin?' Elizabeth asked him now.

Colin looked at her. 'Yes,' he said.

Elizabeth clapped her hands. 'Splendid! Well that's settled, then. Ah – champagne: wonderful. Dotty – you take him later to get his things, and everything – and can Brian drop him back?'

'I'm sure. Mm – lovely, lovely: it's *ages* since I had champagne. Well,' she checked herself, 'not *that* long.'

Lulu was trying hard not to listen to anything – felt a bit of a gooseberry, but where else could she go? Not upstairs – no. Now she eyed the bottle of Moët as the bar steward poured it, and then she looked away.

'So,' said Elizabeth, taking an appreciative sip at the flute. 'What are we all up to tomorrow? To your liking, Colin?'

'It's quite nice, actually,' said Colin. 'I like the bubbles.'

'I *adore* the bubbles,' laughed Elizabeth.

'Never mind *tomorrow*,' chimed in Melody. 'What are we doing *tonight*?'

Dotty slumped back in mock exhaustion, and splayed her legs and arms – it looked now as if Mrs Potato Head was bobbling above a sackful of assorted chums.

'You're *kidding*,' puffed out Dotty. 'I've absolutely *had* it – and anyway, I've got little Dawn to see to, haven't I?' Mm – can't wait.

199

'What about you, Elizabeth?' asked Melody. 'You up for a club, or something?'

'I *couldn't*, Melody – just couldn't. God knows where you get your energy from.'

'She just wants to show off her tan,' smiled Dotty.

'Yeah,' grinned Melody. 'I do. Well who'd know a good place round here, d'you think? I know – I'll ask the barman – he's bound to know.'

She downed the rest of her champagne and skipped up to the bar, leaving Elizabeth to raise her eyebrows as if to say This Kid – Just Watch Her Go.

'Any decent clubs round here?' Melody asked of the small and squat possibly Italian, Greek maybe, barman with the quite black moustache; couldn't rule out Spanish.

'Clubs?' he queried, as if the concept was a new and maybe nasty one.

'There's a very good place not actually that far from here,' said a voice by Melody's side. 'The Meridiana – pretty civilized crowd, good cocktails, open till late.'

'Yeah?' said Melody, turning round. 'Oh *hi*! We talked at the thing, party thing, yeah?'

Miles nodded. 'Miles,' he said.

'Yeah, Miles, right. Melody. So it's good this place, then, is it?'

Now hang on, Miles old lad. You don't wanna get into this. Yes she's the best thing around –

apart from that bitch who blew me out in the lift (don't think she's seen me standing over here) – but look, this is the one with the bleeding *baby*, isn't it? And you know the rules, mate: you don't get involved with women with kids: Christ, wasn't there enough of all that at home with Sheil and her two? Our two.

'Thought you'd be looking after your little one,' smiled Miles. 'Not out grooving.'

Christ, Melody hated it, just *hated* it when people, men, assumed that just because she had a fucking baby that somehow she wasn't a *woman* any more.

'What little one?' she asked – sounding genuinely surprised. 'Oh the *baby*, you mean! Oh no – that's not mine – I was minding it – for a friend. You see her – over there? Not her, but her, yeah?'

Miles craned the neck in the direction. Yeah – I see her: looks like a bloody blancmange.

'Well it's *hers*,' said Melody, thinking Christ, you know – sometimes I wish it bleeding well *was* hers: or anyone's, really.

Miles's face broadened into expansive relief and leery welcome.

'Well in that case . . . would you care to . . . ? I mean I'd be delighted to . . .'

'Great,' agreed Melody. 'I'll see you in the lobby, foyer thing in, what? Hour?'

'One hour,' assented Miles, inclining his head. 'Your carriage will await you.'

Oh *terriff*, thought Miles with gusto, as Melody

went off to fill in her friends on the latest. I mean yes, OK – this afternoon hadn't been a total write-off: turned out it was that receptionist kid's half-day off – what was her name? Pauline – yeah, right. So OK – had a few drinks, few laughs – got her up to the room after a hell of a while. And yeah, she'd been OK – not world-class, know what I'm saying? But OK. Filled in the afternoon, sort of style. But this Melody – different league. Right, Miles – it very much looks as if you're on, my son: time for another Bacardi and Slimline.

'I can't remotely see what she sees in him,' sniffed Elizabeth, once Melody had skittered away.

'Well,' said Dotty, 'he's a man and he's *here*, I suppose.' But God, she was thinking, how could anyone want to go out with some complete stranger (jigging around in a lurid hell-hole) when they could be warm and cosy and caring for their very own little baby girl? Who I am now going to pick up from the creche: can't wait. And they'll give me all those soft and white and faintly peachy baby things – Dawn will grip my little finger, and I shall inhale her talcum.

'Elizabeth – I'm leaving. Thanks so much for the day. Come on, Colin – we'll just collect little Dawn, and then we'll get someone to get us a taxi.'

'Why don't you phone Brian?' suggested Elizabeth.

Because there is no phone at the château, dear Elizabeth: there is no bloody *anything* – but there

202

will be soon, there will be soon when I have little Dawn there, in my arms.

'Oh, I don't like to trouble him. A taxi's fine – it's no distance.'

'But Dotty,' protested Elizabeth now: 'there's still some champagne left!'

'*You* drink it,' smiled Dotty. 'Come on, Colin – we're off.'

'Now Colin,' Elizabeth called after the retreating pair, 'I don't quite know where I'll be when you get back – probably up in the room, but if not I'll tell them at Reception to let you in.'

Colin signalled Message Received and Elizabeth poured more Moët into her flute. Turning to Lulu, she said as if struck by huge inspiration:

'*You* wouldn't like to help me out with this, would you? Everyone seems to have deserted me!'

Lulu looked up. Oh thank you, *thank* you for talking to me: I so much want to talk back.

'That's very kind,' agreed Lulu. Yes – pleasant change: pour some champagne into me instead of over me, why don't I?

'Where is your husband this evening? Cheers.'

'Cheers. Oh, John. We're sort of doing our own thing, tonight. You don't *always* want to be together, do you?'

'Well you know it's funny you should say that,' replied Elizabeth, leaning forward and warming to the thing. 'Because *my* husband – Howard, his name is Howard – he was all set to come on this holiday because that's what we do, and

– well, it's all a bit boring and complicated to go into why he actually *didn't*, but I thought it would be pretty grim without him, frankly – of course, I've got Melody and Dotty: I didn't *introduce* you, did I? Oh God I'm *awfully* sorry – anyway: next time. Yes – what was I saying? Oh yes – Howard. But actually, I'm quite enjoying it. The freedom. I rather like it.'

Lulu smiled. Freedom. Yes.

'You know what I think we ought to do?' proposed Lulu, with a naughty-girl-midnight-feast-in-the-dorm expression in her eye – reaching out and fingering the neck of the empty bottle. 'Get in another of these – *my* treat, this time. OK, Lizzie? It is Lizzie, yes?'

'Well actually it's – well yes, Elizabeth: no one's ever called me Lizzie before, but I think it's rather fun. Yes – I'm Lizzie. Call me Lizzie.'

As Lulu turned to gesture to the bar, Elizabeth was thinking You know it's amazing the sorts of things you do, the sorts of things you say, to utter strangers somewhere else. I like Lulu: I really do.

John Powers was locked into despair, adrift amid the vastness of his luxury suite: just so much stupid, dead and empty space, now that Lulu was gone. He had begged her not to leave, begged her, while knowing that she would – and who could blame her? The curse is, the curse is – oh God, oh Christ, I'm being eaten *alive* by this – is that now, now she really *is* oh God *fuck* knows where – and with whom, with whom? Hey? Could be anyone. Anyone at all – anywhere. He had promised not to follow her – she was steely, while John's face had been steeped in tears – and after she left he had sat there for, oh, minutes before rushing to the door, swearing at the lift, bounding down the stairs – willing his eyes to be heat-seeking and radiant as he stuck an anguished head around every single door. Gabbled to the concierge (he must have thought I was crazy – and I was, I was: I'm crazy *now*), who rather thought *yes*, Mrs Powers has just left the hotel in a taxi. In a taxi! In a taxi! Taxis can take you anywhere – to meet anyone, anyone at all. So where was she? Where did she go? Was she laughing? Was she giving that wonderful, musical laugh and throwing up her eyes the way she did? And what smooth bastard was drinking it in? Whose eyes were feasting greedily on the sight that was John's and John's alone? And would he reach out and touch? *God*! God God God! I can't bear it, I can't stand it, I'll go *mad*, with this. Maybe there was more than one – maybe she was surrounded by dark-clad and moodily handsome men with deep assured voices and glistening amusement alive in their eyes. What if they take her – roughly and now: right here where they found her – the hard men's harsh and swift invasion of all that was most tender! Drink, drink – another drink: oh Christ the bottle is nearly empty. Get another one, order another one, that's what to do, that's what to do – and she'll be back, back soon: any second now the door will be opened and there will be Lulu who will tell him she loves him and he will quite willingly die at her feet and offer up his soul to his Lulu – oh Lulu, my Lulu: there is no end to the depth of my passion: how can you *do* this to me? Why can you not see just how much I *love* you?!

It hadn't been an entirely wasted day, from Brian's point of view. Spent ages on that damned table – a lot of these jobs, you know, are a good deal trickier than at first they may seem: we're talking serious man-hours, no mistake. Then he gave the whole of the outside of the caravan a really good slungeing: queued up for a few buckets of water (quite a good way to get to know your neighbours, as a matter of fact: seemed a nice crowd, on the whole) and got to work with a couple of flannels. Hadn't really needed doing, if he was honest, but it was a lovely day and it filled the hours. Had a pie at the pub – can't think why Dotty was going on about the place: seemed all right. Kept a good pint, anyway; Brian had had quite a talk with the landlord about various ales (you can keep your keg rubbish – bloats you up) and then he filled him in on the optimum route from here to London, assuming you wanted to avoid any black spots or snarl-ups – no easy thing at this time of year, let him assure you.

He'd found quite a nice vase sort of thing in one of the cupboards (Brian was no expert on ornaments, he would be the first to say, but it did seem, as he says, a nice-ish thing: orangey china, pottery, with blackish sort of swirls). So he'd bought a few flowers at the garage – maybe give Dotty a bit of a lift for when she came back: splash of colour. Also brought home a few more pies from the pub – all we have to do is give them a bit of a warm. So everything's ready, really, for when they came back. (And I have kept anguish at bay: have not dwelt on the sheer and awful hopelessness of my position – the peril in which I have placed my family.)

Who, unless I am very much mistaken, are finally home. That *was* a car door, wasn't it? Let's just sneak a peek: yes – not wrong, here they come (they must be tired). Oh no – Dotty hasn't been *buying* things again, has she? I've told her and I've told her – blue in the face just doesn't come into it. And yet still there she was – oh, no – wasn't that sort of thing at all, it was . . . it couldn't be, could it? It was, it was – just before Dotty opened her mouth to speak he glanced down into her arms and was speared by what he saw there. A hot mire of not, then, suffocated memories humidly stirred within him.

'Now I know what you're thinking, Brian,' said Dotty, briskly (and Brian thought well no actually you don't, Dotty, but do continue), 'but I promise she won't be any trouble at all – will you, little Dawn?' Dotty's face was irradiated as she talked to the baby. 'No you *won't*, no you *won't* – you's a good little girly, aren't you? Yes you are – yes you are.' Looking up now she said: 'Oh for God's sake *move* yourself, Brian – you're always in the way.'

Dotty took carefully the two steps up into the caravan. 'Now I'm sorry, little baby, that you are in this horrid little place, but that's your Uncle Brian's fault. But never mind! We'll have a good time, won't we, you and me? Yes we will. Oh yes we *will*.'

'It's,' muttered Brian, very softly to Colin, 'well – it's: you know why she's, you know – doing this?'

Colin nodded. 'I know.'

It's not something they ever talked about. Along with so much else.

Brian nodded too. 'And her hooter must be giving her gyp, by the look of it.'

'What's that *smell*?' accused Dotty now, as if she had detected not so much the warming of food as the whiff of treason among the ranks of her most loyal and trusted servants.

'Pie,' said Brian. 'Sort of pasty thing. I'm heating them up for us. Why is Dawn here, Dotty? Melody not well?'

'Well you are very welcome to your loathsome *pie*, Brian – I myself am not hungry, and Colin is going back to The Excelsior where I am sure Elizabeth will treat him to something a lot more appetizing than *that*. And no, it doesn't actually matter *why* Colin's going back – just drive him there, can you?'

'Yeah,' put in Colin, 'but not just yet, Dad. I'm going to have a bit of a walk, first – 'bout half an hour, OK?'

'All right, Colin me old lad. Whenever you say.'

When Colin had left (funny time for a *walk*) Dotty said: 'Here, Brian – make yourself useful, for once: put Colin's things together – there's clean pyjamas in one of the cases and his washing things are in the criss-cross bag, there. Is you a hungry little baby, Dawn? I think you is – I think you is! Brian – hand me those – no, not those – *those*, those: over there! Yes, those. Now we'll have to warm the bottle. You's got to be patient, little baby, because we've got to make your bottle nice and warm for you, haven't we? Yes we have. Yes we *have*.'

Brian put the bottle in a saucepan half filled with water and recoiled just slightly as the gas popped alight (he'd done this before – long ago, a long time ago) and then he set about getting together all of Colin's things.

'Why's Colin staying there, all of a sudden, Dotty? And you didn't answer me – why's Dawn here? It's all a bit odd, isn't it? I mean – it's a bit *funny*, isn't it? I don't get.'

Dotty looked up. Let's let him have it, she thought.

'If you really want to know why Colin is going back to the hotel, Brian, it is because he *pleaded* with me – pleaded – not to have to spend one more night in this – I do believe he said "rust bucket". And of course the only way that was possible was if Dawn came back with me. Also, I wanted her to. Answer all your questions?'

Brian nodded. Can't do much about it, can I? As per usual. He placed Colin's criss-cross wash-bag on the table, which immediately and clatteringly flapped back down, sending the orangey vase (with blackish sort of swirls) spinning to the floor where it smashed and all Brian could do as Dawn set up a howling that could cause feedback in your bones was to stare down at the spray of mixed pinks and a few bits of fern sprawled still and awry amid the water fast spreading towards Dotty's (was it still bad?) foot.

'Oh God *now* look what you've done, you totally stupid, *stupid* little man! She was perfectly all *right* . . . shoosh-oosh-oosh, all right, little Dawn, all right, little baby: it was only silly, clumsy Uncle Brian – nothing to worry about . . . perfectly all *right* until she came here and saw *you*.'

But already Dawn's sobbing was subsiding; Dotty was playing one of her own fingertips just over the pink warmth of Dawn's sweet lips, and now the baby was quiet, and smiling – so soon gurgling in peace and contentment. Brian had seen this before: Dotty just had a way about her.

'Well,' he said (best make light of it). 'A brand-new Dawn!'

'Just get the bottle, Brian. And then clear up this mess.'

No, thought Dotty: wrong. Not a brand-new Dawn, no. What I have, here and now in my arms and already deep down in my heart – what I am gazing at and holding is a brand-new Maria.

★   ★   ★

'Hi,' said Colin, as casually as he could, when finally – is it? Is it her? Difficult to see – yes it is, is her: Carol – came ambling over the dune (great jeans). He had thought it best to try to appear as if he had just happened along – maybe she liked to be alone? He didn't want to butt in, or anything. In truth he had been hanging about for twenty minutes, nearly, and it was actually getting a little bit chilly. The sea made a cold sound, sloshing around in whatever way it was going; bit scary, too.

'Hi,' said Carol in return, with practised indifference. 'It's nice here, isn't it? At night.'

'It is,' agreed Colin – although actually, while he had been sitting there, he hadn't seen anything remotely nice about it. I mean – *why* was it nice? Half dark, nothing to see, itchy grass – not *that* great, is it? But Carol struck him as one of those types who probably reads poetry, or something: maybe even *writes* it, who knows? What he *had* been thinking was well, she did say I had lovely hands, didn't she? Made a point of telling me more or less what time she came here. I mean, short of a copperplate invitation it seemed plain enough; but you never knew with girls – they behaved very oddly. Or so Colin imagined, anyway. At least if I do something terribly wrong it'll be way too dark for her to see me blushing.

Carol sat down fairly close to him, and began to pluck up handfuls of sand for throwing, most of it spattering down like dry rain on the scrub, the rest gusting back into their eyes – oh God ouch – so she soon packed in that little game.

'How old are you, Colin?' she asked, simply.

'Fifteen,' said Colin. 'Nearly. I think I've got some in my – urgh – mouth.'

'I'm sixteen,' said Carol. And then, after a pause, 'actually I'm not – I'm fifteen too, pretty close. I sometimes say sixteen.'

Colin nodded. *Why*? he thought.

'What do you *like*, and things?' pursued Carol.

Oh Christ this wasn't easy. What do I like? What do I like? Well – all sorts of things. No point saying that, is there, because she'll only come back with Well What Things so I might as well be more, what is it, specific at the outset. But I can't for the life of me think of a single thing I like – except . . . yeah, well: can't say *that*.

'I mean,' went on Carol, obviously fairly correctly surmising that she could well grow old and grey if it was Colin she was waiting for. 'Do you like sailing, say? Boats?'

'Love them,' said Colin, with emphasis. 'Love it.' Never actually been on a boat, but they look so great in films.

'My Dad said I could ask you out on the boat one day, if you'd like to. We're going out tomorrow, actually.'

'Oh yeah!' enthused Colin. 'Great!'

'And you've got all the gear, have you?'

'Oh yeah – sure.' Gear?

'OK,' said Carol, brightly, 'well let's say we'll

meet right here, then: ten, tomorrow.'

Colin nodded eagerly. 'Terrific. And you're sure your Dad won't mind?'

'Oh no – he's great, my Dad. Terry's a bit of a pain, but Dad's really fun.'

Ah, thought Colin. Terry, yes: forgotten about him.

'*My* Dad's not fun,' was all he said.

'Poor you! Look Colin – I've got to get back, OK?'

'Yeah, right – I have to go too now, actually.'

They were standing, and Colin was trembling. Here was parting sweet sorrow time, right? What should he do? What should he do? Carol was hanging around to maybe find out. What he *really* wanted to do – oh God oh God – it was almost as if his wrists were drawn like magnets to some cruel and irresistible force: he could barely restrain them from twitching up, his fingers splaying outwards. What he did was, eventually, no more than incline his face towards hers – pausing a bit (give the girl a little time to see if she felt like slugging him) and then (all clear, I think – who knows?) carrying on down until at the very last second she averted her whole head and said:

'Cheek!'

Colin's skull nearly blew off as a result of so volcanic a rush of blood as he had never felt before in his life.

'Oh Christ I'm so *sorry*!' he practically cried out,

213

feeling luminous. 'I didn't *mean* to be –!'

'No,' clarified Carol. 'I mean my cheek – you can kiss my cheek.'

'Oh. Right,' said Colin. And he did that, for what it was worth (this side of a Roman orgy, yeah?)

'Until we know each other *better*,' sang Carol, skipping away. 'But you really do have lovely hands, you know, Colin.'

Colin nodded as he watched her go.

'Tomorrow!' he called out – and her voice came back faintly: ten, is what Colin was pretty sure she said.

He sighed. How maddening. But girls were, weren't they? Famous for it. Colin turned to go. Fat lot of use lovely *hands* are, he was thinking, if they never bloody managed to latch on to anything *decent*.

As Howard drove up to his gate, he could already see the clients across the hedge hanging around Brian's house, in the way that clients do: bending low and peering through windows, arched fingers serving as a visor – craning up at the roof, they could not have told you why. Now the couple were only ambling halfway down the side of the house (is this a drainpipe? Yes it is) and, yes, they were turning and making their way back again. Howard had seen all this a thousand times – an elaborate variation on the way prospective secondhand car buyers will kick a tyre, or peer down shrewdly into the murky and fathomless innards of an engine.

214

Annoying they were here so promptly, actually, as Howard had been hoping to nip home first for a quick shot of Scotch: a pleasure that would have to be deferred.

Howard bustled up the drive, exuding just the right degree of urgency and bonhomie to befit his profession, the dark blue suit on so warm a day speaking for itself, he thought.

'Mr Street,' stated the man, with no enquiry. 'I can see the gutters are going to need work.'

'And you will be Mr and Mrs Davies,' beamed Howard. 'Let's go in, shall we? The owners are away on holiday, just at the moment, so you'll have plenty of time to . . . you know – get the feel of the place.'

The hall was sunlit and roomy and pretty normal, thank Christ – it was all the other rooms Howard was worried about. He hadn't liked to say anything, but he was quite convinced that if only the house wasn't so filled with all the fallout of Brian's well-meaning enthusiasms, the place would have shifted months ago.

Howard threw open the door of the drawing room, stepping back so that Mr and Mrs Davies could precede him. Yes, he thought – and Dotty too has to bear a good deal of the blame: just look at all this *stuff*.

'Unusually large front room,' said Howard. 'Benefiting from another one equally large to the rear: quite deceptively spacious, in fact.'

'Isn't it funny,' said Mrs Davies (who thus far

215

into the game had seemed to be in the grip of a trance – but people viewing houses often drifted up and away like that, Howard had observed). 'I mean,' she made clearer, 'the things they like to have about them.'

Yes, dammit – this was the trouble: they weren't looking at the high ceilings and the original features and the working fireplace and the connecting doors and the good half-panelling, were they? No – they were just impaled by all this bloody *stuff*. Every wall had fixed to it rows of dark wood racks and mini-bookcases and these were ranked and festooned with all manner of thimbles and spice jars and teaspoons and miniature teapots (miniature teapots!) and ladies in crinolines and balloon sellers and little china children wiping away their tears and kittens with cocked heads and *sties* full of winsome piggies – and there, over there: pride of place on the mantelpiece, just east of the clock-cum-barometer set into a pottery thatched cottage (lights up at night, Howard can barely stand to tell you), is the *pièce de résistance*, the *objet* to end them all: a huge and coloured Capo di Monte circus fucking clown, slumped and doleful in the wings. I mean: what can Howard tell you?

'One has to,' tried Howard, 'try to see *beyond*.'

The Davies duo nodded in a desultory and fairly unconvincing sort of a way, and made plain that they were ready to move on. Howard would dearly have loved to skip over the other living room, but at its most basic it was a really fine and lovely

216

space (Howard and Elizabeth used their next-door equivalent more than any other room in the house). It had the most wonderfully ornate and original ceiling rose, for starters, and grand and full-length french doors leading down a few steps into the hundred-foot garden (which was both mature and well stocked, let Howard tell you).

What it also had was Brian's manhole covers. Mrs Davies's startled reaction to this mass of menacingly dark and deadweight iron could not have been more pronounced if Howard had nippily goosed her with a feather duster.

'The garden . . .' tried Howard.

'What *are* these?' gasped Mrs Davies.

'I reckon,' said her husband, with foreboding, 'there's some sort of loony lives here.'

'Of course,' went on Howard, 'in the event of a sale, we would guarantee full vacant possession – I mean, everything would go, if you see what I mean.'

Mr Davies pulled the knob on a cupboard door, but that door, baby, was having none of it. Howard rather hurriedly suggested they go upstairs, because he had had plenty of experience with Brian's cupboards: none of them opened easily, it went without saying – but put too much into it and either you're reeling backwards with the knob in your hands, or else the whole bloody door is torn from its hinges; either way, not a selling point.

'Actually,' amended Howard (they seemed trustworthy enough), 'maybe you'd like to wander round, just the two of you? Often the best way. Anything you want to know, just call down to me – I'll be here. The top room – the large room at the very top is truly spectacular, I have to say. Then you can come back down and see the kitchen and garage and so on.'

That met with approval (always did) and so the Davieses plodded off upstairs, and Howard wandered into the little den just off the dining room. Elizabeth had tricked out their version as a very pretty little breakfast room (ideal in summer – looking lovely right now, in point of fact, because just this morning Zoo-Zoo had put out a bright and fresh custardy yellow gingham table-cloth, and set a small bowl of margueritas at its centre). Difficult to say, quite, what Brian and Dotty saw their little room as being; if he was honest, Howard had chiefly been hoping to find a bottle of Scotch or similar lying around (nothing in the other rooms – he'd checked) but here too there seemed to be nothing on offer. So he hung around, mooching; what's this? What's this great big cardboard box? Let's have a look. Candles. White candles. OK, candles: nothing wrong with that – but what sort of people bought two gross at a time? (Exactly what Dotty had asked when Brian had heaved them home; they were a bargain, he said.)

Howard poked around the debris on top of what once had been quite a nice little desk (*God* this place was run down – even the carpets, once Brian's pride and joy, his *life*, for God's sake

– even the carpets were in mourning, just look at them).

Now what was this? Some misshapen piece of metal – could have been a part of absolutely anything from a lawn-mower to a jet engine (state-of-the-art sculpture? Unlikely.) And there were signs of whittling, look: offcuts of timber, half carved, wholly abandoned. Hey – he wouldn't be likely, would he, Brian, to keep a drop of something in a drawer, maybe? Worth a look? Well what's to lose – the Davieses could be here for ages, yet (can't hear a sound upstairs – which home improvement has leapt out and assailed them?) Howard slid open one drawer, and it seemed to be filled with nothing but crumpled newspaper: rooted around in that for a bit, but what you saw was very much all you got, unbelievably: just crumpled newspaper, and nothing else at all. The next drawer clinked, which briefly raised Howard's spirits, but what we had here was no more than a couple of very old and truly quite nasty bottles of, what was it, let's read: ah yes, sewing machine lubricant, very nice.

Maybe I'd better hurry up the Davieses and get myself home; hang on – what's this? No – leave it: shouldn't be poking around Brian's desk anyway, should I? *I* wouldn't like it, would I? But look, whenever there are four or five envelopes with a band around them, it's always pretty tempting, isn't it? What decided Howard to go on with the thing was the bold inscription in block capitals across the topmost: DO NOT OPEN UNTIL 1st

JANUARY 1998. Well – ages ago: can't do any harm now. Howard slid the ungummed envelope away from its fellows, but before he could extricate the single sheet within, he was struck by what was written on the one beneath (and this in Brian's hand, all right, block capitals or no): DO NOT OPEN UNTIL 1st AUGUST 1997. And the next? 1st JANUARY 1997: strange. Howard slipped out the paper from the most recent (Brian's normal writing, now – joined up and washable blue-black) and this is what he saw: 'By the time you read this, I shall be dead. I am more use to all of you that way. Believe me, this hasn't been easy. My love. Brian. P.S. Sorry.' Each of the letters was identical, and would seem to have been written at more or less six-monthly intervals – the end of the summer and just after Christmas. Well good God Almighty – Howard had no idea: I mean, yes – life hadn't been going too well for old Brian just lately, but Howard would never have thought that he would have contemplated . . . well, well, well: poor old sod. Hadn't gone *through* with it, obviously – but nonetheless, just imagine the sort of way you have to feel before you can *write* such a letter. Let alone five of the bleeding things.

'Hello? Hello? Mr Street – are you there?'

Howard shot back the letters into the drawer (it was as if he had been stung by bees) and whirled round to greet Mr Davies.

'So!' he announced – and then more quietly: 'How did you . . . ?'

220

Mr Davies nodded. 'We've had a good look round – yes, Edna?' Mrs Davies confirmed by way of a simper that yes indeed, here was no lie. 'And frankly, Mr Street, we like what we see.'

'*Good*,' said Howard. *Really*? Are you *sure*? How utterly astounding.

'But,' went on Mr Davies, hardly unexpectedly, 'obviously they're asking far too much for it. You see I'll tell you what I like about the place, apart from the size and the area – and the garden, I have to say, has very great potential, in the right hands.'

'Cyril is a wonderful gardener,' put in Edna Davies, touching his arm – and Cyril smirked and liked that a lot.

'Well,' he qualified, beaming from ear to ear, 'let's just say I know my way around. But no, what we were looking for, you see, is something with plenty of space and completely unmodernized – tear out all this rubbish and start again.'

Completely unmodernized! Oh God if Brian could hear those words he'd beetle off and compose another sad farewell – there was no moment of the night or day when he hadn't been working on *something*, here.

'Well,' said Howard, thinking You know: I've been in this business how long? I never would have thought we had even a cat's chance with these people, but it very much looks as if . . . 'You seem to have found the place!'

'All very well,' came back Cyril Davies, sounding

a good deal gruffer. 'But I don't have to tell you of *all* people, Mr Street, that the work needing doing here is going to cost a small fortune – and not such a small one, either.'

'I think,' said Howard, with professional caution, 'that to within certain degrees the price is negotiable . . .'

'Tell you what I'll do – I'll ring you in the morning: you in in the morning? Yes? Right – I'll ring you in the morning and I'll make my offer. It'll be final, mind – I know this house has been on the market a while. If it's accepted, I'll get a survey straight away, get my people on to the search. If all looks good, I'll exchange as soon as you like – complete within a week, if you want. Right?'

What could Howard say? 'Right' sprang to mind, so he settled for that.

'Good,' approved Cyril Davies. And then, conspiratorially: 'Let's get *moving* on this one, shall we?'

Mrs Davies tittered. 'That was quite funny, dear.'

Cyril was perplexed. 'Was it? What was?'

'When you said *moving* . . .'

'Yes. What about it?'

'Well . . .' teetered Edna, looking very much as if she wished she'd never started the thing, 'you know: *moving* . . . ?'

Cyril looked at her briefly. 'No. Sorry. Don't get. Anyway, Mr Street – the morning, yes?

Around ten, I should think. Oh and by the way – you haven't got any lowdown on the *neighbours*, have you? I mean – what are they like, people round here?'

'If I hear anything,' promised Howard, 'I'll let you know.'

'It's *such* a beautiful day,' Edna was enthusing, as she got into the car. 'I just bet you're itching to get down to that garden on a day like this, aren't you, Cyril?'

Cyril grinned and turned to Howard with his parting shot (this in confidence): 'Mind you make sure every bloody one of them is out of there, if we go through with this. What sort of people is it anyway who want to go around collecting *manhole* covers?'

Well, thought Howard, as he slumped with relief into his own armchair – this could be a bit of good news for Brian, when he gets back – if we play it right. But God knows where on earth he's going to live then; Howard had never gone into the extent of Brian's liabilities, but he knew that things were far from good.

The phone rang just as Zoo-Zoo entered the room – he had the easy amble of a mannequin, to Howard's eyes. As Howard went for the phone, he opened wide his eyes and pointed to the whisky decanter (*would* you?)

'Katie! Hello. Surprise. Everything all right? Having fun?'

'Yes fine, Daddy. Everything's great. Look, Daddy – you know my Amex card?'

'Oh *God*, Katie – how much this time?'

Zoo-Zoo placed a large glass of Scotch, touch of water, into Howard's ready and eager hand. Howard caught his eye, and now was pointing to his aching shoulder – been bugging him all morning.

'It's just that, well – Chicago is a *very* expensive place, and I *know*' – going gooey – 'you want me to enjoy myself and you *are* the very best and sweetest Daddy in the whole wide world . . .'

'Yes, all right, Katie – never mind all that: get to the point.'

Zoo-Zoo had found the spot on Howard's shoulder and he kneaded it well, and Howard was softly sighing because he needed it badly, and now Katie's squawk was again alive in his ear.

'Could you maybe up the limit a bit, Daddy? To say – eight thousand?'

'Eight –!'

'Oh *please*, Daddy? Lovely sweet Daddy?'

'Oh God all *right*, then, blast you Katie. What will you do when I'm dead and gone, hey? Ooh Katie, by the way – I've just been showing people round Brian and Dotty's – I think they're seriously interested.'

'God – about time. I thought that would be one of the ones we'd *never* get rid of.'

Zoo-Zoo's fingers were now at the nape of

224

Howard's neck, and it was all he could do to stop his gurgling.

'Oh and Katie, now you're on the line – have you been hearing anything on the grapevine about Norman, at all?'

'*Nor*man!' she sang out – and that stopped him dead in his tracks: Norman had been idling his lips around Katie's nipples, as she had instructed him to do, alternating between gently nibbling on first this one, then that – which, she had made clear, was the way she liked it, right? Now he goggled up at her in not quite fear – well, looking at it, *was* quite fear: pure and uncut.

'What *sort* of thing?' pursued Katie, grinning at Norman and actually licking her lips in a wouldn't-you-like-to-know way which was already frankly killing him. 'Really?' queried Katie. '*Really*? No – news to me, Daddy. Yes. Yes well – you know what Norman's *like*.'

This sent the lad into paroxysms: he was up and striding around the room batting his arms in mute frustration and mouthing at Katie *What? What? What am I like?*'

'Actually no,' went on Katie, quite chattily. 'Probably somewhere ghastly like Bognor or Magaluf, knowing Norman. He didn't actually tell me where he was going. You'll just have to talk to him when he gets back next week – I'm sure there's an explanation. Anyway, Dad – Ellie and me are going out soon, so . . . yeah: yeah: you too, Daddy – and thanks *so* much for the – yeah. Love you lots. Bye!'

The second the receiver touched base, Norman was on to the case – you bet he was: Christ, you know – this could be life-on-the-line-time!

'What? Tell me – what? *What*? What about me? What? *Answer*, damn you – what? Has he found out about us? Oh God – he's found out about us, hasn't he? How did he find out? *You* didn't tell him, did you? Did you, Katie? God knows you're capable of anything. Oh Christ' – white knuckles between off-white teeth, now – 'he'll kill me. You do know that? He'll *kill* me, kill me: he *trusted* me. Oh Christ. I feel so awful.'

Katie sighed. 'Oh don't be such a *prat*, Norman! Come on – get changed: we're going out. It's nothing to do with *us* – Daddy thinks I'm here with *Ellie*.' Katie smiled. 'It's funny – I've grown quite fond of Ellie: miss her. I think I'll send her a postcard: "Dear Ellie, wish you were here." Oh *God*, Norman – you're not wearing *that*, are you?'

'Well what was he *saying*, then? How did my bloody name come up? Huh? Oh God *tell* me, Katie, for the love of God.'

'All he *said* was,' said Katie, placatingly, 'was that he'd heard from Steve Torrington at Bixby's that you'd been bleeding the company dry. That's all. Nothing to *worry* about.'

Norman went pale: quite an achievement, as seven-eighths of the blood in his body had been sloshing around his ankles since, oh – since his bloody name came up, really.

'And as you obviously *haven't* been, there's

nothing to worry about, right? Now come on, Norman – let's go. Do you really *have* to wear that awful thing?'

Norman nodded, wide-eyed and slowly – as if acceding to his own execution had mystifyingly become the best and inevitable option from among a fanned handful of plenty of others on offer. 'It's not *that* awful,' came a voice from nowhere, as he glanced down at the acetate bomber with BULLS on the back. I am, he thought, finished then. 'Anyway – I don't have much of a choice.'

Which, if he was actually talking attire, here (difficult to know – the man's mind is in some disarray, just currently), was pretty much the truth: he was still down to the stuff he had bought from the impromptu and disgraceful little shop which had by now almost certainly ceased trading, because just one hour before, give or take, Norman had fielded a call from a very nice American woman on behalf of the airline who had brightly informed him that she had good nooze and bad nooze:

'Well, Mr Furnish, your case did eventually turn up – in Dallas.'

'Ah!'

'Unfortunately, Security didn't like too much the look of it, Mr Furnish – I have the notes, someplace. Anyway, I have to tell you it was destroyed in a controlled explosion.'

'Oh.'

'We can offer you the standard forty dollars

227

compensation – yeah? But your insurance should cover the true value – kay?'

'Mm.'

Norman had hung up thinking well, at least she doesn't Wish I Had A Nice Day; mulling it over, forty bucks is probably over the odds, considering the contents. Can I have it now, please?

'Well,' said Katie – back in the real world – 'since darling Daddy has come through with more dosh, I could be sweet and buy you something really cool – but I'm not going to, I'm going to spend it all on *me*! Come on, Norman – put together whatever you can and just try not to look *too* bloody awful. The night is young!'

Lucky old night, thought Norman: I feel fucking medieval.

As the evening wore on, so the bar in The Excelsior Hotel seemed to become much larger and yet more intimate as the tables thinned out and couples and parties had drifted to dinner. Elizabeth could see dappled reflections of all aspects of Lulu in the smoky mirrored columns, which winked back elliptical glimpses too of shadily soft and glowing lamplight, hinting at a deep plush and wine-coloured sanctuary. They had both agreed about one-and-a-bit bottles ago that neither of them was pushed either way as regards dinner; between them they had made severe inroads into various deep glass bowls once brimming with olives (black, yes – but also the small, yielding and just-sour green ones, pouting pimento); pretzels, too – and fat and oily salted commas of cashew.

'At first, of course,' said Lulu, now – jacket undone, and sprawled back almost fabulously against the giving and downy banquette cushions – 'I quite *liked* his possessiveness. If I'm honest, I *needed* it. I was so fed up with men – oh, you know – men who once they've oh – *got* you, don't seem too much to mind what you do or where the hell you are, so long as you're around when *they* want. And when they say they'll *call* you, and you say Fine, Great, OK – *when* will you call me? And they say Oh, you know – *some* time.'

Elizabeth dipped her eyes and wagged her head in sisterly sympathy as well as a mute and ironic wonderment at just how men could be.

'And *I'd* say,' went on Lulu – emptying her glass (bit warm, bit flat – is there any more? No. Let's get some more, then) – *'I'd* say Well I'm awfully sorry but *some* time just isn't good enough!'

'Bravo,' nodded Elizabeth, her palms nearly meeting in a single clap.

'*When* – just tell me *when* you'll call, and I'll make sure I'm here. It's not *unreasonable*, is it? So they'd say a time and you'd wait like a lemon and then you'd wait longer and soon the whole bloody evening was gone and you'd be *seething*. And then if they were home late, yes? Why is he late, I'd go. He's with another woman: I'll kill him. And then you think no, don't be daft – he's just held up in traffic, that's all. And then it gets too late for

229

that, right, and you think well that's it: he is with another woman, the swine – or hang on, wait – maybe something's happened, maybe something's *wrong*.'

Elizabeth clucked her appreciation of *that* particular scenario.

'So then you think oh darling, darling, *please* be all right, be safe, I love you, please come home. And after a while you think should I phone the police or what do I do? What do you *do*? What is it that you're supposed to *do*? No one ever tells you. Maybe he's been attacked – maybe he's in a crash: maybe he's *dead* and here you are cursing him. Then you get back to the other woman – you can almost *see* her, now – almost smell her. And you hate her – you hate her hair and her eyes and the way she moves and the scent of her and the way that she's taken away your man – and Christ, she maybe doesn't even *exist*, this woman, and you're going absolutely *crazy*. And then you think well if I've got a choice, I'd prefer the bastard was *dead*. In the long run, it's easier, isn't it?'

Elizabeth snorted out a too-true chortle. 'Do you think we dare a nightcap? Too naughty?'

'I'd *love* just another glass, actually, Lizzie. Lizzie – I'm not *boring* you, or anything? I mean – I don't mean to –'

'Lulu,' said Elizabeth, softly and certainly, 'I can't *remember* when I've had such a good evening. It's so good to talk to someone who really *understands*.' And then, more reflectively: 'Course, *I've* been married so long now, I can't even quite *remember* why I . . . I mean, Howard is perfectly *sweet*, of course, but –'

'But they don't really *get* it, do they? Any of them.'

Lulu caught the eye of a waiter, and with one stiff forefinger indicated in turn each of their glasses, smiled briefly, and then swiftly returned to the burning issue.

'Then when I met John – oh God, it couldn't have been more different! He went with me everywhere – shopping, theatre, all the things men are completely hopeless at. Phoned me three times a day, sent flowers for no reason at all – never left my side. I was in heaven!'

'I can understand,' smiled Elizabeth. 'Dream man!'

Lulu nodded, and then she shook her head. 'Well,' she said more softly, 'as it turns out, no. Not.'

The waiter arrived with a further bottle of champagne in a silver bucket, glistening with the cold, a stiff white shawl about its shoulders. Lulu glanced with amused consternation at Elizabeth's face, her eyes mugging *Jesus he's brought us a bottle*, did we *mean* a bottle, but all she saw there was a what-the-hell and indulgent drop of the lids and that relaxed her, so she just watched the man pour it.

'He's so terribly *insecure*, that's the trouble. He hates his job, which doesn't help. Doesn't let me go to work any more, predictably: might *meet* someone. God – if you can believe it, he even doesn't like it when the milkman comes!'

Elizabeth let loose the sort of sneezy and easily uncontrollable eyes-tight-shut and fizzing laughter that tends to be part and parcel of three bottles of Moët (it comes free inside) and that set Lulu off as well. For a time, if you had closed your eyes to the semi-stifled wheezes issuing down from their two tightly-held noses, the effect would have hurtled you back in time to the great days of Steam. There was the wiping away of tears to come (with mouths held ajar), much languid sighing and a weak 'oh God' or so, yet. When things were once more on a relatively even keel, Lulu swigged champagne and set off again:

'He's a journalist – did I say? Well: *journalist*. He writes these endless sort of middle-brow articles for the glossies – you know: 100 Things To Do With £100, crap like that – and he gets roped into all their ghastly promotions, and things. Anything they're plugging, he has to go into raptures about. Must be pretty awful. I don't know if he's a *real* writer, or anything. I've never known. I've never really wondered. Anyway. Our second anniversary at the end of the year. I don't know. This – *jealousy*, though, Lizzie: it's just become crazy, now. It's a mania. It's totally mad because I don't actually *want* anyone but John, not really. It's never even crossed my mind.'

'But,' qualified Elizabeth, 'you can't go on like this.'

Lulu let her head sag down – gave in to the full insistent weight of her head. 'No,' she said, quietly. 'No.'

'Howard doesn't seem to care what *I* do. Or where I go. I'm not quite sure if I mind. I don't think I do. Maybe I do, I don't know. When you've been married a long, long time, you just sometimes don't *know* any more. About anything, really.'

And then the shadowy reflection in Elizabeth's eyes flicked back up into light as she glanced across the bar towards the big glass doors, wedged open.

'Colin!' she hailed. 'Colin, my sweet! Come! Lulu – I didn't, did I? No I didn't. This fine lung man – *young* man, I mean: oh God – *lung* man – Lulu and I have been extremely naughty, Colin, boozing and gossiping. Anyway – this is Colin, my friend Dotty's boy, and Colin, this is my *new* friend Lulu. She was here earlier – 'member?'

Colin lobbed over half a bobby-dazzler of a grin in Lulu's direction (he was pretty knackered, if he was honest, and also he had *things* to think of – and plus, in the morning, he was due to man the high seas – Christ, hope it isn't choppy; anyway, Lulu didn't really qualify for the whole damn thing – Elizabeth did, sure, but you didn't squander it on just anyone, this thing).

'Do you *want* anything, Colin?' asked Elizabeth in a tone so broadly encompassing as to infer that anything up to and including all the tea in China

233

might well be on the agenda, and all he had to do was say the word. 'No? Sure? *Quite* sure? Well look, Colin – I'll just give you the – where's the . . . God, I was sure I had it in my bag: I remember *putting* it there . . . oh God, *there* it is – staring me in the face all the time. Right, Colin – here's the key: you go on up and get a good night's sleep, yes? If there's anything you need just ring down, hmm? I'll be as quiet as a mouse when I come up: promise. Don't lock. Sweet dreams.'

Colin strolled away to the lift thinking You can make as much bloody noise as you like, Elizabeth – why don't you leap on me screaming, and proudly bare your fine woman's torso? Please yourself, of course: it's just a suggestion. And talking of Elizabeth – I wonder how Katie's tits are doing? Wonder what they're up to.

Doing good, boy! Doing just fine: just you watch 'em go – dancing away along with just every other part of her in the hot and heaving depths of a moody blues bar snug at the base of a pink neon-lit spiral staircase in downtown Chicago. Deep bass Muddy Waters throbbed up to the curved and low-vaulted ceiling and slithered down raw brick walls to ooze around soulful soles, each jerked and then luscious inflection of the groovers' bodies taking up most of the slack. Katie – sinuous, now – was lost in sinful pleasure; Norman, for his part, was simply lost.

He had been dispatched to the rear to bring back

more Buds. And it wasn't difficult – you fought your way through the throng (smiling apology, stonewalling the reciprocal scowling) and then there was a sort of a dog-leg bend at the end and through a little arch and there was the bar. Had to shout your bloody head off, of course, because the volume of the music was such that Norman's skull, for one, had long ago been rendered as glue from all those thick and sticky blues. Getting back, however, was altogether a different matter. Norman could have sworn that he had retraced his steps, but somehow had landed up somewhere altogether else – some bit of the club he had never even seen before with large glass and coloured lamps that were not so much flashing as sulkily pulsating like the eye of a frog. Norman didn't frankly care for the place – couldn't remember the name of it, but no matter: this was just not at all Norman's sort of place – as he had said to Katie, fairly and squarely, right at the outset.

'I don't *think* so, Katie . . .' he had said, doubt and reluctance hanging there heavily like twin bed curtains – plain as day for anyone to see and then swish away to the side, if they had a mind to: not Katie, though.

'What do you mean you don't *think* so – you don't think *what*, Norman? This place came recommended. Meant to be one of the best blues joints in the entire state of Illinois.'

Norman was eyeing the narrow and shadowy street, only the club's pink and unreal neon thrown back from the slimy sidewalk. The taxi had been ages getting here, wherever they were (still hadn't got a bloody map) – and Norman had made plain that he had been more than happy in the *last* place – the place with all those gorgeous young girls serving you burgers and beers. God – Norman had never seen anything like it: Hooters, it was called, and all the waitresses – what they wore, all they wore, right, were tiny little sawn-off T-shirts with an owl printed on the front and the legend 'Hooters' (how they got away with it, Norman supposed) and there were to be no prizes for guessing just where the huge and googly eyes occurred, no indeed (young Colin would have simply passed out). Add to this heady mix very brief and shiny orange shorts and white trainers and socks and multiply by a factor of maybe forty and you had a situation which was more or less guaranteed to bring a lump to your throat, and that was just for starters. And (being American) most of the girls had looked about twelve – perfect and honed, honeyed limbs; of course (being American) they could equally have been a bussed-in contingent of hugely cosmeticized and restructured pensioners – but who, at this moment, actually cared too much, huh? Not Norman – he had liked it there. Hadn't, admittedly, extracted all the welcome goodness on offer from his half-pounder with double melted Monterey Jack and ice-cold Miller Lite (on account of he had kept on altogether missing his mouth) – but look, you could eat and drink *anywhere*, right? This was more of a spectator sport thing, surely.

Katie had been unimpressed with both the place and the girls; according to her, every one of them was deformed. She kept on pointing out bony ankles, big feet, sticky-out ears, uneven teeth, dyed hair, chewed fingernails, bumped noses and all manner of defective bits and pieces that to Norman's way of thinking were totally and utterly irrelevant, not to say invisible: it seemed to him that in between all these (wholly illusory) buck teeth and rabbit ears at one end and size twelve flippers at the other, a whooole lot of big compensation was going on. Anyway, they left (of course they did: Norman didn't want to, Katie did) and then they descended into the hell of whatever this place they were in *now* was called (of course they did: Norman didn't want to, Katie did) and here he was still awash among millions of dankly perspiring and so-cool cats clutching a couple of simmering Buds and beginning to slightly panic (and then *truly* panic, no bones about it) about just where it was that Katie might be, and whether he'd ever set eyes on the woman again.

Norman was aware now of a large, red and shiny face peering down and pressing itself ever closer to his, and now this man was snarling:

'You *pushing* me, boy?'

'Pushing?' checked Norman (although of course he'd heard, of course he had – it's just that when fear is piled sky-high on top of panic, you play for time, don't you? Final cigarette before you're blown away – so why not make it a kingsize, and suck on it long and slowly?) 'No – sorry – I'm *being* pushed. From behind.'

Which was true: as he spoke, Norman was pressing back his rump as hard as he dared against whatever swell it was propelling him further towards Mr Fury, here – felt like nothing so much as one of those jolly and long-suffering bobbies with tilted helmets who linked arms to hold back surges of prepubescent girls in those heady early days of Beatlemania.

'Just back *off*,' warned the angry guy, splaying stiff and wide his fingers and thumb and placing them five-square across Norman's chest, then exercising no more than a twanging flick – but enough to send Norman careering backwards as far as the crush would allow, only to ricochet away from some other mammoth and rock-hard body back towards his new-found chum who by now was looking dangerously as if he might be close to toying with the suggestion that the two of them should maybe just step outside (boy) and settle this thing man to man and once and for all; which would have been fine except that Norman (boy) did not currently have a single man about his person, and it is difficult to project quite how this confrontation might have been concluded (not well, it is fair to say) had a blissfully familiar voice not just then assailed him.

'Norman!' bawled Katie. 'Where in Christ's name have you *been*?'

'Hither and yon!' screamed back Norman, who had now dropped a bottle of Bud perilously close to King Kong's foot, so he was mighty eager to be hustled away, depend on it. Katie tugged his arm, and the rest of him followed keenly.

Katie took him to a small and dim area which in context could maybe have passed for an oasis of calm – there were inches to the left of Norman, inches to the right of him – and to make himself heard he had only to bark like a (hoarse) seal.

'Norman,' said Katie, her eyes agleam, 'this is Rick.'

'Is it?' asked Norman, while having no concrete reason to doubt the girl's word. He looked up at this new thing called Rick (maybe this was a club only for blues fans who resembled seven-foot cylinders of sinew, and Norman had slipped in unnoticed?)

'Rick,' went on Katie, 'has been telling me about Chicago at night. Everything's fabulously lit up, apparently, and there's this amazing fountain and the colours keep changing. He's got his car right outside.'

'Ferrari,' put in Rick.

'Oh – I don't *know*, Katie,' came back Norman, with large foreboding. I mean Christ, he was thinking, this person could be just *anyone*, couldn't he? And anyway – Ferrari: bit of a squeeze for three. It was as Katie gathered up her bits and the two of them turned their back on Norman and made for the stairs that he became aware of the seepage of an inkling that there was maybe a subtext lurking here that he had quite possibly missed out on the first time around.

As his heart and various other assorted organs jostled at his throat in their reckless bid for freedom, so did Norman put down his remaining bottle of Bud just anywhere handy, and more frenzied than he could have imagined, canter after the retreating pair and half-lost sight of them, his lips twitching into the formation of semblances of words which so far his brain would have nothing to do with. He didn't catch up with them until they were outside, and twice Norman had banged his shin badly on the spiral staircase because OK, *yes* he had approached the thing faster than was prudent, but pink neon, let him tell you, may be all very pretty and good, but it contributed absolutely nothing by way of illumination, that was for sure.

'Katie!' he said breathlessly, holding on to her elbow. 'Katie – you're not, I mean – you're not *seriously* . . . ?' And his face was now at war with the mind behind, becoming as elastic as that of a marionette in its super-duper effort to convince either or both of them that here was just the gag to end all gags, yes? This was not (couldn't be) a serious proposition?

'You'll be OK, Norman!' laughed Katie. 'You've got the name of the hotel written down, and you've got money and everything.'

'But *Katie* –' was all Norman could manage, this time.

'Here,' offered Rick, waving ten bucks in his face. 'Buy yourself a Popsicle for the journey.'

Norman was stung by this and he set his face and took a step towards Rick with fists clenched, before altogether coming to his senses and taking two steps backwards, pronto.

'Don't, Rick,' said Katie, softly, touching his arm (touching his arm!) 'I'll see you later, Norman. Don't worry. Bye!'

Katie was slipping into the low Ferrari, the splice of pink neon dancing all over the glossy redness for an instant recalling to Norman all the comfort of Heinz Spaghetti on toast before he quickly snapped out of all that and made a dive for the door handle and now he was imploring:

'*Katie* –?!'

'Look, buddy.' Word came down from the mountain that was Rick. 'I've been nice so far, huh? Mr Nice Guy. You be nice too, hm?' And then he bent low and whispered darkly into Norman's ear: 'Else I got friends here who'll break your fuckin' bones, one by one: capeesh?'

As the gurgling engine pulled the Ferrari away and the tail-lights twinkled back scorn at Norman (just standing there) so the feelings of intense disbelief took him over utterly. I *love* this girl: I *love* her. What is it in Christ's name that she is doing? What if something *happens* to her? What if . . . ? Oh my God. She has gone. Gone. Katie, whom I love (we are on *holiday* together, for God's sake – we're meant to be *together*), has just sailed

241

off with a perfect stranger – who threatened to damage *me*.

(And I doubt whether it would have helped Norman to know that although, yes, Rick was a stranger, he wasn't actually a *perfect* stranger on account of he and Katie had already met, just once before: on the plane, in point of fact, while Norman had been nursing an erection full of hope in the dull steel and trembling lavatory – soon to be the recipient of copious expectoration down to a shocked old American in a baseball cap with Coca-Cola on the front – so had Katie been the subject of attention of an oh-so-cool and young American in a Brioni suit, who just happened to have a duplex in Chicago overlooking Lake Michigan, and there's this blues club, honey, that I can tell you is the best in town: meet me there Toozeday, ten o'clock; here's my card. Ciao, baby.)

Norman stood on the pavement. People passed him on their way into the club, glanced at him nervously: in this city, nobody but nobody just *stood*. But what else could Norman do? How did this happen? How has this come about? Why is it that whatever I do, the pain is always mine? I don't *want* to get hurt: don't *want* to. And then he heard the very words in the quickly cooling air now tingling around his ears: Don't Want To Get Hurt – too right, I don't. Maybe here is delirium: I think that whatever I feel, however huge the hurt, I must get a cab back to the hotel: entrench myself and wait.

'You hear me, man?'

Norman turned to this same wheedly voice, more insistent, now. A small, thin and hostile man in a shiny black windcheater stood very close to him; his fists were thrust forwards into vertical pockets, forming aggressive buffers. Norman could only look at him with a degree of puzzled enquiry.

'I *said*,' said the man, slowly, 'you don't want to get *hurt*, right? Now you just walk into that little side alley there, guy, and you're gonna be just fine.'

Norman was shaking, even before he had worked out the full impact of this. He walked into that little side alley there – he must have, he must have, because down its dark and narrow gauge he now surely found himself.

'Just turn to the wall,' the man said. 'I gotta knife.'

Norman stared at the rough, crudely distempered brick-work. This, he thought, could well be the very last thing I ever see.

'Now just hand me back all the money you got, mister. Don't hold back on me, now: I gotta knife.'

Norman fumbled in pockets. He was actually thinking I mustn't pull out the money too quickly, too jerkily, because then everything else will come too and then there will be a comb and some mints and a hanky all over the pavement. Sidewalk.

He handed back all he had – about three hundred

dollars, not much more. Maybe he should have taken up Rick's offer of an extra ten.

'You sure that's all?' queried the man. 'OK. I'll trust you.' And then, in lighter tone, slapping the back of Norman's bomber jacket (which made him leap as if electrified): 'Hey – you support the Bulls! Nice! Everyone in Chicago loves a guy who backs the Bulls!'

Then he raised something dull and weighty in the air, and brought it down heavily on to the back of Norman's neck; he watched as Norman jerked once, pitched forward into the wall, and crumpled on down to the ground.

'Me,' said the man more quietly, grinning with malevolence and tucking away a wrench, 'I'm from outta town.'

'It's weird,' whispered Lulu. 'This room is absolutely identical to ours.'

'Sit,' whispered back Elizabeth (Colin, she had reminded Lulu, during their teetering journey down the corridor, is sleeping just next door). 'God, I'm exhausted. But in a nice way.'

Lulu perched herself on the corner of the bed.

'I'm going to have a beast of a hangover, tomorrow,' she smiled. 'I don't care. Thanks so much, Lizzie, for – everything. I've loved this evening. I don't really want to go back. Dreading it. He'll just go on and on.'

'Stay here!' suggested Elizabeth. 'It's like Musical Chairs tonight, so you might as well. If I know Melody *she* won't be back tonight: new man.'

Lulu shook her head. 'I'd love to. Oh *God* I'd love to – but it would only make it worse. Christ – the explaining I'm already going to have to do is bad enough . . . if I was away all *night* . . .'

'Maybe he's asleep.'

Lulu could only snort at that. 'Joking,' she said. 'No,' sighed Lulu, rising and sucking in her stomach and patting it flat, 'got to go. Good night, Lizzie,' she said, moving to the door.

'You sure, now? You're very welcome if you want.'

Lulu smiled. 'Really,' she said, leaning forward to kiss Elizabeth lightly on the cheek – was half into the impulse to draw back and make for the other side of her face, but didn't: hovered there for just a second. She felt Elizabeth's soft touch on her shoulder, and flicked up her eyes to reassure herself that Elizabeth's eyes dwelt deeply on hers, as she knew they did. Their lips just touched, but the warmth that flooded into Lulu when she barely increased the pressure was both lush and shocking.

'Good night,' she said quickly, slipping out of the door, which closed noiselessly behind her.

Elizabeth stayed there in the stillness of the room, but turned away when she could not truly know what it was she was listening for. As she walked across the room, the pad of her forefinger was pressed into the centre of her lips. Very gently,

245

she eased open the door into the sitting room: there was Colin's form, long and angular, barely discernible in the hugeness of the surrounding gloom. He looked, thought Elizabeth, even taller – infinitely more elegant – recumbent, like that. She had only ever once before seen him lying down, and that was on the beach – seemed days ago, but wasn't: only hours – when she had urged into his skin with insistent fingers cool and protective cream. And he wouldn't turn over. Elizabeth took one step into the room, and then checked herself. She turned away quite quickly, and the door closed after her more or less as silently as it had opened.

Colin's eyes flew wide open. He had been so aware of the swishing of her clothes, the rich and feminine scent of her. Oh Christ *why* did growing up take so bloody long? How could he know what he felt, but never know what he should *do* with it? He sighed, and looked up at the dusky ceiling. His hand strayed yet again back down over his stomach to nestle between his legs. He stroked himself as he would a panicked friend who craved assurance, who needed to be calmed. When people like Elizabeth and Katie and Carol go to bed (alone) do they touch their secret places as I touch mine? Maybe they do; maybe we are all locked into the warmth of night, caressing the parts that others dream of.

In the corridor, it was maybe the full flush of champagne that washed over Lulu; she was red and heady, tired and dazed and yet charged with an energy that made her eager to be back in her room, now, dealing with whatever she found there. Was it silly to wait for the lift? Only one floor, after all (the whole too-hot, softly silent landing smelt of new carpet and maybe lavender: why have I thought that?) She decided to take the stairs, and had turned to do just that when the lift doors rushed open and she glimpsed that hateful salesperson with – yes, that was her, wasn't it? Lizzie's friend Melody, giggling alongside, looking pretty gone. Lulu hoped she had made the staircase before either of them had noticed her.

'Who was that?' said Melody, leaning hard against Miles.

'Christ knows,' answered Miles: honestly hadn't noticed – had far more urgent matters on his mind (this woman is *hot*, I tell you).

'She gave you a hell of a look,' was all Melody had to say to that, before adding on: 'Which way, then?'

'Come on,' grinned Miles (see – told you: *hot*).

Miles was still half holding her up when they reached his room (don't think she's *too* far gone – bloody well hope not; and even if she is, even if she falls asleep, so fucking what? Just *do* it, right?) but Christ it's hardly surprising she's in a bit of a state. What an evening they'd had! What a bloody evening!

They'd started off in a pub around the corner – too early for the Meridiana, Miles had thought

247

– although you got to be careful in these seaside places: not like London. Leave it *too* late and the place is bloody closed. Melody had got rid of a couple of large Sea Breezes without any trouble at all, and while Miles pulled steadily on just the one Bacardi and Slimline (straight tonic from here on in: the idea was to get the bird smashed, not your bleeding self) and soon got around to saying all the things women always wanted to hear, Christ knew why. Miles had learned all this caper years back: tell me about yourself, why don't you; I just know there's more to you than meets the eye – you run deep; what a fabulous dress – very few girls could carry it off; what star sign are you? I knew it: we're soul mates; you're a very exciting person to be with, and yet I feel so at *home* with you – like I've known you for ages; you're not a type, that's what I like about you: really unique; I could get lost in your eyes.

By the time they got to the Meridiana, Melody was saying that if she just so much as set eyes on another glass of cranberry juice she'd throw up for sure, so it was straight vodka on the rocks after that. She had not so much danced as undulated before him – and when she raised her arms high and vertical above her head and pouted in fat-lipped kisses to the beat of the music, wild hair striping her face, all men gazed at her, their half-lidded eyes semi-veiling not quite covert thoughts.

The upside of being out of London, of course, is that when the nitespot of the moment finally clicked on bright and unfriendly lights and politely asked the diehard stragglers to please remember that this was a residential area, and could they please refrain from undue noise and car door slamming on leaving the premises – well then, there was truly nowhere else to go at all, and so it was back to the hotel and let's see, shall we (I think we will), whether all that Smirnoff Black Label was worth the bloody candle.

Miles managed the lock like a master, and as soon as they were inside the room Melody turned to pinion him against the door, and really quite roughly tugging on the short hairs at the back of his neck, she drew his face down to hers and kissed him so hard on the mouth that his teeth felt compressed and his lips quite bruised. Melody broke away and walked reasonably steadily further into the large and cool, nearly dark room. She took in the drawn curtains, the single lamp on way over there and the vast and mirrored wardrobe doors. She took in also the naked and sprawling girl, arms spread in supplication and handcuffed to the bedhead, huge and rolling eyes that were imploring, and a black gag that forced open her mouth into a grotesque and gummy grin. Miles noticed only Melody's silence, and came forward to join her.

'Oh Christ yeah,' he muttered. 'Shit. I'd forgotten all about *her*.'

He stepped up to the bed and released the silk scarf from the back of the girl's head.

'You still here, then?' he attempted (best in

this sort of situation, isn't it, to try to lighten it up?) But the receptionist – what was her name? Pauline – yeah, Pauline, right – was not at all best pleased; you could tell this. Her mouth drew back and contorted into even worse shapes than before, and her slavering lips seemed to be arguing with one another as to just what words they would first cooperate into forming; what won was:

'Bastard! You – *Christ*, you – undo these – get these bloody –!'

Miles had one arm loose already, and Pauline – who could not look at Melody – scrabbled at just anything with which to partly cover herself. Melody – who could not take her eyes off Pauline – slumped back into an armchair, her eyes alight with amusement and a disbelieving delight at so unexpected a cabaret.

Pauline was up now and swathed in a sheet that she tripped over repeatedly in her eagerness to get to Miles and pummel on his chest, but he caught her wrists and just looked at her as she wailed:

'Let *go* of me! I *hurt*, you bastard – I *hurt*. Where in Christ's name have you –?!' At this point she whirled round to Melody and screamed: 'Stop *looking* at me, you! What are you –?!' And then back to Miles: 'What *is* this? Some sort of *relay*? What – is there another one waiting in the bloody corridor?!'

'Look,' said Miles. 'I'm sorry – er –?'

'*Pauline*, you shit!'

'Pauline, right. I just went to get some fags and

I had a drink and it just sort of slipped my mind: happens – OK?'

Pauline's eyes blazed hate and a withering disgust into Miles's whole being – which, if she had known the man (and certainly she was well down the road into a crash course of learning), she would have seen to be a complete waste of both time and effort.

'It slipped your . . . ?! I've been chained to that bloody bed for more than eight hours!' And then – glaring at Melody – 'Will you stop bloody *looking* at me! Christ I can't *believe* this! This is such a nightmare! Oh God I feel so . . . oh Jesus – I'll have lost my *job*, thanks to you.'

'Why?' said Miles. 'It was your afternoon off. You didn't have any shifts or anything: you told me.'

'*Because*,' said Pauline steadily, through tightly clenched jaws, 'every member of staff will now know *everything* – and even if I'm not sacked, which I will be – they're absolutely red-hot on just *anything* in this place, never mind . . . I'll never be able to look anyone in the *face* . . . oh Christ I wish I'd never set eyes on you, you bastard. You *bastard*.'

Pauline turned away, spent and defeated, and began to gather together her clothes.

'Will you,' she spat at Melody, 'for Christ's sake for the last time stop bloody *looking* at me!'

'I like looking at you,' said Melody, softly. 'You're pretty.'

Pauline held the gaze for one incredulous second.

'I don't *believe* this!' she nearly screeched. 'This cannot, cannot, cannot be *happening* to me!'

Pauline continued to struggle with tights and a dress and oh Jesus where's the other bloody *shoe* – and by now she was muttering more to herself than trying to make anything even approaching a *point*.

'And I'm broke too, broke. Absolutely broke. I was *depending* on this lousy job just at least to see me through the summer . . . till college starts . . . it was only a summer thing, yeah – but what am I going to do *now*?'

Pauline was as dressed as she was ever going to be, and Melody moved over to her and placed a hand lightly on hers.

'Stay,' she said.

Pauline glanced at Melody – and Miles did too; neitherwasinanydoubtastothesuggestionsparkling all over her face. Hm, thought Miles – could be interesting: does it have legs?

'You have got to be –! Oh *Jesus*, you're both *disgusting*!'

Nuh, it don't.

Pauline made for the door, but Miles quietly intercepted her; he held out to her one hundred pounds in twenties.

'What in Christ's name do you bloody think I *am*?!' stormed Pauline.

Miles cocked an eyebrow. 'Broke?'

Her eyes glared into his, until the flicker of indecision took her; Pauline snatched the money and would have been out of there for good if only she could have managed the bloody *lock*.

Miles went over to help. 'Look,' he said, in as caring a tone as ever he would achieve in his lifetime, 'I don't see why you think anyone will know about this – I mean, no one here's going to mention it, are they? And you weren't late for work or anything, so –'

'I'll *tell* you,' cut in Pauline. 'I'll tell you *exactly* how everyone in this entire bloody *town* is going to know. *Because*' – and here Pauline's face slightly caved in – '*because*, hours and hours ago when I was just lying there, just bloody gagged and chained and *lying* there, a chambermaid called Clothilde in complete bloody silence and without even *looking* at me turned down the counterpane and put two fucking mints on the *pillow*!'

This was very much the limit for Melody, and although both her palms were well advanced in their journey up to her mouth (maybe someone should gag her) the belly rumble of unstoppable laughter was now a shriek and then a hooting that filled the room and Miles's face squirmed up sideways almost immediately and he was honking down his nose as Pauline with mouth agape just stared at one and then the other before stamping out and slamming the door behind her. Before its juddering had quite faded away (God knows what the people in the next room were making of all this

– depends on the people, Miles supposed) Melody had suddenly come at him from way over there and her leg had hooked around the back of his own and it seemed as if her face was bent on devouring him, as her white hands pressed into his cheeks and urged his whole mouth to be eaten by hers. He made a token movement towards the bed but a breathless denial from Melody, followed by the shedding of her skirt made it clear that this was to be here and now and hard and fast and her hands were moulding him as she spun around and threw her back against the wall so he came up into her and gripped her hair and with each hard thrust of him the air was beaten out of her as her shoulders crashed back and she dragged nails across his jaw as she made as if to squat while pulling him up and pulling him in and so as the gasps thudded out of him, as the gurgle in his throat fought with the lunatic heartbeat, so then did Melody's own gasping become a brief sigh and then short, shocked shrieks were coughed out as both their eyes were opening wide with wonder and ready for the killing, and finally the shuddering that electrified and flooded him made saplings of his buckling thighs but not until Melody was done with clenching him, not until her own great gushing allowed him to stagger, not until then could they slide off each other's sweat and slither to the ground in an entanglement of white-hot breath and quite spent limbs – and now with just the heavy stench of all that discharged lust to warm them,

254

they slowly began to recede into the cool of their own beings, until behind heavy and dragged down lids, damping down the fire of frenzy, still Melody's eyes were alive and dancing.

See – told you: *hot*.

Later, much later – so much later that lateness had almost run its course and lay poised upon succumbing to the raw and the new – Miles and Melody lay in a jumble of sleep across the breadth of the bed, she silent while he was deeply droning. Farther along another humming and twi-lit corridor, the weight of alcohol and fatigue had finally clasped hold of Elizabeth, and she too lay in oblivion; just one door away, Colin had been vanquished in his unequal struggle with both the fever of the night and the threat of morning, and so his body had long ago surrendered to sleep, as his flickering dreams took his mind on journeys.

Dotty would have been pleased to know that her son was at least at rest – he needed it, didn't he? He needed it. Just like little Dawn. People maybe forgot, did they, that if a baby lay trapped in redness and heat and screaming at night, then it was not just those who were struck awake who became the victims – the baby, ultimately, was stranded too. But not tonight: no, not tonight. Tonight, the only one who had not so much as closed her eyes, who had not winked into sleep for even just a second, was Dotty herself – and nor would she till the dawn became warm, when she would ready herself for the baby's twitching and blissful arousal. Dotty had been gazing, just gazing endlessly at this little being, with an intensity that was utterly total.

Brian knew this because he had been watching her, silently dabbing his eyes and invisibly watching her. He had seen Dotty in the grip of such ardour before, but here was no sense of vigilance – her rapt concentration had none of the exhausted dissipation, nor the acute and heart-clutching anxiety of those pained and endless nights when she had pined for the soul of her little Maria. Dotty was in love – this was all she had ever wanted – and Brian, from his not too distant bunker, was well aware of all she felt. For his part, all he could feel was in the way: the sense of loss was all over him. Tomorrow, he thought (or today, it must be), was as good a moment as any other to settle all that – and this time it must be once and for all: I just simply can't face it any more, and nor can I face it again.

Finally, too, Lulu had been dragged away: sleep had been tugging at her for hours and years, but John was not about to give her up – he had her now, he had her back, and not yet if ever would he yield her up to a higher power.

'Please, John, *please*,' she had pleaded, just the sound of her own faint and fractured voice filling her with tiredness and pity. 'I've told you and I've *told* you – I've just got to get some *sleep*. You said you were sorry, you said it, Johnny, and now you're doing it all over again – I just can't stand it, John, I just can't *bear* any more, not tonight.'

'I just have to be *clear*,' said John again – still standing in the middle of the room: couldn't sit down, couldn't. They mustn't sit down, mustn't. 'I just have to get it all straight in my *mind*.'

Yes – oh yes *please*: please God just let some tiny part of this become straight (not too warped) within my mind. His eyes felt wet and large but as hard as coal. The swings his whole being had been through during the hours that Lulu had been gone at times had come close to forcing him to teeter on the verge of derangement – this made more bewildering by the passages of almost awesome lucidity that had punctuated this fraught and abandoned state: times when he had been calm and even quasi-content – had come close to smiling with self-deprecation at the blush-making scale of his folly. Then did something other start burning within him and he was up and swigging yet more whisky from an upturned bottle and fishing around in drawers and pockets for lost cigarettes and he would light one and drag it down and then he would weep quite suddenly and grind it out in an ashtray, on a table – once, when his slashed and lacerated assassin thoughts seemed to be distanced from his body by oceans and continents – into the soft palm of his hand: he gazed at the burn, but inhaled hissingly not in pain but from the realization of just what it was he had done, for no one in their right mind, surely, could do such a thing?

It was Lulu's fault that he was like he was: look at him – just *look* at him, for pity's sake. I mean, Christ – this isn't *me*, is it? I'm not some wild thing. I used to be calm – I used to be happy: beautiful wife, steady job – where has all the turmoil come from? It's her. It's her. Of *course* it's her – who else could it be? Why doesn't she *stay* with me? Why has she *gone*? Why can she not see just how much I *love* her?

And then he thought, look: look look look. Steady. *Steady*, for God's sake. You saw something, little something, in the lift. She explained: she dropped her map, she stooped to pick it up, her towel fell loose, end of story. You overreacted – wildly overreacted, just as you always do. And what then? What then did you inflict upon your fabulous Lulu? You (oh God, can't bear it, can't bear it – did I really? Yes I did) threw her around and then you – *no*. No I didn't; but you *did*. Didn't; can't have – could never do that, not ever. But you *did*. No! No . . . no. From now on, from this very moment (hear me?) I didn't. Just didn't.

And where is she? Hm? Why doesn't she come back? She's been gone for – oh Christ where *is* the fucking woman?! With a man: got to be. Of *course* she's got to be – what bloody else on earth could she be doing? Playing *bingo*? I don't think so, I don't think so – with a man, that's where she is, listening to him, watching the muscles in his face

258

working, working, as he works on her. Maybe two, maybe two men – maybe she is at the centre of a circle of manhood, a circle that gradually closes into one hard and uncompromising wall of man that has just Lulu beating at its heart. When she comes back (she will come back? Will she? Come back?) I shall *assail* her. No. No. No I shan't: I shall *adore* her, yes: kiss her tenderly and pray for her forgiveness and all will once again be well between us. *What*! Kiss her where still her cheek (*mouth*?) is alive with the kisses of so many others? I think not: I shall *assail* her, and then, maybe then, she will *understand* me (for who, what, does she think I am?)

Still haven't heard from the publishers: will I ever? Sorry? *Sorry*? What thought is this, now? It is one of my alternative thoughts, parallel thoughts – a thought that is usually with me, lurking, but has now come to save me from others. My organs are being eaten away and so I must dwell upon a crushing and nagging anxiety, rather than go on juggling with blades. I wrote that novel so that I could escape; I toiled upon it for years just as a forgotten soul in the bleakest dungeon would work away at his priceless scrap of twisted metal with a bent and rusty nail hoping one day to fashion it finally into the key that would ease open that too vast door and lead him if not somewhere, then at least to the way from here. You wait three months until you ring them; John had waited four, and still he could not dare: just to have it out there (he imagined it aloft, and hovering) is better than to have it crash back down to earth, broken but still just barely throbbing.

All this was mad talk. Mad. I must be calm. Calm and rational, because soon Lulu will walk through that door, and I shall tenderly enfold her and our eyes will meet in knowledge and in love – not one word will be said, and the bond between us will be as fine and as strong as ever it has been. But come soon, Lulu – please come soon: I cannot be alone for longer. Come *soon*, you bitch, or I'll *smash* you.

And when she did come, when finally and at last his Lulu, his wonderful, wonderful Lulu had actually stepped into the room and stood there before him, so had John cast himself, prostrated himself on the floor and sobbed and reached out for her and Lulu had said Oh Christ's *sake*, Johnny, get up for *God's* sake – what on earth do you think you're *doing*? (I'm tired, I'm tired, Johnny: please just let me go to bed and don't *do* all this.)

The interrogation, the massive accusations – these followed soon after: round and round they went, John's excited vision of Lulu's orgiastic evening cut by Lulu's gasped out incredulity – his acceptance of his insane stupidity, craven pleas for her to forget all that, forget everything I've said and her acquiescence to do that just before he whirled round and called her the whore to end all whores and how, he beseeched her, how could she bring herself to *do* this to him?

'So what was his name? There was more than one of them, yes? Was it the same man? The man in the lift? Or was it some other man entirely – a new man. Or men. Was it?'

'I've told you and I've *told* you – I've just got to get some *sleep*. You said you were sorry, you said it, Johnny, and now you're doing it all over again – I just can't stand it, John, I just can't *bear* any more, not tonight.'

'I just have to be *clear*,' said John again. 'I just have to get it straight in my *mind*. So there *was* no man – you swear? You swear it, Lulu?'

Lulu let out a sigh that was close to a muted howl.

'I *swear* it, Johnny. I swear.'

'Not even . . . not even just one look. A kiss.'

Lulu turned on him eyes that were dead and resolute.

'John: listen to me. The last man I kissed was you. I haven't kissed a *man*.'

Lulu was asleep almost before she had fully closed her eyes. John watched her in repose. Well, Lulu, that was a very nice speech, but I do hope you don't seriously believe that I have fallen for so much as one single word of it. You met some woman called *Lizzie* and you drank champagne and had a really nice chat about this and that: yeah yeah – and I've just won the Booker Prize, honey. Very funny, Lulu – big, big joke.

It must have been that man in the lift – well it was, must have been. He would have pursued her, wouldn't he? Course he would – one glimpse, one whiff of the essence of Lulu and no man could let it alone. And she will have succumbed. John had worked out all this, oh – hours before. It was just that he had needed confirmation, that was all. He had decided too that harm should come to this man, whoever he might be (and by tomorrow morning, first thing, you may depend upon it, John would know absolutely everything there was to know about this interloper, this rapist, this marriage breaker – this rat who brought with him all the slime and stench of the sewer).

And then John had thought no, it *can't* be true: you must have it wrong – it must just be a mis-understanding. Can't just *damage* a man because you imagine . . . ah but I'm *not* imagining it, am I? Not. This is *fact*: good Christ, Lulu as much as admitted it herself, the filthy little cow.

John looked at her now: beautiful, as ever, in sleep. How could so graceful and tranquil a face mask the evil she has done to me? But I have thought again about damaging this man. This was my first idea, yes, but I see now clearly that this is not the right thing to do – what do you want to go hurting him for? It's stupid, isn't it? Dumb. No – if I am to survive this – if Lulu and I are to walk away from all this in any way *clean* – then this man must die.

CHAPTER 5

The last thing Norman wanted to do was attract any more attention to himself than was, he supposed, utterly inevitable – so maybe he shouldn't have rushed into the foyer of the Sheraton Hotel, damn near tripping over his feet, as if the street outside had possibly just erupted into a ball of fire and napalm and here was the just-reached well of refuge which in those circumstances would truly have been (who could deny it?) a fully-fledged emergency. So everyone *looked*, didn't they? Did indeed – the hardly-there glance soon to deepen into out-and-out peering. And what did they see before them? Norman, but of course, his recently acquired black bin-liner protruding well below the unravelling hem of his nasty nylon Bulls bomber jacket (the T-shirt, the people at the hospital had said, was a total write-off – believe them – what with the blood, and all) and both of his hands forming a bony and makeshift yashmak, Norman's red-rimmed and hunted eyes flickering just to the north, as if sneakily peeking out at a world quite other than his own, one which maybe isn't even fit for glimpsing.

All through the night – for yes, it was early morning now (the sun was high and the sun was hot) – Norman had been frantic about just never mind *anything* but getting back to Katie. He had no idea how long he had lain in that alleyway, like so much trussed-up trash, until the flashlight and the prickle of water and the shaking of his shoulders pulled him back from where his mind and body had been resigned to slumping – and as he winced, squinted and flinched, so he became aware only of aching and a sense of displacement.

'You sit up?' he heard the man squatting down to him say. Policeman? Think so. Has to be a policeman, got up like that: black leather and more badges than a boy scout; silver shield on a cap above a glossy peak – will he direct me to Bloomingdale's? Or will he shoot me for not having been male at the airport?

'C'mon, buddy – get you cleaned up. More blood come out of you than a Texas gusher. You walk?'

Norman stood – there were two cops, two (at first he had thought it was his eyes), and round the back of him there was more hurt – not quite his head, not quite his spine, but it was all behind him, this new and dull unease.

At the hospital, Norman remembered unsmiling efficiency: he answered questions as they patched him up. All he had wanted to do was phone Katie – she'll be going crazy by now. Had she maybe already contacted the police? Missing persons?

Nope, said the cop: we'd know about that. And then it was too late for phoning – just get me back there, will you? He had run from the squad car – spun into the Sheraton, acutely aware of all the hours that had passed – and yes he was aware too of the rustle of his makeshift bin-liner shirting, but more than anything he could not for a second ignore the rigid and pinching cast that constricted his nostrils – the tug on his cheekbones from two broad strips of corset-pink sticky plaster, snaking away from his nose and clinging tight like leeches. He had risked just the briefest snatch of a reluctant half-look in the mirror, and what he saw there was quite as bad as he had feared, and somehow terribly in keeping with all he felt: fractured and taped up, as if just barely being held together.

Norman was almost literally out of breath by the time he reached the room – had to stop no more than halfway down the corridor when his door was actually within sight of not striking distance, simply because his lungs just weren't having any more: he imagined them like an old bellows whose stiff and creaking leather concertina sides were barely doing the business, wearily worked as they were by a tired old man, resignedly and with much wheezing giving it all he had got (knowing it could never be nearly enough). Norman held his heart, and denied the irksome stinging in his nose that breathing hard now brought about.

He tapped lightly at the door. Could she have fallen into fitful drowsiness – the frazzled yielding after a night of anxiety? Norman hit the door with a little more force – *open*, Katie, *open* – I have to know you're safe: you must see with your own eyes that still I am alive. Also, Katie, I must lie down: I have to get my rest. He was saying her name out loud, now – queryingly, and increasingly loudly. By the time he was pounding on the panels with alternate fists, Norman had become convinced that she had overdosed on cocaine. Then the vision of her shock-white and stiff young body, dead glazed eyes still brimming with surprise, simply galvanized Norman and he stood stock-still, strung out in this vast and silent corridor, entranced and completely incapable of more.

A chambermaid with a trolley (they had come from nowhere) eyed him remotely in some way or another: the things they heard, the things they saw, these people – how could the message on their faces ever be clear?

'I can't,' said Norman, quite piteously, 'get into my *room*.' Which was, quite simply, no more nor less than the truth, his eyes were tacking on, but please don't ask me to say another word because I just haven't got any more.

Did she understand? Or did she just want to be rid of something that surely wasn't on her schedule? Norman couldn't trouble himself to wonder – but just as she had clicked and then extracted her chained-up master from the lock, so Norman was through the door and fast closing it behind him – only now half-simpering his gratitude (so the maid who had now trundled away her trolley could never have known it, not even had she hung around, some).

The room was exactly as Norman had left it: the bed had been turned down, but otherwise untouched. He sat down heavily and his hands rushed up to his face but all he felt there was something hard and unfamiliar – but the tears, the hot and helpless tears: he was no stranger to them, and here they came again, coursing down thickly over antiseptic ridges. He roughly dashed them away (thinking I'm not about to do *that* again in a hurry – nearly had my bloody nose off altogether) and set to forcing, forcing, forcing himself to think, think, *think*. I call the manager, yes? Or the police: missing persons. Oh God oh God – I'll never *forgive* myself if anything's happened to her – I can't live without Katie, can't do it: already I feel bereft. Right: that's what I'll do, then. So why didn't he move? Phone was over there – not too much of a journey, so why didn't he move? Don't know. Don't *know*: I maybe do sort of know what to do (do I?) – but why won't somebody just do it *for* me?

Norman had barely started out of his skin at the implosion of the door before Katie was there – radiant, eager and sweet-smelling before him.

'Hi!' she sang out. 'You're up early. Christ – what on earth have you done to your face, Norman – you look absolutely *grotesque*!'

'Kadie!' he gasped. 'Oh thang *Gob*, thang *Gob*!'

267

And even while he was gasping, Norman could deny it no longer: had not even allowed the tang of suspicion to smack him until now – well look, he was already well on the wrong side of his threshold of pain, and he had been cowering away from the heat of risk, simply refusing to believe that there could be any more to come: wrong, of course – seldom safe to think a thing like that.

'Oh God you're not going to be making a noise like *that* all the time are you, Norman? What did you do to your *nose*? Is it broken? Does it hurt? Christ you are a *prat*, Norman.'

'Kadie,' said Norman quietly. 'Where hab you *bead*?'

Katie fell back on to the bed as one would into a sunlit hammock – or one would, anyway, if starring in a commercial for life assurance and making quite plain to the punter that now you've got your policies sorted out, well then all there is to be done with the remainder of your days is to spend them suspended between a couple of trees.

'I have had the most *fab*-ulous time, Norman. This is the most wonderful, thrilling city – I'm so glad we came – it's just amazing.' Katie lifted high long skeins of her hair, letting it filter away slowly from her fingers. 'Oh and Norman – apparently there's horse-drawn carriages that take you all over the city, so we can do that right now – and I've got the address of a cool sort of underground bar and a really knockout steakhouse: steaks as thick as anything, and really juicy.'

'I thawed you didden ead mead. Bud Kadie – you bead god all *nide* . . . ?'

'I only say I don't eat meat to Mummy because it drives her *mad*,' laughed Katie. 'Love it, really: steak and lamb are my favourites. Oh lighten up, Norman – we're supposed to be on holiday!'

More tears. Sorry: can't help it. They just come without notice whatever I try to do, and they're coming right now – yes, I feel it.

'*Kadie* . . .' sobbed Norman, softly. 'I *lub* you!'

'Why are you wearing a dustbin bag, Norman?'

'Do you *hear* bee? I *lub* you. Lub you lub you *lub* you!'

Katie let out a shriek of sheer pleasure as she took in Norman's patched-up and crestfallen face as she leapt up from the bed. She cooed, mock solicitously, and pinching his cheek – just this making him cry out as if burned:

'And I lub you *too*, Norman. Come on – let's get you out of this season's rubbish-wear and into something clean. What have you got?'

Norman thought that maybe drifting into automatic might save him now – protect him from all the deep down bruising, as well as the bubbling hurt.

'Nod much,' he said, fishing around among all that remained of what couldn't really be called, could they, his summer things? 'Diss D-shird. Do you *really*, Kadie?'

Katie looked at the T-shirt in frank disbelief.

269

'Christ Almighty,' she murmured. 'Do I really *what*, Norman? That is *terrible*.'

'*Lub* me – do you *lub me*?'

'No of *course* not – I keep telling you I don't: you really are terribly thick. But this is *misprinted* – I mean, I can't understand why you want to go round wearing things with slogans on in the first place – but what's this I'VE BEEN TO *HICAGO*? Huh? I mean – is it a *joke*?'

Norman shook his head – could never have conveyed the twin poles of numbness and sentience walled up behind so dull and sad an action: he just stood there and shook his head.

'Well look – use this felt pen, for Christ's sake, and stick a "C" on it, OK? At least then it won't be *quite* so embarrassing – just add a "C". And get a *move* on, Norman – I want to feel like a princess in my horse-drawn carriage! Then we'll check out that bar.'

Katie applied make-up at the mirror, and Norman took up the felt pen and held it between his fingers. Was he really about to write on his T-shirt simply because Katie had just ordered him to? Yes. Apparently so. Yes. Katie's hair appeared to be still damp from a shower; Katie's hair appeared to be still damp from a shower.

Soon she was heading the way down the corridor towards the elevator, and behind her trailed a mortally disconsolate Norman, his T-shirt beneath his blood-spattered Bulls bomber now reading I'VE BEEN TO HICAGO, SEE. Look – if it pleased the woman: what could there be left to lose?

'*The Untouchables*,' said Katie, stomping down the fruit in her cocktail with the long and translucent mixing stick. 'That was probably the most famous of them – when the pram went bouncing down all those steps at the railway station, remember?'

Norman nodded, the pad of one finger tracing the rim of his glass near maniacally (round and round, round and round – don't really want this drink, now – don't really want it): yes indeed, he remembered *The Untouchables*; maybe that's what he had become – he had maybe become one of those: an untouchable.

'But they've made absolutely loads of other films here, Rick was telling me,' chattered on Katie. 'He knows about *everything*. *Home Alone* – the one with that kid, yeah? And *North by Northwest* – God, I think Cary Grant was just *so* handsome – and *The Fugitive* and, oh God, I've forgotten them all: Hudsucker something – that was one – ooh and that *Harry Met Sally* thing, I'm pretty sure he said. I thought that film was stupid, actually – I mean, it's *obvious* you can't know a guy without sex, isn't it? What would be the *point*?'

Well if Norman had been barely hanging on to staying just this side of smashed to bloody pieces, that had surely toppled him over: I'm gone, now – fragmented. Don't much care what happens,

271

now: couldn't matter less. But I think I must *say* something.

'Barry be! Barry be, Kadie!'

Katie was halted mid-swizzle '*Huh*?'

Norman leaned forward across the small bar table with urgency, his eyes lit with need, though dimmed by supplication.

'Led's ged *barried*, Kadie – I lub you bore than anything in the word! Blease doan say dough!'

Katie's whole face was set up to rain down on Norman scorn the like of which even she had never mustered – but then something checked her and she lowered her eyes and said with heavy foreboding: *Look*. And Norman did look, of course he did – though with no sense of anticipation, no – more because a pause had to be seen to be enacted, here, for the pretty big reason that Let's-Just-Get-This-Straight was hanging in the air above them, winking off the multi-coloured spangles of the Tiffany lamp dangling on a thick bronze chain just barely over the level of Norman's fucking bloody stupid nose.

'Norman,' cranked up Katie. 'Let's just get this straight, shall we? I don't *love* you – I never have loved you, and I've never *said* I love you. Have I? Hm? I'm not sure I even knew what love *was* until . . . and as to getting *married* – well you just *have* to be joking. I'm young – I want to *see* things, *do* things, yeah? But even if I *did* want to, oh God – settle *down* – I hate that: settle *down* – yuck. But look, Norman – even if I did, it wouldn't be with *you*, would it? I told you back in London – you're around because you're *around*: it's convenient. At the moment. I mean you've got to admit – you're not too great a prospect, are you? You're not much of a *catch*. Christ – most of the time, Norman, you're just plain bloody embarrassing!'

Norman took a pull at his drink (which he did really want, now – wanted quite badly) and settled down to looking at the thing. Never mind the pain – there's plenty of time for all the pain later on (all the time in the world). Just try to focus on the *facts*, shall we? And the facts spoke for themselves, didn't they, Norman? She was right: Katie was right in what she said. Just take today – forget all the bloody cock-ups leading up to this morning, let's just look at the most recent ones: the newly-minted crop. Katie and Norman hadn't been allowed into the cool underground bar that they had spent ages tracking down (the bar where they found themselves now was very much B-grade, as Katie had not ceased to point out since first they had set foot in the place). And the reason they had not been permitted to even so much as sniff the expensive and rarefied air of this hallowed and trendy dungeon (a very dark sort of place where people went to get blind) had been that Norman was improperly dressed. Well of course he was – we know that; what with the rags and his sticky-taped plasticine face, Norman's get-up would maybe only have qualified him to compete for one of the much envied top three places in the Escaped Fucking Lunatic Of The Year contest (having earlier been found wandering, and apparently in some state of confusion – not to say the mismatched halves of jim-jams long ago abandoned by nutters of the past).

And what about the horse-drawn carriage? The carriage of Katie's dreams – what about that, then? Nightmare. First he had had to explain that he had no *muddy*, Kadie – completely broke on account of he had been robbed. All Katie had said in response to that was that he sounded so completely weird, the way he was talking with that *thing* on his nose, that it sounded to her like he'd just said he'd been *robbed*. There had been no time to go into it further, of course, because Katie was already climbing up into the bloody carriage, wasn't she? So Norman had clambered aboard too, and just before the trit-trotting had begun, one of the horses had let out the most outrageous and saxophonic fart – and although all and sundry had done the decent thing and laughed their heads off, it was only a matter of a very short while before Norman found himself behaving in a horribly similar manner – and don't even *ask* him if it was psychosomatic, or psycho-anything-else-for-that-matter: he didn't know and he couldn't have told you – all that was clear was that these derisive raspberries were ripping out of his backside like billy-o, by now, and thank Christ it's an open carriage, that's all, or else we have one asphyxiation situation on our hands here, ma'am (make no mistake about it).

274

Then it got worse: Norman knew all about sea-sick and plane-sick and car-sick – Christ, he could have written the textbook – but horse-sick was a new one. New or not, it surely had all the ripeness of venerable age and long-held tradition, and the oh-so-familiar rich and deep-down rumblings of severe and mutinous disquiet were now joining forces with the wet and cold, quite white face, and Norman was soon pleading to be let down from this at first queasy and now heartily dyspeptic gondola of unease, while meanwhile remaining wholly unable to dampen any of his new-found vigour on the flatulence front.

And you should have seen the look on Katie's face when he had to call her back to pay the man and his horse for their aborted tour – because Katie, when anything was over and done (bar the paying), had this habit of just wandering away. And then they couldn't even get into a bar simply to have a drink because, as has been said, while the bartenders wore little claret-coloured bolero jackets and big-winged bow ties, Norman carried with him all the aura of the man who had come to see to unblocking the bogs.

So yes – *not* a great prospect, was he? No great catch, let's face it: just plain bloody embarrassing, in fact. And let's look, while we're looking, at the broader issues, shall we? How much did Norman earn? Never mind how much he *stole*, let's just concentrate on salary for now. Pitifully little, is the answer. And is there any chance of more? No

– because he was unqualified to do *anything*, if he was honest. That's why he had become an estate agent; it was either that or a teacher. And property? Assets of some kind? Nope – rented a grotty little room, didn't he? Soon, no doubt, to be dumped in favour of something shamingly similar. (Why? Don't know – couldn't tell you: you live like this, you tend to move on.) As to *stuff*, well – there never had been much, but as we already know, whatever had once existed was now just history on account of he had hocked it all in order to buy for Katie the latest fripperies of the day. The very same Katie who now sat across the bar table from him, scowling, and telling him in no uncertain terms that no, Norman I *don't* love you – I never have loved you and I've never *said* I love you. Have I?

No – no, it must be said you haven't. And nor ever did the only other woman with whom I have had what may or may not be termed a serious relationship (was his relationship with Katie serious? One-sided, certainly – he tended to find himself in tears, while Katie just went on laughing in his face: it was seriously *something*). And did I say to this woman, the other woman – the first woman – that I loved her? Yes – almost from day one and every day that followed. Well, I had kissed her by then, hadn't I? And that set up some sort of jangly feeling within that might just as well be love – well mightn't it? But as usual, I wanted commitment – she didn't, it almost goes without saying (because yes, since you ask, all this business about prospects and being any

276

sort of a catch – yes, all that had come up and gone down). And then suddenly (there *were* reasons, but I can't really get into it all now because I am after all trying to keep together this *Katie* thing at the moment – don't quite understand why I'm going back on all this stuff at all, really) I found myself, yes – more or less committed to her, and she to me. But I didn't like it. Didn't like it as much as I thought I would: didn't, in truth, care for it one little bit. And yet I want it again, and yes I want it now – which is why, I suppose, I have just asked Katie to barry be – and in addition to my most obvious shortcomings (which Katie doesn't even have to list or recollect, because manifestations of just about all of them continue to bombard her on an almost hourly basis) maybe she smells just what it is I am. If so, I deeply wish she'd tell me, because I am sure that I have not the slightest insight into even so much as my nature.

'Anyway, Norman,' Katie was saying now, 'I've got to shoot. See you back at the hotel later on, yeah? Only I don't quite know when.'

Norman looked up, jogged from his reveries and slapped by this.

'Where are you . . . ?'

'*Told* you, Norman – this amazing steak place. I'll be late if I don't go now – and I don't think Rick is the kind of guy who likes to be kept waiting! Do you know what we ate last night? Shiitake crab cakes – the most fantastic tower of ratatouille, crab, shiitake mushrooms – they're amazing – and a slice of really crispy dried tomato, all stuck on a sort of dagger thing with zigzags of yellow pepper sauce and, um, green basil oil, I think he said.'

All Norman could utter was:

'God dough muddy, Kadie: bead robbed.'

Katie was standing, and very much in I'm-outta-here mode; opened her mouth to maybe say something – but look, there just isn't the time to get into it all, is there? Christ – bloody Norman: he really can be such a fucking *drag*. She dropped a hundred-dollar bill on to the table just next to his hand and didn't wait for any reaction. It would have been a long wait: Norman was fresh out of reaction.

He continued to sit there, long after she'd gone. Must have been a fair while because some guy – barkeep – had said 'Getchanother drink?' and Norman had said Yeah; he was back in what seemed like no time at all with his 'Getchanother drink?' – and Norman said Yeah. Then this woman came over – sat down before him in the chair that years ago Katie had flown from. Norman looked up, but he did not see Katie – it was Katie he had been eager to see, but no – there in her place was this woman.

'You was lookin' kinda lonely,' is what the woman said. 'You – whaddur you? French? You a European guy?'

'Igglish,' said Norman.

'Oh yeah? English, huh? I just *lurve* your accent.

278

Weren't it just *offal* about Princess Di? What's your name?'

'Norbum,' said Norman.

'*Nor*-bum? Rilly? Gee – you crazy English guys! Hey, Nor-bum, you wanna buy me a drink?'

Not particularly, he thought. 'Sure,' he said.

She signalled to the bar: done it, hey – how many times before?

'So tell me,' she said, batting her thickly-clotted brand-new black eyelashes. 'Chicago your kinda town?' And sweet Jesus – how many times had she had to come across with *that* one for the guys? He didn't seem too much of a talker, this John: maybe it's his beat-up nose that's getting to him, huh? 'Jew know, Nor-bum,' she ploughed on, 'that Chicago's called the Windy City?'

Unfortunate that the anarchic state that was Norman's whole bottom plumped for that very moment to discharge into the bar a citrus fart of industrial proportions and profundity, but he was totally beyond caring about any of that.

The woman was not to be put off (credit where it's due).

'Hey, honey – why don't we get it on, huh? How bout a hunnerd bucks?'

Norman gazed at her: I'm not sure I'm getting all this.

'*Swede* ob you, bud really eye bokay – *god* muddy, dow. Already godda hundra bucks – bud thangs eddyway.'

279

The woman was now to be put off (there is a limit).

'See you round, *Nor*-bum,' she sighed (not at all sure she was getting all this) as she ambled back to her stool at the bar: *Jeez*: hey, baby – do I pick 'em or do I pick 'em?

Did I say something wrong, thought Norman: am I guilty of having offended her in some way? She left with the same speed and eagerness as Katie had done. Maybe it's just what I have become – I have maybe become one of those: an untouchable.

Dotty was back at the caravan with little Dawn still cradled in her arms before Brian was even properly washed and dressed. He had become so very weary by the time morning had begun to sunnily insinuate itself through the lacy and crossover curtains, their interstices casting complex patterns on to dappled galley surfaces and rounded cupboard doors. Weary, yes – and aching too from having lain so still, because he did not want Dotty to be aware of his watching her, just sitting there and watching Dawn: such would not be good for either of them, he felt, while not being able to go on to quite define why this should be.

As soon as Dawn had stirred – the second that consciousness had imposed corrugations on her brow, but before her mouth could become agape with discontent and any potential protest, Dotty had scooped her up and was whispering with love and urgency into her eyes; the bottle was ready warmed – a plastic bath prepared, gentle soap and lotions with tiny and sweet-smelling clothes alongside. It was then that Brian had let himself drift away into a fitful and jerky sort of semi-sleep – sometimes aware of Dotty's motions, and then barely hovering at the rim of a quirky oblivion, before plunging in and out of it.

Dotty had carried Dawn down to the hateful little pub (could, in theory, have left her in the caravan, safe with Brian; wouldn't, in practice, have dreamed of doing any such thing). She was eager to make contact with Elizabeth and Melody – Colin too, of course: the other child.

'Dotty! Morning,' Elizabeth greeted her down the line. 'Did you sleep at all? Could you hear yourself think?'

'I slept like a log,' said Dotty. 'Dawn was as good as gold. Elizabeth – have you got anything planned for today, only –'

'Thought we might go down to the beach again – no particular plan. Did Dawn *really* sleep through? Maybe she was just exhausted.'

'She wasn't exhausted: she was happy. Anyway, listen – I was thinking, it's going to be another gorgeous day, by the look of it – and I was thinking wouldn't it be fun if we could do all sorts of really *summer* things: you know – really sort of holiday-by-the-seaside type things? I'm sure Dawn would love it – she doesn't want to be cooped up in that awful little creche place all day long – not on a day like this.'

'OK, Dotty – OK. I'm not quite sure what sort of things you *mean*, but – yeah, OK, sure: sounds fun. Listen – Melody isn't even *in* yet, after last night –'

'That Melody . . .'

'But I was talking after you left last evening with this really nice person called Lulu – like that pop singer. I don't know if you saw her? She was at our table in the bar. Beautiful shirt – blonde.'

'Yes,' agreed Dotty, 'I remember.' Yes, she thought: I remember too well – she had looked absolutely stunning in every possible way, while Dotty must have come across as so much deep-sea salvage.

'Well I don't *know*, but I think she might like to come along on these jaunts of yours – is it OK with you if I ask her?'

'Sure,' said Dotty. 'Course. More the merrier.'

Yeah – why not? Don't care who comes or doesn't come, so long as my little Dawn is there.

Colin had come on the line, just then, and he said something about having met this boy yesterday whose father had a boat – so he was coming back to the, er – *house* (he nearly said it, he nearly did – he nearly let loose with *caravan*) to change and stuff. Melody, it was tacitly understood between Dotty and Elizabeth, would be otherwise *engaged*, hem-hem. Brian? Oh God – can't think about *Brian*; he won't want to come – might have to put his hand in his pocket. Don't *care* what Brian does, actually, Dotty thought gaily: he can mend or break something – keep him happy.

Dotty had filled him in on the outings – pointedly hadn't asked him to come, and Brian had just as conspicuously failed to suggest that he tagged along (all he was thinking was A boat, ay? Lucky old Colin – I wouldn't mind a day at sea; or would I? Wouldn't it, in the event, be just another day to be got through? The beginning right now, the middle in a while, and then later – once again, once again – what bloody else but just the end?)

'What will *you* be up to, Brian?' Dotty asked now, not much minding.

'Me? Oh don't worry about me – I'll be fine: always things to do.'

Well: one thing, actually – just the one. But it has to be done, this thing: it has suddenly (once again, once again) become something of a must.

'What is it like?' asked Zoo-Zoo, 'being married?'

Howard sipped whisky – put down the glass; picked it up again and sipped some more. '*Like*? What is it *like*? Helluva question, Zoo-Zoo. I don't really know what it's like – it's like everything else, I suppose: it's just the way one lives.'

Zoo-Zoo was looking normal in jeans and a T-shirt, standing at the triple sink just rinsing out a couple of glasses, a couple of plates, before they went off somewhere Howard had told him was lovely for lunch. In the bed-room, still on the floor, lay a tangle of peachy and soft silk lingerie and the

283

blonde and wavy wig: with Zoo-Zoo's colouring, it was never as convincing as the jet-black and straight number, but Howard rather enjoyed a little variety in this department: having a blonde from time to time was all right, pretty good – really quite OK, if it's anyone's business bar his own.

'Will *I* like it?' went on Zoo-Zoo, casual as you like.

Howard shifted in his chair. Wasn't at all sure he cared for all this: part of the essence of what he had with Zoo-Zoo was that it was unreal – the only thing that made him wholly *alive*, it has to be said, so real enough from that point of view – but not a normal relationship in that yes, OK – you say this and now I'll say that and before you know where we are we're having a perfectly regular conversation just like people do. No – didn't want all that, didn't feel right. And all this talk about *marriage* (not the first time, either: he'd brought it up before, young Zoo-Zoo, but that time Howard had successfully deflected it: this time not, it would seem). I mean – apart from the obvious incongruities of the situation (leaving them aside) Howard was certainly no expert on the married state. Look – you get married, right? People do – everyone of Howard's sort of age had been getting married, so why not Howard? So he'd married Elizabeth – loved her, pretty sure. And she hadn't had to go to work (a lot of women didn't, then – and Howard was OK for money) and so she looked after the house and kept everything lovely and cared for her husband really well. Then she wanted a baby: fine by Howard – loads of couples were having babies around that time so yeah, let's have a baby, why not? It's what you do – right? So Katie was born (lovely little thing) and Elizabeth was marvellous with her but then decided that one was quite enough, thank you, didn't want to go through all *that* again – and that was fine by Howard: a lot of people were sticking with one in those days, so we might as well go along with that: why not? Whatever Elizabeth wanted.

And the years pass and the baby becomes a – well, *woman* I suppose isn't putting it too strongly (on holiday in *America* – can hardly believe it: seems no time at all since she was combing out the purple nylon tail on Her Little Pony and wearing a yellow plastic bracelet that had come free with that week's copy of *Twinkle*; stay safe, my Katie – be safe, my sweet). And one gets older and one's *wife* gets older and I really can't bring myself to think too much beyond that: more of sort of the same, I suppose. And that, Zoo-Zoo – if you want it – is what being married is *like*: nearest I can get to it, anyway.

'I don't *know* if you'll like it,' said Howard. 'It's always . . . different. You might. Let's go, shall we? If we're going. I'll just quickly try and get Elizabeth again.'

Howard hit the redial button and this time Elizabeth answered almost immediately.

'Ah – caught you at last,' said Howard.

'Did you ring earlier, darling? I've just had the most divine head-to-toe massage! I feel like jelly. Is everything all right at home, Howard? Are you *eating* properly?'

'Everything's fine. Listen, Elizabeth – I've just realized I don't have Brian's number. Got some news for him: finally got an offer on his house.'

'Oh *that'll* please him,' said Elizabeth. 'I don't know about Dotty, though – she really loves that house. Well – she *used* to. But what are the people like? Will I like them? Oh I *hate* it when neighbours move – particularly when they're friends. Did you get a good price?'

'Well this is it – it's not *great*: thirty thousand below what Brian was asking, but frankly I don't see any other offer even faintly on the horizon. I'll advise him to take it. So yes anyway, Elizabeth – can you give me the number of where they are?'

'You know it's very *odd*, Howard, but I don't have it. Isn't that stupid? Dotty's been phoning *me*. Look, I'm seeing her in just a bit so I'll either get the number or tell her to tell Brian to ring you, yes? It's really *silly* I don't have the number. Is it sunny in London, Howard? Gorgeous, here.'

'It's very hot – quite sticky, actually: envy you your sea breezes. OK, Elizabeth – do that, then, and I'll call you some time, don't quite know when – tomorrow, maybe.'

'All right, Howard. Now take care, yes? Promise?'

'Don't you worry about me,' said Howard. 'Bye, darling.'

'Goodbye, my sweet.'

And that, Zoo-Zoo – if you want it – is what being married is *like*: nearest I can get to it, anyway.

John Powers read the note again: he was willing the characters on this hastily torn off sheet of hotel notepaper to scramble and gang up again into some sort of message that had true meaning, something he could understand and believe in – because *this*: this was nothing short of flagrant *lies*. How could she? How could his lovely Lulu be *doing* all this to him? How could she not see that he loved her so much? The whore. *Right*: right. Let's just read this one more time – is there a subtext? Has she betrayed herself in any small way? Is there anything absolute I can nail her for?

'Dear John,' – bloody good start, isn't it? – 'Dear John, I met Lizzie in the massage room, and we're going out for the day. I think this is best at the moment, Johnny. Lulu. X.'

Well she knows what she can do with her bloody 'X', doesn't she? Shove it right back down her own bloody throat: yeah. So – we're spending the day with our phantom little 'Lizzie' friend, are we? This wouldn't be the Lizzie, would it, with the shitty bloody smirk and that fucking moustache who you've been bonking non-stop since we arrived in this bloody place? I think it bloody might be

– I think it just bloody might. Massage? *Massage*?! I'll fucking *massage* her when I get hold of her, the lousy little *slag*. Oh Lulu! My darling Lulu: I *love* you, I *love* you, I *love* you. How can you even think of *doing* this to me?

John twisted open the very last miniature from the minibar – didn't bother looking to see what it was. Christ – eleven in the morning and I'm practically smashed already. Well – am, still am from last night. But oh God what can I do? I don't know where they've gone, do I? Or even when they left. Could be anywhere, anywhere. Oh Christ in heaven, what can I *do*, what can I *do*? I can't go *looking* – can't do that, can I? Where do I look? Where do I start? Can't just check out of this fucking hotel and go back home, can I? Can't do that – what, and leave the field wide open for this fucking bastard and my bloody *wife*?! Wife – hah! Fine bloody wife Lulu turned out to be. And what would home be like? How could he be at home without his oh-so-sweet and tender Lulu? How can all this be *happening* to me? How could that bitch have brought me to this?

John clicked shut behind him the door and just stood quite still in the corridor, his back firmly turned against the luxury suite that laughed in his face. What could he do? Had to do something – had to set in motion his body so that he could put it somewhere else. Anguish swept over him, now, and he passed a trembling hand across his face (hadn't shaved, hadn't bothered with it – what would be the point of *shaving*?)

Some people were ambling towards him, and John quite instinctively and literally pulled himself together: squared the shoulders, tugged at his sleeves, began to remember how it went – this placing of one foot in front of the other and then repeating the process and then trying to ease into the rhythm of the thing and yeah I've got it, now – I'm walking, I'm walking: away from nothing and onward into anything at all.

John went on walking (plod plod plod – don't know what I'm doing this for) and more bloody people were hanging around, now – waiting for the lift, were they? Yeah – waiting for the bloody lift. Why wait? Why bother? Why not leap on down into the black bloody shaft? It's quicker: if you want to get to the bottom, that way is quicker. Wait! What? There – there! At the end, down there: *him*, isn't it? Pretty bloody sure – and a woman skittering and giggling in front of him: no prizes for guessing *who*. Marvellous! They haven't gone yet – this is *meant*, just has to be: God is giving John a chance. Wonderful, wonderful – thank you, God: now I am filled with the thrill of a mission, for all I want to do on earth is *kill* him. And do you know what, God? I'm going to do it now – right this bloody second.

John was stepping up the pace – it *was* him, wasn't it? Christ alone knows I don't want to kill the wrong man: no – it *is* him, it is: I remember the

289

bloody swagger of the man. He'd opened a door – right at the far end of the corridor, he'd just gone and opened a door and the both of them – damn! – the two of them had gone inside (run, run – never mind how it looks – just run, don't lose him, don't miss this chance) – and God, yes, I'm *here* now, here, but the door is shut: small door, odd little door, and it is shut in my face. It says Housekeeper on it. Why does it say Housekeeper on it? Good God – is Lulu already engaged in keeping his *house*? No no – mad talk, John – that's crazy thoughts. Settle down, concentrate: you've got them cornered – all you have to do is wait. Yes but how can I just stand here *waiting*, knowing what they're doing inside?

John lowered his eye to the keyhole: nothing – key stuck into it. How am I playing this? With stealth? Am I going to wait and then am I going to pounce? Or do I kick the fucking door in – smash into the panels and kill him with one of them. And then there was a voice, a man's voice, *his* voice – muffled, but audible. What could he be saying? Would it be interesting to hear the bastard's very last words on earth? Yes – John could see that there was a certain macabre joy to be had from that. Right, then – cup the ear and listen to whatever it was the man was saying and then just kill him when he's done.

Inside the little storeroom, Miles had Melody's face between his hands and he was saying You are, aren't you? You're a right little sexpot, aren't you? You just can't get enough.

John stood there, white and now shuddering.

Inside the little storeroom, Miles watched as Melody pulled away from him, and while holding deep and cheeky contact with his eyes, she slid up her dress to her hips and then higher to her waist as she widened her legs and Miles said I'm not going to fuck you again you little nympho – you get over here and go down on your knees for me – do it, just *do* it.

John stood there, his heart coping badly with searing fire, as his soul ceased its choking and flew away from him.

Inside the little storeroom – Ugh! Miles was grunting, as he held tight on to Melody's head as it bobbed before him. Yes – yes yes yes – uh – *errrrrr*! Ah – good – lovely. Great. Jesus. OK – get up, you sexy sod – come up here and let me kiss you.

John stood there, the tip of his nose now touching the door, his eyes screwed up as tightly as his fists.

And then all he saw was a dazzle of lights before blackness as the door was slammed into his face and he was reeling now and unable to find his head with his hand and he staggered into the wall and slid on down to the ground.

Melody inhaled sharply and froze as Miles looked down at the creep – probably knocked out, but maybe coming round a bit, now.

'Leave him,' he said. 'He's a fucking nutter. Bloody pervert – he's only been *listening*, hasn't he? Come on, love – you go and do what you have to do and then we'll have a great lunch at the Palace, like I promised. Come on, love – never mind him, he's all right. Let's go and have us some *fun*.'

John, still blinded, could hear their hushed footsteps as they walked away, cushioned by the carpet he was now inhaling; he became filled with the silence they left behind them. This is blood, is it? Yes, I am bleeding. Yes, it would seem so: bleeding – and my darling Lulu just walks away to have lunch at the Palace, hand in hand with her lover: maybe I'll kill her too.

'My hair! My hair!' screeched Elizabeth, not for the first time. 'Oh my God my *hair*!'

'It doesn't *matter*!' yelled back Dotty, over the rush of wind. 'Your hair's *meant* to be all blown about – that's the whole point of these buses. It's really fun!'

They were sitting right at the front of a bright yellow open-topped double-decker, the light quite blinding as it glanced off the sea. The bus was trundling along fairly slowly and hugging close the meander of the coast; soon it would swing away and climb the downs from where the view, Dotty had become really breathless while telling them, would be really breathtaking, believe her. Elizabeth continued to clamp down to her head both of her hands with fingers stretched out as far as they would go – truly as if in fear that her hair would rise up from her scalp and take wing. Lulu's face was pointed into the wind, the elegant arch of her nose like that of a lean and pedigree hound; her glossy black wraparound sunglasses were spattered with diamonds of the summer sun's making and, although her thick and golden hair was thrust back and away from her face, whipped and gushed over by alternate breezes, still it managed to look club-cut and sculptured.

Dotty, for her part – what with hair gone wild and boiling red face slashed by glee – looked nothing so much as demented. She was unaware and careless: Dawn's eyes were alight and she gurgled with laughter whenever Dotty swooped down again to tickle her tummy. This is, thought Dotty, just heaven. Then she started singing – terribly off-key, and loving it:

'We're all going on a – *sum*-mer *hol*-iday! No more *work*ing for a, um – what is it? Week or *two*, that's it, isn't it? Tum-Tum Tumty-Tumty Tumty-Tumty-*Tum* – and make our dree-ums come *true*-ooh-*ooh* –!'

'Oh *God*, Dotty,' was Elizabeth's verdict – trying as best she could to roll in a moan with a shriek (Christ this *wind* – my hair will be just . . . oh God I just can't *think* what my hair's going to look like at the end of this. This bus, you may care to know, is one of Dotty's much vaunted 'summer things': God alone knows what else she's got lined up for us. She can be such a *child*, Dotty, sometimes – which yes, I suppose, is no bad thing.)

As the bus veered inland, the ringing ferocity of the wind level dropped away to merely sub-gale force, and Elizabeth decided Oh to hell with it and let her hair fly around as much as it bloody well liked: she had to admit it was easier and much more fun, that way – just have to avoid mirrors, that's all. The lane was barely wider than the bus, and Lulu, Dotty and Elizabeth all instinctively ducked down when heavy overhead branches came looming, although the clearance was actually yards. At the highest point, the track opened out into a frankly ugly and rather disappointing tarmacked square – a coach from Yorkshire and just three cars were twinkling, hotly – and over there was a pub-cum-cafe-cum-tacky-souvenir-shop.

'Forget all that,' said Dotty, as she carefully led the way down the bus's winding staircase, negotiating each tread as if it might be mined, and holding so close to her her precious cargo. 'It's the view that's the thing – we'll see the whole town from up here – and the sea until it vanishes around the side of the bay. You can see France, sometimes, apparently – if it's really clear.'

'Anyone want a drink, or anything?' volunteered Elizabeth. 'I'd die for a glass of champagne, but I don't suppose they'd have that in a place like this, would they? Doubt it.'

They hung around staring out to sea for a while; the air was good – Lulu made quite a play of

sucking down stacks of it deep into her. Dawn
was in a little pushchair, and Dotty was crouching
down to it, repeatedly urging the baby to see the
lovely sea.

'Let's try anyway, shall we?' pursued Elizabeth.
'They're bound to have *something*.'

'Oh – balls!' said Dotty, quite suddenly. 'Look,
Elizabeth – in the shop: they've got those lovely
coloured beach balls. Ooh – I must just buy one
for Dawn.'

Dotty did that, while Elizabeth idly wandered
around – not quite sure on which expanse of
frankly nothing much she should now be focusing.
Lulu slid out postcards from a revolving rack: slid
them back in again. In the bar (God – it seems so
dark in here doesn't it, suddenly? Coming in out
of the light) Elizabeth was seduced by the sight of
a yellow-green bottle of Chablis, casually leaning
and afloat among ice in nearly half of a brass-bound
barrel: she traced a finger through the beads of
cold sweating that wetly pimpled the bottle from
capsule to hip.

When they were settled in the corner, sipping
cool wine, Lulu leaned across a finger to Dawn.
It didn't come from the heart, this gesture – she
had had a run-up to it several times already – just
felt she had to make contact with what in Dotty's
view, certainly, was very much the star of the show.
Lulu was undecided on the matter of babies: she
had assumed, when she married John, that such
things would follow, but none had so far. Which

295

was, if she was honest, a relief: Lulu was undecided now on the very matter of marriage, and if that's how you're feeling, you don't really need things like babies, do you, making it all that much more complex a mix.

'When did you have her?' asked Lulu.

'I had her,' said Dotty proudly, 'yesterday.'

Elizabeth laughed at the consternation that tweaked at Lulu's face.

'What Dotty *means*,' she explained, placing a reassuring hand on Lulu's forearm (no – you haven't gone mad), 'is that yesterday she was in sole charge of Dawn for the very first time. It's actually *Melody's* baby – Dotty is just –'

'Oh!' said Lulu, flooded with new comprehension. 'It's *Melody's* baby – I thought . . . ah! Right – got you.'

'But it's mine now,' said Dotty, quietly – and when Elizabeth looked at her: 'at least for another day. And then – who knows? I think the bus might be leaving quite soon, actually. Drink up, girls – I thought we'd have a really traditional sort of seaside lunch, if that's OK with you two; you know – cod and chips, or something – with huge ice-creams to follow!'

Both Elizabeth and Lulu laughed their good-humoured assent to that particular scheme – last mouthfuls of now quite warmish Chablis were downed, and soon they were back on top of the bus, generally looking out to sea because the sea, you see, was clearly the business.

296

'Look at the boats!' sang out Dotty now, just as the bus pulled away from the carpark and began its jolting descent to the coast below. 'Look at that one with the purple sail! Colin's out in a boat today – did I say? I hope he brought his jersey. Look, Dawn, look – see that pretty yellow boat out there? Do you see it? Do you want to wave? It's maybe got Colin on it, that little boat. Wave, Dawn – give a little wave. That's right – I think he's seen you, and now he's waving back. Do you want to wave again? Come on little Dawn – one last huge wave for your big grown-up brother. There! What a *good* little girl – aren't you? Is little Dawn my very *best* little girl? Yes she is. Yes she *is*.'

Colin wasn't actually on the pretty little yellow boat with the purple sail (not too many surprises there) – in fact he was on the I suppose no less pretty little white boat, and the blood-red sail on it was being loosened and unfurled right at this very moment. But not by Colin – no, not by Colin: Colin was not at all in an unfurling state of mind, even supposing for one second that he possessed even the vaguest idea as to just how to go about such a thing. Standing, you see, was next to impossible, so let's just forget here and now any idle talk of letting up one's grip on just anything at all within clutching distance, let alone actually moving about and seeing to things.

Carol's father had explained that trainers were all wrong for the deck of a boat (too true: they were already soaked right through and the soles were as slippery as fish) – and did he not possess a waterproof jacket? No, Colin did not – what Colin wore was a polo shirt and jeans – a jersey was loosely tied by the arms around his waist, but he soon put it on properly because although the sun seemed as warm as ever, the skin on his arms looked plucked and felt to his touch as cold as cold; trouble was, as soon as he'd got himself togged out in the jersey (no mean feat, I might say, when you can't actually let go of anything at all with either bloody hand) suddenly he felt like he was about to cook, so he tore that off again and it snagged on something and hit the deck and it was sopping now, along with just about everything else. It was very strange – the sea appeared to be perfectly blue and as calm as you like, and yet the floor beneath Colin's quite foolish and deadweight trainers kept on leaping up at him: leaping up, and then ducking down. Leaping up and then ducking down. Oh God. I feel a bit . . . no no – think of something else, think of something else. Look at Carol, that's a good idea – look at her raise her arms to that sort of sticky-out crossbeam thing, helping her brother Terry to buckle down some sort of auxiliary sail, must it be? Some little triangular sort of sail. Both Terry and Carol looked as if their shoes (thick stitched leather with little brass eyelets) were bolted to the deck: they didn't waver once. Carol's Dad (and she was right about him – he was great: dark tan face and making lots of really decent jokes) was halfway up the mast, jigging around some rope or other – looked pretty cool, actually, in his royal blue and orange jacket, and a proper sort of skipper's cap perched quite rakishly on one side of his head.

'Hey! Hey you! Colin, or whatever your name is!' This was Terry calling over; Colin had judged it only a matter of time before he did. 'You going to help, or what? Or are you going to just stay sitting there?'

Wasn't a question, was it? No sort of a question that called for a spoken answer, even if Colin could be sure of being heard (the wind was getting up, now – the red sail billowed and Colin's ears were singing like tuning forks). He rose very gingerly to his feet – *whoa*! That was a – *whoop*! Oh Christ, hang on, hang on – nearly had me over, there. Now he was standing, but bent over double because his hands were wise things and wouldn't be parted from the brass handles they were glued to because they knew the danger, could smell the risk. So Colin stood like that for a while, looking as if he was placidly awaiting a rigorous birching, and then one hand thought it might just chance it for a second or so – ready to fly back to safety if the going got in any way tougher than it already was.

There's another brass handle over there, look; maybe if I could manage a swoop that could some-how incorporate a dive and something approximating to a low and deadly tackle, then maybe I could just about reach that, and from there I could possibly clamber along that handrail and then I'd be pretty much in striking distance of where Terry was standing and now shouting at me again – so better make a start on it, yeah? Yeah, do it now – *right* now, for preference, because I've just suddenly become aware again of the floor beneath me leaping up and ducking down: leaping up and ducking down.

Colin began his endless journey – clammily grabbing, lurching back a bit, some force or other urging him on again (the odd collision, a knee buckle or so hardly helping), and before maybe even a week had passed he found himself so close to Terry and Carol that he could now hear her saying Oh *leave* him, can't you, Terry? You can *see* he's a bit shaky – and Terry coming back with Shaky? *Shaky*? He's acting like a fucking cripple! And then it was that some surge from deep down below sent Colin skittering forward and across the deck (look – no hands!) and right into Terry's chest, where his nose collided quite painfully, and Colin – now assuming the stance of someone well astride a corpulent camel – looked up with penitence into Terry's dark and glaring eyes and even before his body had alerted him to even the remotest possibility of any such thing, Colin had spewed out his very guts up and over Terry, who looked at first quite as amazed as Colin was, but the expression was quick to change into something altogether more dangerous, and up came Terry's arm now, and he brought it down across the side of Colin's face which had him performing a fairly hasty rumba to the other end of the deck where the back of his head hit something or other that was sticking out and that pitched him forward on to his hands and knees – and while he was down there, staring glassily at the glaze of the deck, what remained of his innards must have decided to reassert themselves by way of a rousing encore, and a fountain of just about anything else was sprayed out everywhere.

Colin just lay there – spreadeagled now, as if in sacrifice (certainly he felt like death). His hair hung into wetness (maybe spume, maybe worse) and he could distantly hear Carol now saying Oh Dad look at him – he looks absolutely *ghastly*: we'll have to turn round and take him back – we can't go on with him in this state. And Terry said Christ Almighty what a *joke* – I thought you said he was a sailor, Carol – he's nothing but a bloody stupid little *kid*. OK, said Carol's father – we'll change tack and take him back.

Colin just lay there – coated from head to toe in coldness, while covered by a shame that smouldered at first, but now took light and burned him.

Brian eased out the master copy from the buttoned back pocket of his wallet, which contained only this and nothing else. The paper was so worn and grimy along its folds that Brian had to go about this with care. There – just spread it out on the little table (which I think, actually, I've finally got

301

to stop flapping back down) and let's just go over it once again, shall we? 'By the time you read this, I shall be dead. I am more use to all of you that way. Believe me, this hasn't been easy. My love. Brian. P.S. Sorry.' Yes, I think that just about says it all: I could go into all the ins and outs – Christ I could write a bloody book on it – but I think that with this one simple note all the salient points are adequately covered. There is a dignity about it, I feel: a certain purity. The only thing I have left in the world is my life insurance – the only thing I didn't cash in. They'll be all right, Dotty and Colin – there'll maybe be enough for a fairly decent little house: flat, say. Enough for them to just about get by.

And how many times in the past had he written this note? Meaning it, always meaning it: every single time quite determined to see the thing through, and yet always just something had held him back – sometimes plain fear, other times a conviction more complex: a deep-seated but unpronounceable feeling that just said Oi, no – this ain't right. Once or twice there had been purely practical reasons for aborting the thing – like that time when he had the cover off the power-point, live wire sticking out and challenging him: his bare feet were in a basin of cold water and he was crouching down low to the skirting board, backside of his trousers getting slightly wet (of course, of *course* this couldn't, in context, matter less – Brian knew that, of course he did: bloody uncomfortable, nonetheless). All he had to do was grasp hold of the nettle – his hand was well nigh halfway to doing it. And then Colin had clattered home early from school. Well – you can't, can you? Lad comes home – complaining about homework, hunting for crisps – you don't like to just electrocute yourself in the living-room, do you? Upsetting. So he'd screwed back together the power-point (realigning it while he was about the thing – it had always been not quite square, this one, and it was irritating, that) and then he'd gone upstairs to change his trousers, scooping up for filing his latest note to those he would have left behind him.

Brian rolled a sheet of paper into the rather old portable typewriter that he had found at the back of another of the cupboards (let's hope it has more staying power than the short-lived quite nice little vase – orangey china, blackish sort of swirls). Of course it had been encrusted with ages-old filth, this tinny Olivetti, but Brian had stripped it down, hadn't he – a thorough scouring out, a proper oiling and I'm telling you, mate, it's good for another fifty years. Brian's normal custom was to hand-write his suicide notes (more personal – and anyway, he was no typist, let him tell you – and as for computers, please leave him out of it) but it would be nice to test the machine – and Brian had nothing else pressing to write, just currently: Farewell Cruel World was very much the message of the moment.

He'd tried pills in the past, of course; he had been rather agitated on that occasion, Brian seemed to recall, and although he'd swallowed fistfuls of Panadol he felt nothing strange at all and so he started shoving down his throat just any pills at all that were lying around: cod liver oil, Rinstead Pastilles, Boots Multivitamins – even started crunching up Alka-Seltzers. Was on the point of dispatching down the hatch ten whole packets of Bob Martins (he'd got them cheap – didn't have a *dog*, or anything) but just at that moment he felt very violently ill and had spent the remainder of the evening chucking up in the bathroom; Dotty had offered him a Rennie that had somehow survived the Swallowthon, and Brian had gagged again at just the sight of it.

So he was off pills, as a result. Another time he had decided on a kitchen knife – long and serrated. He ran his thumb lightly along the edge: was it up to the job? Didn't want a botch on his hands, did he? Semi-severed arteries were no good to man nor beast. So he got out the honer and sharpened it and then he remembered a little old-fashioned sort of sharpener driven by discs that he'd had knocking around for, oh goodness – *ages* now: top drawer of the desk, unless he was very much mistaken. But it was rusted solid – so out came the Three-in-One oil and a bit of wet-and-dry and that was soon working its magic so the kitchen knife was as deadly as a cutlass in no time and then Brian had thought Well look, now I've got all this stuff out I might as well do all the other knives as well (can't bear leaving a job half done), and by the time all that was over he was quite worn out and Dotty was saying his tea was ready and I don't know – the moment (as is the way with moments) sort of passed away (which was more than Brian had managed to do).

Head in a gas oven? Been there, done that. Actually, that was probably the worst of all because look, I'm not saying a word against Dotty, here – no aspersions, believe me, are being cast for a minute – but maybe, I don't know, that month she was a bit behind with the house, or something (it can happen, it can happen – God knows it can happen in even the best-run homes), but the inside of that cooker, I am telling you, was far from savoury. Thinking about it, it was maybe *too* savoury – all the oleaginous residue of roasts gone by – not really the sort of thing you want to be confronted with at close quarters, but if you're on your knees with your head thrust deep within the blackened guts of the thing – well then it's just part of the deal.

Brian had not cared to grip the slatted shelves (slimy, sticky – not nice) so he held on to the rings above (no great improvement). And then he thought oh Christ, it's not, is it? I honestly haven't the faintest idea – but if this gizmo is *electric*, then we're dead in the water at the outset. No, no worries – gas: this'll be sweet as a nut. Christ, though – gas has a truly nauseating stench . . . oh Christ, this is making me ill, and that's not what I meant: *yes* I want to die, but I don't want to feel bad about it. Any decision as to whether or not to stay down there was swiftly removed from him when suddenly (God – even now I don't understand it: maybe I twiddled a knob or something, did I?) blue flames were shooting up at him and hissing like vipers and if he hadn't pulled out in double-quick time his face would've ended up as so much crackling on a plate. Talk about a close shave: I'm telling you – it can be a killer, this suicide lark.

And what was it to be this time? Couldn't tell you – haven't a clue. All I know is it's got to be done. I'll never find a buyer for the house, will I? There's no one in the world wants to buy my house; Christ – I even tried to raise a bit more cash for this Godawful holiday by offering for sale all my manhole covers – and nobody bloody wanted them, either – which is frankly amazing. So it's the only way, the only way. Right – that's the note done (ribbon's a bit faint); now I'll just quickly do the envelope: NOT TO BE OPENED UNTIL 1st AUGUST 1998. That's tomorrow. So today's the day: yes – very much so. It's always either mid-summer or else soon after Christmas: just can't stand those times, don't know what it is.

Brian propped up the envelope in front of the taps (she'll be bound to see it there). I really am sorry to be doing this to you, Dotty – it's not, I realize, the greatest thing to have to deal with when you're down at the seaside for the week, but believe me, it's all for the best in the long run. And you've got little Dawn, now: that's all you'll ever need. I'd only be in the way.

Picking up a copy of the local paper, Brian glanced around the caravan (he was a great one for last looks on earth) and then walked out into the sunshine, locking the door behind him. Bit of a walk, I think – bit of a walk, bit of a read, and then put my mind to how best to dispose of myself: at the moment there isn't a single idea in my head – I do hope something occurs to me soon.

Brian wandered through the avenues of caravans – took to the high ground, and soon they began to thin out. Found himself on a high and remote piece of land where scrubby grass grew starkly from patches of sand: quite breezy, up here. He walked on, and soon he came to an unprotected deep drop down to the sea. He took one pace nearer; then another. His head was already urging him to get back, get back, as he closed the gap between himself and a sheer vertical wall of air. He peered over, and then he peered down: it was a very long way.

Brian retraced his steps, and settled himself into the sheltered crook of a dune. Have a bit of a read, I think: always made a point of buying the local rag whenever he was away from home – catch up on anything that was going on. The headline and most of the front page were given over to the news that some bloke who for thirty years had sold this very paper from a stand outside the Festival Gardens was now no longer going to. Inside there was a picture of a maybe human being in a home who was a hundred years old. The stop press said: 'Burglars

307

flee empty-handed from property in Argyle Road.'
Dear oh Lord – they'll have a field day with me:
Man Found Dead.

Right. Well. I think I've wrung all the goodness
from the paper, so now I'd better, um, attend to
business. Brian stood and again approached the
edge of the cliff. He stood as close to the verge as
he dared, and with arms straight down by his sides,
he closed his eyes and his face to the dying sun, the
eyelids before him now warm and alive with bright
red blood. I will, he thought, count up to ten.

Miles and Melody had just taken their seats at the
rather nice circular table in the corner farthest away
from the kitchen in the conservatory of The Palace
Hotel – were at the napkin-flapping stage – when
the head waiter placed an envelope on the table.

'For the lady,' he said.

They looked at it, and then they looked at each
other, both sets of eyebrows hoiked up in a mildly
curious way.

'Is it from you?' asked Melody.

'Of course it's not from me,' came back Miles.
'I'm *here*, aren't I? What would I be writing you
letters for?'

Melody shrugged as she worked her thumb into
the envelope and jerked away jaggedly. 'Thought it
might be a surprise.' She unfolded the single sheet
of paper and looked at it. She went on just looking
at it for so long that Miles could contain himself
no longer and tweaked it away from her.

'It must be some sort of a joke,' said Melody, sounding quite amazed. 'Are you *sure* you didn't send this, Miles?'

'Of course I'm – now, then – let's read. Christ Al-bloody-Mighty – what the hell's all this? "The game is up, darling wife of mine . . ." You said you weren't *married* – I don't *do* married birds any more.'

'I'm *not* – I'm *not*: of course I'm not married – Christ, I should know! That's what I mean – it's a joke, or – oh no, *I* know – it's just gone to the wrong person. Oh golly,' laughed Melody, quite wickedly, glancing around the half-full dining-room, 'I wonder which of them it's meant for? He sounds like he means it, whoever this bloke is.'

Miles read on: '"You have been caught out in your vile betrayal and you will pay for it . . ." – Jesus, this can't be for real, can it? "As for your lover – he is dead. My love, as ever – John." Who the fuck's John?'

'I told you – I haven't the slightest idea. Don't know any *Johns*. It's for someone else – must be.'

Miles summoned over a waiter and asked for the maître d'.

'Look,' said Miles when the man was there – bent and attentive – 'this letter – where did it come from? Who gave it to you? It's not meant for us – it's got to be for someone else.'

'The gentleman was specific, sir. He handed me the envelope about half an hour ago in the lobby and asked me to give it to the lady accompanying Mr McInerney for lunch. That is you, sir?'

Miles nodded. 'Mm. Yes. 'Tis.' He looked at Melody with increasing suspicion, while she mugged back her wide-eyed and total mystification. 'Can we see the wine?' concluded Miles.

'Miles look –'

'You *said* you weren't married. Why did you have to lie to me?'

'*Look*, Miles – I'm not *married*, OK? I don't know what the hell this is all about!'

'Well presumably this "John", whoever he is, knows his own bloody wife. Why did you tell him we were coming here?'

Melody banged down her bread knife and turned on Miles the full thousand watts of her I-cannot-believe-I'm-*hearing*-this glare of uncut outrage.

'Miles – try to learn this: I don't *know* a John, I didn't tell anyone anything and I'm *not* – hear me? – *not* married: we're both of us the same, you and me, and that's why it's so good – so don't *spoil* it. I have no kids – you have no kids; I'm single – you're single. Right? OK? *Trust* me.'

That's, of course, if he's not fobbing me off with a pack of lies, thought Melody, with a sudden twinge of rancour: he *looks* married – he's got that *look* about him.

Miles nodded slowly: well look – I had to say that, didn't I? She was going on and on in bed that morning about hoping this wasn't just a summer *thing* because she'd had those in the past and this time she wanted it to be *real*. So yeah, OK – if that's what she wants to hear: it's *real*, Melody – of course it's not just some summer thing – all my life I've been looking for someone like you: this could truly be it. Not the time to tell her about Sheil and the kids, is it? Tell her whatever she wants, right? Keep her sweet. What she is is a fucking good lay for the rest of the week: she's mad for it, I'm telling you. And then it's sayonara, cootchy-coo.

I think, thought Melody, that this is some sort of test: of *course* Miles is behind this stupid letter – who else could have sent it? Well I've proved myself – I mean what I say. OK, yeah – but I just had to lie about Dawn, didn't I? It's obvious he hates kids – a lot of men do, whatever they say, as I know only too well. But I really go for this guy – I could actually settle for this one. About time I had somebody to pick up the tab – like Elizabeth has with Howard. And Miles – he seems pretty loaded: just signs for everything.

'OK,' said Miles. 'Let's just forget the whole thing.'

'Fine,' agreed Melody. 'Miles – you do *believe* me? I will never lie to you, darling – you must trust me. And you're the same, yes?'

Miles nodded, and reached out for her hand: eye contact, now. 'Yes,' he insisted. '*Yes*: I don't lie – what would be the point?' he averred, as realistically as anything. I'll give her the lot, will I? Yeah – what's to lose? 'I *love* you, Melody.'

Yeah – worked: just look at the melt at the back

311

of her eyes. Great: she'll be even hotter in the sack this afternoon.

'I think,' said Miles evenly to the sommelier who had oozed alongside, 'we'll have the Dom Pérignon.'

It was dark when Norman finally left the bar (I haven't really been quite *staying* – it's just that I haven't until now got around to quite *leaving*) and – woo – must have had quite a few drinks, then – yes? Feel a bit . . . well, I'm *OK* – just a bit, you know: fragile. How many drinks, then? Dunno: wasn't counting. Norman dug his hand into his trouser pocket and hauled out the crumple of bills half swaddling the clank of not too many coins: about sixty dollars' worth, looked like. Oh well: so what? Nothing could harm him now; when you are raw and roaring with pain, it is easy to feel that you have crossed over some shimmering line, way beyond the reach of any more harm. Back to the hotel: has to be. There's nowhere else I can think of being. Maybe Katie's already there, and waiting? Norman shook his head – allowed a good half of his mouth to twist up – I suppose they call that *ruefully*, do they? No – Katie would not already be there: Katie would not be waiting. Would not the vast and empty hotel room prove to be just a tad depressing? Yes, oh yes – wholly, colossally; but so would everywhere else on earth – and at least it's warm, in a cold sort of a way. Look: Katie was with Rick. Whoever *he* might be – this Rick who fell out of the sky, one night. And Norman was heedless of the lush and glossy sleekness of Chicago by night: for Norman, the bright lights of the big city had all winked out – one by one, and for ever.

Would the weight be eased if he made Katie a part of the pain that invaded him? Should he not have it out with her? Disbelief washed over Norman, then (where am I, actually? Is this the right street? Think so, think it is – and if it's not . . . well then it just isn't); this can't be *true*, can it? Just a couple of days ago he had been lying in a bath and filming her fucking him – and now . . . oh God, can't think, can't think – I just can't think about whatever it is she might be doing right *now*. But look, but look – I know it's hard (oh *Jesus* is it hard!) but can you try to quell just enough of all that to enable you to at least try and look at the thing *rationally*: as rationally, anyway, as one near unhinged may be expected to view a situation so way beyond credulity. *Look*, Katie, I'll say: this just can't go on. How's that? Mmm – not too great, is it? There's only one possible retort to that, you see: *What* can't go on, Norman? OK – to which I say This . . . *thing* – yeah? And she says *What* thing, Norman? Hopeless, right? You could play around with it all night and still be nowhere by dawn. Except it wouldn't *be* all night, would it? No. No, if *last* night was anything to go by, well then no: Katie wouldn't be back, would she? Wouldn't be back till morning. Having risen warm from the bed of Rick.

OK – I'll tackle the thing headlong: *look*, Katie – OK, you've met this I suppose quite glamorous guy (oh Jesus! Oh Jesus! Is there much more of this? I *sting*, I tell you – I *sting*) and, er . . . you were, yeah, *attracted*, flattered and, er . . . all that. It happens. Particularly to young girls in a foreign country – famous for it. But you've got to *see*, Katie (oh *please* see – *please*), that it is *I* who loves you – me, Norman, in person: *love* you, Katie – see? Want to *marry* you, want to have you (to hold you) for ever and ever and . . . *Rick*, right . . . well: he's just one of those summer *things*, see? So let's put it all behind us, shall we? Start again: clean slate. I'm willing to forgive and forget and we'll never even mention it in conversation again – OK? How's that? *Pitiful*: she'd laugh you to death before you'd even got to grips with your half-time wedge of orange – no hope whatsoever: complete non-starter, I'm afraid, Norman: sorry and all that, but it's got to be said.

Yeah, you're right: it's no good at all. Well what I'll *do*, then, right, is – hang on, hang on: didn't I just pass this bloody enormous building about fifteen minutes back? Or was that another bloody enormous building altogether? I don't think I'll ever learn this city – and I know, just know, that I'll never be back. No listen, what I'll do (this *is* right, actually – I know now: hotel's just around the next corner, pretty sure, or maybe the one after that); yeah – what I'll do, OK, is just ask her a series of short and very much – and, yes, painfully – to the point questions and just see what sort of answers she lobs back at me. Let's try it out: Katie – do you have a better time with this Rick person than you do with me? Ha! Easy one: *yes*. Right. OK. He's got a lot of money, hasn't he? Uh-huh. Hm. And you're obviously . . . attracted. She nods. And seeing as you're suddenly spending most of your time with him, it wouldn't really worry you too very much, would it, if I wasn't even here at all? Nope: got it in one. OK . . . OK . . . so what would you say, Katie, what would you say, in fact, if I told you I was booked on to the very next plane to London? Bye, Norman! Oh God, of God – I'm not at all sure I can take much more of this.

I find that I am in my hotel room: how perfectly weird – I don't even remember the lobby, have not the slightest recollection of the lift. But here I surely find myself – so I think now that I'm here I shall have twelve drinks. Yes – lay thcm out (what a delightful clink): start with the little transparent ones and work my way on up to all the little golden ones. I don't really have to put these questions to you directly, do I Katie? Not really necessary. So why don't I spare myself the hot cuff of shame? I have sold everything I possessed for her; I have stolen repeatedly from my employer – who is, God help me, her father – and just look, just *look*, will you, at what *Katie* did!

I think what I must do is drink my drinks and then stow with care this slashed red heart and an ash-grey soul into my Big Brown Bag and leave you, my love: at least that way I shall be spared all the vivid morning agony of knowing just what it was that Katie did next.

And nor would Norman be cheered to know just what it was that his employer – her father, God help him – was actively engaged in at just the moment: sitting in the office and poring over records, looking up stuff in ledgers – even, occasionally, logging on to his computer (hated the thing, hated it). Zoo-Zoo was over there by the window, at the little desk where he pretended daily to more or less attend to some sort of mindless chore (well – there had to be an excuse to have him here, didn't there? Otherwise people might talk – you know what they're like.) Now he spoke up, in that disarmingly direct way that he had about him:

'But even if he *has* been taking money, does it really matter?'

Howard looked up. 'Matter? Well of course it matters, Zoo-Zoo – it's my money, isn't it? My company. I mean – everything I give *you*, that's different, that's fine – but I don't want you going round helping yourself, do I?'

You don't, ever – do you?

'Yes, I understand that,' said Zoo-Zoo, equably, 'but what I mean is – if this whoever-he-was from Bixby's hadn't told you about the rumour, would you ever have suspected Norman of doing it? You haven't noticed any missing money, have you?'

You don't, ever – do you?

316

'Well no I haven't – if indeed it *is* missing. I don't quite know yet – it's hard to tell. I do find it very difficult to believe that Norman *would* do anything like this – I mean, I pay him quite well, I think. Can't imagine what he'd need any more money *for*: not as if he's married with kids, or anything – no mortgage. Never even seen him with a girl. He's a quiet one, Norman.'

'Maybe,' said Zoo-Zoo, 'he's got a boy.'

'Ooh no no,' responded Howard quickly and intuitively. 'Norman's not that type at all.'

Should I in fact have said that?

'What type is that?' asked Zoo-Zoo, sweetly.

No, in fact, I should not.

'Well – you know,' Howard coughed. 'Type that prefers, er, males.'

'I'm not that type, you know,' said Zoo-Zoo. 'Do you know?'

'Yes,' said Howard slowly. 'I *do* know, I think. You see it's rather odd, Zoo-Zoo – yes, I suppose it is – but *I'm* not that type either. I mean, what I mean is – I think you are very beautiful, and you know how much I am attracted to you and all the rest of it, but if you'd happened to be a, you know – *girl* . . . well, that would have been perfectly fine by me.'

Zoo-Zoo nodded. 'Yes. I understand that. I think that's more or less what I feel too. I find Katie very attractive.'

Howard looked up sharply. 'Really?' is all that came out.

317

Zoo-Zoo was nodding again. 'But Katie, of course, I could never even dream of approaching – she scares me, a bit. And she completely ignored me when I first came here, you know. As if I was invisible – never even *spoke*. And you did – that's all.'

'Yes,' agreed Howard, slowly. What, actually, is one to make of this? I mean – I understand completely what the boy is *saying* (pretty sure I do, anyway – *think* so) but it's difficult to apply all this to the people we are actually talking about, here: I know what I feel for Zoo-Zoo (that's one thing) and I know what I feel about Katie (quite another) but all this talk is . . . I don't know: *confusing*. Will that do? Confusing? It'll do for now, anyway – might point it up later. But God, you know, I do wish we didn't have to have these conversations – he says one thing, then I say something back, and here we are suddenly in the middle of a *discussion* and that's not at all anything to do with what I *want* out of this.

'And,' added on Zoo-Zoo, 'I think Elizabeth is very attractive too – although I only saw her once from the window.'

'I think,' said Howard, 'we've done all we can do here for the day. Let's pack up and go home, shall we? Have a drink. Christ – I do wish Brian would ring me – I've had that Davies man on the phone all morning. If I can't confirm that Brian is accepting the offer, I'm telling you – he'll settle on another property. He's that keen to get something. And he's with other agents, I know that for a fact.'

'Did you hear what I said?' asked Zoo-Zoo.

'Yes,' said Howard. 'I did. Come on – let's go – I could do with a drink. You don't think Elizabeth's forgotten to pass on the message, do you? It's ridiculous I can't contact the man.'

Zoo-Zoo was standing now, and chucking the files he usually stared at back into their drawer. 'How should I know? Does she forget things? I've no idea what Elizabeth is like: she's *your* wife.'

Howard looked at Zoo-Zoo from the doorway (halfway out of it – need that drink). Was he *very* naïve, this child? Or was he just so chillingly and insinuatingly brilliant that it quite frightened Howard to even think about tweaking aside even the hem of it? Don't know. I just don't know. Oh, to hell with it – let's just lock up and go and have a bloody *drink*, Godsake.

'Mm – Dotty!' said Elizabeth, suddenly, through a muffled mouthful of roast cod and chips – now bringing down her knife and fork to the sides of her plate, one stiff finger indicating that all this masticatory action was not done yet, but the second the big gulp came, then information was coming in Dotty's direction, depend on it. Here we go – just a dab of the napkin and we're off:

'I completely forgot to tell you: Howard's had an offer on your house – wants Brian to ring him.'

'Oh really?' said Dotty, quite passively. Yes well

– she supposed, if she thought about it, that one day it was bound to happen (everything sells eventually) but God, so many people had traipsed round the house in the last six months – none of them liking it, all of them commenting in one way or another on Brian's fucking manhole covers – that the possibility had become increasingly remote. Dotty did not want to move. It was not that she loved the house, or anything – had done once: had loved lots of things once, before they either left or were taken from her – but change was not a big part of Dotty's existence on earth: upheaval was anathema. Plus, of course, she liked to be just next door to Elizabeth; and (yes, this is the one – this is the one I just can't bear to think about) wherever they all end up will be worse by far: Brian had never talked about this, which said it all, really – confirmed every one of Dotty's very worst forebodings.

'But he did say,' Elizabeth went on, 'that it was quite a bit less than the asking price – don't know how much,' she lied. Well – don't want to depress poor Dotty – just look at her: so happy to be caring for Dawn, almost crouched in hiding behind so small a being – but in every other way . . . oh dear oh dear. I mean just look at her dress: it was never much even when it was new – but *now*! And she'd put on weight – it showed – and an A-line sleeveless number wasn't really very clever, was it, in the circumstances? I mean God – Elizabeth knew that Brian was having a bit of trouble, and everything – but surely he could have afforded to get her just a few new summer things?

'I haven't the slightest idea how much we *are* asking,' admitted Dotty. 'I think I did know at the beginning, but we've dropped it twice since then, pretty sure. I don't get involved. I must say this cod is terribly good – so *fresh*.'

'My sole's divine,' said Lulu. God, she was thinking – I wish I didn't have to watch that baby eating: quite disgusting. Her mouth and chin were glazed with brown and still Dotty went on applying to the same general area ever more brimming spoonfuls of something that could very well be on the lines of stewed dog with prunes. Not the baby's fault, I suppose – but still: off-putting, very.

'So you will tell Brian, then, Dotty – yes?' pursued Elizabeth. 'I got the impression from Howard that they're cash buyers, and these people don't hang around, as you know. Like gold dust.'

Dotty nodded. 'I'll tell him this evening.' Yes – I'll tell him then, whereupon he'll drive down to that insufferable little pub and try to make himself heard on the phone over the bugling blare and babble of a thousand clanking and winking machines, all laid on courtesy of Idiots Anonymous for the diversion of the locals; and then, in all probability, he'll eat a bloody pie.

'Why don't we get a cab out there now?' suggested Elizabeth, brightly. 'I'm dying to see this fabulous estate of yours.'

'Mm,' approved Lulu. 'It does sound fantastic, from what you've said.'

'You know,' came back Dotty, wide-eyed with simple-minded sincerity, 'it's the craziest thing but there's only one *key* – can you believe it? And Brian's got it on him, and God knows where he's gone off to. Said something about a long walk somewhere, I think. Crazy, though, isn't it? About the key. We've been in touch with the landlords about it, of course, but so far – nothing. It's a shame – I'd love you both to see the place. Another time.'

One she'd prepared earlier, adjusting the seasoning to taste.

'I think we'll get some more Evian,' said Lulu. 'Drink gallons of water in summertime.'

'We drink tap water at home, now,' said Dotty; might as well say it – no point in not. 'I think all this bottled water is a con.' No I don't – don't at all. The difference is plain for all to see and actually I happen to *love* mineral water, particularly Badoit, but Brian says paying for water is *out* – hear him? *Out*.

'Oh yuck,' said Lulu. 'Do you know I read somewhere that the stuff you get from a tap has passed through the human system at least six times?'

'Oh *God*,' shuddered Elizabeth. '*Really*? How revolting.'

'Yes but,' countered Dotty, 'some of it must have started *out* as Evian, mustn't it?'

Lulu could not bring herself to even begin to dwell on *that*, and for some reason turned her attention to Dawn, whose entire face now appeared to have taken the brunt of the fallout from an exploding cow-pat and so Lulu thought she would forgo pudding (chocolate mousse? I don't really think so) and why don't we get back out into the lovely sunshine, yes?

But the sun seemed to be on temporary hold: a light and gauzy drizzle was in the air, and so the three of them ran dartingly across the road – Dotty steering Dawn's buggy like a go-kart racer and laughing out loud like a schoolgirl, Lulu concentrating on keeping her breasts from bouncing up and bouncing down (she had been taught the technique in a Lausanne finishing school) – while Elizabeth instinctively thought My hair! My hair! But her hair, she knew, was a write-off anyway: must book an appointment in the salon when they get back to the hotel.

Whatever the resort on Britain's coast, sooner or later you always end up at least once in W.H. Smith's; this is now where they found themselves (I don't think the rain is settling in, or anything – it's only a shower, no more), Elizabeth swooping down on *Vogue* and *Harper's* while Lulu took up the slack with most of the other fat and shiny monthlies (weighed a ton). Dotty dangled a succession of silly furry toys and silly plastic toys in front of Dawn's blue and dancing eyes (her face had been sort of cleaned up, Lulu had been disgusted to observe, by Dotty having licked her handkerchief and applying it with a gentle vigour to the worst of the caked-on purée) and settled upon the sweetest one and then went back and bought all the others as well. Brian had been in Smith's just the day before, he had been droningly telling her: bought *Good Woodworking* and *Practical Caravan*, which shouldn't cause too many shocks in anyone who knows him (there isn't a magazine on collecting manhole covers: maybe he should start one up).

After that (look, look – I was right: the sun's breaking through all that low-lying cloud: it's going to be nice again – I told you it would) Lulu had seen some absolutely gorgeous pinky cream and strappy shoes in the window of some fairly swish shop and just had to had to have them; Elizabeth bought some black slip-ons in the same place – didn't really need them, but they were rather lovely – and Dotty crouched by the entrance and lowered on to Dawn's little button mushroom nose a tangerine spider from its lime green web; the laughter, as two tiny hands made a grab for it, flooded Dotty's heart.

They walked the length of the front – three ice-cream cornets from the shop just by the pier with the yellow-and-white striped awning (Dotty bought some rock, she didn't know why – then she bought a sticky cloud of denture-pink candy floss, and that had Dawn looking like a psychedelic Smurf in next to no time). Soon it was the call of the cappuccino – ooh yes please, with lots of chocolate flakes on top: actually I'm completely *exhausted* – we must have walked miles (thank goodness, thought Lulu, I'm not actually *wearing* those gorgeous pinky cream and strappy shoes – they're not remotely practical, but they'll be absolutely divine with that beigey sheath dress I got from Donna Karan).

'I think,' said Dotty – the lip below her scarlet nose now sprouting a cream and frothy moustache, 'this is the best holiday I can ever remember.' And yes, we know what she means.

'I'm loving it,' said Elizabeth. And she was – more, much more than she ever thought she would.

'Me too,' said Lulu, 'but I don't actually think I'll be staying for the whole of the week. Not now.'

'Oh *why*?' implored Elizabeth. Oh don't go – *don't*.

'Oh it's *John*, isn't it? I just know he's going to get more and more impossible – it won't be the first trip I've had to cut short because of this stupid way he behaves. I mean *God* – loads of men get a little bit jealous, I know that, but John – he's really something else.'

'Maybe I could talk to him?' offered Elizabeth. Don't want to – don't at all *want* to, but I don't want to lose Lulu, either.

Lulu shook her head in an if-only-it-were-that-easy sort of a way. 'If only it were that easy,' she said. 'Don't you think I've tried talking?

Sometimes I feel all I ever *do* is talk and talk and talk. I tell you, Lizzie, it's just so *tiring* – after a while it just wears you out.'

Elizabeth nodded: yes, it must be – yes, it must do.

Dotty said, 'I didn't know you liked being called Lizzie.'

'I don't mind,' smiled Elizabeth. 'Quite like it.'

'I'm dreading going back to him tonight. Casts a shadow over the whole day.' And Lulu shook her head in maybe sorrow.

Elizabeth thought she looked so vulnerable and young, just then – so touchingly pretty. 'Well,' she said, 'my offer of the room still stands – God knows if we'll *ever* see Melody again: I very much doubt it. God – once she's got her hands on a man, everyone else can just go to hell.'

'Even Dawn,' said Dotty, quietly.

'*Particularly* Dawn,' confirmed Elizabeth.

'Anyway,' said Dotty.

Elizabeth drank the last of her coffee. 'The way she is.'

'Why do we *need* men?' Lulu now wanted to know. 'I mean, in the end they're nothing but *trouble*, aren't they?'

'Must be awful to *be* one,' opined Dotty. 'I've never wanted to be a man – have you, Elizabeth?'

'I can't imagine it . . . no, I don't think I'd swap – I *love* being a woman, love all the feminine things. I think it must be so *boring* to be a man. And you've got to *work*, and everything.'

'The only time I ever suffer from penis envy,' smiled Lulu – and that sure as blazes got everyone's attention – 'is when there's a queue for the ladies' loo . . . .'

This brought about general merriment and the smack of recognition – and then Lulu added on near wistfully, and certainly in a lower key: 'Mind you – I've often wondered what it must, you know – *feel* like . . .'

'What . . .' groped Elizabeth with care, '. . . when they . . . ?'

Lulu nodded. 'Yup. What it actually *feels* like. Much different from our . . . from us, apparently. Must be pretty exciting when they actually, you know – come all over the place, like that.'

Elizabeth was thinking well I'm not quite sure what you mean: *Howard* has never come all over the place, like that – while Dotty was thinking I really can't enter the great debate about female orgasms versus male orgasms because I've never had the one and I couldn't give a fuck about the other.

'Probably,' said Elizabeth, 'the only good thing about *being* a man.'

Lulu nodded. 'I think a lot of men would agree with that.'

'Let's go back to the hotel, shall we, girls?' suggested Elizabeth. 'I'm dying for a long, hot bubble bath – and I'd really like to get my hair done before dinner. A drink would be nice, too: champagne.'

'I'll go straight back with Dawn, if that's OK,

Elizabeth. She's pretty tired, I think – poor little mite. She's had a long day.'

'Are you having her again, then, Dotty?' queried Elizabeth. 'Oh joy! Sorry, Dotty – but you obviously have the golden touch: with me and Melody she just goes berserk.'

'Didn't I say? Yes – Lulu and I bumped into Melody this morning when we were waiting for you – tearing hurry to be off with you-know-who, of course.'

Lulu nodded: she certainly had been. It was an odd little scene all round because Dotty and Lulu didn't know each other yet and so they had been sort of chit-chatting in a forcedly lighthearted but actually quite wooden sort of a way – and there had been this man there, Lulu recalled, peeling away the wrapping from a tube of Extra Strong Mints and Dotty (couldn't tell you why she did this – an impulse thing: didn't even particularly like Extra Strong Mints) had just gone up and *asked* him for one and of course he smilingly complied, and then he offered one to Lulu too and she took it for politeness' sake but didn't actually put it into her mouth because she for one actually *abhorred* Extra Strong Mints and always had done. Melody had galloped up, then, and Dotty had asked her if it was all right if she kept little Dawn for another night, and Melody – Lulu had seen this, all right – Melody appeared to have completely forgotten about Dawn's entire existence and had said airily Huh? Oh yeah, Dotty

328

– great, that would be really great. Some mothers (such as Dotty, Lulu supposed) are just born, while for others (like Melody – and one day, maybe Lulu herself) it's, well: different.

'Anyway, Dotty,' said Elizabeth – outside again now, hard to believe it had been all dull and rainy just an hour or two ago – 'don't forget to tell Brian about the house – oh and Colin: tell Colin that if he wants to come back to the hotel tonight that's absolutely fine. And as I said, Lulu – you're very welcome too. Lizzie's Board & Lodging! Cheapest rates in town!'

'Thanks, Lizzie,' grinned Lulu, 'but I've got to face it some time. He's probably climbing the wall as it is. Come on – let's move. You've got me thinking about that glass of champagne, now.'

Dotty, amid much waving, watched them go.

'We don't want any champagne, do we, Dawn? No we don't – no we don't. We want some nice warm milk and some strawberry pudding and then a lovely bath – that's what *we* want, isn't it, my baby? And then before he goes off, your brother will maybe tell us all about his little boat trip: I bet he loved it. I do hope he took his jersey, though, cos it can get jolly chilly bobbing about on boats, can't it, little Maria? Yes it can. Yes it *can.*'

When finally Colin had got back to the caravan, no one else was there, thank God – it would have been just too awful to have to *explain*, on top of everything else. And Jesus – what a journey! This just has to has to has to be the very worst day of my entire life on earth. Oh God – what a prat, what a *prat*: what must Carol *think* of me? Well – bloody stupid question: she *won't* think of me, will she? Not ever again. Why would she? If I were her I know *I* wouldn't bloody think of me.

Carol had left him at the little harbour – he with a complexion like that of the processed pea, she with concerned enquiry zipping all over her face. Are you *sure*, now, you're going to be all right, Colin? Yes, honestly – truly, yes. *Sure?* Mm, feel fine now, Carol, really I do – I'm so terribly *sorry* about . . . oh God. Don't be silly don't be *silly*: just so long as you're OK – sure, now? Yes, honestly – truly, yes. Oh Jesus – all that took years; and Terry, bloody Terry, just standing there on the deck and eyeing Colin as if he was no more than all that remained of a parched and foolhardy gringo spreadeagled in the Mexican desert, after the buzzards had gorged and gone.

And of course he had no money for a taxi – gave up in next to no time even *trying* to decipher the impossible bus timetables and so there had been nothing for it but to walk – and God Almighty what a bloody walk it was – right through the town, out on to the main road (no proper pavement – not like in London: just grass and bloody nettles) and then past the new estate and then finally up the lane to caravan heaven. And the stink – oh God, the stink of his clothes had almost had him retching again; the jersey he had slung in the sink

330

– the jeans were kind of OK. As for the T-shirt –
he had just crammed that into a vast litter-bin close
to the outside tap: some things were just beyond
the beyond.

Much later on, and yes here it comes: Mum's
back – billing and cooing to the bleeding baby,
as per bloody usual. Mind you, if Dawn's here,
does that mean I can . . . ? Yes – apparently yes.
Elizabeth has said it's OK to go back to the hotel.
Great. Get some decent grub, have a decent night:
something, I suppose. And yeah, Mum, I had a
great time, thanks: fabbo. Yeah yeah – we sailed to
Australia and back, raised the *Titanic* on the way –
and I brought you back a barrelled chest brimming
with doubloons: Christ Almighty, what do parents
want to *hear*? They always expect you to go *in* to
everything and then they get all funny when you
just shrug a bit and grunt – but shrugging and
grunting is great, if you want to know, because it
can be made to cover most things, and can get you
out of the sodding lot. And even if you *did* talk –
even if you answered all their dim-witted questions,
they wouldn't *listen*, would they? I mean – look at
Mum now: fooling around with that bloody baby
again – *talking* to her. Baby can't talk back, can
it? No it bloody can't. *I* can – I can talk back,
but no one ever says a bloody thing to me: not
Mum and Dad, anyway – nothing worth listening
to. When is it, I wonder – at what precise point
in one's childhood is it that both your parents,
in tandem or independently, go absolutely bloody

bonkers? They just go mad, I don't know why; and it's irreversible, pretty sure of that.

And then she wanted to know if Colin had seen his father. No I haven't bloody seen my bloody father. I saw *Carol's* father – who is really great (oh Christ oh Jesus – he must think I'm a real little *kid*, acting like that: probably laughing his head off about it right now, along with bloody *Terry*) but no, I haven't actually set eyes on my own father, no. Wouldn't much mind if I never did again. I mean – what's the *point* of a father, actually, if there's so obviously just no bloody *point* to him?

Right, then, he'd said at the door: I'm off, then. Mum? Did you hear me? I say I'm off. Can you give me some money for a taxi? Mum? *Mum?* Christ that bleeding *baby* – she's just not taking in a single bloody word. Sorry, Colin – what did you say? Money, Mum – for a taxi, yeah? There's ten pounds up there, look, near the stove – do you like that pudding, little Dawn? Is it yum-yum-yummy? OK, Mum – see you. I said *see* you, OK? Oh sod you, then.

But Colin wasn't going to the hotel – not right now, anyway: would later on (in a bit) but not just right this minute. OK, granted, it was a hell of a long shot – Christ, you think *I* don't know that? – but I've got to give it a go, haven't I? I mean – she *might* turn up: she might. Not for *me* – no, obviously not for *me* – but because she just likes it up there, for some reason, listening to the sea, watching the sky – and maybe scratching at your arse on account of all the sand round there, and the prickly bloody grass.

Colin sat there. Went on sitting there. Stood up. Sat down again. Sat some more. Christ – when somebody says they really like *doing* this, what bit is it that they actually *like* about it? I mean – there's nothing here for *anyone* that I can see: it's a bit like being dead.

And then he heard the rustle, swish and crunch of approaching feet. Oh Great. I think. Oh God – I don't know, now: maybe being here isn't actually a good idea at all.

'Oh Jesus look!' jeered Terry. 'Just look what we have here – Sir Francis bloody Drake.'

'Oh *God*, Terry,' squealed Carol with exasperation. 'Do you *always* have to be so utterly *beastly*?'

'So what brings you up here, Colin?' went on Terry, heed-lessly. 'If that's the expression I want. What – sneaked out for a quiet puke, have you?'

'Leave him, Terry – leave him alone.'

'D'you know what, Colin – this is the first time I've seen you when you haven't been covered in some sort of shit or another. Your Mummy give you a bath?'

Colin jumped to his feet and with crimson face and hard lips pulled well back from his teeth he hurled himself at Terry who with one hand smacked his face and that had Colin flat on his back and dizzy as hell, so really none of this took very long at all. As Carol knelt down to Colin, Terry let out one fat laugh and ambled away. ('Don't be long sticking him back together, Carol – Dad's doing supper.') Colin looked up into Carol's face: oh God – oh bloody Jesus – she was tending to him *again*. On the boat he had been flat on his face and green and now he was the other way up and seething – but prone and useless one more time; in essence it was only just more of the same.

And just as on the boat Colin had been inno-cent of all knowledge as to the imminence of his burgeoning spew, so now was he quite astonished to find that he had come to the brink of sobbing: thick, hot tears jerked out of him now and were creasing his face – he looked for all the world as if he was straining every muscle available in some supreme effort to penetrate the joke. Carol too was seriously amazed, but now discovered that she was kissing Colin's forehead and then moving on to his eyelids, this round of wet fluttering further astounding the pair of them. Something like anxiety flitted into her eyes in the millisecond before the sight of them was closed down to Colin as she moved in to him and brought down her lips with weight and assurance on to the centre of his mouth – the surge of warmth and the light of fright making him gasp and making him quiver.

It was growing dark, but Colin was now irradi-ated. More of Carol's body was upon him, and he felt the urgent press and jostle of breasts that were hard – but only in the way that rubber balls are hard and would it be all right if he touched one, could he? He had one now – and Carol was kissing him hard. He had it still, and it took him to the brim of swooning; he was aware too of his own straining against her and heaven oh heaven, if only he knew what next he should do!

And then suddenly she was up and away from him – stiffening yet lithe as she hovered above, like a cat on the prowl. Colin reached out for her because he needed more.

'*Sh!*' she hissed with urgency. 'Listen!'

Colin let the sounds of the air surround him, urging himself to hear beyond the boom in his brain.

'I can't hear –'

'*Listen!*' insisted Carol. 'There's someone out there – someone near. I can feel it. I can sense it.'

'There's no one,' whispered Colin. Don't care if there's anyone – there could be an army, I simply don't care: just please don't let us stop what it is we are doing.

Carol was inching away from him – on all fours and crouching low; Colin's groan came from so deep within, but what could he do but just follow? She crept over the stunted hill under which Colin had been couched so briefly in a cradle of pleasure – and now she bristled and was pointing.

'See! There – there. There's a man over there.'

'I can't see . . .' began Colin – and then wait! He did sort of see, yes, that could I suppose be the outline of a figure – someone just standing there, it looked like. 'But Carol – no one can

335

see. If it *is* someone, they can't see anything from –'

But Carol was already edging closer – staying low and moving fast – and Colin was right behind her. Yes – was someone. Christ how weird. But hey – and yes, didn't have to say anything because Carol had seen it too: he wasn't looking – couldn't see – because he had his back turned squarely towards them and still he just stood there at the very edge of the cliff – plain now, quite plain and stark against the unbroken darkness.

Much nearer, now – and Christ, you know, it . . . Christ. Carol's eyes flew to Colin as he leapt bolt-upright and strode on with stiff legs and had stopped now and was cupping his hands to his mouth as he let out ringingly:

'Dad!'

Brian's whole body tensed and jerked and with a sigh of air was suddenly gone, leaving to Colin only the distance, and the deep blue night beyond it.

CHAPTER 6

Lulu could not have been more relieved when as silently as ever one can really manage these things, she let herself into the room. What a happy surprise: John was not so much asleep as deeply unconscious – truly out of it – sprawled across the bed: the top half of his pyjamas more or less on, trousers vaguely undone, and some of him under the covers. The room smelled stale and fetid – empty bottles idled longways on the floor looking as if they might have been spun in some fortune-telling game – and look over there: a clutter of dead miniatures by the telephone; a serious number of cigarettes had been stubbed out not just in ashtrays but other places too.

Lulu snapped off the television – the citrus colours of CNN had been fizzing noiselessly, but now an unforgiving harpy in quite stern hair was instantly cut dead while only some way into giving the universe an unsmiling and damned severe talking-to. Lulu moved to the bathroom and undressed, slipping on the hotel's white and rather harsher than it appeared monogrammed bathrobe. She brushed

337

her teeth, going to elaborate lengths to prevent the slightest thing clattering – although she well knew from the state of John (she had seen it before, this state of John) that little short of an earth tremor so violent as to pitch him face first to the floor was likely to stir him.

Just one standard lamp was alight, quite close to the bed. Lulu fumbled around its neck, running fingers some way up into the pleated paper shade, but couldn't seem to locate the . . . ah, down there, leading away from the thing: a foot-switch set into the flex. Lulu trod on it and with arms out-stretched made her way to the bed, only slightly assisted by the grey light of shadows just less dark than the rest.

The bed was vast, and Lulu was grateful for that – not simply because there was less chance of disturbing this now quite audibly droning and dead drunk husband of hers, but also for the reason that she needed to be far away from him: maybe no distance, now, could be too great. I can't, she thought – easing herself on to the length of the bed (leave the sheets – forget all that) – go on like this. Short and long term – it just can't go on, not like this it can't. She couldn't continue running off for days out with Lizzie and then stealing back like a criminal – well could she? I think, she thought, we'll have to go home tomorrow – it's easier to bear at home (pain and deprivation so often were – they knew their place, at home). Dear Lizzie – I hope I know her for ever; already I think of her as a good and true friend. And Lulu had meant what she had said to her earlier: why in fact *did* they need men? In the end they're nothing but trouble, aren't they? Well *aren't* they?

And Lulu must soon after have drifted to sleep. She had not thought herself able, despite an aching fatigue both without and within – but now the light of morning was filtering in between the flickering layers of spliced bits of dream, and Lulu was rolling her whole body and soul away from it, reluctant deep down to meet this day. But just at the moment consciousness took her did Lulu joltingly remember that she must on no account stray from her self-imposed coffin-space – too late had Lulu remembered that, for now she was colliding with the deadweight of John who grunted once as if he had been impudently interrupted mid-oration – and was not now a good deal of chapped and dry lip-smacking going on? It was as if John was assimilating appetites, discerning the nature of some insinuated flavour. An angry yawn like the muted growl of a tormented bullock was now making Lulu flinch, for soon his arms would rise and reach up stiffly and then his mouth would open wide, and so would one eye. And then the other. And as his legs were stretching in their reach for the bottom of the bed, so were the nails on one hand scraping questingly across his face – alive with gin-gery prickles – and now, dear Lulu, John could no longer be said to be asleep (and this is why she was tensed and bracing herself for all that came next).

The bathroom was always a good place to be at times like these, but Lulu was not even halfway there – mile upon mile of powder-puff carpet yet stood in her way – before John had sat up and even while wincing at the pain and confusion that so abrupt an action had caused him was barking out the first of his blunt-nosed accusations:

'*Caught* you this time, haven't I, you fucking *tramp*. Come here – don't go in there – come here. Now. Come –'

But John was taking no chances: he had stumbled over the edge of the bed and shakily at first but more firmly now he was coming to get her, you bet he bloody was. And maybe no more than just so tight-coiled and pent-up a night made Lulu wail out loud in her extreme desperation:

'*Pleeeeeease*, John – *stop*: I can't stand any more, John, please – I just can't *stand* any more.'

John held on to her shoulders; she tried to shrug him away, but John held on to her shoulders.

'*You* can't stand any more! *You* can't! You just try it from *my* side, Lulu! My wife has just this minute crawled back after being fucked senseless by someone she's only just *met* –!'

'John! What are you *saying*?! Listen to what you're *saying* – what do you think you're *saying*?! You're mad, you're crazy – I really do think you're *mad*, John. I don't *know* any men – it's all in your *mind*. Please stop. Please stop.'

'In my mind – I see.' John was quieter, now: the threat was very much still there (Lulu trembled still) but let's just give her some rope, shall we? Give her a little bit of rope. 'So – what are you telling me? I suppose that yesterday you went to lunch with this non-existent *Lizzie* person, did you?'

Lulu's eyes were wide with *trying*.

'*Yes*, John, *yes*. I went to lunch with Lizzie. She's *real*, John – real. It's everyone *else* who doesn't exist – this man, men, whatever it is you're dreaming – it's *them* who aren't real: it's all just in your *mind*, I'm telling you.'

'Uh-huh. I see. And when you were lunching with your "Lizzie", no one gave you a *letter* or anything, did they? I suppose I'm making that up too?'

Lulu just stopped dead and stepped back. Oh Christ. I think he maybe really *is* mad: look at his eyes – he seems so crazy. I'm scared. I'm scared.

'John,' she said, as steadily as she could cope with. 'I just don't know – *letter*? I've had no letter! From who?'

'You're very cool. So *cool*, Lulu. But unfortunately for you I happen to *know* that you received that letter because I paid the waiter twenty pounds to deliver it personally and he assured me afterwards that this is exactly what he had done. Explain *that*, please, Lulu.'

Lulu wanted to cry. I'm so unhappy – I don't understand. I'm so unhappy and I just want to cry.

'I'm waiting, Lulu.' Yes, I'm waiting: I can *afford* to, can't I?

Lulu gazed at John with pleading. 'John . . . ?' was all she managed.

'And what else would you like me to believe? Hm? That in fact you *weren't* with a man in this very hotel first thing yesterday morning? No? Another – yet *another* bit of nonsense I've just dreamed up, is it?'

Lulu was so *puzzled* – can't think, couldn't think: where was he *getting* all this from? There *is* no man, I haven't even *spoken* to a man – it's just . . . oooh God, oh God: you know what all this is about, don't you? Oh God I just can't *believe* it – all this, oh Christ it's so *laughable*: that bloody stupid thing with the man in the lobby with the Extra Strong Mints: John must have been watching, and out of just that he had woven this insane and blinding fantasy!

'John – for God's sake: that was absolutely *nothing* . . .'

John's eyes bulged like those of a furious toad, and he gripped her more tightly. Shall I go on gripping her? Or kill her now?

'Nothing?' he repeated, blankly – and then with real red anger – '*Nothing*?! What are you talking about, *nothing*?! He only bloody *gave* you one, didn't he?'

Lulu simply couldn't believe what she was hearing. In anguish she replied:

'Well *yes* he gave me one – of course he *gave* me one – so bloody what?'

John was now mesmerized. 'So bloody *what* . . . ?'

Lulu rushed a hand through frenzied hair – what on earth else could she add? What is it that he wants? Will *this* help?

'But I didn't put it in my *mouth*, John.'

John sprang back from her as if shocked.

'That's *it*,' he said, more darkly than she knew. 'I am now going to . . .' John stopped and turned a struck face towards her. 'You can actually stand there and say to me that this man – this complete and utter stranger – he *gave* you one, just *gave* you one in broad bloody daylight but this is nothing because you didn't bloody *suck* it?!'

Lulu shrugged. 'Well I didn't – I hate the *taste*, it's so hot: you *know* that, John . . . look, what exactly is the *problem* here?'

John was walking to the door in the manner of a tin-plate toy, just wound up.

'I am going now to kill this man, Lulu. And then,' he added, just before the door slammed shut behind him, 'I'm coming back for *you*.'

My husband, thought Lulu – while she just stood there – has this morning gone mad: lost his mind. Utter basket case. Was it *me* who drove him over the brink? Am I that kind of woman? We haven't been married for even two years and he is mad and my nerves are in tatters and I might even be in physical danger. It hadn't *been* like this, not at the beginning; but now it's like nothing else, ever.

I must speak to Lizzie. What time is it? Oh God – it's only . . . it's not yet . . . oh I *can't*, I *can't* go

343

and bother her now, she'll still be . . . oh but I've *got* to, got to – I've got to talk to someone and I have to do it *now*. I'll just quickly do my hair, will I? Oh – to hell with it – can't be doing with *hair*: I'll just go, shall I? Ring her first? Or just go? Just go – just go: Christ Almighty of *course* just go: John is right now at this second stalking the corridors, haunting the areas, seeking out a man to murder.

Where's the key? Never mind the key. No – got to have the key. Doesn't *matter* about the key – here, oh here's the key, here: right – go. Go now. Corridor's deserted – a diminishing perspective of doors that didn't want to know, each one guarded by a heavy and slumped copy of *The Times*. Lulu was on Elizabeth's floor before she even realized that she had done with the flight of stairs – and she'd have to knock quite loudly, despite the hour, despite the closed sentinels of silent doors and unruffled newspapers – have to bang like crazy to be heard.

To her surprise and relief, the door opened almost immediately, and there was blissful Lizzie in a beautiful dark pink satin gown, raising her eyebrows in welcome and ushering her in. Even more surprising, though, was the sight of Dotty in some sort of track suit thing, over by the window, coffee cup held aloft, mid-sip. Lulu was overcome by the curious and perplexing sensation that all that happened here was that she had just turned up, as summoned – slightly late for a long-ago convened and formal conference.

344

'So,' said Dotty. 'We three meet again. And at bloody dawn, too: how weird.' And for once Miss Lulu looks less than wonderful: wonderful.

At the mention of dawn, Lulu instinctively looked about her – and yes, there she was, little Dawn: perfect in sleep.

'Hello, Dotty,' said Lulu, hurriedly. 'Lizzie, look – something rather awful's happened . . . at least I *think* it has – it's so hard to tell.'

'What *is* it, Lulu?' asked Elizabeth, all concern. 'God – what a *morning*!'

'Well it's . . .' started Lulu. 'Oh God it all sounds so *crazy*, but – John – my husband, yes? John? Well he says he's going to kill a man. And I almost believe him. He's gone absolutely *mad*.'

'*Kill*?' queried Dotty. 'Kill who? Brian's gone mad too, as it happens.'

'Well this is just it,' despaired an exasperated Lulu. 'I don't even know who it is! You remember – Dotty, you remember yesterday morning? That man? The man in the lobby with the mints?'

'Vaguely,' said Dotty. 'Oh yes, I remember – I asked him for a mint.'

Lulu nodded, very much aware of the impossibility of what she had to say next: 'Well, *him*. He says he's going to kill him.'

'Oh Lulu,' cautioned Elizabeth, 'are you sure you've got this right? Why would he want to –?'

'Because the bloody man gave me a *mint*, apparently – I told you John was crazy, Lizzie – I *told* you. Convinced I had *lunch* with the man – *crazy*.'

345

'Look – have some coffee, Lulu. Sit down and have some coffee,' urged Elizabeth, patting the chair next to her. 'I'll just tell him you had lunch with *us*.'

Lulu sighed and slumped into the chair. 'I'd *love* some coffee, actually, Lizzie. Black, please. He won't listen – he never listens. What can I *do*?'

Elizabeth shook her head. 'I don't think you can really do anything, Lulu. He can't be serious – he doesn't even know the person's *name*. He's just still upset with you, Lulu, that's all. Just showing off. Men do.'

'You're telling me,' agreed Dotty. 'That's just what Brian was doing last night: showing off – just trying to get attention. And the *trouble* he's caused everyone you wouldn't *believe*.'

Lulu didn't actually care too much what this Brian, was it, person had been doing – *far* more concerned with John, who could well be mid-slaying right this moment – but better enquire, yes? One raised eyebrow should do it.

'Shall I show her the letter?' asked Elizabeth.

'Read it out,' said Dotty. 'You want mad, Lulu? Just you listen to this.'

'It is,' agreed Elizabeth, 'pretty incredible – even for Brian. You don't know Brian, do you Lulu? No. Probably just as well. Ready?' Elizabeth logged on to her higher-pitched and prim reading out voice. '"By the time you read this, I shall be deaf. I am more use to all of you that way. Believe me, this hasn't easy. My lobe. Brian."'

346

Lulu let out a gasp – puzzlement, disbelief, most things like that.

'There's more,' sighed Dotty, wagging her head.

Elizabeth resumed: '"P.S. Worry."'

'Now,' said Dotty. 'Be honest – crazy or what?'

'But Dotty,' urged Elizabeth – while Lulu shook her head in wonder – 'tell her what he *did.*'

'You won't,' said Dotty, '*believe* what he did. I can barely believe it myself. Last night – and it was Colin who told me all this: just happened to be there at the time, which was pretty lucky for Brian, as it turned out. Near our house, where we are – you know – *staying*, there's these sort of cliffs – not rugged type cliffs: pretty steep, though. Well Colin was playing around with this boy he's met, apparently – the one he went sailing with, yes? Ooh Elizabeth, meant to say – had a *marvellous* time, he said. Loved it.'

'Good,' approved Elizabeth. 'I'm glad.'

'So anyway, this boy, whatever his name is – don't know if Colin has told me his name . . . anyway, the boy suddenly sees someone standing at the edge of the cliff – just standing there – so they walk up to him, OK, and well – can you imagine what Colin must have thought? It was his *father* – it was actually *Brian*, just standing there. So Colin started talking to him – you know, usual thing: hi, Dad – what're you doing up here, sort of thing – and Brian – this is the amazing bit – he just starts slithering down over the edge. And it was pretty dark, apparently – well, must have been – and so Colin couldn't see what was going on. He called and called him, but nothing. So of course he ran back and told me but *I* couldn't do anything, could I? Couldn't leave Dawn – and even if I could, what use would *I* have been? So I told Colin to go down to the pub – there's a pub just near: lovely oldy-worldy sort of place – thatched and everything, really pretty. Run down to the pub, Colin, I said, and – I don't know, well – what do you *do*? Phone the police, I suppose.'

'Why didn't you phone from –?' put in Elizabeth.

'So Colin raced down there – oh, I don't know, Elizabeth – you don't really *think* properly when things like this happen, do you? So anyway it turns out there were a couple of coast-guards in the pub and they phoned their, I don't know – *people*: whoever they phoned, I don't know – and Colin showed them where it all happened – and they found him straight away because at the bottom of these cliffs, right, there's this incredibly thick *mud* – does that happen when the tide goes out? Must do. Don't know. Anyway there was the idiot Brian stuck face-down in all this filthy *mud* – so deep, apparently, they needed waders and hoses and oh God *everything*. So they pulled him out and just in time – one of them said he could easily have drowned, and all his nose and ears and mouth were full of mud and they washed off all they could and he sort of came to but he couldn't *hear* –'

'Why do you think,' asked Lulu, 'he was so

determined to become *deaf*? It's so odd. And what a funny way to do it.'

Dotty snorted. 'Well he *is* odd, you see – Brian. Probably fed up listening to *me*, I should think. So they took him to hospital – Colin went too: he's been really wonderful in all this – I think he's still with him. Been up all night, poor little boy. Turns out he's broken his neck.'

'Oh no!' exclaimed Lulu.

Dotty nodded. 'Bloody fool. Not as bad as it sounds, apparently – not spinal, or anything. Actually I don't *know* if it's broken, but he's got to wear a sort of a brace thing, whatever they wear. Can you believe all this? I've just come from seeing him now – he looks so stupid just lying there, wasting everyone's time – surrounded by people who are *really* sick. Of course I'd read this stupid letter by then so I said to him Well I hope you are very *proud* of yourself – I hope you're very *pleased* with what you've done. And then I felt a bit . . . oh God – he looked so pathetic and his ears were all red and raw because they'd really had to scrape and scrape to get the mud out and there's still about a ton of it down there, apparently. So I said How are your *lobes*? Well he'd singled them out, hadn't he? In the letter. I actually didn't know that the lobes had anything to *do* with hearing but he's obviously been into it all. He does that: goes into things.'

'And what did he say?' asked Elizabeth.

'"What,"' replied Dotty, with a shrug. 'He said "what": *deaf*, you see.'

349

'Amazing,' said Lulu, softly. What an amazing story.

'Oh well – there you are,' sighed Dotty, pretty philosophically. 'Anything to spoil my holiday – that's Brian all over. And you notice he wanted me to "worry"? Of course, we'll have to go back, now. I don't want to be cooped up with him down here, not with him helpless like that. Bad enough at home.'

'Oh *Dotty!*' lamented Elizabeth.

'Can't be helped,' shrugged Dotty. Don't actually *mind*, to tell you the truth – can't stand another day in that bloody little caravan. Anyway – holidays are for young people: people like Melody. And *I* won't be selfish – not like Brian. *I* won't spoil Melody's holiday, just because I've got to cut mine short. No – I'll take little Dawn back home with me. Yes. And then Melody can go on enjoying herself. Because that's the *kind* thing to do.

'But what about poor *Colin?*' pursued Elizabeth.

'Oh I *know*, Elizabeth – don't you think I feel awful about that? And just when he's made a new little friend. But what can I do? It's all Brian's fault.'

'Well he can go on staying *here*. God – we've only got the place for a couple more days and it's a shame to *waste* it: all *paid* for and everything. Yes, Dotty?'

'That's so sweet of you, Elizabeth. He'd love that, I'm sure. So you see, Lulu – men *do* go mad. It seems that ours have chosen to do so on the very same day – that's the only odd bit about it.'

Lulu nodded. 'I suppose my holiday's ruined too, now. I'm going back today, Lizzie: I'm sorry but I've decided. I know what Dotty means – it's just about bearable, when you're at home. It's just not quite so awful.'

'You could be lucky,' put in Dotty, with a cheeky and girlish smirk. 'Your bloke might have been arrested by now for the calculated and cold-blooded murder of the person who gave you a peppermint.'

A snort of laughter escaped from Lulu, and Elizabeth was laughing now too: it was just too *ludicrous*, wasn't it? What *is* it about these men?

'But what will *I* do?' Elizabeth asked now of each of them. 'Everybody's *leaving* – all my friends are *going*! Melody I haven't seen since the second we *arrived*.'

And then, while both Dotty and Lulu were clucking consolation, Elizabeth came up with one of her famous brain-waves: Howard would have heard the whoosh and plummet as it came down low and homed in unerringly to its chosen target.

'Look,' she announced – quite like a compère outlining the coming attractions on next week's show – 'I've just had the most brilliant *idea*. After the weekend, yes? When everyone's back home and *I'm* back home and Katie and absolutely *everyone*, we'll have the most marvellous reunion party at *my* house. Yes? It'll be wonderful – and it'll be so nice for Howard because he hasn't even *had* a holiday, poor lamb, and summer things like this are *sort* of holidays, aren't they? And maybe he could talk Brian out of wanting to be deaf – he's quite good with Brian. Oh Dotty – did you pass on the message about the house?'

'Well I *didn't*,' admitted Dotty. 'What with Brian being buried in mud and breaking his neck I didn't get round to it. Anyway – he wouldn't have *heard*, or anything. I love the party idea, though, Elizabeth. I just *adore* summer parties.'

'We'll have it in the *garden*,' insisted Elizabeth. 'I'll phone Howard and tell him to hire the most wonderful *marquee* – wouldn't that be lovely? It'll be the best summer party of all – forget Buckingham Palace: anyone who's anyone is coming to Lizzie's!'

'Sounds great,' laughed Lulu. 'But . . . well – I'd have to bring John along, you know, Lizzie. He'd just go crazy, otherwise.'

'Just be sure you don't serve *mints*,' warned Dotty, quite roguishly. 'Wholesale slaughter all round.'

Lulu laughed again. She's right! She's right! It's just too stupid to even *think* about: John was just wanting to be the centre of attention – probably even jealous of *Lizzie*, never mind some bloody *man*. And then Lulu put into words a good deal of this, and enjoyed the feeling of being bound into a sisterhood: it's great being with these two – really great.

'It's just the same with Brian,' averred Dotty. 'They just can't bear it if anything else, anything *better* comes along. The only reason Brian did all this – believe me, I understand men, not that there's anything much to understand about them – all this was because of that little angel Dawn: he just couldn't stand it – it's just so *typical*. And look at her – just look at her sleeping, good as gold. Only a man could resent the loveliness of such a little *doll*. *And*, I said to him, you're lucky – luckier than you deserve, Brian. Just a little bit further down the coast, apparently – so Colin was told, anyway – there are all these jagged rocks at the bottom – not mud: the sort of rocks that smash things to pieces. Don't you *see* how stupid you've been, Brian, I said to him – just a matter of a few more yards and God – you could've gone and *killed* yourself.'

John had been slumped in sleep at the little corner table in the breakfast room. He knew this only because some vague and distant clattering noise had now roused him, and God he felt worse than ever in his life. Why am I sitting here? Bloody coffee's gone cold. Why am I sitting here? And why is that waitress person over there so pointedly *looking* at me? I suppose because of the way I – oh Jesus, my head, my head: what a bloody blinder – I suppose because of the way I appear: mad hair, mad face – unshaven and troughed by shadows; pyjama jacket and cotton trousers – classic madman's combo. Yeah – that's why she's looking. Well let her look; what possible difference can it make to me if someone wants to *look* or not?

It's still so bloody *early* – no one at all seems to be around, yet. I remember what the hell I'm doing here, now. Stormed out of the room, didn't I? (Couldn't believe, could not take in, just how *brazen* Lulu had been – I *love* the woman: why on earth can't she *see* that? But do I love her still? I think I must do) – and Christ I was ready, boy was I ready. If that McInerney person had shown his face to me at right that moment, I would have ripped it off him. But then this complete blank fell down all over me – and I felt bad, really bad: still do – I'm feeling mighty bad because this is no hangover – I'm still smashed and stunned and wounded. Hangover comes later: icing on the cake. Couldn't remember, couldn't remember for the life of me what his bloody room number was (because yesterday I had found it out, you bet I had). Jesus – I was ready to smash down doors, as many doors as it took, but that was no good, that was no use. So I came down here, then – maybe get some dozy pillock to tell me the room number, maybe get a squint at a registration? Don't know – hadn't thought it through; all I knew was that soon I had to kill that man, and only then could I sleep again.

The smell, that wonderful smell of deep-roast coffee – that's what took me. Christ I needed *something* – and I just followed the waft, went for the warm aroma of comfort. Yeah, that was it. And then we fast-forward to now, do we? Somehow I just fell back into this hammock of exhaustion, and now, yeah – now I'm awake again (get some more coffee – need some – didn't even get around to drinking the first batch) and Christ, I feel even worse than I did before. You – yes *you*, the waitress who keeps on looking at me: can you see what it is that I'm doing now? You can? Flapping around a napkin is what I'm actually up to – that and pointing down at my cup. Can you make sense of this, or is it beyond you? Oh yes of *course* – the first time I actually *require* her attention and what does the stupid girl do? Leaves the bloody room altogether; well, what can you expect? Only looks about twelve.

Then did the slice of pain near cut him in half as he newly realized the enormity of what had been done to him. Lulu! My Lulu! Oh God – I must just quickly kill this man: it simply must be done. Three fourteen. Three fourteen. It has just this moment come to me – the number of his room is three fourteen, so here I bloody come: I'm already on my way.

Miles rolled away from Melody and tenderly touched his moustache, rather as if to check that it had not come away and attached itself to the other party at some hot point during their latest bout of lusty combat.

'God, Miles,' sighed Melody. 'You'll *kill* me, you will. Oh God you're so wonderful.'

Miles smiled. 'I know,' he said. Well I bloody should be, he was thinking: I don't do all this in any lily-livered sort of a way – for me, this is a lifestyle. I'm a professional – I can sell anything to anyone at any time of the night or day, and this includes myself.

'And me?' pursued Melody. 'Do I please you, Miles? Do you think I'm wonderful too?' Why are men like this, actually? I shouldn't have to *ask*: no matter how good the sex, I always end up feeling let down.

Miles turned her cheek towards him and kissed it. 'Magical,' he said. 'Wonderful isn't the word.' No, he thought – it's not: average but enthusiastic, I think would be the summing up. The only really good thing about you, Melody (something you women never understand), is that you happen to be *here*: this week, you're the lucky one – capito? All the rest's just chat.

Melody was gently stroking the quite dark hair on his chest.

'Miles . . . ?' came her voice, now – tentative and probing.

Miles sighed in utter silence – something you have to learn to do if you're around women a lot of the time, cos they can really wear you down with all their bloody stuff, you know, but you don't want to shove it in their faces, do you? And then he gave out the mandatory 'Mm . . . ?' – cos otherwise she

356

was never going to go on with it, was she? I mean, he was hardly going to refuse her permission to speak, was he? But without that 'Mm . . . ?' all she was going to do was come out with another interrogative 'Miles . . . ?' – right? So let's not waste any more of the day – let her say whatever she wants and then just bloody agree with it.

'When you said you loved me . . . ?'

Here we bloody go. 'Mm . . . ?'

Melody was now propped up on an elbow, eyes alight with an eager sincerity. 'Well, you did *mean* it, didn't you? You didn't just – *say* it?'

'*Told* you, love – I don't tell lies. When I say something, I mean it: depend on it. I *love* you. See? Said it again.'

'Oh *Miles* . . .' came the swoon of relief and yielding from Melody. 'I don't ever want to be parted from you. You do know that, don't you?'

Well in one sense I know it (I get this a lot) but in any *real* sense, darling, what we've got is two or is it three more days and then you're just going to have to bloody get used to it.

'You don't ever have to be, Melody: I'm here for you, aren't I, love? Now,' he said – bringing down her head to his chest, which she kissed, and then drawing it down further and on past his stomach. 'Why don't you show your appreciation?'

Miles could not have told you which had come first – the thunderous, sudden and now explosive noises or the nip of teeth on his most prized and tender part, but he was up and out of bed and

357

wild-eyed and Melody was quaking and now he was striding over to the door to see just what the bloody fuck was going on, here.

As soon as the door was wide, John barged his way right in – but whatever his immediate intention had been he was pulled up short by the sight of Miles who was standing completely naked before him. The shock was equal for both of them, but it was only a matter of a very short time before one of them (which one?) said *something*.

'Fucking *hell*!' roared Miles. 'It's bloody *you* again – what the bloody fuck do you think you're up to, ay?'

And by now John had taken in a fact that he had not previously sanely registered: this man was huge – he was looming way over John's head, and – among much else – he wasn't even wearing shoes. Maybe hitting this man was not a clever move, always assuming I could even reach his face.

'I have come,' said John – and the voice was high-pitched and trembly – 'about my wife.'

Miles hurled shut the door and grabbed at the lapels of John's pyjama jacket and drew him close; John did not enjoy this, as now they were touching all the way down. *Fuck*, Miles was thinking – jealous, crazy fucking husbands I *do* not need – why did the stupid bitch have to bloody *lie* to me?

'Miles!' called out the stupid bitch from the bedroom. 'Christ's sake – who *is* it? What's going *on*?'

'*Right*,' said Miles, grimly – letting go of John.

'We're going to settle this once and for all. In there.'

John stumbled in to the bedroom, and Miles was pushing him on. Melody had the sheets up to her mouth and was staring at the two of them.

'Oh my God,' she said, 'it's *him* again.'

'Jesus!' cried out John. 'You've got *another* one!'

'Look – just shut it for now,' said Miles. 'Melody – you told me this bloke *wasn't* your bloody husband.'

'He's not! He's not!' she wailed. 'I don't know *who* the fuck he is – he just keeps turning *up*!'

'Of *course* I'm not her husband!' ranted John. 'Of *course* I'm bloody not!'

It was Miles's turn to be dumbstruck, this time.

'But *look*, you fucking nutter – you just *said* –'

'Not *her* – not *her* – I don't know who your latest bloody tart is! I'm talking about –'

'Don't you call me a bloody tart!' screamed Melody. 'Miles – *do* something – get *rid* of him: he's *mental*.'

'*Look* –' bellowed John to Melody. 'You may not know or care but *my* wife is the one this bastard bloody had right before he bloody had *you*.'

And now Miles sort of saw it: that little receptionist girl – what was her name? Pauline. Yeah, Pauline – right.

Melody set up a hoot. 'Oh *her*!' she laughed. 'No, actually – I *don't* care – I thought it was hilarious: she was hand-cuffed to the bed for *hours*!'

And that did it for John: he rushed at Miles, who more or less picked him up and threw him on to the floor.

'Look, mate,' said Miles. 'I don't want to hurt you, so don't make me, OK? That little thing I had with, er – oh Christ, I've forgotten her bloody name again –'

John stared up from the crumple he had become: he couldn't remember her *name* . . . ?!

'– that was just nothing: believe me. That's all over. Didn't even begin. Things like this *happen*, mate – just some stupid little summer *thing*, OK?'

John scrambled to his feet and was denting his face on Miles's chest again before Miles got hold of him and said *Right*, mate, I'm sorry but this just won't do: it's time for you to go. He bundled him to the door and flicked him out into the corridor and John spun around a few times before his head clonked into a fire extinguisher and Miles slammed the door on the sight of him reeling badly and maybe about to topple over.

'Forget him,' said Miles to Melody, as he ambled back to her. 'He's just a bloody nut – we won't see him again. Hey, love – it's not worth *crying* about.'

But when Melody raised up her eyes, he saw that her shoulders had been hunched in laughter. 'Oh *Jesus*,' she whooped, 'what an absolute *creep*! But oh God – can we *blame* him, being married to that silly little *Pauline* person!'

Miles grinned (oh yeah – that was it: Pauline).

'You were *terrific*,' gushed on Melody. 'So *manly*. Oh Miles – I do love you so much. You won't, will you – you won't ever leave me, will you?'

Miles folded Melody into his arms.

'You don't listen,' he said. 'Do you? Now then,' he added now, pressing down on her shoulders until she was kneeling before him and gazing up in wonder and adoration as might a supplicant at the sight of a creamy icon sweetly oozing tears of blood.

Yes, he thought, as she began to work on him – and then after, I'll have a shower, and while you're having your massage or your sauna or whatever it is you do down there, I'll nip out and buy a couple of incredibly expensive and real knockout toys for the boys – get that out of the way. Ooh – ooh – *now* she was exciting him: now this was beginning to make him feel deep down real good. Maybe get some bit of bleeding junk for Sheil, while I'm at it.

Howard replaced the receiver, not knowing quite what to think. The stuff that Elizabeth had just been saying had pretty well amazed him: how on earth can such things happen in just a few days? And what had Brian thought he was up to? And now of *course* she had to round the whole thing off with one of her huge and loony schemes, but naturally – and who, exactly, would be arranging it, do you imagine? And who, might you suppose, is to pay for it all? Yes – quite.

But he had been pleased to hear from her (was

361

actually on the verge of ringing) because, as he had said to her more or less immediately:

'Look, Elizabeth – have you *given* that message to Brian or what? This Davies person is getting –'

'Ah no – I mean *yes*, yes I have – I told Dotty, anyway, but look, Howard, quite a lot has been going on down here what with one thing and another so just let me fill you in on it all, all right?'

'Yes but Elizabeth *look* – if Brian doesn't get back to me soon –'

'You'll probably be *seeing* him later on – just let me *explain*, Howard – it's no good butting in all the time.'

'OK, Elizabeth – all right, fine: explain.'

'Right. Well the first thing: Brian. Last night Brian apparently decided that he wanted to go deaf –'

'Wanted to go *what*?!'

'*Deaf*, Howard: do listen. I don't know *why* he wanted that, but apparently he did – maybe very Freudian, I really couldn't say. Actually, Howard, between you and me I think he's a psychiatric case, but I didn't say that to Dotty – probably *knows*, of course. Well – would do, living with the man. Anyway, what he did was fall over a cliff – or jump off a cliff –'

'Jump off a –?'

'Yup. Anyway, there was all this mud at the bottom, so he wasn't killed, or anything – but he did sort of break his neck. At least it *might* be broken, no one's quite sure – but it's OK: he can *walk* and *talk* and everything. But he can't hear very well. Which is what he wanted, of course.'

Howard did no more than click his tongue: *what*?

'*So*,' resumed Elizabeth, 'he and Dotty are coming home – today, pretty sure – so you can talk to him then about the house, and everything. Maybe Howard too you could tell him that going deaf isn't maybe such a brilliant idea, hm? *Talk* to him, yes? Of course if he can't actually *hear*, there's not a lot of point. Maybe shout. Now *Colin* – Colin is staying on with me till the weekend, OK? I'm coming back on Sunday, as arranged. Melody I've barely spoken to since we got here – seems quite head over heels about some *man* she's met – with him all the time. She says it's more than just a summer thing and that he *loves* her, if you can believe it.'

'Really?' commented Howard. Bit of a pang, there: silly – I have no claim, no deep feelings for Melody any more; still, bit of a pang – no point in denying it. 'What's been happening to Dawn, then?'

'*Dawn* – yes: it's the most extraordinary thing – Dotty's become a sort of second mother to her: *dotes* on her – won't be parted. Which, of course, suits Melody right down to the ground. Dotty's bringing Dawn back with *her* – so she'll be next door until Melody gets back. I think that's everything. Now, Howard: listen – I have had the most marvellous idea!'

363

Oh no. 'Oh yes?'

'Mm – now listen. Because everyone's just so all over the place, I've decided that the most wonderful thing to do would be to have a lovely summer party in the garden – a sort of reunion and everyone can come. I've met the most adorable person called Lulu – oh yes: *Lulu's* leaving early too – bit complicated: her husband's gone a bit mad and wants to kill some man because he gave Lulu a peppermint – oh God you wouldn't *believe* it!'

'Elizabeth – have you been drinking?'

'It sounds like it, doesn't it?! I know – it's crazy. It's all so mad. So anyway, Howard – I thought you could hire a marquee, yes? From that firm you use. Doesn't have to be huge, or anything – oh and *Katie*, have you heard from Katie? I haven't heard a word, just lately.'

'I haven't, no. Well – not since she rang me about – oh you know: usual. Money.'

'Oh God that child! Anyway, she'll be back by then – Tuesday, Howard: we're having it on Tuesday. That'll give me buckets of time to do the food, and everything. She can maybe bring Ellie along – I do hope they're having fun. And *you*, Howard – everything all right, yes? Not too lonely? I *can* come back early if you want me to – God, everyone else seems to be doing it. All so terribly odd.'

'No no, Elizabeth – that would be silly. You're enjoying it, aren't you? Stay – of course stay.'

'Well I *am* enjoying it, yes, Howard – but it

364

won't be the same without Lulu. But I'm going to keep up with her, and everything. She doesn't actually live too far from us – and *God*, she's as crazy about shopping as I am! She's quite like me in a lot of ways, if I think about it: a really, really lovely person.'

And that was more or less all she had to hit him with; she mentioned the marquee and the party another six or so times, made him promise faithfully to take care, and then said that she had to dash because she had a facial and a mud bath booked – but not to worry because hers would not be at the bottom of a cliff, OK?

And the surprises were clearly not yet over for the day, because not at all long after Howard had replaced the receiver (not knowing quite what to think) who should walk into his office but Norman Furnish – looking fairly apprehensive and maybe more than marginally ill.

'Norman!' exclaimed Howard – the warmth and well-goodness-me-I-hardly-expected-to-see-*you*-here-so-soon tone of voice maybe only slightly dimmed by the shadow of the little bit of business that possibly had to be gone into, and afterwards, we do hope, dispensed with entirely.

'No, well,' grinned Norman – half in relief (it actually really *was* good to be back: wish to God I'd never left) but also with the air of one who at any given moment might have to hurl himself prone in the face of an aerial and out of the blue rat-a-tat attack. 'I, er, came back early. Cut it short.'

'Obviously not a very brilliant holiday, then, Norman. Where were you? Where did you go, actually?'

Argh: hadn't thought of that – where was I? Where did I go, actually?

'Cornwall.' Why had he said Cornwall? Don't know – bit flustered. Hope Mr Street – Howard – doesn't *know* Cornwall, or anything, because I for one have never set foot in the place in my life.

'Oh I *am* surprised you didn't go the length in Cornwall,' deplored Howard. 'I've had many happy times in Cornwall. Which part were you? South?

'*Sort* of south,' agreed Norman. Oh God – this is awful: Mr Street – Howard – was one of the few really straight people that Norman had ever encountered, and yet all the time he was forced into lying to the man, and deceiving him, and robbing him (not too long before that comes up, I suppose – this could be my very last day in work), and even all that leaves out of the frame all the *Katie* business, doesn't it? Who does indeed appear to be out of the frame for good and all: how else could it be? After the way it had gone and the way he had left?

That long, sad and darkening evening in the Sheraton Hotel had elongated further into the undeniable finality of night, and Norman had taken his rags and his carrier bag away from that room and down in the lift and into a taxi – counting and counting as the cab wove its way

366

to the lights of O'Hare the forty or so dollars that were left from Katie's hundred and praying that it would be enough for just this ride and then a tube from Heathrow back to the dead and useless stuff in his dark and empty room; because the only other thing that Norman now possessed was the blood in his veins, and anyone at all was welcome to that because what good now could it be to Norman? When again would he need to be ruddy?

He had written to Katie a letter, filled with such outpourings – charged with an ardour with the power to melt a platinum heart. He knew she would laugh her head off at all that so he folded it neatly and slipped it inside his Bulls bomber jacket (there was no pocket there, but what was left of the tattered lining afforded a makeshift and gaping space). He then extracted another sheet of hotel notepaper from the slatted rack, and wrote just this:

'Katie. I have gone back to London. I hope you enjoy the rest of your holiday. I'll see you, I suppose, at work. I love you. Norman. X.'

He then drank a good deal of a can of Coke from the minibar (toyed with beefing it up with a slug of something, but his stomach was playing him up, if he was honest – probably no more than fooling at the foothills of limbering up, working out and getting on down and then steadily building before exploding in a no-holds-barred and truly awesome fashion when finally the fearsome plane engines made him shudder

367

and jolt with their thrust and roar: probably no more than that).

And just before he left (Goodbye, America! I'll be back – but please God next time don't make it *personal*) he wondered whether or not his punished soul and his headlong heart could bear to watch again Norman and Katie's joint little porno production, and while he ached to have back that wonderful moment, he decided that yes, on balance, he could just about cope – but five minutes' meddling told him what he might already have guessed: that there was no way on God's earth that this bloody machine was even going to begin to cooperate – so he just added the video to the pitiful haul in his Big Brown Bag and quit.

Norman survived the flight by becoming alternately ratarsed and convulsively sick – his apple-green and shaky form a familiar sight to fellow passengers as it ricocheted from this fixture to that in his latest pressing need to more deeply investigate the depths of the stainless steel and comfortless lavatory. Finally he got home (Home! Home! Oh God I hate this place more than ever – I'll have to move, have to get *another* horrible room, somewhere: that's if I've still got a job) and found that he had left in his pockets just exactly one pee: great, he thought, I am not penniless. Didn't *smirk* at that – didn't find the observation in the least bit *amusing*: why would he? Would *you*?

So Norman had washed a bit, slept a bit, and had then fished out from the back of the crate that posed as a cupboard a few clothes (anything – but *anything* was an improvement on the duds that had entrapped him for days) and now here he was, as unstale as he could manage – back in the familiar and comfortably faded office, so ridiculously short a time after he had left it – wondering now whether Mr Street – Howard – would be assailing him with a succession of cruelly accurate and razor-tipped banderillas and then, when Norman became irreversibly maimed by the onslaught and was staggering groggily, dispatching him with the swift and pole-axing coup de grâce; or would he just deliver the one merciful bullet to the back of his head, a booted foot then toppling him lifeless into a fast dug out and shallow grave, all of his own creation?

'Well look, Norman,' said Howard. Was he shifting with unease? Was it the approach of some unpalatable deed which prompted that decided swivel to which Howard's buttocks had just been subject? Time will tell, Norman: time will tell. 'Look – sit down, will you? I'm sorry you didn't have much of a holiday, Norman, but there's a certain something we must just briefly discuss – get out of the way, yes? Now Norman – I trust you, you know that?'

Oh God yes I *do*, I *do* – that's what makes it all so *awful*. Oh *God*, Mr Street – kill me now and spare us both. Howard.

'Yes – I do know that,' mumbled Norman.

'I'm *glad* you do, Norman – glad you do. So you

will not take any of these questions as *accusations* of any kind, no? It's just that there are certain things I should like you to tell me – and I don't have to ask you to be honest, Norman, because I know you will be. OK?'

'Yes of course, Mr Street. Howard. Understood.'

'Good. Well look – we won't draw it all out: here it is, plain and simple. Have you, Norman, ever offered one of our clients a private deal? One in which the commission does not come to the company but, um, to yourself.'

Norman's eyes were as wide as a pair of flying saucers – he looked for all the world as if, one dawn on some remote and windswept moor, he had with these own wide eyes of his witnessed the slow and humming vertical descent of a pair of flying saucers.

'What . . . ?' he struggled to understand, forehead crumpled in confusion. 'You mean – *I* go to a client and offer some sort of inducement to pay me instead of the company? Oh *God* no, Mr Street. Howard. I didn't know such a thing was possible – it has never entered my –'

'Well of course I *knew* that, Norman,' beamed Howard. Oh thank God – couldn't bear going through the business of interviewing anyone else for the job: doubt I'd get a replacement so cheaply. And the police and things would've been involved, wouldn't they? Messy; unpleasant. 'Good – that's settled, then. Hope you didn't mind my . . . ?'

'No, Mr Street – not a bit. Howard. It's your company, after all – if you suspect any irregularities . . .'

'Well it was just a bit of rumour-mongering, if you want to know: opposition stirring up trouble – no more than that.' And I won't go into all the petty cash business, adjudged Howard: can't accuse the lad of stealing *twice* in a day.

'Actually, Mr Street – just touching on money . . . um – Howard. I was in fact *mugged* in, er, Cornwall . . .'

'Oh my *God*, Norman – were you hurt?'

'Well – my nose . . . can you see? Bit of a bump.' I left the cast and its plasters in the trash at the Sheraton: some souvenirs you just don't need. 'But the point is they got all my money, and –'

'Oh Jesus – so *that's* why you've had to cut short your holiday! Oh poor old Norman.' Oh *shit* – here I was charging him with theft, and all the time the lad's a bloody *victim*. 'Look, Norman – tell you what: your salary's due at the beginning of the week, yes? Well let me give you, say, a hundred to tide you over, OK? God – who would've thought a thing like that could happen in *Cornwall*?'

'Well that's terribly *good* of you . . .'

'No it's not: basic duty. And listen, Norman – think of this as a summer bonus, yes? You don't have to pay it back. God – what a time you must have had!'

'Oh really, Mr Street – I *couldn't* . . . Howard.'

'Too late now: I've written the cheque. Here.'

Norman accepted the cheque. Weird: members

of this family keep giving me hundreds. He left the office feeling as if the population of the world was *regarding* him, clucking its vast collective tongue in reproach, and extending a zillion accusatory fingers. Look – *look*: conscience is one thing, right? But a man has to *live*, doesn't he? Yes he does. Or at least get by as best he can.

'Right, then,' summed up Lulu as gaily as she could, surveying the massed ranks of their luggage just inside the living-room of the suite, and trying hard to avoid the chill eye of John. 'I'm pretty sure that's everything.'

Oh *God*, she prayed, just let the porter arrive and let's be *done* with it. All the violence seemed to be on hold, for now, but steel-bladed malice still glinted, and only when they were home, thought Lulu, could anything come back down to some sort of normality. Normality? Unlikely – but a state closer to blunted antagonism: could we just maybe tolerate that? Until one or two conceivable futures could be not all that closely looked into.

Earlier that morning, Lulu had not known quite what to expect when she heard the scuffling at the door – it was such a funny noise, she did not know how to react to it. Did it denote crumbling masonry? Or was maybe a frisky dog brushing the panels and snuffling? Lulu opened the door, and as John fell inwards as a result of just his most recent shambolic collision, she reached forward to catch him – fluffed it, and he hit the floor like a stone.

Lulu suppressed a yelp and kicked shut the door and tried to help him as he tried to help himself and now he was more or less half up and Christ that was quite a nasty lump on his forehead there and a fair deal of spittle was glistening at the corners of his mouth and as Lulu half carried and half hauled him into the bedroom and on to the bed she was thinking I think I must now telephone the hotel doctor – or will he already be dealing with John's assailant, who might quite well by now be dead? And listen: John was almost raving.

'Leave me! Leave me! I'm quite badly awake!'

'Look John, just – oh God you're so heavy – here, John – just – can you get your feet up there? Yes – one last push, John – there, OK – better, Johnny? Better?'

John lay on his back on the bed and roared up to the ceiling:

'All I am – all I am is quite badly *awake*, I tell you!'

Lulu was concerned and quite frightened. Was he *really* mad, then? Does it really take so little time, so few days, this undulation from sane to gone? Or is it always there, darkly lurking, and we glimpse its teeth only when the pouncing's done?

'What do you *mean*, John? What are you saying? Look – I'm going to phone the doctor – you just lay still.'

And already she was jabbing out numbers while John's hoarse ranting descended sharply to little more than a guttural whisper:

373

'I mean, I mean . . . all I mean is I'm *awake*, I'm *awake*, but I'm really not doing it all that *well* . . . is all I mean. Is all I mean.'

It took an unendurable while for the doctor to arrive: Lulu just sat in mute acceptance and denial of all John's wild and gutsily furious opprobrium, each lewd and hideously painful dismissal of her worth weighed down by the thick and silty phlegm of loathing. I think, thought Lulu, this man is mad: I hope that's all it is.

The doctor sniffed at John's husked-out breath and thought I'll ask no questions: he dressed a graze on John's right cheekbone, applied something other to the swelling on his head – got him to take a few pills to make him sleep. Lulu all the while was braced for a rerun of his barked-out and accusatory obscenities, but all John muttered was I'm awake, I'm awake – but really *badly*.

As he dozed, and the doctor began to pack away his things (it's the same every bloody summer – they drink too much, they get into fights: no one learns, not ever), Lulu enquired of his opinion as to John's, um, mental fitness.

'He certainly appears to be very stressed,' considered the doctor, with unctuous ease (your husband is probably just an overworked, overpaid alcoholic – we get a lot of them here). 'Maybe you might think of a week or two at a health farm?'

Lulu smiled, despite – oh, *everything*. 'I don't think so,' she said – and then more softly: 'I was thinking more of maybe a psychiatrist?'

'Possibly a good idea: certainly worth thinking about.' You can, thought the doctor, send him to a health farm, consult a psychiatrist or else shoot him full of holes and dump him in the sea – I really couldn't give a flying fuck: I've five more malingerers and idiots in this hotel, all requiring attention – and it's not yet lunchtime. He smiled, with professional concern, and let himself out.

John had woken maybe two hours later; Lulu had by then packed everything into suitcases, informed Reception, and filled in Lizzie on the latest. It was awful to be leaving Lizzie (and going home to oh God – *what*?) but she had her address (yes I've *got* it, I've *got* it, Lizzie – you've given it to me *twice*) and goodness – the number of times she'd mentioned the party! But actually – sounds crazy, I know (so much does) – but I'm not so much looking forward to Lizzie's summer party as *living* for it: it's the only good thing on the horizon.

And now finally the porter was here and they followed him into the lift and it seemed to Lulu that John was a good deal calmer (maybe the pills – could it be the pills the doctor gave him? Nice man, the doctor: appeared to genuinely *care*, anyway) and God was she grateful for that. John, for his part, was indeed feeling pretty tranquil – was I ever otherwise? Can't quite recall the sequence of events. But Lulu, certainly, seems very excitable, these days – I wonder could it be anything to do with her hormones? You read things, don't you, about women who behave strangely due to some form or other of hormonal imbalance – all I am wondering is, could it maybe be this? Why else would she behave so outrageously, so irrationally – so wholly out of character? Unless she's *mad*, of course. That would explain a very great deal: with madness, it all becomes clearer.

In the foyer, as a concierge loaded the cases into their car (I'll drive, John – OK? I'll drive, yes?) John had made to go over to Reception, but Lulu quickly indicated that this too had been dealt with. And while she was glancing across there, she just happened to catch sight of that *man*. Now OK – fair enough, he had been completely and utterly innocent of anything at all – must have been startled out of his wits when John had that morning attacked him just because he had given Lulu a bloody Extra Strong Mint which she hadn't even *wanted* – but still he did not have to inflict such severe retribution on her hapless and misguided husband, did he? *Look* at John – just look at him: his face is a mess. And this other man doesn't even have so much as a mark on him.

John was now moving towards the glass revolving doors, and Lulu was briskly following. On impulse, however, she wheeled round and back to the Reception desk and in front of an astonished cluster of comers and goers brought her hand hard across this big bully's face and all he could do was clutch it and stare at her, his big red mouth wet and agape. Lulu immediately turned and swished out of the hotel and into the car without even for a moment even breaking her stride. John – who was stunned – tagged on gamely.

It was not until they were close to the motorway that he said:

'What did you do that for?'

'Can you look out for the right intersection, Johnny? It's confusing, this bit – I don't want to get back on to the ring road thing. Do what?'

'That bloke. Hit that bloke. Who on earth *was* he?'

Lulu fell silent. Oh my God – it's *this* bad: this morning he was out to kill him, and now he doesn't even remember who he was: this man needs professional help – and bloody quick.

'Johnny,' she said, as soothingly as a nurse who has been trained in all this sort of thing, 'he was the man with the *Mints* – yes?'

And John nodded, which seemed to relieve her. Well I don't know, he was thinking: the man with the *mince*? You can't go round smacking people in the face just because they've got a funny *walk*. Christ, he thought now, as the car swung on to the intersection and joined the flow: this woman needs professional help – and bloody quick.

Some way down the very same road, Dotty was now urging the rented Vauxhall that she hated to get her home faster, faster – wanted to be a million miles away from that caravan, yes (never, not ever, in the whole of the rest of her life would she again set foot in a caravan of any description whatever), but what was truly exercising her was *Dawn*, do you see – because little baby Dawn was in the *back*, wasn't she, unhappily perched upon the bony knee of Brian. Why should this be so? Because Dotty, of course, had been doing the driving, Brian being trussed up the way he was (Dotty could not yet even begin to describe just what it was he resembled, but maybe some sort of simile would come to her soon); and so of course she couldn't be nursing Dawn.

And didn't Dawn know it! The ceaseless screaming was breaking Dotty's heart, but what on earth could she do about it? All she could do was urge the car to get on, get on – faster, faster – and shout over her shoulder at the ludicrous lump that was Brian. She eyed him now in the mirror: his expressionless and moonlike face rose up out of a creamy gauze and padded collar, heavy and rounded wings needling his nostrils – it was quite as large as that of an Elizabethan courtier, while of course most pointedly lacking all elements of swagger, style and allure. The awful thing was, it occurred to Dotty now, that the ghastly contraption actually *suited* the man – being forced into upholstered constrictions *became* him. One day, all that time ago (and Dotty's mind contracted with the attendant shudder), I actually looked long and hard at this person and said Yes – I will marry you. How do these things happen? What in the wide world is it that prompts one to *do* such things?

'Brian!' she barked. 'Can't you for heaven's sake

378

do something? She's not *happy*, is she? Can't you talk to her – play with her? God's *sake*, Brian – the screaming is driving me crazy!'

Brian looked up. 'What?' he said. 'Say something?'

Dotty just wagged her head and slammed her foot to the floor. Let's just get back, shall we? Faster, faster – let's just get back, get back (get back to where we once belonged).

Dotty is less than delighted, thought Brian; and little Dawn doesn't appear to be having a barrel of fun, either. Myself, I feel quite strange. I don't think I've quite got over it all. Hearing's not too good: that's to be expected, they had said, for maybe just a day or two. And Dotty had bawled at him Well that's what you bloody *wanted* isn't it, you stupid little man! Or at least I *think* that's what she said. Don't at all know what she meant, and truly don't mind too much. Eyes felt itchy – and I don't think breathing is quite as easy as it was before: not so much the lungs (don't think it's got anything to do with the lungs per se) but more the actual *nose* – bit gummed up, maybe: nothing a Vick Inhaler won't sort out. And the neck? Can't actually feel the neck – except that it seems to be rather stretched; can't turn it, of course: feel like a bloody lamppost (maybe more of a Belisha beacon). Well – that's the price you pay, my son. It's your own bloody fault, lad – you've only got yourself to blame: the ultimate act of DIY and you buggered it up yet again. How many attempts did *this* make, now? Can't count. Oh *God*, thought Brian all of a sudden: I really feel like death.

Doctor said I needed rest – said I should maybe *talk* to someone. That's as may be – but who in turn is going to talk to *me*? And *rest* – what does that mean? I sometimes think I've been resting for years, and what bloody good has any of that done me? You can't just rest for the rest of your life. However long it may be.

God, though – what a funny feeling, waking up in the hospital, like that. Colin – that's the first thing I remember: Colin, looking down on me. Just as he always has. There was a smell of sweet sewage – maybe merely the mingling of mud, blood and bandage. Christ it had given me a shock when I shot off the cliff like that (I'd been miles away) – must have been a fair bit of an eye-opener for Colin as well, I shouldn't wonder. *We-ell* – not what you expect, is it? Darkish night – your father perched like a zombie on the edge of a cliff, and the next minute – *whoosh*, gone: fifty feet down and up to his neck in muck. I sometimes think it's no wonder the two of us fail to *relate*; he probably wants me dead, Colin. About the only thing we agree on.

Messed up the holiday well and good, haven't I? Well – not much to mess up: Dotty hated it (except for Dawn, and she still had her; funny – of all the things you can bring back from a holiday by the sea, you don't really think of someone else's baby). At least Colin's going to get a couple more days out of it – and staying at The Excelsior (can't be bad).

380

And what, actually, is it that I'm going home to? If 'home', indeed, was at all the appropriate word. Dotty had finally got round to telling him about the offer on the house, just less than half an hour back. Brian's first thought had been Oh Good – and then he thought Oh so *what*? Even if the bloody thing sells, here is just one more stepping stone leading me further, yet further, into the mire. Anyway – talk to Howard about it. Then he'll have to ask him that *favour*: joys to come. Hadn't liked to broach it before – little point until a sale came even within whispering distance. But he'd have to, now. And if these buyers, whoever they were, were really even remotely serious – if they really did have cash (which according to Dotty according to Elizabeth according to Howard they did) then Brian would just take the offer. Even if it was low. Even if it was pitiful. Because he had to: only way. Even if it brings us low – even if it renders me pitiful.

I tell you something else that's funny – well: seemed bloody funny to me at the time. While I was propped up there in that hospital bed – as clean as they could get me, when Dotty and Colin had been and gone – do you know the very first thing that popped into my head? You'll never believe it (it surprised the hell out of me, I can tell you): sex. Yep – that old thing. Now I tell you why that's funny, son – because I can hardly remember the last time it even so much as crossed my mind. Well – you get so involved in your *hobbies*, don't you? Takes you out of everything, an interest (I think, you know, one thing I might do when we get back is rearrange my manhole covers into order of *date*: that way they'll be neat and ready for wherever – if we're moving – I next unpack them). Yes – sorry, just lost myself there . . . hobbies . . . manhole covers . . . oh yeah! Sex.

I think it was maybe that nurse who had just swished by; it wasn't that she was a beauty, or anything (Brian had never had a beauty, or anything), but it was maybe just her rather starchy air of capability – that, and quite large red hands which could easily, Brian felt sure, handle most things. And suddenly, he was transported back to a time when all this sort of thing had actually happened: had more or less come to a complete halt after little Maria had died.

But oh! Well do I remember those nights: every other Saturday, as I recall. Never very late, because Dotty always wanted to make sure that afterwards she had plenty of time to strip the bed completely, turn the mattress and change the linen and follow that with a shower and then a good, long soak in the bath: I was always asleep by the time she got back.

Now look – don't get me wrong: I'm making no claim here to being any sort of a Casanova; I mean by that I've never seen myself in any way a sex object – but quite how I appear to others, of course, it really isn't for me to say. No – what I mean (all I'm saying) is that like any other job you want to step back and be proud of, your sexual act needs all sorts of preparation – that's always the key to a good job: preparation – you just got to ask anyone who knows what they're about. Now granted, to some men this may be seen to be just so much farting around – but I'm telling you, son, you come with your one slapdash coat of magnolia on unprimed plaster and the finish you get is not what you want. You've heard of sugar soap, haven't you? You're no stranger to Polyfilla and sanding down? Same principle: you don't want to go rushing at it – bit of priming, takes time.

On the other hand, there's no bloody sense in overdoing it – five minutes is about tops, by my way of reckoning: any less and you could be guilty of skimping the thing – more, and you've maybe lost sight of the point; I mean – preparation or no preparation, the aim in any job of work is to get to the *finish*, right? Then you pack up your tackle and call it a day.

So what you do is, right – the way you get going is you get your woman and you put her on her back (and despite some of the things you may have heard, this is always favourite: best have everything to hand and where you can reach it because there's nothing worse, is there, in the pitch dark than groping around for some part and you just can't lay your hands on it). You then make sure you make the woman in question feel both lovely and desirable; I've always found that saying 'You look both lovely and desirable' can usually be depended upon to do the trick, but I'm not putting this forward as a foolproof game plan. You might well find that some other combination of words works just as well, like (for the more poetically minded) 'Roses are red, Violets are blue – Get ready, darling, cos I'm going to do *you*'; it's all just down to a question of being sensitive to their needs, see? (It's a bit of a handy short cut, knowing this – it was years before I even twigged that they had any.)

Now next what you do is you hold one nipple (right or left, depending) between thumb and forefinger and treat as if you were giving a ball bearing a really good dose of Three-in-One – or maybe freeing a wing-nut. I'm not saying it's much fun, or anything – but the ladies, they like this. Now next you really ought to kiss her, but I'm only too aware that a lot of you lads would just as soon cut this bit and advance to the next stage, but you'd be well advised to show willing in this department: you don't have to go the whole hog with *tongues* and all the rest of it (I often feel sure it's only people in films who do this, and what else can you expect? They're paid, right? And you're not.) But I'll leave it up to you, that side of things.

It gets better, now. With your right hand (always assuming you have positioned yourself well to the left of the lady) you get hold of her right thigh (oh – I forgot: if we're still in a nightie situation, now is the time to divest her of same) and sort of shove it, the thigh, away from you (not roughly – she's not a piece of meat), and then you grab a fistful of the other one and kind of yank it your way. What you should have now is a perfectly symmetrical V-shape which very conveniently allows direct access to all the gubbins. Well – home and dry now, aren't you? You should find that the male coupling slots neatly into the female housing, and now lad, the time has come to put your back into it; elbow grease is the name of the game from here on in. It's a bit like giving something a damn good kicking with your hips – sounds grim, I know, but don't despair: it's usually all over in a jiffy, and then you have earned the reward of a very nice feeling indeed – makes all that hard work worth while. Withdraw with care, and carefully wipe away all excess seepage: she'll take care of any making good. Tool's needing a rub down so as to be ready for the next job in hand, which – if you're anything like me – is a fairly lengthy widdle.

Brian was reined in quite suddenly from his reverie: car doors were slamming and Dawn was taken from him and almost immediately she ceased her wailing. Well well well – just look where we are: home sweet home. Where did all the miles go, along with all the time?

'Thank God that's over,' said Dotty. 'Get out.'

Which was funny, in its way: that's quite often how she used to round the whole thing off, all those years ago. Every other Saturday, as I recall. (Before it fell off altogether.)

'I just feel,' said Melody – eyes making a huge

385

show of skipping just everywhere, as if to in an instant please a thousand paparazzi, 'too *wonderful* about it all.'

Elizabeth nodded, and smiled with indulgence. Yes indeed, she was thinking, what I see before me now is very much the new improved and biological Melody with added mystery and priceless ingredients. But maybe give her the benefit of the doubt, yes? Sometimes, people could be so eager for happiness (contentment? Some settled state) as to will themselves away from the flimsiness of the here and now and into something else that was too *wonderful*, possibly? Don't know. Only *glimpsed* the man, after all, while Melody – well: Melody, shall we say, knows him rather better. Well maybe this *is* finally the man for her. She deserved it, really, poor love. That was the one thing Elizabeth could never really understand about Melody – this apparent need for one man after the other. I mean – apart from anything else – how can she be bothered? Such a lot of effort for so tragically little return, surely? Elizabeth, speaking for herself, had never ever seriously considered anyone at all since Howard; indeed, she had considered very few before – and only one of these had even come close to making the grade but Elizabeth had decided quite quickly (he was becoming fearsomely earnest, which is always tedious at the early stages – or even the later) that he had funny feet and she simply couldn't picture herself entering shops and parties and restaurants with a man who could manage to look so effortlessly foolish by the simple expedient of placing one foot in front of the other. His name was Carlos and he was very good-looking (in the way that such a name would imply) and actually rather rich but that was not the *point*.

And now – so many years later – Elizabeth was quite happy with Howard (sweet old thing). And *he* would never stray – Elizabeth was quite sure of that: too lazy, for one thing. And Howard was a good provider: of money, she meant. Rather older, yes – less lithe, so much less boyish – but which of us would not be affected by the advancing years? Which of us did not have to bravely address our autumn, aware of the inevitability of winter and then black-out? Spring, for us, could be no more than a rumour and a memory.

But Melody, you see, had never really settled; I mean, granted she was a fair deal younger than Elizabeth – but not so young as all that. Once – some years ago, now – Elizabeth had become convinced that Melody was having an affair with an older married man (yes – *that* old thing) and it didn't really appear to bring her much joy; odd that Melody had not chosen to confide in her. Elizabeth had once thought she might talk about it with Howard (canvass his views) but fairly predictably he didn't seem at all interested: just grunted in that way he had: typical Howard – anything to do with anyone else always seemed to bore him terribly.

Then there was another man soon after that; Elizabeth had not got the impression that here was the passion of the century, but initially Melody had seemed happy enough (content? Some settled state). Of course, in each of these cases Elizabeth had never actually met the man in question, so she could only judge by what she heard and what she saw. Anyway – we don't have to, do we, dwell on just what happened next: Melody was pregnant, and the man was gone. Well – not much new there. And Melody, let us face facts, is hardly ideally suited to motherhood, is she? As far as Elizabeth can see, she just regards it as an unjustly inflicted impediment – and dear little Dawn, she's so sweet (if raucous).

There were other brief things, of course – some-one she met here, someone she met there, friend of a friend, all that sort of thing – but those, Elizabeth felt sure, were little more than ego boosters – or, even more basically, just something to do. But this time – *well*: they had been sitting in The Excelsior foyer for what, now – quarter of an hour? More? Could easily be more – and Melody had yet to talk of anything else bar this *Miles* person. Quite boring, actually – but people did, of course, behave in this way as Elizabeth well knew, when afflicted. Miles this – Miles that . . . oh look, if I am not very much mistaken, here comes the man himself. Yes – that amble; Elizabeth well remembered the amble. Didn't at all *care* for it, it must be said: too practised, too cocksure, too . . . don't know – just something not *right* about it. Oh but God! Look at Melody! Just look at her – quite as that Bernadette person (was it Bernadette?) must have seemed at Lourdes, I think – when the Virgin woman had appeared (of course it needn't be that at all – I'm *so* bad at Catholic things: I know it's supposed to be sort of the same as us but it's *quite* different, really, isn't it?)

'Hello darling!' breathed Melody with open delight – all but bounding up to him like the overall best of breed at Cruft's and covering his face with a good-dog (down girl!) choc-drop licking.

'Yeah, right,' said Miles, managing to combine the wink of an accomplice with an oh-blimey-what's-this glance over to Elizabeth.

'Elizabeth,' said Melody, with proprietorial pride – and just the hint of a pause for ceremony's sake: 'this is – Miles.' It was as if she had in fact said Now Look – you will of course have heard of the Supreme Being Almighty God? Well here he stands before you (can't get away from this divinity thing).

Elizabeth smiled and extended her hand – which clearly hadn't been anticipated. But Miles had the grace (?) to remove one of his own from the side pocket of his pretty tasty Calvin baggies and briefly put a finger to one of Elizabeth's (Sistine Chapel? Let's not overdo it.)

'I know they say this,' said Elizabeth, at her very most hostessy, 'but I *have* heard a great deal about you – and *yes* I promise you it was all very good.'

Melody laughed lightly – and Elizabeth's mirthful cluck was hardly heavier; Miles compressed and extended his lips as if he had been jollied into saying

389

Cheese just once too bloody often by some hack snapper at a function.

'*So*, Melody,' he said, jerking his head in the direction of the revolving doors.

How rude, thought Elizabeth: I really don't care for this Miles person – not one little bit. None of my affair, of course.

'Oh *Elizabeth*,' said Melody – suddenly and as an after-thought, maybe just at that moment remembering that Elizabeth was indeed a friend of hers. 'We're off for a sort of lunch thing – would you . . . ?'

Elizabeth did not have to catch the light of alarm that had sprung up into Miles's eyes: it was all around. 'No no no,' she insisted. 'You two go off – I've planned to do a few last *summer* things, as Dotty calls them: see a bit more of the sea, and so on. And I said I'd be back for Colin, later on, so I can't be too long.'

'Oh – OK,' agreed Melody, looking full into Miles, now.

'*So*, Melody,' he said, jerking his head in the direction of the revolving doors – quite as if someone had rewound the scene just a smidgen (no that's too much – forward a bit) and then hit Play. And yes, thought Elizabeth, my initial impression was entirely correct: rude – quite intolerably so.

'OK, Elizabeth,' sang out Melody – her arm now tucked into the crook of Miles's and already they were on their way. 'If I don't see you before, you know – tomorrow . . . I mean I'm sure I shall, but if I don't I'll ring, yeah?'

Elizabeth nodded: just don't mention the *party*.'

'And then there's the *party* – I haven't forgotten. Miles – Elizabeth has invited us to this fabulous garden party when we all get back to London: I'll tell you all about it.'

And then they were gone, which Elizabeth didn't mind a bit. Oh well, she sighed philosophically, it is only a *party*, after all: everyone enjoyed themselves at parties. The more the merrier, yes?

Carol was standing over there – way over there by the window. Colin still clung on to the door handle, though: not quite sure now, if this was such a good idea. I mean – *wanted* it, yeah, sure (thought about nothing else since, oh God – since I was *born*, it sometimes seems), but it's all down to me, now, isn't it? Yes it is – all down to me, because Carol, I don't know – Carol is just standing over there – way over there by the window, just looking out of it, pretending that the only reason she accepted Colin's invitation up to Elizabeth's suite was so that she could idle by the curtains, taking in the view.

But Jesus – what if she wasn't pretending? What if – oh God – what if, when Colin had said Well actually *yes*, there is somewhere we can go, as a matter of fact, because Elizabeth – she's my, well – just the person who lives next door, really, but I suppose I think of her as some sort of relative, now, because she's been around since I was little: aunt, sort of thing, maybe – she's out this afternoon (she told me). What if, when Colin had said that (by the scrubby grassland at the head of the cliff that his father had dropped off – up there), then maybe Carol had just said Yeah? OK Then as in Yeah, Why Not? I mean – what I *mean* is, if he'd suggested an ice-cream cone or a bus trip or a paddle then maybe she would have just said Yeah? OK Then to those as well and the fact that they were now alone in this endless sitting room with Colin's current bed so huge and bloody in between them was just where they happened to be and nothing more than that – no big deal at all. Look – what I suppose I'm, oh God, *getting* at here (why don't they give you *instructions* when all this stuff starts happening?) is, um, oh God I've lost *track*, now – oh yeah, got it: if I now said Well anyway, this is the room I was talking about – now let's go and have an ice-cream cone or a bus trip or a paddle, would she (a) think I was Wimp of the Century (and God knows why she doesn't already – maybe, Jesus, she *does*) or (b) just stand there and say Yeah? OK Then? I just don't know, is the answer, so quite a lot hinges on what I say next.

'Why don't you come over here?'

It was Carol who said that, not Colin – for which much relief all round from Colin's point of view because he had been only too aware that the silence was now edging into uneasiness and he only would have blurted out the first thing that had come into his head which could very easily have entailed ice-creams, buses or even, oh Christ, *paddling* and then would not so God-given and golden an opportunity have been lost to him forever?

Colin came the nearest he could to strolling over to the window – tried to make it look maybe as if he was just popping across the road for a paper (do it all the time) and yes I'll be popping right back in a couple of minutes. No sooner had he arrived than Carol put up a hand and touched his hair. It was good, just the lightness of that touch: you never really feel your hair, do you, till someone else does too.

'You know, Colin,' said Carol, softly, 'I really like you?'

Colin nodded, just prior to shaking his head. 'Do you?' he said.

Oh God, *dumb*, he was scourging himself: *do you? Do you?* Of course she bloody does – wouldn't have *said* so would she, if she – oh Christ *say* something, *say* something. That's easy for you to say – what do I say? Go for this:

'I think you're wonderful. Carol. Just wonderful.'

OK – pretty good; more than pretty good – huge and maybe secret smile coming up and now spreading all over her face. I think this is very much the right track.

Colin put his hand to the side of her face – remembered again how frighteningly soft and warm it was: is this how faces generally feel? Their lips were touching, Colin did not know quite how – had been aware of no volition of any kind – but now did a flood of heat rush into him as he felt the wet and quite electric insinuation of Carol's tongue between his teeth, now lolling all over his own, stuck deep into him. Colin went to heaven, then, as each of his hands latched on to the utter fabness of those tennis ball breasts and he gagged and damn near choked on the seven or eight tongues that the two of them now seemed to be sharing and the distension in his jeans was compellingly rigid in its absolute determination to be altogether elsewhere – more so than ever before – and Colin was aware of charges from the deep where before there had been little more than spangles of light playing upon him and teasing his sensitivity. His hysterical hands were now tugging on those oh God I can't *believe* it tits of hers – yeah, this way and that, quite as if they had been granted free rein over the control panel of the Starship Enterprise – and now as her hand snaked down to the belt loops on his jeans – one thumb (can't be sure) just hanging there a bit – so as her fingers began to sift through the evidence was Colin at once overcome by the most sublime and catastrophically magnificent quite dreamy horror. The feelings that coursed up and through him were of an intensity that left him numb and gasping and still squirming urgently against the firm pressure of the palm of her hand and so *that* was what it was all about – all those longings, all that questing time and here it was: my life has come, thought Colin – and now, oh Christ, it is surely over. He pulled away from Carol, shame quenching everything.

'What is it?!' gasped Carol. 'Don't stop touching me!'

There was space between them now, and all Colin could say, the only thing that would come out of him now was:

'Look, Carol – I think this is maybe not such a good idea.'

She stared at him, and Colin cringed away from that as well as the lie. It was the only good idea he had ever had during the entire course of his life on earth, and now he had rendered Carol hurt and quite as if she had been slapped. But how else could he have done it? How else could he have arrested her discovery of what had assailed him – the amazing, unforeseen and wholly overpowering assault he had just been subject to, deep down where it mattered, the immensely disorienting aftermath of which he was now just anyhow coping with (and please don't think it was easy)?

'Colin . . . ?' went Carol, her hand out and coming for him again. 'We've got to *do* this . . .'

Colin gave in to a fairly energetic round of head nodding and wagging while looking down at the floor and thinking Yeah well we can't, can we, because I at some point must have started without you and now I've already bloody well done it all on my own – and also, oh God, the awful thing is I still want to touch her and I can't do that because if I do that she'll . . . oh God, oh God! I've really messed this up so bloody *colossally*.

But Carol had got the message, now: the *wrong* message, admittedly, but anything – just *anything* was preferable to her discovering the truth. She buttoned up her shirt (had Colin undone all those buttons? Had it been he or she who had deftly slipped open each of those tiny buttons?) and was immediately busy being as sniffy as you like.

'OK, Colin: fine. Let's get out of here, now, shall we?'

'Look, Carol –'

'I don't want to *discuss* it, Colin. Let's just *go*, OK?'

'It's just that – maybe Elizabeth will come back, and –'

'Yeah well – it doesn't matter now, does it? Look, Colin – I'm going right now – you coming or not?'

Colin nodded and followed her to the door, never so ashamed and unhappy in his life (despite the still tingling miracle), feeling too, and not at all incidentally, as if he was waist-deep in Cow Gum and further that his boxers had now asserted their moral and constitutional right to put into train the genesis of their metamorphosis from workaday cotton into corrugated cardboard. All this stuff, he thought, as he stood next to Carol in the lift – both of them staring dead ahead at the vertical slit dividing the doors – is, I can see, going to need work.

Walking through the foyer towards the revolving doors – Colin now making like a semi-extended gate-leg table in his plywood pants and thinking maybe actually I should have let Carol go on without me because OK, yes, it would have been just about the rudest thing possible on earth coming on top of the last thing, but on the up side at least then I could have – oh yuck – changed.

Both of them were caught short by Elizabeth's whoop from just inside the bar.

'Colin!' she called out. 'You've *come*!'

That had Colin looking as startled as a caught-red-handed sneak thief before he settled right down and beckoned to Carol to come on over.

'I'm *so* pleased to see you,' went on Elizabeth, from the depths of a Chesterfield – and she really seemed so, making bulbous her eyes and flicking up the brows above, Colin thought in order to indicate her sheer desperation to be rescued from whatever man was sitting alongside her. She now turned to him.

'My friends are here, now,' she said – and although all of Elizabeth's honey thickly coated the words, there was no disguising their intention.

'Right, then,' acquiesced the man – shooting to his feet with such energy as to suggest that his next stunt was to be performed on the parallel bars. 'I'll be away, then. Fascinating to talk to you, Elizabeth.'

And he wandered away, his wispy hair catching a draught and flying into his eyes – he now far too busy rummaging in his pockets to care about anything of that order.

'It may have been fascinating for *him*,' tut-tutted Elizabeth, patting the sofa invitingly and turning enquiring eyes on Carol. '*I* have never been so bored in my *life*. Won't you introduce me, Colin?'

'Oh God, sorry, yes. This is, er, *Carol*,' he insisted (as if making sure), 'and *this* is, er –'

'Elizabeth, yes,' interjected Carol. 'We've just been upstairs in your terrific suite. Wonderful views.'

Have you now, thought Elizabeth: now what, if anything, do I feel about that? Something, quite sure – not sure what, though.

'It *is* lovely, isn't it? Be quite sorry to leave it – but it's always nice getting back home, isn't it? Are you on holiday too, Carol?'

Carol nodded. 'Going back the same time as you and Colin. Back to the Smoke!'

'Oh well then you *must* come to my party – have you asked Carol to the party, Colin?'

'Didn't know there *was* a party,' said Colin, frankly.

'Oh yes – it'll be splendid. Now make sure you come, Carol – Tuesday, so make a date. Colin will tell you where, and everything. We're having it in the garden – it'll be splendid.'

'Oh thanks. Yeah. Love to. Thanks.'

Yeah, Carol was thinking – I *would* love to, actually: thanks. Because I really do want to see Colin again and *he* wouldn't have done anything about it: boys don't, unless they're creepy. I really really really thought we were going to *do* it, up there, just then. God I've waited for *ages* – dying to get rid of it. Horrible *Michael* at home wanted to – could've done it with him any time, but God he's so *creepy*. Colin's really nice, though. Maybe that's why I think he's so nice – cos he wouldn't: probably thought he was protecting me, or something. Which is really sweet. Takes a lot of will power, that, I should think. If you're a boy. Oh God that's really *sweet* – and I was so beastly to him, after. So yeah – I will come to this party (God – there's weeks and *weeks* till school, and sod-all to do) and then maybe he'll see how much I want him. Cos he lives right next door to Elizabeth – isn't that what he said? I actually think I love him, now. Think of him all the time, so I must do, I think. Sorry – what's that Elizabeth said? Oh, drink – yeah, I would like a drink, as it happens: thanks.

'Orange juice and soda, please,' said Carol. 'I've really got to get out of always having that – it's a bit naff, really.' And then she laughed. 'It's just that it's become a sort of tradition, a sort of joke thing with my Dad. He has a citron pressé.'

Colin nodded. 'My Dad's got a Volvo Estate,' he said. 'Didn't use it this time, though, for some reason.'

The hesitation in Elizabeth was only just palpable – Carol smiled roguishly, but let it go; Colin, oblivious, stirred the peanuts with his index finger – first clockwise, and then the other way.

'I'm terrifically glad you both arrived when you *did*,' expanded Elizabeth, sitting forward and tracing the rim of her champagne glass with an opalescent fingernail. 'That *Derek* person – that was his name, apparently – God, as if *I* cared – he was a *systems* analyst, whatever grislier than usual sort of thing *that* might be – and, oh God!' Elizabeth laughed now at the recollection, two fingers pressed up to her nostrils: 'It was *so* ghastly I didn't know where to *look* – he said he had every single episode of *Eastenders* on video and he and his *colleague*, as he put it, took turns to watch them all! And he lives in Dagenham. Can you *imagine*? Tell you – never so bored in my *life*.'

After a while – all that had passed was chitchat, nothing more, with Elizabeth making most of the running – Carol stood up and said she must go, now.

'Told my Dad I'd be back early – he's booked some restaurant or other in the town. I'm sorry I can't *ask* you, or anything, Colin, but –'

'Oh God no,' said Colin, waving away even the remotest possibility. 'No no – you, er. No. I wouldn't dream . . .'

No – I don't think so, even if I *was* invited. Bloody Terry would kick off the proceedings by hitting me with a chair or smashing my face into the wall – and I doubt if Carol's Dad would actually care to sit at table with me – not unless he was wearing his oilskin and souwester and had an umbrella handy.

Carol kissed Colin on the cheek, while Colin devoted time to an in-depth scrutiny of the skirting board and the way it abuts on to the doorframe, like that. Elizabeth drank all this in, smiled in a sort of a way, and then found herself studying the very same thing. When the waving was done – reminders of the party thrown up by Elizabeth and fielded by Carol as she walked from the bar – then did Elizabeth turn to face Colin and with eyes quite bright at the prospect, she said:

'*So*, Colin – what shall we *do*?'

First off, Colin had replied, I think I'd like to change. Oh *yes*, Elizabeth agreed – it's so nice to change one's clothes in the evening, isn't it? Yes it is – and a particularly pleasant prospect when your smalls have turned to earthenware while you've just been sitting there – so Colin moved away starchily, his gait now more like that of a saddle-sore cowpoke (aware too of a certain scratchiness that had not hitherto troubled him, but was now giving gyp to his tender loins).

What they eventually did, Colin and Elizabeth, was go to what Elizabeth had heard was the absolutely top-flight numero uno whizz-bang restaurant in town and both of them ate far too many truly good things and Colin was really getting quite a taste for this champagne stuff now, if he was honest, and those petits fours looked absolutely *irresistible*, Elizabeth had said, and so Colin had tried them and she was right: they ordered more. Back at the hotel, they could hardly *move*, they were both so stuffed. *God*, Elizabeth had puffed, holding her stomach – I'm so stuffed I can hardly *move*. Me too, said Colin: me too. But upstairs in the room, Elizabeth had the wire off yet *another* bottle of champagne because, she said, it is quite brilliant for the digestion. Is it? Colin queried. It is, averred Elizabeth: have some. He had some – had some more. They laughed a bit about Christ knows what and then suddenly Colin entered a decline, and all he wanted to do was sleep, sleep – oh God just let me *sleep* – I'm so tired I can barely keep my eyes open.

Much later – and Elizabeth now has woken up suddenly, quelling the rising panic that always assails her in any dark room that is not her own. Not, actually, so totally dark as it had been before – so daylight was maybe well on its way. She lay flat on her back and stretched her whole body slowly and with an insistence that did truly make her feel luxuriously tautened on a downy rack of dreamy pleasure. All was grey in the room – as if fog had invaded – and the silence was profound.

Elizabeth turned on to her side in the vast and now it seemed quite bluish, the bed. Her fingers mingled softly with Colin's tousled hair. She thought, then, of Howard. I wonder, is how the thought went, what my partner in marriage down all the years would think or say or do if he were to come to know that right at this very moment I was sharing my bed with a young, so young, and beautiful boy? A thing, indeed, during just such dusky hours as this, that Howard had wondered himself – oh, so very many times before – and maybe even at this very waking instant, as gradual morning stalks and whitens the last of the night.

PART 3

After

CHAPTER 7

Katie hadn't *rung*, or anything. That's what Norman was thinking, yet again, while just sitting at his desk in the office – the desk beneath which Katie had crouched (right there, just at that spot in the void between Norman's gaping and now quite pointless knees), and oh God don't even think about the touch of her, the featherweight fusion of those long, cool and inflaming fingers of hers, and the bob of her head as hair fell over her eyes while she stooped down lower and . . . no, don't think about that: cast it out. Not going to do you any good, is it? Thinking like that. Not going to make her suddenly *appear*, is it? And nor can what has passed be so easily erased: what happened, happened – right? She's still there, in Chicago, with . . . with that *American* person, and you, Norman, are back in the office, just fooling around. The old and flyblown, ridiculous office that seemed, along with absolutely everything else, empty beyond measure.

Still, though – he thought he might have heard *something* from her, even if only an enquiry as to whether he was still alive (he had ages ago put away any dreams about the clamorous phone that he idly picks up and from the other end of it bursts open a breathless, agitated and tearful Katie imploring him to take her back, begging his forgiveness, protesting her undying devotion now that light has finally dawned – yes, I think we can safely set that one aside). No – Katie hadn't *rung*, or anything: wouldn't, now. Due back was it tomorrow – *if* she came back then or at all: no knowing – not with Katie. And if she does come back – what? What then? They go on? They don't go on? *What?* Christ alone knows – Christ alone. The phone rang shrilly, then, and Norman's heart booted him hard.

'Look it's Cyril Davies again,' came the weary but clearly impatient voice. 'Have you heard yet or what? What the hell's going on?'

Oh God yes Norman *had* heard, of course he had – he'd just been too distracted and miserable to remember to pass on the news. Never *used* to be like that, not before – used to be bang on the ball, as Mr Street – Howard – always had told him. (Oh God – I'm so sorry I'm me and not the man you think I am.)

'Ah yes, Mr Davies – how funny you should ring right now – I've just this second put the phone down and was about to call you. I *have* spoken to Mr Morgan – been ringing him all day but he was out – yes and – good news – he accepts the offer.'

'Good. Bout bloody time.'

'Yes. He did want more, of course, but I made it quite clear you were sticking.'

And then – inspiration. Here was no plan, no careful manoeuvre – no stratagem of any description. It just *came* to Norman, as these things (and only these things) tended to do. Already in his mind he was spending all the money – lavishing it all on Katie, buying her back for whatever it took.

'Look, Mr Davies – reading between the lines – um, I trust I can speak confidentially?'

'Course you can. What are you on about? I want the survey done this afternoon – my people have already got the search, and that's OK. I'll exchange in the morning, if all is well – let's get going on this one. And I want a fast completion.'

'Yup – of course. But my point is, Mr Davies, I might be able to save you quite a lot of money on this deal.'

A silence is all that Norman got: it was often the way. And then Cyril Davies said:

'Go on.'

'Well – I shouldn't really be saying all this, of course, because Mr Morgan is, of course, our client – but it seems to me that he's so absolutely desperate to sell that he'll actually take less.'

'Well why didn't somebody bloody tell me that before? Made the offer, now – and he's accepted it. Can't offer less *now*.'

'No but look – this is my idea. Strictly between ourselves, yes?'

'I *said* yes. What?'

'Right. OK. Commission the survey and just before exchange say that something or other fairly major came up and you're dropping by twenty thousand.'

'Twenty thousand! He'll never wear that. The price is low as it is. And why *are* you telling me this? That lowers your commission.'

'No – this is the point. If he accepts – if Mr Morgan says OK – and he will, he will, I assure you: he's truly desperate, believe me. If he goes along with it, then half of your saving is payable to, um, us. Cash, it would have to be, I'm afraid.'

Cyril Davies turned it over.

'Right – let's get this straight: I offer twenty grand less at the very last moment – Morgan calls me every bloody name under the sun and says yes. I give you people ten on top, and I've saved ten for myself. Yes?'

'That's it. Absolutely. Yes.'

'OK. Let's do it. Let's get moving on this one. Tell Morgan my surveyor will be round at three. Good thinking, Mr – er?'

'Furnish. Norman Furnish.'

'Furnish – right. Even if he *doesn't* bite, I can't lose, right?'

'Right.'

'Right. Get on to it.'

Norman grinned maniacally. 'Will do,' he said.

But oh God, he thought, as he quite slowly replaced the receiver – I really *am* sorry, Mr

Street, that I'm me and not the man you think I am. Howard.

And who but Howard wandered into the office, not that much later on, when Norman had utterly done with wrestling with his conscience – he now stood proud like a hunter, one foot aloft on its once-noble, still warm and caved-in form, while slickly extracting a blade from the heart of the defeated beast that it was. And behind Howard there trailed that young and very strange Peter person – who was actually supposed to do *what* exactly around here? Norman had never worked it out; and on at least one occasion he had overheard Mr Street calling him 'Zoo-Zoo', or some other silly sort of thing, which just has to be about as weird as it gets.

'All right, Norman?'

'Fine, Mr Street. Howard. I've just been on to Davies – been phoning him all day, but he was out. He's pretty pleased, obviously. Survey's on for three this afternoon.'

'Good good,' approved Howard, rather vaguely. 'It's a bit rough on poor old Brian, though – Davies really has got it for a song, you know. Still – bird in the hand, right? Beggars can't be, um . . . oh Christ, my mind. What is it beggars bloody can't be?'

'Choosers. And the marquee people phoned with their quote.'

'Oh Christ – tell me the worst. *Choosers* – that's it.'

Zoo-Zoo yawned, then, with the indulgent air of a weary and dutiful wife who has as requested attended the football match, yes, OK – but don't you think a lengthy postmortem on the ins and outs of the game is really asking a bit too much? Enough is enough – yes?

'Sorry,' apologized Howard. 'Won't be much longer.'

And Norman had heard that sort of thing before too. I told you it was weird. Still – none of Norman's business: he had enough, don't you think, without bothering about any of all that? I should say so.

'Well,' said Norman, 'the actual hire charge isn't too bad – it's the huge ones that really cost – but look at what they want for putting it up!'

Howard glanced at the Post-It held out towards him.

'Oh bloody hell,' was his verdict on that. 'Three times the bloody rental! Oh sod that for a lark – I'll put it up myself. We'll manage it, won't we? The three of us. Can't imagine why Elizabeth actually *wants* the thing, if I'm honest. Useful if it rains, I suppose – but we do actually have a perfectly good *house*.' Howard rolled up his eyes in mock and mute suffering. '*Women* – hey? What can you do with them?'

Norman said nothing – what on earth could he say about that? And Zoo-Zoo said nothing either: looked at Howard, though, in some sort of a way or other, Norman couldn't have told you what.

'Right,' resumed Howard. 'That's settled, then. Right, OK – we're off. Sorry,' he said again to Zoo-Zoo. 'You'll be OK on your own – yes, Norman?'

Norman nodded: oh yeah – I'll be fine. On my own. Got to get used to it, haven't I? Again.

'I actually asked Dotty along,' said Elizabeth to Lulu, and then she said 'hoop' as the taxi swung tightly around a Kensington corner, catching Elizabeth unawares and sending her slithering down the bench seat and into Lulu. 'I sometimes get a bit sick in black cabs,' she went on.

'I know what you mean,' said Lulu. 'It's when they sway.'

'And if they've got that cardboard deodorant thing hanging up it's just the *end*,' deplored Elizabeth. 'Where are we? Ah – just coming up to . . . there, soon. Yes – I did ask Dotty but she said she couldn't. God – I don't remember a time when Dotty and Melody weren't ready and eager to go shopping, but they're both suddenly so, I don't know – *changed*.'

'Other things to think about,' smiled Lulu. 'Are you on the look-out for anything in particular, Lizzie? Or just looking round generally?'

'Well I absolutely *have* to have something new for the party . . . I think you're right about those two, actually – having other things to think about. I've never *seen* anyone so besotted with a baby before – and it's not even *hers*. Actually' – and

411

Elizabeth had lowered her voice, now, in order to render the imminent betrayal of a secret considerably less of a sin – 'Dotty did tell me in absolute confidence that she and Brian were going to *adopt* – legally, and everything. Talked to Melody about it on the *phone*, apparently – she of course doesn't give a *damn*: it's almost as if she's swapped poor little Dawn for this awful *Miles* character. That's still very much *on*, by the way. And if I see some sort of summery gardeny *shoes*, I might be tempted. But generally just looking around – what about you?'

'Anything, really – whatever catches my eye. Oh look – here we are. This is near enough, isn't it, Lizzie? We can get out here, can't we?' Lulu glanced up at the soaring flank of Harvey Nichols and with bogus lover's ardour sighed out: '*God*, I've missed you!'

Elizabeth – who hadn't been looking – said simply: 'I've missed you too, Lulu. It's so lovely to see you again. And isn't it great to be back in town? These seaside places are all very *nice* but how do people actually *live* in them? I'd go mad. God it's so hot – I wish I hadn't worn this jacket, now.'

Yes – back in town. All those seaside sorts of summer things were over and done with, and now it was the time for others. Did Elizabeth mention that tomorrow she's having a garden party (with a marquee and everything)? And that for it she absolutely *has* to have something new? OK, then: here we go.

Elizabeth and Lulu wove their way through

the scent and cosmetic counters and made for the escalator. There was urgency in the air – a sort of female and quite contagious excitement that lent speed and almost bustle to their every movement: it was as if they anticipated a massive and restless queue that signalled the electric and dangerous possibility that the very best of all the good things had already gone.

'I do hate it,' said Elizabeth, just as they stepped off the top of the escalator, 'when they squirt you in shops.'

'I know,' agreed Lulu. 'It always clashes so horribly with whatever you're already wearing. I put Cristalle on today – I used to use it all the time but I'd forgotten all about it.'

'I've had that,' said Elizabeth. 'And Coco – Coco's nice. I actually can't *remember* what I'm wearing – isn't it awful? Oh God, Lulu – they've got all the *autumn* things in: look at that coat dress – divine, no? I *think* I put on Joy – think it was Joy. Or it could have been that Guerlain one.'

''Tis – Shalimar, pretty sure. Over there, Lizzie – Agnès B. That's all summery. And – oh God, Lizzie – look look! That yellow – isn't that the most *perfect* Chinese yellow? Oh God I've just *got* to try that.'

'And the pink! Look at the pink! Do you think that pink would suit me, Lulu? It's not too . . . ?'

'*Perfect* for you – you try on that and I'll try the yellow. It doesn't matter they're the same, does it?'

Elizabeth shook her head as she gleefully plucked

the pink silk dress from the rail. 'It's not as if it's the *only* thing we'll be getting, is it?'

When Lulu emerged from the changing room, Elizabeth was already there – resplendent in deep shock pink and swivelling herself this way and then that in front of the triple mirror.

'Ta – *da!*' sang Lulu, dipping at the knees and extending her open palms like a self-satisfied magician following the closing move of a successful illusion – and now wasn't she parodying the coquettish twirl that just such a person's leggy assistant might grinningly provide, when urged to.

They both agreed that each outfit was positively faint-making and absolutely *perfect* on them. Gold cards were swiped through machinery and Elizabeth and Lulu swooped on and upward, eyes now eager and hotly stalking the next big kill.

It wasn't long in coming (Lulu's twill and superbly cut trousers – just the very most subtle and kicky-out flare) and nor was its mighty successor: a donkey-brown cashmere drape coat for Elizabeth (not for *now*, obviously, but it'll be just wonderful for wintery evenings – except that everywhere you go is so horribly *overheated*, these days: not here, thank God – but Harrods, Harrods is like a furnace – but anyway I've got to have it, got to – but it's going to be awfully hard finding *shoes* that colour – what colour would you say it actually *was*, Lulu?) Next on the agenda was coffee in the basement – *God* what a fabulous smell – just *got* to sit down or

I'll die: here, over here – there's a free table just over here.

'Was it awful getting home?' asked Elizabeth in a you-know-you-can-tell-me-anything sort of a way. 'It's terribly naughty but I'm going to have one of these gorgeous knobly brown sugar lumps – love it with cappuccino.'

Lulu sighed. 'Wasn't great. But it was better than in the hotel. At least at home we've got different *rooms* to go to.'

'And is John . . . ?' Elizabeth let it linger, balancing her sugar on her spoon and lowering it teasingly into the piebald froth, rather as might a witchfinder who was loving it with a scold or maybe hag on a ducking stool.

Lulu was sighing again, shaking her head and looking down as she slowly stirred her large espresso – sipping some gingerly, now (tsss – bit hot).

'Same. Just the same. Not so *violent*, thank God – and drinking less, as far as I can tell, but he won't *leave* it, will he? Just won't leave it alone. Oh and *God*, Lizzie – the first thing we saw when we got back was a huge parcel – one of those bag, padded bag things and it was addressed to John and he just *pounced* on it and he was cursing and yelling –! I really do think, you know . . .'

'What?' urged Elizabeth. 'Think what?'

'Oh . . . it's just that he's so . . . anyway – it turns out that he's written a *novel* – had no *idea* he'd been writing a novel – never mentioned it –

415

and the publisher, whatever publisher he'd sent it to had sent it *back* – oh God, as if he wasn't in a foul enough mood already – and I looked at the letter with it – well, *wasn't* a letter, just a printed slip sort of thing and it said that they were sorry it wasn't right for their – what did it say? *Lists*, I think: wasn't right for their lists at the present time – something. So *I* said – thinking I'd be cheering him up, like a fool – well that's just *now*, Johnny – maybe they're, I don't know, full up or something – and he went absolutely *spare* and started shouting and ranting that they *always* said that – that's what they *say* – and what it means is the book is a whole load of bloody . . . oh God, all sorts of swearing and words. And *then* – you won't believe what he did then! He went to the fireplace and started throwing logs and papers into it and put a match to it – said he was going to *burn* it and *Jesus*, Lizzie, the house was absolutely *baking* because no windows or anything had been open for *weeks* and there was John lighting a log fire in the middle of a heatwave . . . !'

Elizabeth just had to laugh – and Lulu briefly joined in with yes-but-it's-not-really-funny-is-it undertones before resuming with some animation.

'Anyway – he got the fire going and everything – and I was saying oh for God's *sake*, Johnny – there are *other* publishers, aren't there? All that stuff. But no – he chucked the manuscript on to the fire and I thought that was that – I mean oh *honestly*, Lizzie, I was so *tired*, I was so worn *out* by him after, oh – everything – I just thought well look: it's his book

– if he wants to burn it, let him burn it – and then suddenly he was scrabbling around in the fire and pulling it out again and he was going ow ow ow and his shirt caught fire and I was *screaming* but he managed to get the thing out and on to the rug – *that's* ruined – and his cuffs had gone out, thank God. Then he knelt down and was picking off all the black bits from the paper and then . . . then he started sobbing. It was awful . . . watching him on his knees just *sobbing* like that. I really do think . . .'

Lulu's eyes flashed up and into Elizabeth's – here was something just for her:

'. . . I really do think he's a bit . . . *mad*. Not actually a *bit* – completely. Completely mad. And I don't know what to do.'

'I must say,' sympathized Elizabeth, 'from what you've *told* me . . . maybe he ought to *see* someone?'

'Yes but *I'm* not going to suggest that, am I? What – I go up to him and say Look, Johnny, I really think you ought to see a psychiatrist because you're absolutely nuts – Jesus, he'd go absolutely –'

They both shrieked out 'Nuts!' at exactly the same time, and that outburst fizzled into isn't-it-awful laughter, this soon simmering down into a new and quite warm sororial complicity.

'And the only things on the answering machine,' continued Lulu – much more easily, now – 'were all these ghastly commissions from his editor – I

417

think he's afraid of her, actually: she sounds a bit of a tyrant. You know – How To Build A Winter Wardrobe For Under A Thousand Pounds – all that – and some feature on a firm that's doing a BOGOF campaign –'

Elizabeth's eyebrows rose: a *what* campaign? Bog Off, did she say?

'Oh sorry,' said Lulu, hastily. 'Yes it *is* a mad name, isn't it? It stand for, what is it? Yeah – Buy One Get One Free. It's *awful*, that world: just awful. You're so lucky, you know Lizzie, having someone like Howard. I'm so looking forward to meeting him – he sounds really nice. And *sane*.'

Elizabeth smiled. 'He *is* nice,' she confirmed. 'And *very* sane – oh yes, very. I can't see Howard doing anything crazy – or even risky. He's very predictable, Howard – no skeletons in cupboards. And he is *generous*.' Elizabeth gestured to the slithering island of Harvey Nichols bags clustered at their feet. 'Just as well,' she tacked on.

'He must have been awfully pleased to see you when you got back – was he? Do you want another coffee?'

'Don't think I *do*, actually. He *was* pleased, I think, dear old thing. He'd bought flowers and everything was immaculately tidy – he'd even changed the bed, which I thought was perfectly sweet.'

'I don't like double beds,' said Lulu, suddenly, not knowing quite why. 'I don't quite know why I

418

said that. I mean for sleeping in. I'd like a bed on my own.'

'I sometimes feel that,' said Elizabeth, carefully.

But not recently. Not at The Excelsior, certainly. Not during those two sweet and quite blissful nights – and God, so very much of the days – that she had spent luxuriously sprawling in the huge and sumptuous bed with that utterly adorable boy. The first morning (she could laugh about it now) neither of them could quite remember quite how it had come to pass: were amazed to find themselves revolving within the same soft white and churned-up sheets. But touching had come easily, and then they came to delve more deeply. God knows how many bottles of champagne they got through, during those brief and endless dark and sunlit hours. Colin had been so utterly boyish – he became so excited, so quickly: quite charming. Elizabeth had had to guide him with quite firm care and then stay quite still, just in order to prolong the moment. How she loved his long slim shanks and the thickness of his hair: he had cried when he kissed her breasts, and then she had too.

Elizabeth and Lulu shared a taxi to Jermyn Street, where Elizabeth bought two shirts and two ties for Howard from Hilditch & Key (because he had had no holiday, poor lamb, and was perfectly sweet), and then later when they parted, Elizabeth reached back into the cab for their final farewell and it came quite naturally to both of them that they should kiss very fully on the lips, and then

419

glance briefly into the light of one another's eyes.

And Elizabeth had been right about one thing: *had* been awfully hard to find shoes that colour, but she managed it, eventually, which was really rather clever of her – don't you think so?

Brian had been busy doing his sums. Apart from being dispiriting beyond measure – here, it soon transpired, was very much a task and a half because he found it quite impossible to bend his neck. He had sat down – usual chair, usual desk – and pulled out a jotter pad and found a cracked and chewed up Bic that *functioned*, anyway, and then made the quite weird discovery that although every fibre within him was urging his face and eyes down there where the page was, he was still staring resolutely at the wall before him. The spongey wings of his latest prison were snagging now in the stubble on his jowls (you can really only think about shaving the main parts when you're wearing a thing like this) and irritation began to kick in the door of incipient despair and he yearned – he absolutely *yearned*, Brian – to be back on top of that seaside cliff, and this time would he not make utterly sure to walk those precious and vital yards eastwards so as to leave no doubt that the fang-like rocks below would gnash and then mash him as the sea flushed away all the bloody bits.

He piled up some books – rotten old books, most with the yellowing and clammy plastic covers slapped on by some long defunct public library, the edges of the pages soft and grimy (God knows where they had come from – not much of a one for libraries, Brian) – and that was fine as far as it went, but still it involved standing and then bending down to the flat of the page, but then sharp twinges in his lower back soon let Brian know that this way of doing things just wasn't on the menu so he went into the kitchen and somewhere here (what cupboard did I stick it into?) there was a weighty and possibly cast-iron cookbook stand that had a broken foot which only needed a touch of welding so as to make it as good as new but some things (yes?) you just never get around to. But Brian was hauling it out now – there it was, behind that box of alarm clock parts – and yes, I do think that should do it. Back in the back room, he balanced it on top of the unspeakable books and of course it lurched to the left (broken foot – hardly surprising) so Brian wedged that with the nearest thing to hand which was a half-eaten Mars bar that he had munched into not one hour earlier thinking Mmmm, just what I fancy – but only one bite told him that in fact it wasn't, wasn't at all: felt quite sick for some time after.

Now Brian could sit down and prop the notebook directly in front of his face, while beginning to write down all the terrible figures with the splintered Bic. His debts and liabilities he knew by heart – knew too the daily rate by which they rose: lumped them all together into their appalling total and then wrote alongside the really quite tragic amount of money he had accepted in exchange for this big, grey and aching house. At the very last second, the bloody bastard had dropped the offer by twenty bleeding grand – it was almost as if he had sensed his desperation; did Brian now always give off that air?

As expected, there was a considerable shortfall – not, maybe, a wholly unbridgeable one, but a considerable shortfall nonetheless. Could possibly any of Dotty's old junk raise a few pounds? I mean, presumably she isn't the only deluded woman in Britain who actually derives pleasure from china frogs and dollies' teapots and bloody silly spoons? And what else? His father's gold half-hunter – scrap value, I should think – but *something*. And maybe if, as seemed on the cards for now, Brian was destined to plod a little further down life's winding lane – would it be better to cash in his insurance for whatever he could get? Maybe, maybe – who could tell? All in all, it seemed that the best possible scenario was that he and Dotty and Colin would end up with absolutely nothing at all in the whole wide world: otherwise, it could go badly for them.

And here's a joke: we're going to have a baby. Well – got the bloody thing already, if I'm being accurate (can you not hear Dotty just next door – now billing, now cooing?) So on the very day I write off all my assets, the responsibilities burgeon (isn't that just always the way?) And what of little Dawn? Her future depends on *me*? Good God. But no –

it was Dotty, wasn't it? Dotty was the whole point here: she would do anything – simply anything – to get that girl a life.

And yes – Dotty next door would have unquestioningly gone along with that: how could it be any other way? Had she not promised as much to Melody during that strange but hugely exhilarating phone conversation just that very morning?

Melody had not long got back to her tiny flat, and Miles was still there with her. He would have asked her back to his place, he said, but the builders were in and believe me, darling, you wouldn't like it. Melody had not minded – she was still glowing with seaside sun and full of the warmth of love for this wonderful man. He had bought her the most fabulous big, white, floppy polar bear (she had thought it was a blissful seal pup, with those gorgeous dippy black wet eyes, but Miles insisted it was a polar bear). She said she would call him Miles so that she could cuddle and stroke him when the real Miles wasn't there. He said *nah* – call him Bum. Bum? Why Bum, laughed Melody, her nose wrinkled up in puzzled amusement (oh God I just love this *feeling*). Bear *Bum* – yeah?, he explained. Bare – bear: get it? Yes! Yes! shrieked Melody – got you, oh yes *got* you – you're so *rude*, Miles: you're really very very naughty. Yeah I am, agreed Miles – and aren't you bloody grateful?

When it had become clear that Melody wanted Miles to stay around even after the holiday had ended, he had become quite wary: hang on, hang on – can't have the bitch getting clingy. Why don't they ever know when the party's over, hey? I mean – that was then and this is now, yeah? But then he thought well look – I can swing a couple more days, can't I? It's not a problem. Not going to do any harm, is it? Pretty hot, this kid – and it's not as if I've got anything else going at the minute, is it? So he phoned the office and they said sure, Miles, sure – take as long as you need (if you're top salesman, right – when you're numero uno bar absolutely bloody none – that's the sort of respect you get: Miles was big on respect). Then he phoned Sheil and spun her some variation on one of his eternal themes and she said OK then, Miles, I'll see you when I see you (which was just about the size of it) and then she said Hang on, Miles – the boys want to talk to you and Miles had said Yeah? OK then – put them on: Hi, lads – you being good boys and helping your mother? Got something mega for you when I come home – all your mates'll be green, I'm telling ya. Your Dad loves you, lads – put me back on to your mother, yeah? Sheil? You there? Yeah – so anyway, like I says – couple days ought to do it: really tasty bit of business come up (well – they can think what they like, can't they?) So let's say Tuesday night, maybe Wednesday, yeah? Don't know really when, but have something ready – OK?

He'd been in the foyer of The Excelsior when he'd done all that. Paused at the bar for a quick Bacardi and Slimline and then went back to his room for an even quicker fucklet with Melody, before they got turfed out at noon. She'd responded quite well to the riding crop side of things, as it happens – and now that they were back in her actually pretty pitiful two-room dump in Christ knew which bit of London it was, Miles rather thought that a touch more of that would maybe not go amiss, and he was well down the road into warming her up when bugger him if the bloody phone didn't ring and he said Oh Christ leave it, leave it – if it's important whoever it is'll ring back (just stay down on your hands and knees) – but Melody had said she didn't *like* to leave it ringing like that and so she picked up the receiver and it was Dotty of all people – wonder why? Oh yes of course – because she's looking after my *baby*, isn't she? God – I've lost all track.

'So,' waded in Dotty, with gusto. 'You got back safely, then? Little Dawn has been as good as gold – I think she wants to talk to you.'

'Yeah?' laughed Melody – trying to detach Miles's hands from her upper thighs while mugging at him Look, there's a time and a place (but God, though – wasn't his urgency thrilling?)

A bit of dribbling and a gurgle or so came down the line, and Melody would have made suitably mumsy noises to that, but just at this moment she had to box clever, yes? In no time at all Dotty was getting down to business.

'I can't *tell* you how much I've enjoyed having her,' she said. 'Of course it's *different* for me – I've got so much time – all the time in the world. It can't be at all easy for you with your job, and everything.'

'Yeah well it *is* difficult.' *Bloody* difficult, Melody tacked on to herself before shuddering deliriously because the tip of Miles's tongue was fluttering around all over and into her ear.

'Melody,' said Dotty now – still lightly, but with serious intent thickly coating the edges, 'I don't at all mind carrying on with it, you know – more or less semi-permanently. Or permanently, even. I mean, you know – we could even *legalize* it, if that would make you feel easier. I mean I hope you know you can *trust* me, Melody.'

Melody really did push away Miles now, no bones about it: this was proper talk, as a flicking in her eyes made Miles realize. He receded with resentment and slumped alongside, looking at her balefully. For Melody's part, she was thinking You know I really do believe that all of this is *meant*: I mean – the only hitch, the only problem was Dawn. If Miles found out she'd been lying about having a kid, he'd be off – she just knew it. Men don't like babies hanging around, do they? It's the woman they want – they want a woman to adore *them* – not some bloody baby. Christ – even Dawn's own bloody father couldn't get away quick enough.

'I think,' she said slowly, 'that that's really worth thinking seriously about' – and she heard, she could swear it, the whoosh made by Dotty's

426

whole heart and soul as they were sent soaring on up to the stars.

And it was tacitly agreed, there and then. One or two other small things were said (See you at Elizabeth's tomorrow – that was one of them) and then Melody put down the phone and turned to face Miles, her whole face lit by something that went far beyond pleasure – it was as if she had been newly released.

'You do mean it, what you said? You really do mean it, Miles?'

Miles smiled: great – we're back on course.

'Course I meant it. Don't think I'd let *you* slip through the net, do you?'

'But *marriage*, Miles – it's a pretty big step.'

'Not if you love someone,' said Miles. 'Hey – come here.'

She went to him, and he kissed the tip of her nose. Yeah – he had actually said about this marriage thing. How it went was, she'd asked him how he felt about living with her and he said Yeah, lovely, nothing better (keep 'em sweet, right? Told you before.) Then she'd said yes but that's completely different to *marriage*, isn't it? I mean – there's no commitment. And so Miles, without even blinking, said What – you want us to get married? We'll get married (it was no sweat – he'd done it before. Room bugged, is it? She's wired up? I don't think so. You see, what you got to understand about your woman is that if she feels secure, then there just ain't nothing she won't do

427

for you. Got it?) And Melody had become wild with delight and then the shadow of Dawn had descended – and now, quite as suddenly, it was gone: no more. Nothing now could spoil the moment, nothing could mar the eternal future.

'Now,' said Miles, 'get across my knee and take your whipping like a good little wife.'

And she did.

Dotty hadn't so much replaced the receiver as dashed it down while hissing out through her teeth whatever build-up of pressure within her now demanded immediate expulsion. She picked up Dawn – oh sweet Lord, the achingly tender soft warm smell of her – and hugged and hugged her as hard as she dared. Should she bother telling Brian? Would it matter either way? He wandered in just then – the shock of seeing that thing round his neck jolting Dotty once again (kept forgetting he had it, kept forgetting it had happened – forgetting anything at all like that) – and so she thought she might as well:

'Brian, I've just been on to Melody and I suggested to her that it might be a good idea –' and then excitement got the better of her and she simply erupted: 'Oh it's so *marvellous*, Brian – we're to have Dawn for our very own! Our very own little baby girl for ever!'

Brian nodded; tried to look what passed for pleased.

'I've just sold the house,' he said. 'Exchanged,

anyway. They seem to want it all to happen quite quickly, though.'

Dotty nodded too: this obviously *was* relevant, but she couldn't be expected to get her mind around it now. 'I'm going to tell Colin,' she said.

'I'm going out,' was the only other thing Brian had to say for himself.

Dotty looked at him. His pale and quite blank face rising up from that collar gave him the air of a giant banana that someone had begun to peel, and then thought better of it.

'Fine,' she said. She scooped up Dawn and went upstairs.

Yes, thought Brian on his way to the door, I'm going out and I'm going to get drunk on the last few pounds I have. And maybe – if I go to one of those lovely old traditional pubs with a sturdy brass footrail all along the bar – I might drink so much as to occasion a helpless fall and just possibly my skull might connect with that rail and do me the goodness of splitting open and with a bit more luck by the time the paramedics arrive their sole and sombre duty will be to rise up from the urn of my ashes and pronounce me clinically dead.

Colin was sitting on the corner of his bed, idly plucking at the strings of his Yamaha guitar. Hadn't plugged it in – was only fooling around: just something to do with his hands as his mind revisited it all – went back one more time with feeling over every contour of each undulation of his rich and recent life.

The first thing he had known was a headache that truly was akin to being blind: sharp darts of colour were running amok, but opening his eyes was subject to all sorts of impossible strictures, most of the features on his face and certainly the surface of his skin kicking up a hell of a row at the very idea. Then he sensed before glimpsing the warmth of that deep brown body, castaway beside him – hair thrown wild and plunged into sleep. The spill of Elizabeth's breasts came close to stopping his heart. (No more, he knew now, would he ever think of these wonderous things as 'tits'. Tits was a schoolboy, silly, smutty word: breasts were altogether different. Maybe girls have tits and women breasts – yes? Colin was now reminded of how he had once thought it would be nice and convenient if all young tits were graded like eggs from Class A downwards – but maybe only so he could exercise free range over them all.)

But these breasts here, warmly lolling alongside – these were not for grabbing, no – these were for folding oneself within. And only then did it hit him like a stone (Looking back, he's pretty sure that although the morning now washed through the windows, he was still as drunk as hell from more champagne than he knew existed.). This is Elizabeth! These are *her* breasts – and I am in her bed. He edged closer – edged on closer still; spent a good time nestling, one hand pressed hard into his groin, lest his arousal roused her. Soon his body heat doubled into boiling as their skins were bonded all the way down – and then, in waking half-sleep, Elizabeth had thrown up an arm, and now were her fingers idly rummaging among Colin's golden hair. And the lightness of so careless a caress went a good way to easing the hot thud that hit him all over the temples.

Colin did not know which of them first ceased to pretend to be asleep – it was maybe a much to be wished for and mutually arrived at thing – but Elizabeth then was giving Colin a fine wide smile of encouragement: it was packed with fondness and goodly overtones of don't-be-shy-and-don't-be-scared-it's-only-little-me, and Colin was grateful for that. At first it was no more than friendly. Pretty soon it became just about as friendly as it gets – but alas, just as it had been with Carol (I have touched two women – two – in not much more than half a day, after all those years of longing), Colin was soon covered with at least embarrassment.

But as the hours passed – room service and more and more champagne kept coming and going – Elizabeth became more coaxing, until big, deep things were fretfully suggested and then quite wildly gone for and then their unqualified and zinging success could be celebrated with nothing much short of hysteria.

Some time later (lunchtime? Teatime? Some time of day when the sun still hung hot and high in the sky) Colin had showered and dressed and

431

after many lingering out-stretched arms reluctantly slithered from his, had torn himself away. He had to, he explained: but he'd be back – my God would he be back – just as soon as he could possibly make it.

Before all this, any of this, had even been thought of, Colin had made a date with Carol. And where else but at the top of the Godforlorn cliff (the one where his father . . . ? Yep: that one) and there he gently explained that he couldn't ask her back to the hotel, not now, because Elizabeth, you see, was there all the time. And Carol had thought What is it about this boy? Can't he see how much I want him? Even love him, maybe (don't know). Is he really protecting me? Maybe he just doesn't care.

And at that moment, Colin could not have told her. Did he care? Impossible to say: I am in the grip of an obsession. Time is running out and I have to get back – I may never ever have such a time again.

And now, right now as he plucked at the guitar while flushing and flinching as a result of it all – his mother was in the middle of barging in: here she is, grinning like a wax-work, and of *course* with that bloody baby in her arms. So anyway – just quickly before Mum starts up – where was I? Oh yeah – so I more or less left Carol just sitting there (her breasts, let's face it, not remotely in the same league) and she called after me But I still will see you at Elizabeth's party?! And I called back Yeah, sure, of course – but all the time I was thinking oh

432

Jesus: Elizabeth's party – that's going to be a bit weird, isn't it? Oh God – Mum's been wittering on while I did that last bit and I didn't catch a word of it: hang on.

'Sorry, Mum? Say again?'

'God you're *miles* away, aren't you, Colin?' came back Dotty with indulgent wonder. 'I *said* that baby Dawn is coming to live with us for good – although we don't actually know quite where, yet, because your father has sold the house. Say hello to your grown-up brother, Dawn!'

More grown up than you think, thought Colin with a smirk. And then he nodded: tried to look what passed for pleased.

Later – oh, so much later – when Colin was just lying there, going over it all just one more time (Dotty and Dawn must have long ago tiptoed down the primrose path that leads to Dreamland) – the doorbell rang, and then it rang again: the sort of insistence that won't be ignored. When Colin saw the policeman standing there he thought God – I haven't done anything *illegal*, have I? And then it flashed into him that yes, he almost certainly had – I mean, they're red-hot on you even buying a tin of lager when you're my age, so Christ knows what they do for banging your Mum's best friend.

'A Mr Brian Morgan live here?' asked the officer, impassively.

Oh great! It was only about Dad! Panic over. 'Yes – that is, yes – he lives here. He's my Dad.

He's not here right now, though – and Mum's asleep, pretty sure.'

'We've got him in the car,' the policeman said now, jerking a thumb in the direction of the street. 'Slightly the worse for wear.' He made some sort of a wave and soon Colin could make out the stumbling form of Brian, half carried and half pushed up the path by another copper. 'We won't be preferring charges, this time. He's sprained his wrist – just had it taped up at the hospital. Tell him when he's sobered up we'll be writing to him.'

Dotty had suddenly appeared. 'What is it? What's wrong?'

'*Mrs* Morgan?' checked the policeman, just at the moment Brian crumpled in through the door. The gauze wrapped snug around his wrist and half his hand was rather cleaner than that of his surgical collar, which looked as if it had recently gone ten rounds with a tanked-up coal sack.

'*Brian*, for God's sake – what –?'

'Gentleman had better sleep it off. We had a report, madam, that a man was reeling around the pavement and clutching a purloined manhole cover. Before we could reach him he had fallen down the hole. Well – wedged halfway, if the truth be known.'

Dotty made many clucking noises of apology to the two policemen (who, Colin felt sure, beneath their bland and professional faces were cracking up at the memory of this drunk old loony trapped down a bloody manhole) and when they had left she said Oh *God*, Colin, we'll never get him upstairs in this state – just help me into the living room with him, will you?

They got him there and had him poised over the larger of the sofas: all he had to do was pitch forward and yes, he managed that all right but glanced off the cushions and hit the floor like a duvet cover packed with spuds. A deep groan of anything from utter defeat to contentment rumbled out of him and Dotty said Oh God *leave* him – just leave him, Colin: you go on up and I'll do the lights, and everything. Colin nodded and turned to go, pausing only to look down on his father: you know – as men go, this one has all the makings of a bloody lemming.

Norman had all the poles in the ground, now. Actually, the whole thing had gone rather well – well hell, I've never put up a marquee before (few have, I should think) and of *course* I was expecting all manner of things to go horribly wrong: freak thunderstorm, smashing my hand with a mallet, impenetrable lawn – all that *Three Men in a Boat* type stuff. But no – an absolutely perfect summer's day yet again – and, it must be said, what a wonderful garden! Norman had never been in the garden before (only been to the house was it twice). Just look at all those sort of, what are they, flowering things over there: red ones. And some tall lilac-y ones behind (not lilac, is it? Couldn't have told you – know absolutely and totally nothing about plants; pretty, though.) And Howard had just gone off to get them all a beer, which would be a very welcome thing, let Norman tell you. So – these long striped panels, if I'm not very much mistaken, slot in here . . . and here . . . but I'll have to get up on the steps for this bit, I think, so someone'll have to . . . where is that bloody Peter person? Just been hanging around all morning doing bloody nothing. For nearly two hours, now, Norman had been waiting for Howard to say something on the lines of Come *on*, come *on* – let's have a bit of effort out of you: but no, nothing. He seems to regard him so oddly. And Peter, make no mistake, is decidedly odd: get this funny, creepy feeling whenever I look at him – just something not *right*. And even when he talks he says the weirdest things, in his whiny little high-pitched voice – not normal chitchat, as you might expect, but all these serious statements and point-blank and in-your-face questions, and then he just *looks* at you as you go through the motions of trying to answer.

'Do you think about clothes?'

Here was another one, I mean – what a question for a however-old-he-was boy (sixteen? younger?) to ask a man in his twenties. And it hardly *looked* like it, did it? Norman was wearing even more appalling duds than usual, today (well – you're not going to dress up to fool with a marquee on a baking hot day, now, are you? Mind you – Howard had invited Norman to the party, later on:

God knows if there's anything I can unearth for that.) Maybe Peter's being cheeky, is he? His way of mocking the way Norman looks? Don't think so – no lurking sneer, that I can see. Peter for his part was wearing very slim and perfectly pressed white trousers which sort of curved into his hip: *weird*, I tell you. And now Norman for reasons he couldn't even begin to fathom was struggling to respond to this kid's ludicrous enquiry.

'Well,' he said slowly. 'Actually – could you just hand me up that – yeah, no: that one, yeah that one. Good. It depends, really, what you *mean*.'

Well it doesn't, actually, thought Norman now – eight steps up on the aluminium ladder and dropping the brass eyelets of the door panel over the hooks on the crossbeam: quite clever, these things – neatly put together. No – it doesn't at all depend on whatever it is you might mean because the short answer is No I don't, not ever: how can one think about *clothes*? The only time he had ever considered any garment at all was when Katie had instructed him to write the word 'See' on his HICAGO T-shirt (later to be covered in his own blood just after Katie went off with . . . oh Christ, oh Christ – I thought I'd stopped myself thinking and remembering, and here it all is again: the sunshine and the lilac-y flowers mean nothing to me, now).

'What I mean is,' expanded the boy known only to Howard as Zoo-Zoo, 'are there ever certain things that you yearn to have touching your skin?'

Norman wobbled on the ladder and nearly lost it, then. What a perfectly *extraordinary* thing to say – was he *sane*, do we think? The only thing I yearn to have touching my skin is Katie, and that will maybe never ever be happening to me again! Why am I up a ladder and exchanging inanities with a maybe psychotic youngster when my heart lies bleeding and my life is in tatters?

'I,' went on Zoo-Zoo, 'simply adore cream silk underwear.'

Norman came down the ladder just as Howard ambled up with three cans of lager. Would Norman have hit the boy or snubbed him or pronounced him an unutterably sick little shit? Couldn't tell you. What he did now was grasp the icy and glistening can, tear off the ringpull and get his laughing gear well around the business end. What on earth could it be that Howard saw in this kid? Nuts and truly weird, if you ask Norman.

'Taking shape,' approved Howard. 'Elizabeth says she wants to start arranging all the chairs and food and so on in an hour, so let's get cracking. Oh and Katie rang, Norman – which pleased Elizabeth, I must say. She's at the airport – be here in an hour, so it's going to be quite a full house.'

Norman went on glugging down beer – simply couldn't decide whether to feel great or terrible: could there be anything for him, here? Or was he well and truly over?

'Mr Street,' said Norman, with care – wiping his

mouth with the back of his hand (is the wetness sweat or lager? Bit of each – hardly matters.) 'I wonder if I might just have a word. Howard.'

'Well can't it *wait*, Norman? We've got this bloody marquee to finish.'

To which Norman could only nod. He turned back and without a word resumed his task. Howard glanced at Zoo-Zoo and touched his shoulder and said softly All right? And Zoo-Zoo's eyelids were lowered as he smiled his reply.

Not much more than half an hour later and the marquee was done: it looked wonderful, Howard said – and a hastily summoned Elizabeth too was delighted when she came out and saw this fine white and yellow striped and rather *medievally-* looking (didn't Howard think?) structure sitting sunlit and four-square at the centre of her just so perfect English lawn. This, she said – actually clapping her hands – will be the party to end them all. And then she looked at Zoo-Zoo for the very first time: now who on earth I wonder can this young person be? And then she thought she had it:

'You must be Peter from the office.'

'Oh God I'm *awfully* sorry, Elizabeth,' blustered Howard – a touch of brow-smiting going on, now – 'I'd completely forgotten you haven't actually met before – I just sort of assumed . . . yes, this is . . . and this is Elizabeth. My wife.'

What a funny feeling, he was thinking: like it, pretty sure.

Why, thought Elizabeth, is he just eyeing me, this boy? And why now is he looking at Howard? Shy. I think he must just be shy.

'So anyway, Mr Street. Howard,' started up Norman again. 'I wonder if, you know . . . I wonder could I . . . ?'

'Oh yes – you want to talk to me, don't you? OK – let's go into the house, then: it's actually *baking* out here, isn't it? And then I'd better see to all the drink stuff.'

'We'll see you later on, then,' said Elizabeth, as the two moved off. 'And thank you, Norman, for all your valiant efforts. It looks just *wonderful*.'

'No problem, Mrs Street,' said Norman. 'Elizabeth. No problem.'

'Now Peter,' said Elizabeth. 'Are you going to be awfully sweet and help me with the *plates* and things?'

She got a nod and a smile in reply to that. Nice smile. Really rather lovely eyes.

Norman didn't quite know what it was he wanted to say to Howard. Just felt certain that he had to rid himself of at least some of the secrets, some of the guilt. Life would be so fine if only I was the sort of man Mr Street believes me to be; that Howard believes me to be. Yes.

'So,' opened Howard, settling himself into a window seat in the breakfast room. 'Fire away, Norman. God, it's hot. I think I'm going to have to change my shirt again. Absolutely soaking.'

'Look, Howard. Yes – Howard. It's about Katie.'

And that made Howard look up: whatever all this was about he surely hadn't expected Katie to be a part of it.

'Katie?' he said. 'But I told you, Norman – she'll be here any minute. You can talk to her yourself. Something at work, is it?'

Norman shook his head. 'No. Nothing to do with work. It's about how I—' Oh Christ: was going to say 'feel' – wanted so much to say 'feel' but I just can't do it: it just won't come.

'Well spit it out, Norman lad!' chivvied Howard, who was now thinking You know, I'm glad I'm not young any anymore: are they all like this, nowadays, young men? Can't speak up for themselves. And he was further thinking Actually, I can't hang around for too much more of this because I haven't yet checked the ice situation and if everything isn't absolutely shipshape for this party thing, then Elizabeth will lose little time in having my guts for . . . oh Christ, what is it? What is it? What do people have your guts for? No – it's completely gone: Christ, my mind. Is this boy ever going to speak? Oh yes, here we go: lips moving, anyway – something might come.

'I love her,' said Norman: that is what came.

'Sorry, Norman? reacted Howard. You do *what*!

'Very much,' sighed Norman. 'More than anything on earth. I'm just – oh God, I'm just *mad* with love for Katie!'

The next thing that popped into Howard's mind

was to tell the lad to stop being so bloody *stupid* but Christ just look at him – seems on the verge of tears. *Garters*, that's it: guts for garters.

'Oh stop being so bloody *stupid*, Norman!' snapped Howard (some things you just have to go with). 'How can you possibly love *Katie* – you don't even *know* Katie!' No you bloody don't – and you're not going to, either. *I* know Katie – it is I who knows her because I'm her bloody father and if and when her first man looms he will not in any shape or form be anything remotely like *you*, young Furnish, because *you*, lad, whether you know it or not, are going absolutely nowhere fast (because let's face it – where the bloody hell did estate agents *go*?)

'I'm sorry! I'm sorry, Mr Street! I just can't *help* it.' Norman's eyes were wide and frantic, his fingers energetically plucking away at his sleeves. He just had to let go of it *all*, now: 'It was fine, everything wonderful right up until halfway through the holiday just before I got mugged and –'

'*Holiday*, Norman? What on earth has this quite ludicrous nonsense of yours got to do with your bloody *holiday*, Christ's sake?!' What *can* he be banging on about? Maybe I was wrong about young Mister Norman Furnish – it sounds to me like he's fucking demented.

'Because she was *there*. On holiday. Katie was with *me*!' And Norman's eyes now were pleading with Howard to please please please *listen* and help me or end it and kill me.

Howard stood up. 'I think the bloody *sun's* got

442

to you, Norman!' Christ I was right – fucking demented. 'Katie wasn't in *Cornwall* – what on earth are you thinking about? She's just on her way back from *Chicago*!'

'Chicago!' bawled Norman. 'Chicago, yes! I was there – I was there in Chicago. With Katie. Me. I was there!'

'Norman,' said Howard, more quietly. 'I don't quite know what game you're playing but I'm telling you that it's stopping right *now*. Hear me? You did *not* go to Chicago –'

'Did! I did. Just got back.'

'*No*, Norman, no – you have just got back from – Christ I don't believe this is *happening*! You have just got back from *Cornwall*.'

Norman was shaking his head as if desperate to be rid of it.

'No! No! Never been to Cornwall in my *life*!'

'But you *told* me –'

'Yes yes yes but I just *said* that, didn't I? Had to say that, didn't I? I mean I couldn't tell you I'd been to Chicago with *Katie*, could I?'

'But that's exactly what you *are* bloody telling me, you fucking *lunatic*, Norman!'

'Yes but that's *now* – *now* I'm telling you, yes, because it very much looks as if she won't *marry* me now, and –'

'*Marry*!' gasped Howard, still just simply not believing this could be *happening*. And then he became quite stern. 'Norman. Cease. Now. I seriously think you are deranged, if you want

443

the truth. All this is so *unlike* you. Are you on *drugs* or something?'

'No,' said Norman, miserably. 'Haven't had any since Chicago – Katie chopped me out a line of coke.'

Howard came bloody close to hitting him. '*Right*, Norman – that's it. We are going to have all this crap out with Katie the minute she walks through the door – clear? It seems to me you have suffered some sort of breakdown and – *no*, Norman – shut up: not another word. Now go into the garden and make yourself bloody *useful*. If you want to go home and sleep off whatever's got a hold of you, that's fine too. We're going to have a very serious talk soon, though, Norman: very serious indeed.'

Norman sighed as if for the very last time. He stood, defeated and abashed. 'I'm so sorry,' he practically whispered. 'I will hang around here if that's all right. Want to talk to Katie. Can't wait to see her again. Oh *God* I'm so sorry, Howard!'

Howard just looked at him. 'Mister *Street*,' he said, quite firmly. 'Let's for now just keep it nice and formal, shall we?'

Norman's face was held as if struck. He felt in the grip of a trance as he walked stiffly back out into the white-hot and now quite dizzy sunshine. I am putting one foot in front of the other. I am sitting on grass. I am standing up. I am too hot. And now I am palely loitering (within tent).

CHAPTER 8

Dotty gasped with pleasure at the sheer and bright prettiness of the sparkling marquee, two pink pennants just about fluttering under glinting finials in the warm and heavy air; this, in such a setting (*God* how does Elizabeth keep this garden so utterly immaculate? Oh yes – two gardeners, no problem), surely had to be the ultimate English Summer Thing. And, knowing Elizabeth, the tent would be filled with not only extremely good stuff (and plenty of it) but the touches that others had maybe neither the time nor money to take care of: flowers, but of course – oh heavens look! Fountains of yellow lilies, confetti explosions of snow-white gypsophila – and also a couple of rows of rich green canvas-backed directors' chairs and lovely gingham cloths and napkins in maybe a delphinium blue (most unusual). Did that not clash with the green? Make strident the yellow? Not at all, oh no no no: the blend and shock of the colours came together quite perfectly. Here was big evidence of Elizabeth, in all her enviable glory.

And enviable too was just everything she *had*.

Yes she made the most of it all (Howard must be so pleased to have her – the ideal wife and mother, yes?) but the luxury she always had of just getting an idea, and suddenly all was gorgeous reality (courtesy of just about anyone, but generally Howard), this did – yes it did – make Dotty now go quite as green as those canvas-backed chairs (and if not that green, then greener) and for the very first time since Dawn had come to her – now as warm as heaven and strapped to her bosom – Dotty slithered and then fell headlong into sadness and regret. Never would she have the things that Elizabeth had; and now the house – the house too was gone, and so all hopes of it ever being even nearly as lovely as this were taken from her completely. The chill of fear entered her now (I have a child – I have a baby: what is to become of us?) but she was straight away cheered as she slipped into the cool of the dazzlingly lit up marquee by the sight of not just Lulu (seems *ages* since I saw her) but also Elizabeth herself – radiant, yes: it's the only word – radiant as a blaze, and Lulu too. Dotty was wearing something lemony and old, and Dawn served very well to mask a hardly younger blemish that no cursingly applied and stringent stain remover would have anything remotely to do with.

A flurry of kissing (a laugh or so at the frontal obstacle that was Dawn – I love it, I love it, thought Dotty: it feels like I'm pregnant but she's already born) and now all that had to be decided was

446

should it maybe be Pimm's or champagne or Buck's Fizz or Kir or what looked like the most wonderful and fruity ice-cold punch (as dark as wine, and marbled with mandarin swirls). And over there, talking to Howard and a couple I don't know – that must be John, yes? Lulu's husband? The one who wants to kill everyone, apparently. Well – what is one to make of that? He does keep glancing over quite aggressively: I do hope he's *safe*. At least bloody old Brian only inflicts damage on *himself*: altogether preferable, I should have said. And here was Brian now; don't ask Dotty how she knew – she didn't have to turn round, or anything. Just knew he had arrived – and it wasn't the sight of Elizabeth and Lulu nearly but not quite imperceptibly rearranging their faces into oh Look oh God oh How Lovely To See You, no: Dotty just felt it. Comes with the years, and maybe never leaves you – the feeling that someone who is so remote, so utterly beyond and outside anything to *do* with you, has nonetheless become a part.

'Oh *God*, Brian,' Elizabeth could not check herself from blurting out, 'what is it that you look like? What I mean to say is,' she amended, recovering herself a little, 'you look very *well*, Brian. How's the neck?' And then, in a quick aside to Dotty: 'Can he hear me?'

Dotty nodded. 'Oh yes – he's not deaf any more. It didn't work.'

'What?' said Brian. 'What are you saying?' Hadn't been listening.

'I *said*!' yelled out Elizabeth – this causing Brian to practically fall over – 'You're looking very –! Oh but I didn't know you'd hurt your *hand* as well, Brian – how did you –?'

'In the wars,' said Lulu, quietly. Didn't know Brian (why *do* women actually get married?) but felt she ought to put in something.

'No no,' explained Dotty. 'You're not up to date. The *neck* he did falling off the cliff, yes –'

'Why,' asked Brian now, 'are you talking about me as if I'm not here? I can *hear*, you know.'

'– but the *hand*,' went on Dotty – and it really was as if Brian at that moment was in quite a different country – 'the *hand*, I have to say – that was done just last night when Brian fell down a manhole.'

Lulu blinked, but Elizabeth sort of thought she understood:

'You mean he fell over one of his covers? Dropped it on his hand?'

'No – fell down the hole. He tells me it was a rare and beautiful cover – I kid you not – and because the silly sod was plastered, he prised it up out of the street and then went reeling down into the bloody hole, if you can believe it.'

And now Elizabeth was blinking too, but she rallied round in huge and true hostess style:

'Well never you *mind*, Brian – I tell you, that sort of thing happens to me all the *time*.'

'Why,' said Lulu to Brian, 'oh – I'm Lulu, by the way – *did* you in fact want to go deaf?'

448

'*What*!' barked out Brian. Go *deaf*?! What on earth was this woman *talking* about, whoever on God's earth she is.

Both Lulu and Elizabeth looked to Dotty for clarification here, and Dotty said Well all I can say is he was hearing perfectly well this morning: it maybe comes and goes.

Brian moved away in quest of a drink. And Dotty can laugh – she can say what she wants – but it was, it was: a very rare and beautiful cover, and just touching it was the only sensation that had stirred the vapour of alcohol that suffused him and kept him safe that night. When he staggered (partly the weight, mostly the booze) he had been surprised to find no firm floor beneath him, but even through the jarring pain of being wedged fast in the manhole, Brian urged himself ever downwards: it did not occur to him to struggle out – he only needed to plummet. Could not move an inch either way, as it turned out, which is why when the police eventually arrived they found him protruding from the ground like the softened nosecone of a battered and quite forgotten missile, peeping up with regret from its abandoned silo.

First: a drink. Second: another.

'Brian!' Howard hailed him.

Damn: want a drink and then I want a bloody nother. Still – it is Howard's party, after all.

'Some people you maybe ought to meet, now the deed is done. Brian Morgan – Cyril Davies and Mrs Davies, Edna.'

449

Brian was all ears. 'Oh! You're the—' Was going to say You're the bastard who just knew from some sixth sense that I was as low as low and would accept just anything, and then you reduced it hugely and further when you smelled I could barely breathe any more. Instead he said, '– purchaser.'

Cyril extended his hand. 'No hard feelings, I very much hope, about the, er, last-minute alteration. The survey, I must say, was far from good.'

Brian just nodded. Nod nod nod. Want a drink.

'We particularly liked the garden,' piped up Edna. 'Or what it will look like, anyway, when Cyril gets going on it. He's *such* a brilliant gardener – aren't you, dear?'

Cyril regarded the outstretched fingers of one hand. 'I keep my hand in,' he said. 'But you might have a rival, I have to say, Howard. Lovely garden – lovely. Are you much of a mulch man?'

'The garden is Elizabeth's territory,' laughed Howard. 'So she is your enemy from now on, not me.'

'So what is it that you do, Mr Morgan?' asked Cyril. 'Brian.'

'I'm in carpets. Was in carpets. Retired, now.' Want a drink.

'Cyril,' said Edna, 'is a psychiatrist.'

'Are you *really*?' And here was a new voice: this was John's voice, John had been hanging back, lurking – eyeing Lulu less than furtively. It was all right at the moment because she was chatting over there with this Lizzie person (who yes all right *does* exist but that hardly made up for all the rest of it, did it?) and also some woman with a baby. The cripple Brian, was it, had been over there too – yes, John had certainly clocked that – but even he didn't see Brian as any sort of a threat at all.

'Howard,' said Brian. 'I'm just going to get a drink.'

Howard nodded – and as John seemed on the verge of engaging Cyril in earnest conversation, he asked Edna if he maybe couldn't refresh that for her and she said that would be lovely and I actually wouldn't mind some of that very tempting smoked salmon and by the time Howard was escorting her there and Brian was at another table (drinking hard) John had already got down to it:

'Look, um – Cyril. I know we don't know each other or anything – and doctors, all doctors, they must get sick of complete strangers buttonholing them at parties . . .'

'No no,' said Cyril. 'Not at all.' Yes yes bloody *yes*, he was thinking. I keep telling Edna that there's a time, a detectable moment to let loose my profession – not among strangers until you know the lay of the land, and certainly not in order to cap some deadbeat who apparently used to flog carpets for a living and now doesn't even do that.

'It's just that . . . *well*,' went on John. 'It's about my wife.'

Cyril nodded. Yes – it generally was. Talk to the wife, of course, and you learn that the problem comes from somewhere quite other.

'Mm-Hm,' he grunted, automatically: it was the noise that encouraged people to go on while Cyril, in his mind, could go off. More guests were arriving now – mostly rather young, by the look of them. Maybe I can steal away from this person and meet one or two of them, just possibly. He had been eyeing a perfectly stunning woman over there since first they arrived – wraparound black sunglasses and talking quite animatedly to Howard's wife, Elizabeth: quite remarkable. Now that Edna's gone, all Cyril maybe had to do is dole out some *Reader's Digest* verdict on whatever it was troubling this clearly deeply neurotic man, and then possibly start to enjoy the party. The champagne, he had to say, was really quite excellent.

'Look,' apologized John, 'I'm sorry to, you know – *do* all this but I had actually been thinking of, you know – *talking* to someone, but I probably never would have got round to it. My wife – that's her over there: Lulu, she's called. Is her name.'

And Cyril glanced in the direction of the knot of three women: not Elizabeth, evidently. 'The one with the baby?'

John shook his head. 'Other one. Sunglasses.'

Well well well, thought Cyril: who on earth would have believed it – a woman such as that with a man who, the more I talk to him, I am becoming convinced could be on the verge of derangement. It didn't do, not professionally, to comment – to say anything at all on the lines of 'Fine woman' or 'What a tasteful dresser' (and certainly not 'Jeeeesus, son, look at the fucking legs on her! I'm telling you I wouldn't mind right here and now!' – of course not) so Cyril, quite wisely, said nothing at all.

'Well the thing is,' John forced himself to go on. 'She's a nymphomaniac.'

'Really,' said Cyril. *Really*? Of course, it must be remembered that the layman almost never knows the clinical definition of nymphomania; I, on the other hand, know exactly what the layman means by it and so all this is maybe not without its points of interest.

'But the really weird bit is,' whispered John now (glass was empty – must get more, much more), 'no – the *really* odd thing is that when she's *done* it – and sometimes it's someone she's just met in a *lift*, for God's sake – when it's, you know, all over, it's as if she has no memory – gone. Or else she chats about it – to *me*, to *me* – as if it was all the most natural thing in the world. So I think I've worked it out and I'd like you to tell me if I'm on the right lines – I mean, is this *known*, this condition? I mean – it's a sort of amnesiac nymphomania, right? Or maybe the other way around. And she does other things, too. The other day – you won't believe this – she walked up to a complete stranger and hit him in the face because apparently, she said, he had a funny *walk*.'

Cyril smiled – a combination of doctorly sympathy and fuck off, twit. 'So,' he said. 'Would you like me to, er, have a word with her? Roundabout word?'

'Oh God I wouldn't *presume* . . .' stuttered John.

'No no, not at all. Often best in a party situation. You find out all sorts of things from general chat.'

'Well I must say that's really very, very good of you,' enthused John, a bit of relief for the first time in ages breaking through this weight of gloom. 'I'm going for more champagne – would you . . . ?'

'Excellent,' approved Cyril. 'And then I'll sidle over.'

Good, thought John, on his way over to all those lous silver buckets packed with gold-necked bottles of fizz – at least he's taking me *seriously*: Christ – how long was it (you just tell John that) – how, in fact, bloody long *was* it since anyone had taken him *seriously*? Not my editor, certainly – not her: she just *loves* to put me down. I tell you, if it wasn't for the money . . . I mean – just look at what came in today. Do you know what I'm expected to do fifteen hundred words on next? Well do you? Just try this for size: tartan. Yeah – tartan. Know why? Because they were already working on the bloody November issue, weren't they, and every single fucking winter in living memory these bloody so-called interior designers reinvented *tartan*, didn't they? Announced it as

454

if it had never been *seen* before. Depend on it – as soon as shop windows are awash with autumn leaves and witches' brooms, so is everyone pushing tartan and red velvet and brown leather – *again*. Same in the spring – candy stripes (peppermint fresh!) and bleeding nautical-but-nice (how many times have I used that one?) blue and white bloody stuff. Anyway – tartan, next.

And the novel. They didn't read it – they didn't even *read* it, John would bet you anything you like. And do you know what was *really* galling? The bit that really got to him? Some bloody young person on the magazine had said just last Christmas that *he* had started a novel, in fact, and John had said Oh yes – really? Glancing down at so pitiful an intention from the vantage point of two whole years' slog and nearly ninety thousand words logged on. The bastard's only just gone and had it *accepted* – wrote it in six weeks flat and got some bent agent to send it in saying that the stream of consciousness and the unforgettable power of the language reminded him of nothing so much as Joyce – and the bloody publisher took it on! And I bet they didn't read *that* either because this bloke, this bastard who was now calling himself a bloody *author*, he told me that he had been pissing himself with laughter because Joyce, it turns out, is his agent's mother-in-law! Publishers? Tell me about it, *please*.

John turned away from the drinks table (super party, Howard!) with a brimful flute of bubbles

455

firm in each hand – well, save him a journey – and did not drop them, didn't, but came extremely close to it (certainly the nerve ends in his fingers were a-jangle: they trembled still as he goggled) for before him now stood Miles and Melody and although he did not know or care that those were their names he sure as fucking hell remembered their bloody faces – and, indeed, most of the rest of their parts and pieces because the last time he had clapped eyes on them they were both stark naked and hot from sex in a hotel bedroom one hundred miles from where they now stood before him – and Miles, at least, was leering – and now these two vile and lewd and mocking monsters had looked him up and tracked him down: here they are to maybe kill me and take away my Lulu to be their sexual slave and conquest. How good it is, then, that suspicion this morning clambered all over me – how fine it feels to have come prepared.

Colin had practically collided with Katie in the hall. She had evidently just come down from changing and was shrieking with laughter about some sort of girl thing with some sort of girl with bright red hair who skittered just beside her. She looked good, Colin would give her that (Katie always looked good, let's face it), and her friend wasn't at all bad either, but Colin was relieved and pleased beyond measure to find that his heart was not gripped and nor was he blushing. Just a glimpse of Katie alone, up till just a week ago, would have been more than enough to set all that off, as we have witnessed with pain – but two girls together, locked in that frightening and so female nubile conspiracy: that would surely have done for him. But no – he was no longer in thrall to Katie's tits: here was an altar he would never again bow down to. No, Katie, no – you have lost your power over me, because I have graduated to your mother's breasts.

'Good holiday, Colin?' smiled Katie.

'Very, thanks,' said Colin, lightly. Most enjoyable, yes: I spent the larger part sleeping with your mother, if you really want to know. 'You?'

Katie nodded. 'Great.' Yeah it was – and now all I want to do is lie in the sun because let me tell you (and that's what we've just been killing ourselves about) I have never in my life been so fucked to bits as I have in the last few days.

Colin passed on into the garden (God it's hot – can't wait for some more of that champagne – what will Elizabeth think as she watches me drink it? I wonder if Carol's here yet.) Katie was close behind him – but oh look it's Daddy! Got to be nice to Daddy – I spent so much!

'Katie you *are* here,' said Howard. 'Expected you about an hour ago. You look well – good time?'

'No I *have* been here, Daddy – I've just been having a shower and all that stuff. Had a *super* time. How are you? I missed you.'

Howard smiled: always reached him, that kind

of talk. 'Sweet, Katie. Look, darling, I know you've just got back and it's a party and everything but there's something I'd really quite like to get straight. It's all a bit – well it's completely bloody insane, if you want the truth, but I just want to hear it from *you* – OK?'

Katie assumed a suitably puzzled expression – and this wasn't one from the repertoire: what on *earth* could Daddy be talking about?

'Look,' said Howard. 'You did go to *Chicago*, didn't you?'

Katie just looked at him. '*Huh*? You *know* I went to Chicago – I brought half of Chicago back with me.'

Howard nodded briefly. 'Right, right – of course, right. No chance at all of your having been in *Cornwall*, then?'

'Daddy – have you been overdoing the whisky again? What are you *talking* about?'

'Not yet I haven't – might well later on. OK – now listen, Katie. Were you there – in Chicago – with a man?'

Katie stopped dead: so *that* was it. Oh Christ. But how did he . . . ? Well if he knew, he knew: had to come some time.

'Well . . . I sort of was, yes Daddy.'

Howard had not expected this. Had been wagging his head to spur on in her a forceful negative. 'Ah!' he said. And do you know, he really had believed that the very first time it had happened, he would have sensed it: would have known. Would have felt a wash of desolation. Just as he was feeling now.

'But any talk of . . .' And Howard had to push himself along, now – throat clearing like he thought they only did in plays. 'There's no suggestion of anything like *marriage*, however. Hm?' He tried to make it sound the most ridiculous thing on earth.

'Well . . .' said Katie, slowly – there was never going to be an easy moment, was there? 'I suppose it's not impossible. He has *asked* me . . . and I truly do think he's wonderful, Daddy.' Well look – if she was actually going to go through with having this baby (only just found out about that side of things) *someone* had to be around to pay for everything, didn't they? Not quite sure who the father is – probably Norman, but there were one or two others, briefly, not that long ago. So it needn't be at all.

Howard moved to the window. 'You're not even eighteen,' he sighed – but already he was making huge beckoning signals with his whole right arm to some distant figure on the lawn. Norman immediately bounded forward maybe not so much like a retriever, but more a cross between a something and a something else. 'But just explain to me,' went on Howard, almost as if to himself now, just as Norman fell breathlessly into the hall, 'why on earth you should want to marry *Norman*?'

'*Norman*?!' shrieked out Katie.

'*Katie!*' swooned back Norman. 'Oh – you've come back – you've come back to me! Oh thank the heavens!'

459

It didn't take Katie long to seize *this* fucking situation by the scruff of its neck. '*Norman*, Daddy?! Who in God's name said anything about *Norman*?! I wouldn't marry Norman if he were the last –'

'But,' stammered Howard (equal measures of relieved and confused), 'Norman told me he was in Chicago with you . . .'

'Well he *wasn't*,' said Katie firmly. 'I don't *know* Norman.'

'That's what *I* said,' said Howard, regaining his strength and rounding now on the just about demolished Norman, trembling before the two of them.

'How can you *say* that?' he gasped. 'I was there – I was *there* – we went *together* . . . !'

Katie actually stamped her foot, and appealed to the linesman for justice: 'Dadd-*eee*?! I went with *Ellie*!'

'That's right! That's right!' roared Howard. 'She went with *Ellie*!'

Norman was useless with tears by now and all he could sob out was: 'No . . . no – There Is No *Ellie* – Katie made the whole thing up!'

'Daddy,' said Katie, with surgical venom. 'I do think Norman is *mad*.' And then she called down the hall.

'So do I,' grunted Howard.

'Hello, everyone,' said a girl with bright red hair, 'I don't think we've met: my name's Ellie.'

Katie grinned and Howard went forward to

460

grasp the girl's outstretched hand (just the rumblings of Hang on, though, who's this *man*, then, if it isn't . . . ?) and it was only the noise of a splintering chair and no-nonsense clump of a head on to wood that alerted any of them to the fact that Norman had just passed out, quite spectacularly.

Colin thought he had just caught a fleeting glimpse of the tail end of Carol as she entered the tent: pretty sure it was her. But even as he strolled across the lawn he was thinking Now why aren't I in a hurry? What am I actually going to *do* about Carol? What is it that I want?

Yes – had been her. What Colin was surely unprepared for, however, was the awful, huge and mocking presence of her brother, gangling alongside.

'Well well,' said Terry. 'If it isn't bloody Superman.'

Was the sneering tone the one he always adopted, wondered Colin. Was this his habitual way of speaking? Or was it exclusive and specially reserved for Colin alone? Terry anyway was now moving in the direction of the drinks (good) and Carol was mugging to Colin several variations of I'm-sorry-but-what-could-I-*do* type looks. And it was true – there was nothing she could have done. Her father had not wanted to come (Can't just turn up at a garden party with people I've never even *met*) but there was no way he was going to have

Carol crossing London on her own; and that had meant Terry.

'It's hot,' said Carol.

Colin nodded: there was no denying it.

'I'm just going to get some orange,' she went on, blushing now from nothing more than the inanity of what she was saying. 'I've missed you.'

True enough, for all the good it did her. Look at Colin: Carol did. And there wasn't really anything there for her. What had happened to Colin? I thought he was truly *keen*, she thought, but he's not even looking at me, not properly. And then she became annoyed. He could have said that he'd missed *me* – or something, anyway. Even now he's craning his neck and who was he looking at? Oh – Elizabeth. And then – don't know why – Carol became really *bloody* annoyed and was about to just turn on her heel and get her sodding orange when suddenly – over there, standing all on his own – she caught sight of quite the most fabulous-looking boy: fairly tall and slim with gorgeous eyes and he seemed to be staring right at her. Without thinking too much, Carol walked over to him. She threw a See You over her shoulder to Colin – didn't mind too much whether he heard or not, just wanted to be sure that he knew damn well just where she was headed.

He did. Suddenly, all of Colin's haughty indifference, his quite intolerable superiority over this super girl quite deserted him. He very nearly called her back. Who *was* this boy? Looked a bit foreign and a bit bloody odd but there was no denying that he was a looker. There were one or two bastards in his class at school who were lookers, and they were usually the cruellest. Colin had been going to walk over to Elizabeth but something held him. Oh God of *course* it's Carol I want (she's talking to him now, this boy, whoever he bloody was) because Elizabeth – well look, that just had to have been just one of these really weird *things*, didn't it? I mean – *wonderful* (not to be missed, never to be forgotten) but it wasn't *real*, was it? It was *Elizabeth* – the next-door neighbour, his mother's *friend*. Colin shivered now, in the heat, for the first time seeing it and not quite believing. Carol is laughing now – a sweet and tinkly sound that was ripping him up. I've got to get her away from him. Yeah – go up to them (do it now). Take her by the arm and swiftly lead her elsewhere. Can't. Why not? Oh you *know* why not – I'm just not that sort of *person*: can't be done. Can't can't can't – and nobody hates me more now than I do.

And then – just like that, truly as if by magic – they were gone. Carol and the boy: gone. Standing there one second – and the next . . . And Colin could have sworn that he hadn't taken his eyes off the pair of them for a single second but very much *did*, obviously: must have done. They were gone. Colin was covered in alarm and now (too late! Too late!) he dashed to where they had stood, and sure enough there was a flapped entrance just there and he flew through that and *nothing* – just nothing:

lawn and flowers and blinding sunlight and the muffled chatter from within the marquee. Colin blundered back in – not sure why – and Howard called him over with a Colin dear lad! Come and have a drink! But Colin stumbled right past him and out of the tent through another flap on the other side and he was thinking The house, the house – maybe they're in the house.

'There's a boy in a hurry,' observed Cyril Davies, who had been chatting to Howard.

'Indeed,' agreed Howard. 'Man with a mission. Bright lad, though, Colin – Colin is Brian Morgan's boy, actually.'

'Ah,' understood Cyril. 'So I am depriving him of his home. Have they actually bought a new place?'

'Couldn't tell you,' said Howard. That's a point, he thought.

'But you've got a good lad working for you,' said Cyril now. 'Talking of lads. Furnish, is it?'

'Oh,' said Howard, gloomily. 'Norman, yes.' Norman – the crazy – sitting up in the breakfast room, now, moaning and a-groaning, silly bloody sod.

'Was it your idea or his? The twenty thousand.'

Howard looked up. 'I'm sorry? The . . . ?'

'I didn't think Morgan would've gone for it. Wouldn't have dared if Furnish hadn't told me how desperate he was.'

Howard, with great subtlety and tenacity, prised out of Cyril the whole bad story, while pretending

464

to be a knowing part of the deal. So. Let's get this straight, then. Norman – who is under the illusion that he holidayed in Chicago with Katie (with whom he is in – ha – *love*) – has diddled Brian out of twenty thousand pounds with a view to netting half of it for himself. Certain, then, that all those other rumours were true. Norman is a crook. Norman is mental. Norman is also out of a job, and might well be facing prosecution.

It was the smell and sight of the enormous roast turkey that alerted Lulu's stomach to the fact that it was empty, and in need.

'*God*, Lizzie – that looks absolutely wonderful. I'm suddenly absolutely *starving*. Didn't have breakfast, or anything. Haven't even nibbled. Here – let me help you. God – it weighs a ton.'

Elizabeth smiled at Lulu's comments while grimacing at the ton-weight which right now she was lifting from the oven. The golden turkey sizzled and darkly glistened.

'I only *just* got it in the oven. It only just fitted in. The hen birds are meant to be better, more tender, but you can't get really big ones, so this year I got a cock. I love doing turkey in the summer – it's always so unexpected.'

'Smells divine,' approved Lulu.

'Mm. It should be really, really good because it's what they call a *bronze*, apparently. Something to do with the feathers. We'll just let it settle a bit.'

'Oh Lizzie – you're so clever. You do all these

things so beautifully.' And she held Elizabeth's shoulders and kissed her cheek. 'And you always look so . . . I think you're very – sounds silly when you say it – *attractive*, Lizzie.'

Elizabeth looked at Lulu. 'Doesn't sound silly. I know what you mean. I feel it too.'

The kiss on the lips was full-blooded and warm, and neither seemed inclined to break it. When they did, it was Lulu who spoke.

'I hate men,' she said.

Elizabeth nodded. I suppose in a way *I* do too, she thought. But all *I* really like is young – young and beautiful: if there is that, then it doesn't too much matter what else they are.

They both turned at the very slight ruffle that vaguely stirred the air and then saw Colin staring at them open-mouthed before he turned and fled back into the garden.

Melody, her hands still ablaze from clutching her wonderful Miles's muscular arm, sidled up to Norman who was now sitting – stunned and forlorn – on a short flight of semicircular brick steps some way to the side of the garden. He had the rarefied air of one who has been banished.

'Hi, Norman,' she said, lightly. 'Long time, no chat. Christ you look miserable. Katie has told me some of it.'

Norman looked up; registered her presence with a nod. 'I love her,' is all he said. 'Doesn't matter now.'

Melody sat down next to him. 'It's getting pretty stuffy in that tent. I've drunk so much champagne!'

'*And*,' sighed Norman, 'I've just lost my job. Quite rightly. So I'll never have anything to do with anyone here, now. Not now.'

'What are you going to do?'

'Don't know. Doesn't matter, does it? I was talking to Brian Morgan, just now. I was going to apologize to him for what I'd done – don't terribly want to get into what I did: done, now. Anyway, he had quite a few interesting things to say about suicide. Thoroughly recommends it. Might take him up on the idea. Who knows?'

'But he's still *alive*,' protested Melody. 'What can he know about suicide? God I *have* had a lot of champagne – I think this is all squiffy talk, isn't it?'

'Yes he is – but it's not for the want of trying. He's really been into it – gas ovens, pills, knives. Threw himself off a cliff just last week, apparently.'

'Is that how he broke his neck?'

'Think so. It can be quite dangerous. Anyway, Melody – there's no point me hanging around any more. Not welcome. Say goodbye to Katie for me, will you? Tell her I love her.'

'Oh you don't *love* her, Norman! It's just that she was *there*. If she'd shown the slightest commitment, Norman, you would have run. You would've been off – you *know* you would.'

467

'No I wouldn't. How do *you* know?'

Melody sighed. 'Because that's exactly what you did with *me*, isn't it? Hm? The minute you discovered I was pregnant you were gone. It's just *you*, Norman. It's what you *do*. I don't suppose you care, by the way, but Dawn's going to live with Dotty and Brian, now; it's probably the right thing. I don't think it'll matter too much if he kills himself.'

Norman was standing, now – touching the soreness at the back of his head. 'I must go. I might leave London, actually. Might not, of course. You know, I never really liked the name Dawn.'

'You should have been around to choose another,' smiled Melody. 'Funny you should say that, though. Dotty's going to call her Maria, she was telling me. Oh yeah – it looks like I'm finally going to get married. Wish me luck? Bye, Norman. See you around, yeah?'

Norman grinned weakly, and just before he turned to go he thought No – no, Melody, you won't: around is what I shall not be. And I *didn't* apologize to Brian Morgan – didn't. I was going to give him the ten thousand pounds from Cyril Davies – at least make good half the loss – but Mr Davies, when he approached him, had said Ten thousand pounds? Ten thousand *pounds*, you say? I don't recall any such arrangement. And Norman had even been witless enough to pursue it for a sentence or so before he finally accepted the inevitable. *Writing*, said Cyril Davies, poking him in the chest and driving it home – always get it in *writing*. Norman sighed heavily now as he trailed away from the sweet scent and colours of Howard's garden party: you just can't trust anyone, these days. Mr Street's garden party, I should say. Who, if he sees me again, might well kill me.

And only then suddenly did he remember the small black cassette of sin and truth that he had slung into his Big Brown Bag before quitting. When the worst has blown over, could there maybe be some sort of way back?

White resin loungers with French blue and white striped cushions had appeared on the lower slope of the lawn, and Howard and Brian lay in two of them alongside. Howard was happy and very warm from sun and too much whisky, and was enjoying the distant tinkerings of people bobbling about here and there. Some were still in the marquee – Elizabeth would be just finishing off the real food, now, and I think that new friend of hers Lulu might be helping; seemed a nice person – very good-looking, if that's the sort of thing you went for. Hadn't seen Dotty for a bit – but wherever she was you can be sure that little Dawn is there too. Colin just went rushing past again, not too long ago – don't know what's got into the lad: not good, running around in all this heat. He had asked Howard breathlessly whether he had seen Carol anywhere, but Howard hadn't the slightest idea who this Carol was, so he was unable to help.

Quite a few new faces around – there's that Ellie girl, the one with the red hair, down by the pond; seemed in fairly earnest conversation with that rather smarmy-looking person that Melody had brought along – Giles, did she say his name was? Couldn't tell you – Christ, my mind. Something of that order, if it wasn't Giles. I think, you know, that it's a rather good thing that I got out of that Melody situation when I did: she could be dangerous – far too unpredictable. And man crazy, according to Elizabeth, who didn't understand why all these men should want her so badly. *Because*, Howard had yearned to tell her, she is quite the most willing and serviceable fuck. Yes indeed. But these days, of course, Howard was into other things. Where *was* Zoo-Zoo, actually? Hadn't seen him for ages. And as to *Norman* – well: good bloody riddance. Nuisance, though: have to start advertising for someone else, now. Ah well.

'So, Brian,' he said. 'Proving to be quite a summer for you, isn't it? One thing and another.'

Brian would have nodded, but nodding was among the things he could no longer do, now, so he went on staring at the trees.

'One thing I have to ask you, Howard. A favour. I hate to – you know – do this, but there's really no alternative.'

'Fire away, Brian, said Howard, expansively. Oh God – he's not going to want *money*, is he? Along with everyone else.

'It's just that – well, you know how quickly this

470

sale has gone through, and everything – I haven't had time to actually get anywhere else.'

'Yes,' said Howard. 'I was wondering about that.' Oh God – he's not going to want to move *in*, is he? Along with everyone else.

'Also, Howard, if I'm honest – money isn't so much tight as non-existent . . . so what I've done is, I've rented a caravan.'

'A *caravan*? Good God. What does Dotty say?'

'Doesn't know, yet. I have this feeling she won't be too pleased. But anyway, Howard, what I want to ask you is whether I can park the thing in your driveway – I mean, well out of the way of your garage and everything, obviously. It's just that I haven't got anywhere else to go.'

Howard was caught by a new and plaintive tone: Brian looked so sad. Had been about to say oh *Christ*, Brian – Elizabeth will go *crazy*, and just think how Dotty's going to feel about this and God I don't want a fucking great caravan in front of the house – everyone's going to think it's a gypsy encampment and I'm supposed to be the star local estate agent and how's it going to *look*?

'OK,' he said. 'Fine.' And brushing away the stutterings of gratitude, he continued to say: 'Brian – one thing's been bugging me. Why did you decide you wanted to be *deaf*?'

You know, thought Brian, I really do think everyone's gone a bit nuts. Why do people keep saying this? He would have turned his head to Howard and widened his eyes in a display of

471

incredulity, but turning his head was among the things he could no longer do, now, so he went on staring at the trees.

Howard didn't push it: maybe he just hadn't heard.

Lulu was back in the marquee for just one more glass of champagne, and even as she caught the merest glimpse out of the corner of her eye of whoever this man was now coming towards her, she was willing him away: go, go – do not approach and do not speak to me because if you do my husband will appear from nowhere – maybe swing down from a tree and burst through the roof of the tent – and in all probability slay you before my eyes (for he is not as other men). Didn't *work*, naturally enough – here he came, party face already in place.

'Hello,' he said. 'My name is Cyril. Cyril Davies – I've just bought next door. Are you a neighbour too?'

'Not, no,' replied Lulu – eyes now flicking, right and left: John cannot be far away and soon he'll come and then I'll die of shame and heaven only knows, Mister Cyril Davies, what it is that *you* might die of: some form of violence, certainly. 'Friend of Lizzie. Elizabeth.'

'Ah – our hostess. I must say she has done us proud.'

Cyril's initial impression of this truly luscious woman was that she was perfectly sane: no sign

472

of mania or neuroses that I can see. Although she did seem rather nervous. Why, I wonder, is she nervous?

'Look,' she said suddenly (the anticipation was killing her), 'I know this sounds rather odd and I really don't want to go into it, but my husband – my husband would not like to see us together.'

Aha! Initial prognosis all wrong, then. Already she is speaking to me as if I am her secret lover. Could well be she treats every man she meets in this way: there could be something in what her husband says. Sometimes, in order to discover the true persona, it pays to be blunt. Let us, then, go for blunt:

'You know,' said Cyril softly, 'I could really sort you out.'

Lulu blinked once and stared at him fully.

'I *beg* your pardon,' she said, with huge froideur.

Cyril moved in closer: the scent of her stormed his senses.

'You know what I mean. See to you. Sort you out.'

Lulu – scarlet and furious – turned away and stalked out of the tent. I simply do not believe he *said* that! Just as she reached the warmth of outside, Lulu felt a touch to her shoulder and, jangled now, she spun around abruptly and who should be standing there but that vile man from The Excelsior – the awful person in the lift.

'Just wanted to say hi,' said Miles.

Lulu bestowed upon him the sort of look that

473

renders plums unto prunes – oh God oh God! These horrible men – I simply can't stand all these horrible men! And then a purple and sweating John had her by the arm and was hustling her away to a quiet and shady part of the garden.

'Again!' he spat through teeth tightly clenched. '*Again* you're talking to that bloody man! Why has he followed you here?'

Lulu was so frustrated and angry she could almost have *cried*.

'I wasn't *talking* to him – I *hate* him, *hate* him – hate them *all*.'

'All! *All*! Who are all the bloody others, then? How many have you screwed since him, then?'

'John! You're *mad* – you're *crazy*. I hate all these people – how many times do I have to say it? If you want to attack someone go and get that Cyril Davies person! Disgusting! He just came up to me and offered to, oh God – sort me *out*!'

John was temporarily becalmed. 'Yes,' he agreed, more quietly. 'I told him to do that. Believe me, Lulu – a good sorting out is what you *need* – can't you see that?'

Lulu just stared blankly at John. This man, she thought, truly is a complete and utter fucking lunatic.

'*And*,' went on John, regaining momentum, 'it's no good saying you weren't talking to your *lover* because I saw you with my own eyes – he touched your *shoulder*.'

And now Lulu was crying: this is the person I

married. I have to, have to be free of all this.

'Listen to me! Listen to me!' she hissed, as her lips curled back. 'I have been in the *house* – yes? Talking to Lizzie in the *kitchen*. Got it? *Understand*?'

John's tone now was all smarmy sarcastic. 'Oh yes of *course* – Lizzie. Whenever I think you're with lover boy, in fact you're with *Lizzie*. So what did Lizzie say, hey? What were you talking about?'

Lulu was flustered and confused by the man's insanity. She struggled to recall something, anything that Lizzie had said – maybe it would appease him until they could decently get out of here – and then, most surely, would she shove this madman out of her life.

'Oh God, John – I can't remember what she *said* . . .' And then – to crush the light of victory in his crazy eyes, Lulu came up with this: 'OK – she said that this summer she'd got a *cock*, yes that's it – and it was so huge – it *was* huge, massive – I saw it – and it's so huge, she said, she only just fitted it in. That's what she said. It was only *chat*.'

John stared at her, stupefied. At least he had quietened down, thought Lulu. And she went on more conversationally:

'Truly big. It's bronze, I think she said. Smelled divine. I actually wouldn't mind getting myself around some of that – it's ages since I had anything.'

John's mind was made up. It was that *man* – that *man* had turned his darling Lulu's *mind*.

How could she say all this to me – John, her *husband*?!

Lulu smiled and licked her lips. 'I like lots of stuffing,' she said.

And a light went out behind John's eyes. Right. That's it. I'm going to kill him. Now. And this time I really bloody *mean* it.

Before Lulu's wide and startled eyes, John set up the cry of a vengeful wolf and loped across the lawn towards Miles. He raced right past him yelling out Just You Wait, Bastard, and screeched to a halt by the drinks table inside the tent and in full view of just anyone around hauled out of a bucket by its golden neck an open bottle of champagne and haring back to Miles now he raised it above his heads and the champagne coursed down his arm and all over his head and down him and quickly formed a slick on the silky grass and John's feet were up in the air before he landed and practically split himself asunder as he slithered up to Miles and the bottle was gone from him – had landed up somewhere – so he dragged himself up and howling now from the pain he was feeling he raised his fist and drew it back and propelled it forward and then it was that Miles's single and devastating punch smacked squarely into the centre of John's face and the light of surprise now threw open his eyes as blood jetted out of his nose and just before he went down he went forward and pitched into Miles and the two fell as one and rolled over together and John was roaring Kill You Kill You Kill You Kill

You as Miles screamed back Look What You've Done To My Fucking *Shirt*, You Berk!

Some people fluttered on the sidelines, uncertainly. Howard had heard the row and was approaching fast. Colin – not even partly relieved of his inner turmoil – was enjoying the show for all it was worth and it was then that a tearful and agitated Carol rushed up to him and threw her arms about his neck and he held on to her as she was shuddering – and glancing just once more at the gory pair grappling on the grass, Colin took her hand, and as hot and greedily lustful as ever he had felt, he pulled her away from all that and together they ran in the direction of the trees and when a barked out *Oi* and then *Oi You* reached his ears, Colin did not run faster, did not seek to hide: he let go of Carol's hand and turned in his track and wheeled back to Terry, who he knew would be there, and Terry's eyes were now widening as he saw that Colin was not about to stop and Colin had rammed into Terry now and as the wind burst out of him Colin swung his fist full into his open-mouthed face and Terry teetered but Colin wanted blood – had to have blood – and he punched him again and then one more time and blood came now from the side of Terry's mouth and he groaned before he collapsed and as Colin ran back to Carol who was jumping on the spot and clapping her hands, her eyes now flashing like coals, he could smell the blood on his fingers and those fingers now took hold of Carol's and they fled together into the trees, through the trees, and they threw themselves down and tore at one another as Colin panted and Carol gasped and he fucked her now and he fucked her hard and swiftly and then he rolled away, content to die, and yet more eager than ever before because it was life itself he was dying for, now.

In common with a good many of the guests, the party had begun to break up. Miles was off, for starters. He'd learned a bloody lesson, he could tell you: when a summer thing is done, then it's done – over, ended, finito, out. Now the bloody bitch had got all clingy – and he'd been attacked yet *again* by this fucking fruitcake and just look at the state of his bloody clothes! Just can't stand being seen like this. And what is that gorgeous Lulu bint doing fussing over the fruitcake? I thought he was supposed to be married to that receptionist thing – what was her name . . . Christine? Something. Right – out of here, and out of Melody's Godawful life. Christ, how she sticks that pit she calls home I do not know.

'Bye, Miles,' she was whispering now. 'I love you so much.'

'Yeah,' he said.

'So when will you call me? We've got big plans to make!'

Miles nodded. Jesus, these women – did they believe *everything* they were told? 'Soon, darling, soon.'

And then Melody threw herself at him and it was

then that he knew his ribs were killing him. It was just as well someone had pulled him off back there, or he would've slaughtered that fucking maniac.

'Oh God, Miles, I'm going to miss you! Hasn't it been heaven? I'm so used to *being* with you.'

'Won't be long, darling, and we'll be together again.' Let me *go*.

Finally, he got away (Say thanks, will you, to whoever's party it was, yeah?) and glanced for the last time into Melody's eyes, struck wide by something close to adoration. God, she was thinking as she watched him go, what a *man*. Christ, passed through his mind, what a bloody woman. That redhead was OK, though – very young and tasty: got her number – might see what gives.

Melody wandered over to where Elizabeth was helping Lulu into a perfectly simple cream linen jacket while Lulu adjusted the towel around John's neck, partly concealing his blood-soaked shirt.

Melody sighed. 'He's gone. I miss him already.'

Lulu looked at her. 'I don't know you very well, Melody, but I tell you I think he's quite the nastiest man I have ever met.'

Melody's eyes were already blazing when John piped up:

'You liked him well enough to fuck him, though, didn't you?'

'What?!' gasped Melody. 'You're crazy, you are! You're just *mental*.'

Lulu nodded. 'You're right – he is. I hate him.'

John looked up at her, in pain: I love you, Lulu

– I *love* you: why do you find it so hard to see?

Lulu whispered to Elizabeth, who whispered back. Arrangements and plans – sympathy and advice were sorely needed: I cannot wait to be alone again with Lizzie – I feel so very much for her. Just as she was hustling John out of the garden and into the street (his eyes were spinning and his hair was wild) he brushed against Cyril Davies and husked into his ear:

'She's *mad*, I tell you. *Mad*.'

Cyril really couldn't give a shit – he was never going to see either one of them again. Maybe she was mad, who knew? Truly luscious, though.

'Well, Elizabeth – Howard,' said Cyril now, gripping the hand of the latter quite appallingly tightly. 'We will take our leave. It's been very – ah – interesting.'

Edna Davies was hanging on to him, now. Where have you *been* all this time, he had asked her. Looking at the plants, she had replied – they've got some lovely ones, but just you wait till you get cracking next door, dear – that'll show 'em! Cyril wondered whether, in the circumstances, he ought to say goodbye to Brian and that wife of his, but when it came to it he couldn't be fagged. Good Christ, thought Cyril now, as Terry wandered past: yet another person covered in blood: what sort of an area have I in fact bought into?

'Nosebleed,' said Terry to Elizabeth, trying on a smile – and that hurt his mouth a lot (the source of all the blood, as was plain to everyone). 'Have

480

you seen Carol? We've got to go.' And have you seen that cunt *Colin*? Because I've got to fucking smash him. 'Carol! There you are. Come on – we're going. Where's your little friend?'

'I don't know,' said Carol. 'Come on, then – let's go if we're going.'

Carol very much wanted them to leave before Colin appeared, because she well knew what Terry was like. Colin had not wished to stay in the shadows of the trees (I'm not scared of *him*) but Carol had eventually persuaded him.

'Well just you tell him,' intoned Terry darkly, and with menace, 'next time you see him, that he and I have got an *appointment.*'

I know exactly when that will be. Tomorrow. I am in love, and Colin loves me and I have never been so happy in all my life. But God – it had been so strange with that Peter person – God I felt so frightened. I only went off with him to make Colin jealous but he was really persuasive, really smooth – and his eyes, his eyes: you could've just melted into those eyes. We went down to the bottom of the garden and there's a sort of a greenhouse shed thing down there and we talked about – oh, I don't know, nothing much, and then he started touching my hair and that was quite nice, really, and then he touched my breasts and I did want that and I sort of didn't and I started to think of Colin, then – it was Colin I really wanted, but if Colin didn't want *me* then why shouldn't I, hm? Why not? Got to do it some time, haven't I? So we were kissing a bit, and touching and I thought oh blow it – I'll do it, why not? So I put my hand down and cupped him and then put the palm of my hand right on to him (love doing that) and I thought hang on, that's funny – and just then he said I wouldn't bother, if I were you (think that's what he said – that sort of *thing*, anyway), and I was feeling and feeling and there was nothing to feel and God I felt so funny and scared and I sprang away and I shouted out oh my God you're a *girl* – and he smiled that sort of lazy smile, and suddenly he looked so sad. Not even that, he said: not a girl, but not really a boy either: there is, he said, just nothing to me. And suddenly it all felt so weird that I just ran and ran and then I saw Colin and I flung myself into his arms and then he took me, took me – took me so divinely – and now we're going to be together forever and I love him so much I think I could die.

Long and dark green shadows were reaching across the brightness of the lawn when Colin emerged from the trees. I'm not hiding, he thought – I'm not hiding from anyone or anything ever again. And the bastards at school? Sod them. I can handle the lot. Carol has given me this. I love her. I am in love and will remember this summer for the rest of my life.

He just caught a glimpse of the receding flurry of her angelic hair as she waved goodbye to Howard and Elizabeth (who had actually been kissing Lulu in the way she used to kiss me – which I think is perfectly sick). Carol and that pig of a brother of hers had moved away and out of sight. Didn't matter. Seeing her tomorrow. Can't wait. Can't wait. Oh my God – I simply can't *wait*.

Elizabeth had covered most of the surfaces in the now richly glowing and golden marquee with little scented candles in pierced brass bowls. The perfume of mimosa along with more late evening drinks were having their lulling effect and conversation was sporadic, Howard for his part quite content to sip his whisky and gaze upon the shadows flickering up and around the canvas panels, the candlelight making even the lilies wink and glint with a special warmth. Dotty was pushing the pram six inches away from her, hauling it back, all the while making clucking noises to the baby, who was nearly asleep. Katie was giggling in the corner with Ellie. Her name wasn't really Ellie – it was Jane: an old school friend that Katie had quite literally bumped into at Heathrow – asked her on impulse to the party, and on the way cobbled up this crazy Ellie thing: God – you should have seen Norman's face! *So* funny. The prat. I wonder if I will marry Rick? He's pretty gorgeous and colossally rich. Bit old, though. I suppose what I really have to decide first is whether or not I'm going through with having this baby. I think I probably won't – don't want to be all fat and clumsy: don't think Rick will like it. Don't think *any* man would like it. How could they? Not natural, is it? That's why I got rid of the last one; that and the fact that I was still in the Upper Fifth. On the other hand, babies are quite *sweet*, I suppose – look at Dotty over there, totally besotted. Yes, but I'm not Dotty, am I? So I think on balance I'll get rid of the thing. Or maybe I *will* have it – it's quite a stylish thing to do, actually, if you're as young as I am because then when I go and collect the kid from school in ten years' time I'll be the youngest and most fabulous-looking mother of the lot. But they probably take up acres of time, do they? Babies? Probably. Yeah – maybe best get rid of it. Rick's coming over in about a week, he says: often flies in and out of London, apparently. Don't know, quite, what he does. Don't much mind. A week's quite a long time, actually. That bloke Melody brought along – Miles. He asked for my number, so he'll call me soon, I expect: quite a hunk, actually. Melody wouldn't like it, of course, but there's no way he's going to see her again: he told me. Hee hee – poor old Melody! Wonder what she's thinking? (Melody in fact was asking herself have I done the right thing with Dawn? Maybe it's not too late to change my mind. And Miles – do you know, I had absolutely nothing of him, not even a phone number – said he was getting a new line put in, or something; not sure if I believed him or not – so I took a card from his wallet when he was in the shower. I hope he rings me soon, but I can't really wait for that; think I'll just ring him anyway. At least I've got the numbers: something.) Oh God – Dawn or Maria or whatever the bloody little thing's name is has started whimpering now

– what a bloody nuisance. Nah – I'm not going through with all that: best get rid of it. Colin looks like he's in a trance: probably drunk too much, silly little sod. And why's Mum talking to that perfectly weird kid Peter? I've never worked out the *point* of Peter – why Dad even has him around. Never *does* anything. Anyway – Mum seems happy enough. And Brian. Look at Brian. Christ – he looked bloody ridiculous *before*, but now with that stupid collar on him . . . apparently, Mum was saying, he jumped off a cliff because he wanted to go deaf. Believe it? He might as *well* be deaf – all his other senses have gone. Just look at him – staring into nothing, not a single bloody thought in his head.

Wrong. Brian was thinking this: you see that champagne bottle over there? The big one? Magnum, I think it is. I reckon I'll take that when we go because it has all the makings of a very nice lamp base. What you do is, right, you cover the lower part with a good amount of Three-in-One (warming it beforehand is a good idea) and then with the drill on really high speed (the bottle, now, is clamped into the Workmate, I need hardly say) you get a nice clean hole for the flex. From here on in it's child's play. Feed through your cable – lampholder wrapped around with a slice of cork for a really snug fit, plug on the other end and you're in business. For a really elegant finishing touch you could soak off a load of wine labels from other bottles and apply with Copydex to

485

a bog standard paper shade: very classy, and no more than an afternoon lost.

'I think,' said Dotty, 'we had better be going, Elizabeth. Maria is getting just a teeny bit restless. And God – I suppose I have to face up to some *packing* tomorrow. There's so much to be done.'

'Are you going to *fit* everything into a caravan, Dotty?' enquired Howard – and Brian had no time to hide. 'I mean – some of them are pretty large, I know – but still.'

Dotty stared at him.

'Oh God!' guffawed Colin. 'We're just spent all week in a caravan and now we're actually going to *live* in one!'

'Caravan?' said Elizabeth, puzzled. 'But Dotty, I thought you said . . . ?'

'Misunderstanding,' said Dotty, hastily. What a shame, she thought now with bitterness, that Brian didn't kill himself when he fell off that bloody cliff. Too bloody selfish to even contemplate it. Never mind deaf – it's *dead* he should be.

Dotty was eager, very eager, to be away now (What's all this about a bloody *caravan*, you bastard? she hissed to Brian. Tell you later, he said: oh Jesus) – but Elizabeth was up and had something to say.

'Listen, everyone – I've just had the most marvellous *idea*.'

Howard chucked up his eyes to the tented roof. Christ, that woman – we're all still in the middle of *this* idea, aren't we? Think I'll have a touch more Scotch.

'Now just listen,' went on Elizabeth, excitedly. 'I know it sounds silly now because it's summer and everything but pretty soon we'll all be putting away our summer things –'

'Getting out our winter things,' said Dotty, reflexively.

'– yes – and look, I mean – apart from poor Lulu's crazy husband we're all really enjoying this summer, yes? I mean I know it's not over yet but you know what I mean.'

Everyone dwelt briefly on their current fixations, and yes, the general consensus (bar Brian) was that so far this had been a good one.

'Well *look*,' rushed on Elizabeth, 'I expect we'll all be going off for a winter break – I know I shall be: God, I'll really *need* a break by then –' (A break from what, Elizabeth, thought Howard. What is it that you actually do? I've often wondered) '– and then we can all get together for *Christmas*. Here – in this house. How about that? It'll be really nice – like an old school reunion.'

There were no real grumbles about any of that – it all seemed so impossibly far away: even now – this late in the evening – it was still so warm in the scented garden.

Everyone made a move, soon after. Dotty (not thinking of caravans, but dwelling on Maria), Colin (filled with light and yearning for tomorrow) and Brian (hefting the empty magnum, and more or less dreading the whole of the rest of his life) – they all slipped away next door, and Katie

487

took redheaded Jane (so recently Ellie) up to her room for some seriously silly girl-type talk. All the goodbyes were done with, and now only Elizabeth, Howard and Melody (who lingered on) were left sprawling in the green canvas-backed directors' chairs – oh, and Zoo-Zoo was still over there, eyes alert and ready.

'Can I *do* anything, Elizabeth?' offered Melody. 'You've done so much today – it was wonderful.'

Elizabeth smiled and shook her head. 'I enjoyed it – apart from John. I'm *so* sorry he set upon Miles like that, Melody – Lulu really has to get shot of him. He's dangerous. I do hope she's all right. And anyway – I've already *got* my helper for the evening – haven't I, Peter? Come on – let's make a start on the glasses.'

Elizabeth and Peter (so recently Zoo-Zoo) each carried a large tray of champagne flutes and tumblers out of the marquee and across the lawn, and Howard watched them go, thinking How pleasingly odd, this is. The house was flood-lit and welcoming, and their feet cut swishing swathes through the lushness of the grass.

'Just put them over there,' said Elizabeth, in the kitchen. 'It's so *sweet* of you to offer to help like this, Peter.'

She briefly kissed his hair, which was as soft as soft and clean and young.

'Now,' she said, in her let's-be-practical voice. 'I'll be the food putter-awayer – what would you like to be?'

The boy came up close to Elizabeth and looked full into her with black and liquid eyes.

'I can be,' he said softly, 'whatever it is you want me to be.'

'Happy, Howard?' said Melody.

'Content – I think the word is content, Melody. You?'

Melody nodded. 'Very. Fresh start. Last week I was a single parent, and now I'm going to get married with no children at all! Quite a change. It's strange, isn't it, how just chance things can change your life for ever? You never, do you – you never know what's going to happen. That's why plans are a waste of time.'

I do hope I've done the right thing. I wonder if he's home yet. I'll have to ring him soon.

'I'm glad you're happy,' said Howard. 'It's about time you were.'

Melody smiled and then she stood up. 'I'm really tired, Howard. God – what a week it's been. I'm absolutely shattered.'

Howard rose and reached down for the last of his whisky: it warmed him as it hurried down. 'Shattered into pieces, are you, Melody? Just like, er – oh God. What was that character, that nursery rhyme – fell off a wall, couldn't be mended . . . Christ, my mind.'

'Oh – Humpty –'

'*Dumpty*!' broke in Howard. 'Of course, of course. Yes – Humpty Dumpty. Christ knows why I brought *him* into the conversation. Come on Melody – I'll run you home.'

'I hear you gave old Norman the shove. Poor Norman.'

'Bugger *Norman*. He's in the past. Over. Did you have a jacket, or anything?'

Melody shook her head. What if it *was* just a summer thing, she was thinking. What then? Do you know – I think I want my baby back.

Once they were outside the tent, Howard hugged her briefly and whispered: 'I really *am* glad you're happy, Melody: truly. I still love you, really.'

It's nice, thought Melody, when someone holds me tight. Trouble is, I don't think there's ever been a time when anyone's held me sober.

'Isn't life funny . . .' mused Melody now, making fairly clear a new and wistful element. And then, when Howard half-stumbled during their walk across the lawn to the car in the driveway, 'Oh God, Howard – are you actually *fit* to drive? You've had a hell of a lot.'

'Course I'm *fit*. Fit as a, oh God – *thing*, Christ, my mind. *Fiddle*. But you're right about life, though, Melody,' expanded Howard. 'The thing is you mustn't, I think, *think* about it. Think about it and it would break your heart. But if you just stagger through, like I do – well yes: life's a laugh.'

Howard smiled in vaguely Melody's direction as the two of them settled into the Jaguar, and Melody, suddenly, had nothing to say.

490